GOODBYE UNCERTAINTY

The Lost & Found Series
Book Three

JACQUELYN AYRES

The Lost & Found Series

GOODBYE CAUTION

Book One

GOODBYE SECRETS

Book Two

Dedication

To all the women who have journeyed back to themselves, after
being lost for so long. It is an honor to walk amongst you.
And to my three beautiful children for being the compass in my
journey, I love you.
You are my stars and I am your moon.

Chapter One

"Ray? Ray?" I cry and try to lean forward, lifting my arms to him. He hugs me fiercely.

"Oh, thank God ... thank God, baby." He kisses every inch of my face. His skin feels hot, and he doesn't look very well.

"Ray ... baby, you're burning up." I touch his forehead.

"Becs?" He searches my eyes.

"What? Ray, you need to go to the ER." I push his hair off of his forehead.

"I'm okay, baby ... stop. How are you?" He holds my hand to his cheek.

"Upset with you." I sigh. He looks down nervously. "You haven't been taking care of yourself! You're here twenty hours a day, and Lord knows you're not sleeping the other four." I push the call light.

"How do you know how many hours I'm here?" He looks up.

"I know a lot of things, Ray. I've had quite an enlightening experience, to say the very least." I kiss his forehead.

"Becs?" He seems nervous, which doesn't help me fight off my concerns. I try to find the right words to say—and then it dawns on me.

"I'm ready to be yours, Ray. I'm ready for us. I'm ready for our present and our future. I'm ready to be all you need now," I repeat the words he had said to me. Whether he was actually the one who said them, I'm not sure.

His eyes fill up. "Yeah ... until tomorrow," he says under his breath.

"Tomorrow, I will feel the same. And the next day, and the day after next. No more Lucy Whitmore, baby. I promise." I chuck his chin, making us lock eyes.

"You know I call you Lucy?" A smile breaks through his lips.

"Yes." I smile. "Look, Ray, I know and understand why you may have some reservations about what I'm saying. Please give me the chance to prove it's true." I lean forward to kiss him, but he pulls away.

"I want to kiss you, baby, but you're right. I'm not feeling very well. I don't want to get you sick."

Just then, the nurse walks in.

"Hi, Jen!" I smile, recognizing her. Jen and Ray both look at me sharply.

"How do you know who I am?" she asks with a slight smile.

"I just know."

"Well, it's good to see your eyes." She grabs my hand.

"Ray was right. The other nurse was hurting me," I inform her. They both get wide-eyed. "Jen, Ray is running a fever and I'm afraid he won't listen to me about getting checked out," I say, raising my eyebrows at him. He stares at me in astonishment. Jen goes over to him with her thermometer, puts a plastic cover on it, and instructs him to open his mouth. After a few seconds, we hear the beep.

"Oh, you are so outta here!" she snaps at him in disbelief. "Down to the ER right now! Dana!" she yells toward the hall. A nurse walks in.

"What's up, Jen?" she asks.

"Please take Mr. McNeil down to the ER with his 104.5 fever!" She gives him *The Look*, and I dart mine at him as well.

"I don't want to leave. She just woke up!"

We all stay expressionless.

"I'll take Tylenol," he adds.

2

"Oh, okay. So, Becca's health and the babies' health are of no concern?" Jen sighs, her voice full of sarcasm.

"Jen!" Ray says with panic and looks at me, petrified.

"I know about the babies." I softly pat my belly and offer a slight smile. "We'll talk about them later. Right now, I want you to go and take care of yourself, McNeil. You. Look. Awful." I poke at his shoulder.

"Babe?" he asks, seemingly confused.

"Go!" I point to the door. He gets up, confusion still lingering on his face. "Hey, McNeil," I say as he nears the exit. He turns, still looking weary. "I love you, baby." I shoot him an air kiss and wink. He flashes me a boyish grin and gets on his way.

"You have a very stubborn man on your hands, lady!" Jen shakes her head.

"Yes, I know ... thank God," I add the last bit under my breath.

"So, before the doctor gets up here and before I take out your catheter, I need to ask you a series of questions," Jen states as she charts in her computer.

"It's 2012, Obama is president, and I'm at Mass General in Boston, Mass. My date of birth is March 5, 1977. Does that cover it?" I smile.

"Works for me, lady! I can't believe you just woke out of a three-month coma in this condition!" She smiles.

"What do you mean?"

"Usually it doesn't look so good for a full recovery when someone is in one longer than a month. But here you are!" She squeezes my hand.

"Thank God for miracles." I smile and rub my belly.

"You didn't even panic or anything. No confusion at all. It's like you just woke up from a nap." She looks at me, miffed, as if she's trying to figure it all out. She pulls the curtain and assists me in bending my knees to get the catheter out.

If she only knew ...

"Oh dear, I have to pee." I go to sit up.

"Bedpan," she says, sounding panicky.

"It'll never happen."

Just then, Dr. Peterson walks in and I have to stifle my giggle. He really does look like Chewbacca's little brother.

"Mrs. McNeil! Where are you going?" He gets on my other side. *Mrs. McNeil? Holy shit! Are we married?* "Mrs. McNeil?" he asks again.

"Sorry, I need to get to the bathroom. Will you help?" I push myself onto the floor and try to steady my wobbly legs. They both help me, though they are obviously not pleased. I then talk Jen into helping me with a shower.

A few hours have gone by. It's now ten in the morning and I have been mindlessly watching TV and waiting to hear anything about Ray. The rush of adrenaline I felt when I first woke up wore off during my shower. I am now experiencing the effects of being in a coma for three months: muscle weakness, unsteady gait, and feeling a little foggy. Although, that could be from the pain meds.

"You're still here?" I ask in disbelief as Jen walks in.

"With the amount of paperwork you gave me, lady?" she asks, but adds a smile.

"Sorry," I offer.

"I'm not! So, listen, Dr. Peterson has ordered a slew of tests to check your psychological, neurological, and physical status. If you get a clean bill of health, you can go home as early as tomorrow."

"Have you heard about Ray?" I ask.

"Oh, yes, I did. He's been admitted with pneumonia. He's very lucky you woke up when you did—and that you didn't get sick!" she says, a bit annoyed. "Actually, you still might, so I'll have them include the symptoms to look out for on your discharge papers," she adds.

"You want to call him a dumbass, don't you?" I laugh.

"Yes, I do! Anyhow, he'll be here for a few days—and you cannot visit him," she adds.

"I guess that wouldn't be a great idea, given my condition." I sigh and rub my belly.

"He should recover soon. You take care, Becca." She hugs me. "I have tomorrow off, so I won't see you. I'm glad you're back. It's been a pleasure taking care of you and your overbearing, overprotective husband." She laughs.

"Thanks, Jen! You've been wonderful. I hope Ray didn't drive you too crazy." I squeeze her hand when she pulls away.

"No. I don't think my husband could say the same, though. I'm pretty sure mine hates yours, considering how I go on about how wonderful he is." She laughs. "Lady, you hit the jackpot with that one! I think he has to be the most loving and attentive guy I've ever met! Your girls are lovely, too! Real sweethearts. Give my best to your family, and when you're up for it, come down for a visit. And bring those babies!" She smiles and pats the top of my hand with her free one.

"Thanks again, Jen." I smile and release her hands, then watch as she leaves the room. So much for waking up without any confusion. I close my eyes and try my hardest to remember Ray and me getting married. Nothing. Ugh! I don't think we are. Grayson would've told me—I'm sure of that!

I stare out the window, watching the snow fall. It's been several hours since I left Grayson. I've wept off and on. But mostly, I've thought about everything he said to me. Feeling exhausted, I close my eyes again to rest.

"Becca, baby?" Elise pats my hand. I open my eyes to find her and Artie.

"Hi ... I must have dozed off. Where are the girls?" I ask with a slight smile. Elise just stares at me. Tears start streaming down her face. "Mama, I'm fine." I grab her hand. "I do have a question, though."

"Ask away, darlin'." She sits next to me and clasps my hand with both of hers.

"Ray and I ... are we married?" I whisper.

"You oughta be!" She gives me *The Look.* "But no. You're on his insurance plan and he put you down as 'McNeil,' and I don't blame him. Now, how's my grandbabies?" She rubs my belly.

"Good, from what I hear." I lean back and smile.

"You gonna let my son make an honest woman outta ya?" She lifts an eyebrow.

"Yes, ma'am." I nod.

"Good." She pats my hand.

"Where are Morgan and Annie?"

"Oh, baby, I'm sorry. We didn't get the call 'til we were on our way down. Raymond's been admitted, by the way. Boy, is he mad!" She shakes her head.

"Well, he needs to rest. I get to leave tomorrow," I say with excitement.

"Damn insurances and their drive-through policies! I don't like how they jus' push folks out," she says disapprovingly. "Nonetheless, they're gonna be so happy to see you!"

"I can't wait to see my girls!" I'm sure if my smile got any bigger, it could swallow my face.

Chapter Two

"Derek, I have some things I need to tell you," I say once we get settled into my truck.

"What's that, Becca?" he asks. It's funny hearing him with an English accent again.

"You're the first person I'm telling this to." I take in a deep breath.

"What is it, Becca?" He takes a sip of his coffee.

"These past three months, I've been with Grayson." I grab the wheel as Derek spits his coffee out everywhere, causing him to swerve. "Sorry." I wince. "Probably should've told you this before we got on the road."

"Becca, I don't know what to tell you ... I don't know what to say." He seems pretty uncomfortable—not a suit this beast of a man usually wears.

"Well, mate, I'll give you the editor's cut." And that's just what I do. Well, the G-rated version, at least. No need for Derek to think me a dirty whore!

"I believe you, Becca," he says when I get toward the end. That took up half of our trip.

"Can I ask you how you've come to believe me?" Honestly, I don't think I would believe me if I were him. There's no *aha* part of my adventure that involves him where I could say, *Well, how would I know that, then?*

"Because, the way you are telling the story and talking," he glances over at me. "I haven't heard you speak that way in over seven years. You've been around my best mate, all right!" He laughs and I see tears spring from the corner of his eyes.

"You were always his 'right-hand man,' Derek. He trusted you with his life. He told me to thank you for standing by and looking out for Morgan and me. We both thank you." I squeeze his arm. "He feels honored that you gave Jasper his name and he said he'll always look after him. He said you're still his best mate—you always will be." I hand him a tissue. Derek is so *verklempt*, he can't say anything. I stare at this huge, six-foot-something, fierce-looking black man and giggle. He shoots me a look and tries to pull it together. "Oh, Derek, I'm not laughing at you! I'm thinking about when I first met you in my 'other state.' I could see this big teddy bear of a family man in there even though you looked as if you would stomp on anyone who approached you." I unbuckle so I can propel myself to plant a big ole kiss on his cheek. "I love ya, mate!"

"Buckle up, Becca. Ray will have my arse if anything happens to you on the way home." He tries to be stern, but can't contain his smile. "You never were afraid of me! Gave me a what for the first time I ever actually met you! I knew at that moment, I was either going to be the best man at your wedding or I'd be bailing Grayson out of jail for stalking you!" He laughs. I join in, thinking about that day out in the Barnes & Noble parking lot. "I wish we could get those days back, Becca." He frowns.

"They were good ... once we got past the whole tag-team-stalking bit." I smack his arm.

"Well, you know, good friends never let friends drink and drive ... best friends never let you stalk alone."

"Derek, that's awful! Don't think you will get a bumper sticker deal out of that one!" I laugh.

"Oh well, someday I'll come up with a doozy!" He shrugs.

"Oh, they are doozies, all right!" I tease. Derek has a very long history of trying to come up with a phrase that will become popular on a catastrophic level. Grayson and I always teased him about it.

"You know, Bec ... Grayson's right, Ray is a great guy." He gives me a sideways glance this time, as there is traffic by Exit 3 on Route 93 North in Windham, New Hampshire.

"I know he is. I've always known that. It's just nice to have my memory back. I felt so much guilt over our relationship, for feeling the way I did about another man, I just completely blocked it all out. Honestly, I don't know how Ray could've stayed with me all of these years. I plan to make it all worthwhile for him ... thanks to Grayson." I half smile, feeling a pang in my heart for Gray.

"It's hard to believe that Grayson didn't have a hard time with all of this." He sighs.

"Oh, he did! For two months he got swallowed up by the delusion. He was very jealous, but in the end, he did what he came to do. My happiness was more important." I stare out the window at the construction vehicles working at widening the road.

"It always was, Becs." He slaps my knee.

"Becs? Uh-oh ... do I detect a bromance brewing?" I tease him.

"Yes, I've fallen victim to the epidemic of calling you 'Becs,' and yes, Ray and I have hung out quite a bit." He laughs.

"Have you gotten him to lighten up on his 'secret' hatred of Grayson?"

"Ugh, finally!" Derek sighs and speeds up as the traffic clears. He looks over at me. "Yeah, I think I have a bit. I don't know, Becca, but in a weird way, he reminds me of Grayson." He shakes his head, as if he's trying to figure it out.

"I totally agree! They're so different in so many ways, but the same, too. Grayson thinks they would've been great mates—if you take me out of the equation, obviously." I grab my phone when I hear the ping of a text.

December 27, 2012 11:53 a.m.
Ray: Are you on your way home, baby?

Me: Yes. Halfway home. Having a great laugh with Derek. How r u feeling?

Ray: Good! Wish I was bringing u home! The truth?

Me: Yes.

Ray: Like shit, babe :(

Me: Ahem ...

Ray: Do I detect an "I told you so" in there?

Me: No ... not me ;-p

Ray: U r a terrible liar, babe!

Me: I know. When will u b home?

Ray: Few days. Stuff is starting to come up now, which is good.

Me: Things tend to always come up with you.

Ray: Yeah, no problem in that dept., huh, babe? ;-p

Me: Apparently not ...

Ray: Becs?

Me: Rays?

Ray: LOL ... okay, just making sure

Me: Of?

Ray: Delayed reaction or anger really.

Me: No. But we do need to talk. I want to do it in person.

Ray: Yeah, I don't like doing "it" on the phone ... definitely better in person ☺.

Me: Not in the mood for sexual banter.

Ray: Uh ... sorry. Were you not doing the same thing a minute ago?

Me: Hormones, woman's prerogative ... whichever one fits the bill. Lol.

Ray: Whatever, text me when u get home.

Me: I love you and I can't wait to see you!

Ray: :)

"Well, that was weak," I say flippantly.

"What?" Derek asks.

"I said I love you and miss you and he sent me a fucking smiley face."

"Grayson?" he asks, and I can't help but go into hysterics.

"Oh, Derek," I wipe my eyes. "Honestly!"

"Shit ... you are going to tease me for the rest of my life about that one!" he grumbles.

"Oh, for sure! That is, until we can actually receive texts from Heaven!" I giggle. Derek answers his ringing phone.

"You sound like shit, mate. Why? I need to ask her. I can't just tell her, you do remember who we are talking about? Yes, all right ... hold on then." He pulls the cell away from his mouth. "Becca, Ray wants me to bring you to his house instead of the inn."

"Why?" I look at him quizzically.

"Because he's afraid you'll dive right into work. He wants you to relax and slowly get acclimated."

"Give me the phone." I hold my hand out, and Derek complies. "Ray, I don't want to stay at your house by myself, and I want to see how things are going at the inn." I sigh.

"My par ... ents are there, and—" he coughs.

"Baby, you sound terrible. Now I know why you got grumpy."

"No, Becca, I got grumpy because you're pulling the same shit!" he yells, but then starts coughing up a storm. He hangs up on me. My phone lights up.

December 27, 2012 12:18 p.m.
Ray: Just do what U r fucking told!

I throw my phone into my purse.

"You're not going to answer him?" Derek once again looks uncomfortable.

"He's sick and crabby ... no, I'm not." I cross my leg over the other and stare out the window angrily. Derek laughs.

"What?" I snap. "Sorry," I say quickly.

"Gray drove you crazy like this, too."

"Damn alpha males!" I seethe, then ponder in silence. Does it aggravate me more that they behave this way, or that I find it to be such a turn-on?

"So ... what are we doing, friend?"

"Well, can I have your driving services for a couple more hours?" I ask as he gets off at our exit.

"Sure."

"Can we pick up the girls, then go to the mall? I have no maternity clothes. I could use some retail therapy. Sorry," I add, knowing this will not be at the top of his hit parade.

"And then?"

"Then Ray's," I say, defeated.

"Okay then." He smiles and heads to the inn. As we park, Morgan and Annie come running out, screaming for me.

"I was so scared, Mama," Morgan cries.

"I know, baby, I know. I have so much to tell you tonight." I kiss her. "C'mere, you!" I hold my free arm out to Annie and hug her just as fiercely. "Look how you two have grown!" I release and take another look at them. "Come now. Get your coats! We're going to the mall. I need new clothes, and your help!" They look at each other with excitement and take off. "Is Hazel here?" I ask Derek.

"No. She's with her sister, Violet, for the holidays."

"Oh." I sigh with disappointment. Within minutes, the girls are back out to the truck and Derek begins his brave adventure of taking the three of us to the mall.

"All set?" Derek looks up.

"Yep." I smile as he grabs the one bag I was carrying. The girls walk ahead with the other several bags filled with treasures for all of us.

"Ray's pleased that you're listening." He smiles. I shrug. "But he's not pleased that I brought you to the mall after just getting out of the hospital. I have to agree with him there," he adds. I'd agree with both of them ... if I wasn't too stubborn to admit the poor judgment call on my part.

The last few days have been filled with visitors and trying to get back into some sort of routine with the girls and work. Well, I've only dipped my toes in at work. Claudia's been doing an excellent job. I gave her a huge raise and put her on our company insurance. Needless to say, she was thrilled.

Since Ray's coming home later this afternoon, I decide to drive into town to get some filet mignon from our local butcher shop. I think it'll be a nice treat for him after eating mainly hospital food for three months.

"Becca!" Al practically jumps over the counter when I walk in.

"Hi, Al!" I smile as he comes around to hug me. I panic when I see the blood all over his white uniform.

"Oh ... justa stains, sweetaheart! You my firsta customa this mornin'!" He smiles, holding his arms open wide. I go in for a super Al hug. I adore this little gray-haired Italian man. He reminds me of my dad—same type of personality. "Look at you, mama ... you belly almost as a bigga as mine!" He rubs it. "You husband musta be a so excited! How is Ray?" he asks.

"Husband?" I hear a familiar voice ask. I turn around.

"Yes, Will, husband," I say. He glances down to my belly. I ignore him and turn back to Al. "He's doing better. Should be home today. Can I have six of your best filet mignon?"

"Only the best for you, Becca!" He kisses his fingers and throws the kiss in the air toward me.

"So ... he knocked you up, huh?" Will says. "Well, I guess he finally figured out how to get you to marry him. I'm kinda shocked, Becca. That's so 1950s." He turns away to place his order with Rosie.

"You know, Will, I'd be careful of what you say to me or about me, unless you want Ray to finish what he started. Ray's kind of the 'big guy' in town—everybody's pal. You're just the town jerk. I don't think you would get much sympathy if Ray's fist accidentally hit your face a few times." I find myself articulating my words like Grayson did when he was passionate about what he was saying.

"Is he a bothering you, Becca?" Al asks angrily.

"Doesn't he bother everybody, Al?" I smile at him. "Al, you remind me so much of my dad!" I kiss his cheek when he brings the meat out to me.

"I wisha you were my daughter! *Si bella!*" He kisses both of my cheeks.

"How much, Al?"

"On the house—welcome home!"

"Thanks, Al!" I smile and go over to Rosie, his sister, and discreetly hold out a few folded bills. "Rosie, put this in the register to cover the steaks." I keep my voice low. She takes the money, giving me a knowing look. Al's sweet, but they can't afford to be handing out filet mignon like it's candy.

I walk up to Will. "You know, it's sad. I considered you a good friend at one time. You're just an asshole!" I snap.

"And you're nothing but a fucking cock tease!" he bites back in a low voice near my ear. "Tell Ray I said, *Good luck, prick!*" He heads out the door. Ugh! I could punch him in the face myself!

I leave the butcher's and decide to quickly run into the jewelry store to order Morgan's necklace from Grayson. As Eric is writing out the order, the bracelet Grayson just "gave" me catches my eye. "I'll take that, please." I point to it.

He grabs it. "Becca, I'm sorry. It's been sold. It shouldn't have been in the case. This was specially ordered by somebody."

My heart sinks.

"Well, can you order me one?" I feel hope rise.

"Sorry, one of a kind." He sighs.

"What? Well, can you ask the person who ordered it if I can buy it off of them? I'll pay them extra," I plead.

"I can't at the moment. The person is out of the country. That's why we still have it." I'm about to be in tears. Nope ... now I am, sobbing included. "Hold on, Becca." Eric raises his finger and goes into the other room. He's on phone for several minutes, waving his hands. He looks exasperated. He comes back out and gently takes my arm. "Let's see how this looks." He places the bracelet on my wrist, then hands me the phone.

I shoot Eric a curious look before I speak into the receiver. "Hello?"

"Yeah ... Merry Christmas, babe!" Ray says with a bit of irritation. "Why the hell are you in the jewelry store? You should be home resting!"

I give the bracelet and phone back to Eric and leave the store. I climb into my truck and cry. Ray has been so snippy with me, and, well ... that bracelet was supposed to be from Grayson! I ignore my phone, which is blowing up—surely by one Mr. Ray McNeil—and just head to his house.

"She's home," Elise says into the receiver when I walk in. "Ray wants to talk to you." She tries to give me the phone. I hand her the meat and head upstairs without a word. I lie down on the bed and cry some more. "Becca?" Elise opens the door.

"Elise, please." I lift my hand. "I'm very emotional, and your son has been an asshole to me all week."

"Oh, Becca, he's just mad he's not here with you, and now they don't wanna release him 'til tomorrow." She rubs my back.

"Let's be honest. He's waiting for the other shoe to drop." I sigh.

"Do you blame him?" she asks.

"No, but he doesn't have to be a jerk."

"Well, I'm not gonna to sit here and listen to you talk 'bout my son like this! You've put him through a lot, missy, and he's been nothin' but good to you!" she says, raising her voice.

"Ha! You have no idea how your son has treated me!" I catch myself before I go too far. I get off of the bed and head back downstairs. "Morgan! Morgan!" I yell for her and grab my keys.

"Becca, what are you doin'?" Elise asks when she catches up to me.

"I'm going home!" I cry.

"Becca, Ray wants to talk to you. Please talk to him, honey." Artie tries to give me the phone. I accept it.

"Ray."

"Baby, please ... take a deep breath and calm down." His voice is soft and comforting now. I walk into the den and sit.

"Ray, I can't help how I was. I had no control over it. It kills me that I hurt you so much. That's not going to happen anymore. It hasn't all week, and I have most of my memories of us back. I know you're upset that you're not home with me, but you've been short with me off and on since I woke up. I know it's because you're waiting for the other shoe to drop. It's not going to. I threw those shoes out ... they were old and ugly! Just bare feet over here!" I begin to hiccup-cry like a little kid. "Ray?" He hasn't said a thing. I hear the door open behind me, provoking me to stand and turn.

"Yeah, baby?" he says with a sigh.

I stare up at him as he walks over to me. He throws his phone down and grabs the one out of my hand.

"You weren't supposed to be home 'til later."

He's so close to me. I lick my lip before biting it.

"Mmm ... there it is." He smiles, freeing my lip so he can claim it for himself. He releases and slides his tongue across the slit of my mouth, begging to enter. He fists my hair as he deepens the kiss. My heart is pounding a mile a minute—we're like a wildfire, unable to be contained. He pulls my sweater up and over my head. His hand caresses my belly. He tilts his head. "Becs ... what did they do to you at that hospital?"

"Oh, that? That's from an injection I received before I went to the hospital. It was a pretty big injection," I add. "But the doctor said a few more months and the swelling will definitely go down." I let my smile hit my eyes.

"Big injection, huh?" Boyish grin.

"Mmm, yeah ... I think so." I lean up to kiss him again. His hands slide up my back and unhook my bra as his mouth travels across my jaw and down my neck. "Did you lock the door?" I ask when he stands back, hooking his fingers under the straps and guiding them down slowly.

"Yes." He stares into my eyes. Stormy blue-gray ... God, I love his eyes! I tug at the hem of his blue cable-knit sweater. We pull it off of him together, followed by his T-shirt. Ray takes in a sharp breath as my fingers trace the skin above the waist of his jeans. My hand travels up his chest, and when I reach his heart, he covers it with his and holds it there. He palms my face with his free hand, then grasps my hair again. He pulls me close to him, our breath smacking each other in the face. "Are you mine, Becca?" he asks softly.

"Yes, baby," I say after mentally declaring a need for a panty change. He sounds so hot when he asks that.

"Theme song?" He crooks his head at me again.

"No, just in need of a panty change." I bite my smile back, and his eyes light up playfully. *There's my Ray.*

"Let me help you with that." His hands dive under the band of my pants and he carefully pulls the waist away and off of my belly, then whips them down with my underwear. I giggle, holding onto his shoulders to steady myself as I step out of them. He kneels in front of my stomach and lays several kisses on it.

"I have a theme song for this." I pat my belly. He looks up at me, seemingly trying to hide his nervousness. "'Glad You Came' by The Wanted." I rub it, encouraging the goofy grin on his face and impending laugh.

"How do you do it, baby?" he asks, looking astonished as he stands and stares down into my eyes.

"How do I do what?"

"How is it, after five years, you can still make my heart leap inside my chest like that?"

I cup his face and lean up to kiss him. Ray has never fallen short on saying the sweetest things to me.

"We do need to talk about this." He sighs against my lips, his fingers caressing my rounded belly.

"I know why it happened, Ray. Right now, I'd like you to just remind me how it happened." I bite my lip, pulling my head back as I work at his belt.

"Cliff notes or full version?" He thumbs my lip free.

"Um ... feeling a bit impatient." I unbutton and unzip his jeans dramatically. "Cliff notes, please," I say, and start to pull them down. He grabs the waistband and does it himself. I turn to lay a blanket on the couch—for sanitary reasons, because these are the odd things I manage to think of even in the heat of the moment.

Ray's lips caress my shoulder, his hands at my hips. My right arm hooks around his neck as I turn my face to his. Our mouths lock; our tongues taste each other hungrily. His hands slowly travel up to my breasts.

"Oh, um ... mmm," I moan against his mouth and fist his hair as his fingers gently knead and pull at my nipples. This only encourages him to be a little tighter—a little harsher. "Ah, Ray ... please," I beg, feeling the powerful surge of the electric current hitting my groin.

"Feel good, baby?" Soft and sexy.

"Yes," I say breathlessly. My left hand grasps the side of his hip.

"Do you want me, baby?" He bites at my earlobe. I turn to him urgently.

"You know I do," I say before my lips attack his fiercely. His light groans drive me even wilder, somehow. He brings me down on the couch. I open my legs without much coaching and lean up to meet his mouth as he climbs between them. I nudge his hip with my leg. He shifts slightly and, in one swift motion, enters me. I gasp from the painfully sweet feeling of my body trying to accommodate his size. *Big* was an understatement.

"Becs ... baby, are you okay?" He touches my face. I open my eyes to gaze into his. I nod and fight the urge to bite my lip. Instead, I try to steady my breath. "Ready?" he barely whispers.

"Yes."

He pulls his hips back only to crash into me again—reaching deeper.

"Oh God!" I cry.

"Shh." He covers my mouth with his. His right hand grasps my left hip and guides it to match his motion. His thrusts quicken with more power and deeper intent, forcing my body to adjust to him quicker. *Country Sybecca is in a white dress, rolling around on the floor singing "Like a Virgin" by Madonna.*

Soon my hips meet his urgently without any assistance. Our mouths keep each other quiet. After several minutes, a soft, whimpering sob escapes my throat as I feel myself climbing higher and higher.

"That's it, baby. C'mon, Becca ... c'mon, baby." He eggs me on as his face starts to scrunch. I squeeze around him. "Jesus, Becs ... oh God, baby," he groans. Forehead to forehead, we come together, relishing in the intensity and sweetness of it. "Jesus, baby." He takes in a deep breath as he pulls out. I wince. He smirks, looking satisfied. I giggle. "What?"

"You love the face I make when you pull out. You always watch me and get that satisfied smirk on your face." I scoot over and turn on my side to face him. He shifts onto his side as well.

"I don't know what you're talking about, Becs." He sighs and watches his fingers trail along the side of my body. "You were so tight, baby. Usually you're snug, but this was different." He finally catches my eyes.

"I think I did Kegels several times a day," I say, then allow a giggle to erupt.

"What?" He smiles.

"Um ... well, I have a lot to tell you about when I was in a coma." I push his hair off his forehead and plant a kiss there.

"Shoot!" He grabs my hand and kisses my palm.

"Well, um, let's get dressed and at least go upstairs to our room. There's a lot to talk about." A shiver comes over me.

"Cold?" He rubs my upper arm.

"A bit." I smile.

"Okay. Let's go." He quickly kisses me. I sit up and grab my bra. Ray straddles behind me, helping me guide the straps back up, all the while planting soft, wet kisses across my shoulders. He hooks my bra for me. I throw my sweater on and grab my panties and pants. I slip them on my legs and stand to pull them up. Ray just stares at me in all of his naked glory.

"C'mon, baby." I hand him his boxer briefs and jeans. He dutifully responds. He stands, buttoning up. I bite my lip, admiring the sight of him. He glances up quickly, then grabs his shirt and returns my stare before putting it on. I move in close to him and run my hands up his chest slowly. "You are so fucking hot, McNeil." I grasp his lips with mine.

"Oh, baby, you better stop, or we will be back at square one here." He pulls away and tugs his shirt on when I step back. He grabs his sweater, then my hand.

"Wait." I pull away and wrap up the blanket to be washed. Ray rolls his eyes and holds his hand out again. We leave the room and head down the hall just in time to find his parents and the girls leaving.

"Where are you guys going?" Ray asks.

"To the inn. We'll be gone until dinnertime." Artie nods at us before they walk out.

"Good. We can talk in the living room, then." I start pulling him that way.

"Uh, well, doncha think we'll be more comfortable upstairs, babe?" He tugs my hips to bring me closer.

"Ray, we have a lot to cover. We don't need the distraction of a bed." I play with the hair at the base of his neck.

"Becs ... a bed has never been the cause of our distraction. It's just been an accessory when available." His forefinger lifts my chin gently. He leans down and caresses my lips with his.

"Ray. Stop, please. I have so much to tell you." I pull back slightly.

"Ugh! Fine." He groans and releases me.

"I'll be right back ... bathroom," I add at the end.

"Do you want something to drink?" he offers, heading toward the kitchen.

"A glass of wine, please!" I call after him.

"Water it is!" he calls back. I head into the bathroom to pee and clean up the spill in aisle *OMG*! "Baby—c'mon!" Ray pounds on the door.

"Okay. Okay, geez!" I haven't even had a moment to contemplate how I'm going to start this conversation. Of course, I've thought of different scenarios all week, but none of them matter now. The moment is here, and I need to rethink everything.

"Becs!" Ray yells.

"Christ, Ray—you're so impatient!" I snap as I walk out of the bathroom.

"Sorry," he mumbles. "You okay?" He has that nervous look again. I close my eyes, inhaling deeply.

"Bare feet, baby ... no shoes," I remind him.

"Yeah," he sighs with a hint of apprehension as he grabs my hand. We head into the living room. The last time I was "here", I was showing Ray the welts on my ass that Grayson gave me. I shake the memory away. Ray watches me intently. "Theme song?" he asks.

"No. A memory. I'll tell you about it in a few minutes," I say and plop down next to him on the couch. "Ready?" I ask as he throws his arm around my shoulders.

"Yep." He takes a sip of his root beer. Eck ... I hate root beer!

"Okay. I guess the only place to start is at the beginning."

"Usually how every story starts, baby." He leans his head back.

"Yeah, well, I need to warn you that you may get mad or upset during this story." I look up at him. He furrows his brow in curiosity before nodding for me to begin.

"Okay. So, last thing here—we were arguing in your truck on the way back to the inn, and we got into the accident."

"You—" he starts, but pauses and looks away. "They were about to pronounce you dead. I begged them to try once more. Thank God ... thank God they listened. I almost lost all three of you." He touches my stomach. I look up at him. His eyes are filled with tears and pain. His chin quivers slightly.

"You didn't. I'm here. We're here, and we're fine." I kiss him and brush away his fallen tears.

"We were arguing because ..." he starts.

"Because I woke up naked in bed with you and accused you of taking advantage of me," I finish.

"I did take advantage of you, Becs." He's barely audible.

"I know. You slipped something into my drink. It wasn't the first time, either," I add.

"How do you know? How do you know about the other times, too?" he asks, looking a bit shocked.

"Well, I'm going to get to—wait! Did you just say *times*?" I sit forward and turn to him. He looks down. "Jesus, Ray!" I place my head in my hands. My knees steady my elbows to support the weight. "How many times?" I look straight ahead.

"I don't know, Becca. What does it matter? I'll never do it again." I feel his hand at my back. "I'm sorry, baby. I shouldn't have done it."

"How many times, Ray?" I ask through my teeth. "If it's too many to count ... how long?"

"Just this past year. No more than once a month." He sighs, sounding defeated.

"I need a minute, please." I get up.

"Becs." He goes to stand.

"Please! One minute!" I snap angrily and head outside onto the porch.

Why didn't Grayson tell me it was more than twice? I wrap my arms around myself and have a good cry. I'm so mad I could scream. I could slap the pair of them! Ray for his atrocities, and Grayson for not telling me the whole truth. Why? Why would he push me to Ray, knowing what he did? I think back to our conversation for any hints. I remember the last thing he said about Ray:

"Ray is a good man. You are lucky to have him. Sure, he loses his temper sometimes. Yes, he's been aggressive, and he's done a few other things that were not okay. He's still a great guy and I don't blame him for most of those behaviors. I can't say I would've done any better. He loves you—stop questioning it!"

What Ray did was really wrong. I've already forgiven him, but he had no hand in actually telling me how many times it happened when I let it go. I'm a bit confused as to where the line of fairness falls. I think back to my conversation with Melissa. I have hurt him and toyed with his emotions for five years—unbeknownst to me, of course, but that doesn't lessen the weight of my part in all of this. He has been very good to Morgy and me. He's tried his hardest to take care of me the best he could. Pushing him away now is not going to erase either of our past actions. We love each other. We're getting ready to add twins to our very happy family. My pushing him away would only be letting the other shoe drop—destroying us both.

"Okay," I sigh out loud, wiping my tears away and taking in one last brisk-winter-air breath before I head in.

Ray is sitting with his head in his hands, fisting his own hair.

"Bare feet, baby ... no shoes." I sit beside him and kiss his shoulder. His head shoots up and he looks at me, obviously shocked.

"Becs?" He palms my face. "How can it be that easy? Don't you want to scream at me? Slap me across the face? Something?" He searches my eyes.

"Yeah, that moment kinda passed for me." I half smile. "None of this has been easy for either of us. So no, it's not that easy—but it doesn't have to be that hard anymore, either." I see a flicker in his eye. "So help me God, McNeil, unless you want me to slap you— no wisecracks!"

He pulls an imaginary zipper across his lips. "I won't mention that some things need to be hard, or where I'd like you to slap me." His comment warrants an eye roll from me. My eyes refocus and close when I feel his lips on mine. "I love you, baby. God, I love you." He kisses me again.

Chapter Three

"Okay. C'mon, let me tell you what happened," I say with a sigh and pull away from him.

"Er, okay." He releases my face. I sit sideways on the couch and he mirrors me, just like a week ago in the new office.

"Okay, so, truck spinning. My very next memory, I'm in my office figuring out wedding and crop schedules. Claudia's begging me for more hours and Hazel's trying to talk to me about slowing down."

"So, a typical day for you?" He smiles.

"Yes, pretty much. Hazel tells me her nephew from England is coming in a few weeks."

"She has a nephew over there?" he asks and furrows his brow, looking as if he's trying to remember.

"No, Ray. It turned out to be Grayson. But my memories of Grayson as my husband had been wiped clear. As far as I knew, I was the widow of George Campbell."

"Wait, George Campbell ... from Grayson's book? The wife beater?" he asks.

"Yes! So remember now that all of my PTSD was altered for the next three months. There were even pictures of me badly beaten." I hit his leg for emphasis.

"Hmm, that's weird."

"Well, it'll all make sense in the end." I roll up my sleeves. "So, in walks Grayson, and it's instant crazy attraction for both of us."

Ray clears his throat and shifts a bit. I squeeze his knee and continue to tell him how quickly and intensely Grayson and I fell for each other, and about Grayson cleaning up my war zone and going over my mortgage and the new POS as well as other new programs.

"Becca, that son of a bitch took credit for what I did!" he snaps.

"No, no. He told me later that you really did it all, and that you were cursing me out, too." I give him an arched look.

"You are the most unorganized person I've ever met in my life!" he states with exasperation.

"Okay, well, yell at me later for it. Can I continue?" I ask.

"Yeah, but I have a question first."

"What?"

"Did you sleep with him?" I can see the internal battle going on within him.

"He's my husband, Ray."

"You didn't know that though, right?"

"Right." I bite my lip.

"How long did it take him to get you into bed?" His nose flares and I can't help but giggle.

"Less than a week." Now his jawline twitches, and I really can't stifle my giggling.

"Stop laughing, Becca!" He swipes my knee with the back of his hand.

"Ray, you do realize that my body was next to you in the hospital, right?" I try to stop.

"You were subconsciously cheating on me."

"Technically, no, I was having sex with my husband." I try to clarify again.

"You didn't know it was him, so technically, you were cheating on me subconsciously." He raises his voice.

"Well, subconsciously, I wasn't aware that we were together. Ray, please, this is very silly." I grab his hands. He pulls them away.

"Did you sleep with Will?" His question is laced with anger.

"No! Never! Not here or there!" I gasp with disgust. "Why would you ask me that?"

"He said you did three years ago at one of your dancing events. He said it right after you kissed him at the bar!" he yells.

"I never slept with him! How could you believe him for one minute?" Now I'm yelling too.

"Because he doesn't block shit out! How can I believe you?" He's all teeth and stormy eyes.

"I don't know, Ray. What does your heart tell you?" I try to fight my tears back. "My heart is telling me I didn't."

"Your heart also told you that you didn't love me," he says, and sighs.

"No! No, that's not true. I always knew I loved you. That's why it killed me to see you with Michelle at the bar that night. By the way, how dare you yell at me for something I know in my heart of hearts that I did not do, during a time when you *were* sleeping with someone else?" He opens his mouth to say something, closes it, then opens it again. "You told me last week. We were sitting on the couch in the—"

"New office in the barn," he finishes my sentence. I gape at him. "Becca, I dreamt that last week."

"Ray, you were going over most of our memories?" I ask.

"Yes ... wait, Becca, c'mon, that was just a dream." He cocks his head in disbelief.

"It was a dream for you, Ray, but you were visiting me in my subconscious!" I almost screech with excitement. "I can't believe that was really you!" I hug him.

"Holy shit, babe, that's crazy! How is that even possible?" He pulls my face back to his.

"I don't know. Maybe Grayson did it—I'm not sure."

"Baby, Grayson wasn't really there."

"Oh, but you were?" I quip. He grabs my right leg and hoists me so I'm straddling his lap and facing him.

"I don't want to fight, baby. It's our first day together, and I feel like the more we talk, the more we're falling apart." He leans his head against my shoulder.

"Well, it might get worse before it gets better, so buckle up." I play with his hair.

"No. Let's just stop talking about all of this and move on." He looks up.

"No, Ray. I need to tell you what happened."

"Baby, I don't really care. All I care about is that we're here in each other's arms and that we love each other," he states passively.

"Ray ... I care." I look down, feeling disappointed. Why doesn't he want to know "where I've been" the past three months? I've done a ton of research online about coma patients and what kind of things happen to them to see if anyone out there has had an experience like mine. The first thing people usually ask them is what they remember, if anything.

"Hey. Hey." He pulls my chin up gently. "I'm sorry, baby. I'm being selfish. Go ahead. I do care, I'm just ... I'm thinking with the wrong head right now. You're on my lap, looking more beautiful than ever, sporting this hot new look." He caresses my belly. "I'm sorry. Tell me." He shakes my hips.

I take in a deep breath. "Come on. I can talk and make lunch at the same time." I get off of his lap and hold my hand out to him. We head out to the kitchen. Ray takes a seat at the table while I pull out plates, bread, and leftover meatloaf from last night.

"So, Grayson hired you for the renovations because you were labeled the best architect in New England by *Architectural Digest*."

"Yeah? Boy, do I wish that were true! I'm definitely not the best. I've never even gotten an honorable mention," he says with a hint of disappointment.

"I think you are, baby—you do beautiful work! Your designs are awesome. You just need that one huge contract that will tell everybody else what I already know," I say as I pan-fry the thick slices of meatloaf.

"Thanks, babe, that's sweet of you."

"It's the truth. Anyway, I had no idea he had hired you. He just said an architect was coming. When you got there, you walked straight past him and pulled me into your arms." I hand him his sandwich. "Beer?" I ask.

"Yes." He smiles, but grabs my arm as I turn away and pulls me onto his lap. "A kiss first, please." *Butterflies take flight.* I lean forward and rub my lips barely against his, pulling back when he tries to capture them. "Stop." There's just something about the way he says that word. I lean in and let his mouth devour mine.

"Okay. Okay—focus, McNeil." I pull away.

"Oh, I'm focused, baby." He tugs my face back to his.

"Focus on lunch." I try to stand, but he holds me still.

"Oh, baby, I am." He bites down my neck.

"Ray!" I smack his shoulder, laughing.

"Oh? You're not lunch?" He gives me a look of confusion. I shake my head.

"Dessert?" His eyebrows arch.

"You are insatiable!" I roll my eyes and climb off his lap to retrieve his beer. I bring it over with the sandwich.

"This is good, baby," he says with his mouth full. Reminds me of a twelve-year-old boy when he does that! I continue on with what happened that day in the office. Ray shifts in his seat and stares at the ceiling. He does have a good laugh at how he and Gray carried on. I get to the part about the binder and what he said, then go on to tell him about the next day—what Grayson did after he saw us kiss. "Could you feel all of this stuff, Becs?" he asks as I scoop ice cream onto our bowls of apple crisp.

"Yes. Everything—butterflies in my belly, touch, scent. You name it, I felt it and experienced it as if it were all really happening." I slide his dish in front of him.

"How could he hurt you like that?" He winces.

"To push me toward you." I half smile.

"Did it work?" He takes a bite and rolls his eyes upward—code for, *Damn, this is good*!

"It did that day. I ran to you. We were in the living room here when I showed you the welts. That's what I was thinking of earlier. That was the last time I was in your living room."

"Our living room," he corrects me.

"So, you rubbed aloe on my bottom ... wait, why did you just roll your eyes at me?" I stop.

"Forget it, Becca, just go on," he says with a bit of irritation.

"No." I reach for his hand. "Tell me."

"Nothing. Just go on, please, babe."

I continue on about our day, then the kidnapping. He laughs about what I had said to them. I take in a deep breath then tell him about being woken up with the indecent proposal.

"You agreed to that?" he asks in disbelief. I ignore him and carry on. He gets a satisfied smirk when I tell him about his early arrival, then about scrapping together. He pulls out his wallet and opens to the pictures. I look up at him in disbelief now—they're the exact pictures, in the exact order. I go on with the story. "So you chose him over me ... with no regard to how it would hurt me? Wow, Becs." He sits back in his chair, staring at me. I continue on, choosing once again to ignore his comment. "I wouldn't do that—you're not the jealous type!" he snaps when I talk about him plotting with Stacey. I get to us out in California and give him an edited version there. "You just dropped all communication with me?"

"Please, just listen." I grab his hand before I tell him what brought us back from the West Coast. The two times we saw each other at the hospital. The mall, the explosion, and the day he brought Annie. He looks away from me when I tell him about what he said— us being a team, and how he felt like we were divorcing. "Ray?"

"What, baby?" He looks back to me.

"I'm striking a lot of nerves, aren't I?"

He nods slightly and focuses on his bowl, slowly spinning it like a top. I place my hand on his to comfort him, but mostly to stop the annoying noise of the bowl against the tabletop.

"It struck a lot of nerves for me, as well. I suppose I needed my nerves struck." I look down, then back up. "I ... why did you stay? I don't deserve you. You're a great guy. You're funny, smart, handsome, and successful—and did I mention hot?" He gives me a boyish grin. "Why me? I don't understand it. You could have any girl you want." I lift my hand when he opens his mouth. "I'm sorry, Ray. I'm sorry for all the times I made you feel alone." He pulls my hand, guiding me up and over to him. I sit on his lap and encircle his shoulders and neck with my arms. He lays his head on the top of my chest.

"Becca, do you remember what I said to you in the office when you asked me that?"

"Yes."

"Then stop asking me, baby." He looks up at me. "Becs, there's not another woman on this planet who has made me feel the way you make me feel. Christ, the depth to the emotions I feel with you is insane. I've never laughed so hard with another woman, or cried so hard over one. You know me, Becs—I'm the 'let it roll off your back' type. It's rare for me to cry—literally cry—about anything."

"Being an alpha male and all," I cut in.

"Yeah, don't act like you don't like that." His voice has a hint of seduction in it. I offer him a playful smirk.

"Can I continue now, Miss Rudeness?" he asks. I nod, playful smirk still intact. "You've got this amazing ability to make my heart leap all over the place one minute, and then crush it to smithereens the next. Nobody gets me like you do. Nobody calls me out on my shit like you do. No one has ever made me feel comfortable or nervous as hell like you. You challenge me, inspire me, interest me, and have helped me become the father I've always wanted to be. Then we get to the outside beauty. Christ, baby, I could stare at you every minute of every day for the rest of my life and never once feel the desire to change the channel. You are my favorite smell, my favorite touch ... taste." He kisses my neck. "And my favorite sound." He picks his head up to look at me. His left hand palms my right cheek, his thumb freeing my lip. "Becca, baby, if you don't stop doing that, you'll give me no choice but to lie you down on this table and fornicate with you like Sister Husband and Mr. Sprocket." A giggle erupts freely from me. His reference to two of the characters in *Where the Heart Is* comes from the several times I've subjected him to watching it with me.

"Hmm, you fall more under the 'Forney' category," I say thoughtfully.

"Yeah, I've always thought so too. Poor horny Forney." He shakes his head with deep sympathy for the fictional character, causing me to burst into another fit of laughter. "You know, the only reason I watched that movie so many times with you was because I was hoping a damn lightbulb would go on and stay on! Sometimes it would go on and I'd get laid. But ... as we both know ... "

"Next day—lights off," I say, and sigh.

"Yep!"

"Sorry," I murmur. His eyes search mine. There's a hint of a smile in the corners of them. He leans up for a kiss, then another ... so on and so forth. "Ray, stop, baby." I grab his wandering hand.

"Please hurry, Becca," he breathes. His frustration lingers in the air above us as he leans back in the chair.

"I'm trying."

"Yeah, you are *trying*." He offers a soft, playful smirk. I smack his chest. He grabs my offensive hand and brings it up to his lips for a kiss. Ugh! Christ, does he know how to distract me. He arches an eyebrow, studying me as he bites playfully at my wrist. I swallow hard ... probably to push the butterflies down. *Pull it together, Becca! Damn hormones!*

"Did Annie get her period?" I ask as I finally think of where I left off. Ray slowly lowers my hand, the seductive expression gone from his face. Yes, that was quite the cock block, if I do say so my-self!

"Yes. It happened just the way you say it did, because my mother must've told you." He looks away.

"Your mom did not tell me, Ray!" I rip my hand from his grasp.

"Becca, c'mon, just move along." He waves dismissively.

"Raymond McNeil, have I ever lied to you?" Oh, I am boiling over now. He shoots me a condescending look. "I have never lied to you!" I defend myself.

"'Ray, you're just my friend ... I don't feel that way toward you.'" He imitates me.

"That's different and not fair!" I say, raising my voice.

"You want to talk about what's not fair?" His voice goes an octave louder than mine.

I grasp his face with both hands and rest my forehead against his.

"Please, baby, please ... I don't want to fight. I'm just trying to tell you everything."

"And I'm listening, babe." He lowers his voice.

"But you don't believe anything I'm telling you."

"Yes, I do. I'm trying to, at least. Please, go on." He grabs my hands and plants a kiss on each palm.

"Well, we went back and forth about our feelings and you got really mad at me and told me about my birthday and how hard I came for you."

"Three times," Ray cuts in. I dart my eyes up to find a satisfied smirk on his face as he stares off into the memory, I think. I suddenly feel like I might vomit, and while I'd like to chalk it up to morning sickness, I'd be lying to myself. I get off of his lap. "Where are you going, baby?" he asks, completely oblivious.

"I just remembered my prenatal vitamin. If I don't take it now, I'll forget. I'll be right back," I answer nonchalantly. Half lie—I only "remembered" now as an excuse to get far away from him. I have a terrible need to sob pathetically, and I have to give in to it. I climb the stairs quickly and run to our room. I close the door behind me. My tears emerge right away, and I head into the bathroom and turn on the faucet to drown out the sound. I put the toilet lid down, sit, and drop my head into my palms. My body shakes, keeping tempo with my cries. *Becca, pull it together!* But I can't. *Even Ghetto Sybecca is crying into her brass knuckles.*

"Becs?" Ray opens the door. He turns the faucet off and kneels in front of me. "Becs?" he asks again softly. "What's the matter, baby?" He massages my shoulders. *God, I can't look up at him.*

"I'll be fine. Can I just have a few minutes?" I ask without moving.

"No. I need to know why you are so upset." He sounds worried, but I say nothing. "Becca, if it's what I'm thinking it is—I am truly sorry. I should never have done that to you, baby. It's not even in my character. I just ... this past year, I started losing all hope for us. I didn't think this day would ever come. I know you keep saying 'bare feet' to me, but it's going to take me a long time before I fully let my guard down. I've been fighting so long for your love. I'm afraid that when my mom leaves, you'll go back to being forgetful Lucy."

"I was thinking we should get a Great Dane and name her Lucy." I look up.

"But your ability to pull shit completely out of left fucking field? Well, baby ... I'm pretty sure that will always stay intact." He shakes his head at me.

"I don't want to be Lucy anymore. I don't want to drive you to do things you wouldn't normally do ever again." I wipe my tears on my sleeves and blow my nose in the tissues he hands to me. He continues to kneel patiently, rubbing my legs for comfort.

"I promise, no matter what happens, Becs, I will never do anything like that again. And just to satisfy the quota for my left-field action, I will never again argue with you in a moving vehicle that either one of us is driving."

"You never let me drive."

"Babe ... you drive like you're competing in NASCAR—it's a little scary." He sits back on his heels.

"Have you ever driven with Stacey?" I ask.

"Just for ten minutes, and never again." His eyes go wide.

"Did she apply her makeup while driving with her knee?" I smile, knowing I'm proving a point as to what scary driving really is.

"Please, I can't talk about it. It was very traumatic. It took everything in me to fight off the urge to suck my thumb and cry for Mama." He closes his eyes and shakes off a shiver. I can't help but laugh at his theatrics.

"Ray, when you said 'three times,' you got a satisfied smirk on your face and you looked lost in the memory. I just don't understand how you can truly be remorseful if you're relishing in it." My nose flares as I feel new tears wanting to spring to life. Ray looks at me thoughtfully. He slaps his knees, then stands up.

"Come on, no more conversation in the bathroom." He holds out his hands. I take them, letting him lead me into the bedroom. He arranges the pillows up against the headboard and sits with his back to them. "C'mere." He pats the bed. I look at him with hesitation. "Ugh! Becs, c'mon, we're talking. That's it. For now," he adds with a grin. I take in a deep breath and crawl around his legs and up into his arms.

"I can see that I'm losing my side of the bed again." I look up at him.

His knuckles graze my cheek. "Our side, baby." He plants a soft kiss on my nose. *Country Sybecca twirls her low ponytails, staring at her picture of Ray. She's wearing a cute little froufrou nighty with bunny slippers. She sways back and forth, hugging herself.* I feel Ray's soft lips beckoning mine open. I willing comply—and he pulls away. "Wait, babe, before we have an intermission."

"An intermission?"

"Yes—a—much—needed—intermission," he says between kisses. "I need to clear something up." His fingers caress my cheek.

"What?"

"I wasn't relishing in the memory of what I did to you. I was relishing in the memory of what you said to me that night, after we made love." He searches my eyes.

"What did I say?" I ask, feeling some relief from this clarification already.

"You said, 'Ray, I'm so in love with you. You must know this. I'm sorry I haven't been able to give you what you need. I'm just scared. There's only one other man I've ever loved like I love you, and he was ripped from me tragically. I'm so afraid I'm going to lose you, too. I know it's silly, but I can't seem to get my mind to push pass that fear. Please don't give up on me. I promise—one day, it won't be like this anymore.'" He kisses my forehead.

"I said all that?" I look up.

"Yes. That's why I slipped you the pill again and again. You have such clarity. You're very aware of *us*. I needed the validation. It was selfish and it won't happen again, but it wasn't just about the sex."

"It's strange that it affected me like that. Isn't it supposed to sort of cloud your judgment?"

"Well, maybe because your judgment is already cloudy when it comes to our relationship, it had the opposite effect on you. In any case, it was very wrong of me, and I'm sorry for every time except the last." His hand travels to my belly. "Are you disappointed that you're having my babies—not Grayson's?"

"What?! Ray, why would you ask me that?" I push away from him.

"Really, babe? You're not sure?" He pulls his shirt off.

"What are you doing?"

"Getting ready for intermission, Becs. Now answer me." He

grabs my sweater and yanks it up and over my head. I stare at him, dumbfounded. He takes in a deep breath and exhales with frustration. "Answer the goddamn question, baby!"

"Uh, well, I'm not happy about the way it happened, but I am happy they're here and you're their father," I say quickly. Satisfied with my answer, he leans in and rubs his lips against mine quite seductively. This warrants erratic breathing on my part. "Ray." I place my hands on his shoulders, trying to keep him at arm's length.

"Becca, goddamn it, we've been talking for two hours. Intermission, baby." He takes my hands off of his shoulders and hooks his right arm under the small of my back, pulling me down so I'm lying completely flat on the bed. I stare up into his eyes, watching them search mine for the *okay*.

Because I love him. Because I need to do everything I can to prove this is real. Because I know the next part of the story may bring him more doubt. Because I'm feeling intoxicated by his scent ... his touch ... his eyes. Because this pregnancy is making me horny as hell, I raise my head up to his and nudge his lips with mine. His response is urgent. I help him remove the rest of my clothing, as well as his own. *Horny Sybecca snaps her whip at the floor. She's decked out in full leather garb and looking to take control of the situation.*

"Damn, baby," he gasps as I push him onto his back and straddle him. He fights against the pressure of my hands trying to pin his arms down. I suddenly find myself upright, his chest pressed against mine as he pins my arms behind my back. He slowly bites across my left shoulder, my neck, and then my right shoulder.

"Ray, let me touch you, baby." I nip at his earlobe.

"It's tough not being able to touch the one you love, huh?" He looks into my eyes.

"Yes it is ... like torture," I add. He releases my arms.

"Don't, um ... don't ever try to pin my arms down again. I need to be able to touch you at all times when we're in bed. Okay?"

"Okay. I won't. I'm sorry." I strum my forefinger across his bottom lip before I lean in to grasp it with mine. I'm so lost in our kiss, I barely notice the slight shift of movement as his arm hooks around my lower back. He grabs my hip to raise me and guide me back down onto him quickly. I whimper slightly through the stretch and lay my forehead against his as we slowly match each other's rhythm.

Ray and I lie in each other's arms, wrapped in post-coital bliss, and try to steady our breathing.

"Whenever you're ready, please go on with the story." He runs his fingers up and down my back so softly it almost tickles.

"Um, where was I?" I wince, trying to think.

"Uh, when I told you—"

"Right, right." I cut him off. "Well, you left and I got sick to my stomach and ran off. Grayson brought me upstairs to rest. He asked me if I remembered my birthday. I told him what I remembered at the bar and how, the next morning, you looked like you knew something I didn't." I stop at the sound of him lightly chuckling. I look up at him.

"That morning was so effin' hot!"

"Anyway!" I sigh with irritation. Ray shrugs. "Later, Stacey tried to talk to me about you, but I went apeshit on her. Grayson decided to give her a what for because he couldn't stand how she was treating me. That's when she told him that you were worried I was going to press charges and to please wait until after Christmas for Annie's sake."

"Wait!" He stops me. "Why would you be pressing charges against me?" he asks, looking confused.

"Uh ... for date-raping me, Ray." I pick my head up this time to look at him.

"*What*? Becca, I didn't ... that wasn't ... no, I wouldn't ... it wasn't ... I ... *no!*" He freaks out, making him unable to finish a sentence. He sits up. The color has drained from his face. "Oh God, baby, I never once looked at it that way. I mean, I knew what I was doing was wrong, but it never occurred to me to think of it like that. Were you going to press charges?" I see his level of panic rising and rising.

"No. It wasn't even a thought that crossed my mind. I just wanted to understand why ... how you could do that to me. So, I called you later."

He grasps my face urgently. "Becs ... baby, is that how you feel? Do you feel like I raped you?" His eyes search mine.

"Ray, what you did is considered rape. I don't know what you want me to say. It is a bit different than other cases. I know I had a hand in driving you to that point." I squeeze my eyes shut.

"No, baby, there's no excuse for what I did. I can't tell you enough how sorry I am. Please look at me." I open my eyes. "Please forgive me."

"I have. I am. Clean slate, Ray. We're both not happy with the way we've behaved in the past. Things are going to be different now. I love you, Ray. I want this. I want us. After today, I don't want us to harp on the things we've done in the past. Can we make a pact?" I place my hands on top of his and get on my knees.

"Anything you want."

"Ray, we're both stubborn and we're both passionate, intelligent people who are used to doing things our own way. We are going to have huge arguments over the years and that's fine. We will get through them. Please, we have to promise here and now that we will never, ever throw what we did in the past in each other's faces. We can tease here and there, because that's how we are, but let's never use it against each other in anger. If we do, it will destroy us, Ray. I know it will. Do you agree?" I squeeze his hands.

"Becca," he says through his teeth, apparently fighting off tears. "Do you have any idea how amazing you are?" He shakes his head slightly for emphasis. "How did I get so lucky, baby?" His lips slam onto mine. He lets go of my face to embrace me. I pull away after a few moments.

"It's a deal?" I ask.

"Yes, baby." He pecks at my lips again and again.

"Ray, we need to finish before I have to start cooking dinner."

He looks past me to the clock.

"Oh, we'll be finished way before." He smiles and tugs me back to him.

"Stop!" I laugh.

"I can't help it." He touches my face. "You're here, and you're beautiful, and you're very naked, and you love me. You smell good." He leans forward and inhales deeply. "You taste good." He kisses at my neck.

"Ah ... Ray—please," I gasp as he tweaks my nipples.

"You respond well to my touch." His voice is becoming more and more seductive. "You feel good." He slides his hands down my body and around to my bum. He massages my cheeks with purpose. Before I know it, I feel his palm slap my left bum cheek, creating the most delicious sting. I gasp, closing my eyes and holding onto him to steady myself. My breathing is so erratic it's beyond control-lable. "Again, baby?" he asks, almost in a whisper.

"Yes, please." I speak in the soft tone that always stirs some-thing deep inside of him.

"Christ, you're so fucking hot, baby," he says just before his hand comes down on my bum again. Ray stifles my groan with his mouth. "Baby." He pulls away, gasping.

"How do you want me?" I kiss down his jawline.

"Grand slam, baby." He grabs a pillow and throws it toward me before he tries to guide my hips. I turn, scrunching the pillow under me as I part my knees for him.

"You gonna hit it out of the ball park, babe?" I tease.

"Jesus, baby, I think I'm gonna fucking hit it into next week!"

he says as his right hand slides up my back and grasps my shoulder before he enters me. He takes my hip in his left hand, and as if someone shot a gun—he's off! Within several minutes, his tempo slows and he thrusts deeper into me, his fingers pressing harder into my skin. "THANK ... YOU ... MA'AM!" he says with each last thrust, then pulls out. He crashes next to me as he grabs my right arm to guide me onto my backside. He slides his hand slowly between my thighs, parting them again.

"What are you doing?" I ask as I finally open my eyes.

"It's your turn." He smiles.

"No, no. I'm good." I wince.

"Sore?" He bites his lip to hide his amusement—unsuccessfully.

"That's a bit of an understatement." I pull his lip free and lean up to kiss him.

"Sorry."

"No, you're not." I giggle.

"Well, I guess that's true." He smiles. "Shower?"

"Uh, yeah ... three times definitely warrants a shower." I push myself up.

Chapter Four

"Shall we continue?" he asks as he plops down onto the couch and throws his legs up, parting them. I sit between them and lean against his chest. I go on to tell him about our phone conversation, the flashback I had in the middle of the night. "Ugh, I was so mad at you that night." He smacks my leg.

"Yeah, I got that." I roll my eyes. I tell him about our texts and us getting together the next day. "Now, Ray, we talked about George. Did you mention George, or was it not part of your dream?" I turn my head back to him.

"No, I mentioned Grayson and told you he couldn't have you, stuff like that. You told me you were leaving in two days, which freaked me out when I woke up. I thought you were going to die and be with him." He hugs me. "Becca, you have no idea. Your heart rate spiked like crazy several times a day, for no reason the doctors could find." At this, I go into hysterics. "What?" he asks.

"Um, well, I know why I was setting off the alarms. Grayson and I were joking about it the last day we were together." My laughter gets blanketed by sadness.

"Why?"

"I was having sex. Every time they went off ... that's why." I sigh.

"Becs, it was several times a day, sometimes a few times in a row," he says, trying to discredit my revelation.

"Yep, that's right." I give him a frown-smile.

"Whatever, Becca ..." He trails off. His facial expression is a mixture of anger and jealousy. I kiss his pressed-together lips in an effort to soften his mood. It works a little and he nudges my lips back.

"When you left, you gave me my Christmas present. Grayson made me watch it right away. It's really beautiful, Ray. I love it." I hug him.

"Babe, what are you talking about?"

"The DVD you made me, set to music. You took your mom's flash drives with all the photos she's taken." I furrow my brow at him. A lightbulb suddenly comes on. When would he have had the time for that?

"Uh, Becs, I only thought of doing that. I, uh ... "

"I know, you haven't had time. But when you do, please do it. And please use the songs you originally thought about. I loved it, and it would be a great reminder of my journey to you if you do everything the same. By the way," I add, "your mother has gone beyond Nanarazzi boundaries!" I giggle.

"Why?"

"Have you looked at the pictures she has on her flash drive?" I widen my eyes.

"No, I haven't 'borrowed' it yet. Why?" He rubs my belly and kisses my cheek.

"Um ... remember when we had sex in the meadow during a riding excursion with your parents? After they headed back before we did?" I ask, trying to contain my laughter.

"Yeah. Jesus, that was hot, baby." He nips at my ear.

"Ahem ... yeah, well, apparently your mother's desire to take some nature shots produced a very interesting take on 'the birds and the bees.'" A giggle escapes.

"No—c'mon, Becs!" he says in disbelief.

"Didn't she come up to you later and tell you to take your time with me and to not be in such a rush?"

"Yeah, she did, but how do you know that?" He turns my face to him.

"You told me."

"No, I didn't."

"Well, then Grayson did through you in my subconscious. You'll see—the pictures are there." I smile. Ray is starting to look a little freaked out. "Well, after all that, I had a hard time not thinking about you. I couldn't bear the thought of leaving you and Annie. I was so torn. Part of me wanted to walk away from both of you, because all I was doing was hurting everyone." I play with his fingers on my belly.

"You were thinking about me even though you were with Grayson?" he asks quietly.

"Yeah. He could tell, too. He kept getting pissed in one instance, and then in the next, he would try to help me to acknowledge that I love you. It was very confusing." I close my eyes and try to fight back my tears. Talking about Grayson, getting close to our last moments—it's becoming painful.

"Baby?" Ray hugs me.

"Ray, I'm sorry. Can I just have a minute?" I tap his hands to release me. He lets go and I get up. I find myself back on the porch, having another good cry. I'm always going to miss him. He will always be a huge part of me. He was right. The years don't add up; it will always feel like he was just here yesterday, now more so than ever.

"Baby?" Ray pipes up, interrupting my thoughts. I turn to him. He hands me tissues. "The bracelet you tried to buy this morning ... that wasn't from me." He thumbs my tears away. "Grayson bought it for you before he died. It was a special order, and Derek picked it up for him. Hey, hey ... shh." He pulls me to him as I begin to sob uncontrollably.

"Ray," I cry, "he just gave me that bracelet for Christmas. That's why I was so adamant about buying it."

44

"Holy shit," he almost whispers.

"Why was it with Eric?" I ask.

"I dropped it off to get appraised so I could insure it for you. His new employee didn't realize it and put it out on display."

"How did you end up with it?" I nudge him, indicating we should go back inside.

"Well, Derek and I have been hanging out a lot. He's a great guy, and he's been helping me understand who Grayson was and your relationship with him. I've actually grown quite fond of Grayson. I think we would've been great friends—if you weren't in the equation, obviously." He smiles hugging my shoulders to him.

"Yes, we girls ruin everything, don't we?" I laugh.

"Hmm ... well, Derek told me he's had the bracelet all these years, but you kept telling him you couldn't handle any gifts from Grayson. You just weren't ready. So he gave it to me to give to you. Of course, after you opened it, I was going to tell you it was actually from Grayson."

"Ray, I'm glad that I woke up knowing everything and ready to move on, because had I not, that could've been very traumatic for me," I say, a little perturbed.

"Any more traumatic then waking up to find yourself four months pregnant without remembering how it happened?" he challenges me.

"Wow, that combo would've granted me a one-way, first-class ticket on the crazy train." I hold my temples and shudder at the thought. "Let's just both be glad I woke up the way I did—thanks to Grayson."

"Thanks to Grayson." He nods with what seems like a new sense of camaraderie toward Grayson. I continue to tell him about the crazy plane dreams I was having, then Christmas Eve and Day with Grayson and Morgan. Ray finds my gifts to Grayson very funny, especially the Shelley ones. I had to go back and tell him the story behind the pictures, and he was practically in tears over what

Grayson had said. "What else did you give him?" He leans on the opposite side of the counter as I pull out potatoes and start peeling.

"Well, Christmas Eve, I gave him one more thing, but that's private. On Christmas Day, I gave him a horse." I laugh at the thought now.

"A horse? How's that working out for him?" He joins in my thoughts.

"Not well, I suppose."

"What was the private gift?" His forefinger nudges my chin up, making me look at him.

"It was private, Ray." I sigh, trying to give him no expression to analyze.

"Was it something naughty?" He smirks.

"It was private. Now, stop asking!" I say with irritation.

"What did he give you?" he asks, changing direction.

"Well, he wanted to wait to give me my Christmas Eve present until after Christmas. Turns out, it's the item in the box he sent me just before he passed away." I grab another potato to peel.

"What was it?"

"I don't know. I've never opened it. I just hold it every year, staring at it." I strike the potato's skin a bit more rapidly.

"Why, baby?" He grabs my hands.

"Um. I guess I couldn't handle the finality of it all. It would've cemented the truth—that he's not coming back—in my heart." I use Grayson's words. He knew exactly why I behaved the way I did.

"Oh, baby, I am very sorry for your loss."

I'm taken aback. Not by the sincerity in his voice, but by the pain he seems to be feeling for me. I'm in awe at the depth of this man's patience and understanding. I put the potato and peeler down and wipe my hands on a towel before I walk around the other side of the counter.

"You are truly an amazing man, Ray. I love you so much, and am so thankful for you." I kiss him with everything I've got.

"Does this mean I get a private gift?" He smiles against my lips. I wave at the ceiling.

"What are you doing?" he asks with a chuckle.

"Waving goodbye to that very special moment you just killed," I reply. He throws his head back to let out a good, hearty laugh, then swats my butt as I get back to the potatoes. "McNeil!" I gasp. He grabs a stool and sits. "By all means ... pull up a chair," I tease him. He always watches and rarely helps me in the kitchen. It's okay. We decided a long time ago—it's best this way.

"So, did he get you anything else?" He hands me the next potato.

"Yes. A PANDORA bracelet filled with sentimental charms. If you don't mind, I'd like to buy what he gave me." I look up, unsure. He shrugs with indifference. "Um. A book, some Cricut cartridges that haven't been released yet, the bracelet, and ..." I trail off.

"And what?" He takes the last swig of his root beer from earlier. "Eh ... flat!" He wrinkles his nose.

"Pilot lessons," I say, my voice on the quiet side.

"Pilot lessons? Why?" He repeats the same face he just made over the flat soda.

"I used to fly Cessna planes when I was seven years old—with a pilot, of course," I offer.

"What? You mean actually flew?" He makes a driving motion with his hands.

"Yes. I was quite the natural. The pilot—Kay was her name, I believe—told my father to make sure to get me lessons when I was older. I fell in love with flying. It's an amazing feeling, to pilot a plane." I start chopping and look up when the long silence feels awkward. Ray is just staring at me, mouth open—speechless. I push his chin up and smile slightly.

"Becs, you have never told me this. Why didn't you pursue flying?" He grabs an apple out of the fruit bowl and takes a hearty bite.

"Well, my aunt's friend, the one she stayed with on the island, passed away. We stopped going out there, and my parents could never afford the lessons." I shrug.

"What island?" He looks at me quizzically.

"Really, Ray? I'm from Jersey. What 'island' do you think a struggling middle-class family would visit often?" I can't help my sarcasm.

"Would that be *Laung* Island?" he imitates my Jersey accent with annoying exaggeration. I throw a piece of raw potato at him. "So, do you still want to do that?" He pulls the piece of potato off of his shirt. "I have to say, I'm really not comfortable with the idea. I'd prefer if you didn't do it." He clears his throat and takes another bite of the apple.

"Well, it's not something I'm going to do right now, but I am thinking about it." I throw the cut potatoes into the pot.

"All I ask, babe, is that you please talk to me before you run off and do this. Okay?" I look over my shoulder at him as I fill the pot with water. "All decisions are made together now, not just the ones about the girls. Got me?" he asks. I give him a half smile and nod. This is going to take a bit of getting used to. "Hey, why were you at the jewelry store, anyway?" He gets up to throw the core into the trash.

"I was placing a special order for a necklace from Grayson to Morgan. He gave it to her for Christmas, and asked me to get it for her for real." I point to my iPod. Ray hands it to me and I put it in the dock, then turn on the Singers and Standards station at a low volume while I cook.

"It must've been bittersweet for him to spend time with Morgan."

I nod sadly. Ray grabs my hand and pulls me into his embrace. We start to dance slowly to "It Had to Be You." We're silent, soaking in the moment. I lay my head on his chest and he twirls us around. I think the period from the 20s to the 40s had to have produced the most romantic music of all time. So innocent and sweet—

it's enough to make you fall in love with love.

"It was bittersweet for him," I finally say.

"I don't even want to imagine." Ray shakes his head. "Becca, I promise to be a better father—more attentive and more equal to Morgan." His hands cup my face.

"You've already stepped up these past few months. I know you will keep at it, and I appreciate it, baby. Morgan loves you. I love you." I kiss him.

"So when did Grayson let you know who he really was?" he asks as we disengage so I can carry on with supper.

I tell him about the nap and my dream. How he had to convince me that it was all real. How my heart broke all over again. The relief I felt, though, at being able to say goodbye. How much he advocated for Ray. The appreciation, respect, and jealousy he felt toward him. I tell Ray what Grayson said about Heaven and the dilemma we'll have when all three of us are there. Ray laughs at this, but not so much at the shag schedule I laughed with Grayson about. I tell him about how quickly time goes by there, and how that's another reason Grayson had such a hard time with his assignment. I tell him about our book and Grayson's encouragement.

"Wait—you wrote a book?" Ray sits up straight on his stool once again in disbelief.

"Um ... yeah." I glance at the pan to season the steaks, then look up when I hear the stool hit the counter. "Where are you going?" I ask as he heads out of the kitchen.

"I need a minute ... by myself, Becca!" he snaps. A few moments later the front door slams. *What the hell is that about?* I pull out a new cutting board and slice up zucchini and summer squash, then throw them in a deep frying pan with minced garlic, cinnamon, and diced tomatoes. I melt butter and blue cheese in a small saucepan, whisking it slowly until it's creamy, and spoon it over uncooked breadsticks. I place them in the oven to bake.

The front door opens, and I can't help the sudden irritation I feel at hearing ESPN blaring from the family room. I head in there and find Ray in his recliner, looking pissed off instead of relaxed. I grab the remote off the side table.

"Give me that!" he snaps and jerks it out of my hand. "I need a break, Becca! Go in the kitchen and fucking cook." He raises the volume. *Oh hell to the fucking no he didn't!*

Ghetto Sybecca sways her head to the tempo of "uh-uh, girl-friend!" I grab the remote back out of his hand and turn the TV off.

"Oh hi, I'm sorry ... I'm Becca ... have we met?" My sarcasm takes center stage and bows. He kicks the recliner into a seated position, stands up, and gets in my face.

"Five fucking years! Relationship aside ... I have been your best friend! Flying fucking planes! Writing goddamn books! Why don't I know this? Why didn't you share it with me? I think these things fall under the big-fucking-deal category!" He's all teeth and anger.

My smart mouth is activated before I can even try to stop it.

"Dude ... you're like the Englishman who went up a hill and came down a fucking mountain!" I say. Ray stares at me intently, trying to stay mad. "Can I get something for you, Ray? A tampon? Maybe some Midol?" I try to keep a straight face. Ray sucks in his cheeks in an effort to avoid laughing. I, however, let my creeping glee escape.

"You're impossible," he sighs, finally allowing a smile.

"Possibly." I wrap my arms around his neck and get on my tippy toes for a kiss. "Ray, I didn't mention the book for the same reason I haven't published it. And the flying? Honestly, I haven't thought about it for a long time. That's all." I rub my nose against his.

"I just ... I don't like not knowing stuff about you."

"C'mon, that's a good thing. Keeps me interesting." I hold my head back to look into his eyes.

"I've never lacked interest in you, just so you know." He sways me a bit. "Can I read your book?" he asks.

"Um ... yes, yes you can." I nod after the initial thought.

"Hey, ya'll ... we interuptin' somethin'?" Elise says. We turn our heads in her direction and are met with the flash of her camera. Both of us burst into laughter. I know we're thinking the same thing.

"Nope, you're just in time. I'm throwing the steaks on now." I let go of Ray and head over to her.

"Are we okay, baby girl?" she asks, her eyes filling up.

"Yes, of course we are." I hug her. "I love you, you know that." I hold her at arm's length.

"And I love you, baby." She palms my cheeks and kisses my forehead.

"Mom ... I took the breadsticks out for you!" Morgan yells. *Shit!*

"Thank you, sweetie!" I yell back. "Let me get out there." I sigh. Ray pulls me back by my hips. I turn my neck up and to the right for the kiss I know is coming. Artie walks in as we pull away and slaps his son on the shoulder; a common greeting between them. Elise and I head down the hallway to the kitchen.

"It's so nice to see you two together again." Elise smiles wide. In the mother-in-law department, I'm happy to say I've been twice blessed. Gosh, I need to call Hazel. I only talked to her briefly the other night. She seemed a bit off.

"Elise—" I start.

"Mama," she corrects me with *The Look* for emphasis.

"Mama," I say with a smile, "have you talked to Hazel? Is she okay? She seemed off the other day." I place the filets on the grill portion of the stove.

"Yeah, honey, she's just sad. You know, sweetheart." She frowns.

"Yes, I do." Duh, why am I such an idiot? It's Christmas and her only son and husband are gone. No! No, it's more than that! I know it is. There's no sense in pressing the issue with Elise, though, because I'm the one who knows Hazel better.

"Mommy, can I help?" Morgan comes up behind me and rubs my back.

"Sure, baby. You wanna mash the potatoes?" I kiss her hair before I bring the pot to the sink to drain it.

"Okay. Regular or garlic?"

"Garlic. Morgy, I have it all ready to go in that pan there." I point and dump the potatoes in the bowl. "Where's Annie-Banannie?" I look over my shoulder at her.

"I think she went upstairs to finish reading the last few chapters of the book she has to do a report on," she says as she grabs a big fork out of the drawer and mashes them a bit before using the mixer, like I showed her.

"Oh, okay." I shrug as I return to the stove and flip the steaks. I lift the lid off the zucchini pan and stir that around. "I'll be right back." I smile and head down the hall. I can't help but overhear Ray arguing with his dad.

"Son, you know we love Becca. This has nothing to do with her. I just can't understand why you would let things go at work! There was no need for you to spend twenty hours a day at the hospital, and now you have no new contracts and you are ready to go under. Not a smart move in this economy, son! You have all these people who depend on you for a paycheck." Artie sounds passionately irritated. I've never heard him like this before—it's quite the opposite of his usual reticent behavior.

"If it was Mama, Daddy, you would've been there every minute you could *and* couldn't, just like me!" Ray yells back.

"I understand, son, but Becca hasn't ever been your only responsibility! You have a little girl to provide for!" Artie snaps.

"I have a family of four to provide for," Ray corrects him.

"Not yet, son. Annie is your priority."

"As far as I'm concerned, Dad, I have two little girls. They are both my priority."

My heart explodes at his declaration.

"How much are you in the hole, son?" Artie changes direction.

"I'm not ... not yet." Ray sighs, defeated.

"Why do you need twenty thousand dollars, then?"

"Because I took it from Becca to cover my overhead. I need to put it back before she realizes." His voice is laced with shame.

"She doesn't know?" Artie gasps.

"No, Dad, how do I tell her? *Hey, babe, I'm going to take care of you for the rest of your life. By the way, I'm broke and took twenty grand from you,*" he says with a bit of sarcasm. "Dad, please, I'm embarrassed enough as it is."

"Ray, what are you going to do next month?"

"Hopefully I'll have stuff lined up. I don't know, Dad." I hear him pacing. I can't take anymore. I know this is killing him. Ray is a very proud man.

"Hey, you two—dinner's just about ready!" I walk in cheerful.

"Baby, did you overhear anything?" Ray asks nervously.

"No. Why?" I give him a "what are you up to?" look.

"Nothing." He smiles and kisses me.

"Hey, can I talk to your dad a minute?"

"Why?"

"It's a secret, McNeil." I roll my eyes.

"All right ..." He leans in for another kiss before he heads out. I close the glass French doors behind him and turn to Artie.

"What's up, sweetheart?" Artie smiles.

"Please listen to everything I have to say before you interject." I wait. He nods, seemingly unsure of where I'm coming from. "Please give Ray a check for fifty grand. I will give you the check to cover it."

"Becca," he tries.

"Artie ... Dad ... your son has been taking care of everything at the inn for the past five years without ever taking a dime from me, no matter how much I argued with him about it. I know for a fact that he only charged me half of what it cost him to build onto my store. He won't take the money from me. You have to be the one to give it to him," I plead with him.

"Becca, isn't this going to put you in a bind?" he asks, full of concern.

"No, Dad. Grayson left me in a very comfortable position." I look down, feeling ashamed.

"I thought you were struggling?"

"No, I've been overpaying on my mortgage and not touching the money Grayson left me because it offered closure that I wasn't ready for. Please do this. It will bide me some time to talk Ray into taking on the renovations I want to do—and the money to cover it." I grab his arm.

"Are you going to tell him you know about the twenty thousand dollars?" he asks.

"What twenty thousand dollars?" I wink.

"You know, lady, you are one of a kind! It'll be a proud day for me when you become my son's wife." He pulls me into a fierce hug, his words taking my breath away. "I was going to lend him the twenty, but I wanted to give him a wake-up call. How do I explain the fifty?" he asks.

"Well, take your time. At the end of the night, tell him that you and Elise talked and you both decided to give him an early wedding gift." I smile at my bright idea.

"Ha! Becca, that's quite the wedding gift, doncha think?" He looks at me warily.

"Well, I'm quite the girl that he's marrying, doncha think?" I raise an eyebrow.

"That you are, my dear." He chuckles and kisses my forehead.

"Come on, dear, sweet, future father-in-law, I've got some good grub out there for you!" I take his arm and we head out and down the hall.

Ray looks over at me from the table and flashes me a huge smile. I return the gesture. We all sit down and hold hands as Elise says the blessing.

"So, Mommy, when are we moving all of our stuff over?" Morgan asks before she cuts into her steak.

"We'll do it slowly so we don't overwhelm ourselves," I say thoughtfully. A box here and there is much more doable for me.

"You girls still have to decide whether you want to share a room or have your own." Ray waves his fork at them before taking a bite of his steak. "Mmm ... this is good, babe." He closes his eyes, a look of pure enjoyment coming over his face.

"Yeah?" I smile. He nods.

"Well, I think we'd like to share," Annie says before taking a swig of her drink.

"Just remember, this is it. You two are going to be sisters now, not just best friends. You'll be with each other all the time. You may want your own space," I try to remind them. I can feel the weight of Ray's stare. I glance over at him, causing his mouth to curve into a half smile. Elise pats my thigh. I look over at her when Ray digs into his food again. Her eyes are full. *What has gotten into everyone?*

"Mom, we want to share." Morgan backs Annie's declaration up.

"Yes, Mom, we're sharing," Annie says again, and my heart leaps at the sound of her calling me "Mom."

"Can we redecorate our room, Dad?" Morgan asks Ray and he drops his fork. Morgan has never called Ray "Dad," not even on a slip up.

"Anything for my girls." He winks at her. The girls get excited and start chatting about color schemes and patterns. "Becs," he whispers. I turn to my left, where he's sitting at the head of the table. He grabs my hand. "I feel like I've won the lottery." He smiles.

"We all did, baby." I lean in to kiss him.

"So, Becca, when's your appointment for the babies?" Elise asks.

"Oh! I almost forgot!" I look back to Ray. "We have an appointment and ultrasound in two weeks. We may be able to find out what we're having!" I clap my hands like a child.

"I don't think we should find out," Ray states flatly. My head whips back to him in shock, as if he stole the cherry right off of my imaginary sundae. "Look ... if it's a boy and a girl, the nursery will be neutral anyway, so what's the big deal? We'll just go with neutral now." He shrugs. I continue to gape at him. "I want to be surprised," he adds.

"Don't you think the fact that I'm pregnant is surprise enough?" I try to stay calm. He stares at me, keeping his face straight for another minute before he cracks up.

"Really—you think I could wait?" He nudges my shoulder. I smack him playfully. Ugh! He knows how to push my buttons!

The table conversation carries on with bets over what they are and which names we might pick. We also agree that we will celebrate Christmas on New Year's Eve. Good thing the girls are out of the Santa Claus stage, or we could've found ourselves in a pickle. I'm glad to get a couple of extra days, as I haven't gone shopping! Today was the first day I felt strong enough to drive.

"You go 'head to the family room, baby. I'ma wash these dishes up for ya!" Elise nods me out of the kitchen.

"No, Mama, let me help." I grab a dish towel and dry off the pot she's already washed.

"No! Now go on! You cooked, I'll clean. Go rest. Have yo'self a nice snuggle with my son." She bats her eyes at me playfully.

"Hmm ... well, when you put it that way ... " I smile and kiss her cheek before I join Ray in the family room.

"C'mere, baby." Ray pats between his legs. I head over and scoot in. He wraps his arms around me.

"What are we watching?" I ask around a yawn.

"*It's a Wonderful Life.*"

"It is, isn't it?" I look up at him.

"It will be now." He kisses me.

"Are you guys going to be kissing the entire movie?" Annie asks.

"No, sweetie, I'm sure Daddy and I will fall asleep halfway through it, like we always do," I answer.

I didn't lie. That's exactly what we do. When Elise wakes us, Artie pulls Ray aside, leaving me to go up to bed alone. I put on my PJs and head into the bathroom for my nightly routine. Ray walks in just as I finish brushing my teeth.

"Wow ... SRPs!" Ray laughs. I think for a moment.

"Sex-repellent pajamas," we say in unison.

"Oh, you don't find my earmuff-wearing snowmen pajamas sexy?" I laugh.

"Yeah ... not really." He winces.

"Well, shop is closed anyway. We're both exhausted." I pat his chest and head into the bedroom.

"But—" he starts.

"Ray, I'm pregnant and tired, which is a surefire mix to making me cranky. Please." I pull the covers back. "There's always tomorrow morning." I smile sleepily after I climb in. He spits out his toothpaste and wipes his mouth.

"What if you don't love me tomorrow morning?" He looks down at the floor instead of me. I take in a deep breath and get out of bed. I grab a flyer out of my purse and write on the back.

I, Becca Kirsten James, on the date of December 29, 2012, promise to still be in love with Raymond Patrick McNeil on December 30, 2012, and every day after for the rest of my life.

Becca Kirsten James

I hand him the paper and climb back under the covers. Ray places the paper on the nightstand before proceeding to undress as well. After a few minutes, he crawls in and wraps himself around me, like he always does, in an effort to share our side of the bed.

"Do I at least get a kiss good night?"

"Mmm hmm." I turn my face and give in to the soft beckoning of his tongue.

My new alarm, called "The Bladder," wakes me up at its new usual time of 5:30 a.m. I slowly try to unravel myself from Ray's death grip. He rolls over and I head in, keeping the light very dim. I sit for a minute, simply because I'm too lazy and too tired to get up. Looking down at my PJs, I realize they *are* quite hideous. I get up, wash my hands, and head out to the bedroom. I open my top drawer and pull out a tank top and panties, then change quickly in the bathroom before going back to bed.

Ray holds the covers up for me and I climb back into his arms.

"You changed?" His hand runs up my leg.

"Yeah. I didn't want to repel you in the morning." I yawn.

"Baby." He kisses my shoulder.

"Mmm ..."

"It is morning." He presses against my backside. A perfect theme song comes to mind—that is, if Ray were actually Grayson. I feel a quick pang in my heart and get lost along that train of thought. "Becca, goddamn it!" Ray sighs with frustration. "Where is your head at, baby?"

"Sorry, I'm still half asleep." Half-truth.

"Fine." He inhales the smell of my hair. "You're a terrible liar, babe, just so you know." He pulls me closer to him.

"Mmm." I drift back off.

⠀

"Is that a new outfit, babe?" Ray stops eating his breakfast to study my appearance.

"Why, yes it is!" I spin for him in my new maternity sweaterdress. It's gray with specks of cream in it. "I got new boots too." I show off my black knee-length boots.

"Yeah, Derek told me you subjected him to the mall the other day. You look pretty, baby." He smiles and continues to eat.

"Well, I had to buy new clothes to accommodate my new look." I pat my belly.

"I have to go to the office today, Becs," he says quickly and takes a sip of coffee.

"Ray! We're supposed to go Christmas shopping today! Can't you go back on Monday?" My attempt at hiding my disappointment is nonexistent.

"No. I really can't, babe."

"McNeil, you pull this shit every year! You just hate shopping with me!" I snap.

"I'm not denying the fact that I hate shopping with you. It's a fucking nightmare," he states in a matter-of-fact tone. "But that's not the reason. I really have to go in. I'll try to meet up with you by this afternoon. Okay, baby?" He pulls me to him and looks up at me.

"Fine," I grumble. "You suck, McNeil," I add.

"That's not what you were saying an hour ago." He smirks, patting my bottom. "I really, really like this dress." He slides his hand down and creeps underneath the hem.

"Stop!" I smack his hand as it travels up.

"Saved by the girls." He smiles and nods over to our two sleepyheads. They sit at the table, eyelids drooping, and I swear their faces will fall into their pancakes.

Chapter Five

"Thank you for still loving me this morning." Ray smiles against my lips.

"I had to. I signed a contract ... sorta." I laugh and wave him off, and he walks out the door.

Ugh! I wish Stacey was here to go shopping with me! She won't be back 'til next week. I was so happy when she told me that Max was moving his consulting firm back east. We'll be having our babies together!

"Mama!" I shout.

"Yeah, baby?" She comes out from the kitchen.

"Oh." I laugh. "I didn't realize you were down here already. I'm going to head out now. Wish me luck!" I grab my purse and coat.

"Okay. See you later, baby girl." She smiles.

As I drive down Orchard Terrace, I realize I have no idea what to get Ray this year! Crap! I mean, the usual stuff is a given, but I have had no time to come up with a special personal gift. It'll come to me. I know it will—it has to. I pull up in front of my favorite coffee shop, The Java Joint.

"Hey, Talia!" I say when she turns around. Talia's the owner. She's a petite little thing, about thirty, with jet-black hair, jet-black glasses, and a silver hoop nose ring.

"Becca!" she practically screams and runs around the counter to hug me. "How are you?" She holds me at arm's length.

"Great, great!" I laugh.

"Look at you—you're glowing! It's about time you and Ray finally settle down." She rubs my belly. Small town ... of course everyone knows. They probably knew upon the egg's implantation! "Your usual?" she asks. I nod.

"Oh, half decaf, though."

"Okay. Freakish warm weather today, huh?" she asks.

"Yeah. You don't need a coat out there at all." She hands me my pumpkin coffee.

"On the house." She pushes my money away.

"Thanks, Talia! I'll see you soon." I head out. One great thing about being in a coma? People want to give you shit for free when you come out of it! I head next door to the Hot Topix spa. Love that name. Very clever; who doesn't catch up on the latest gossip at their salon? I grab gift certificates for Claudia, Hazel, Elise, and Stacey. Next, I hit Claudia's favorite tattoo parlor and get her a gift certificate there. I pop in to see Eric the jeweler and pick up my bracelet from Grayson. I put it right on, then buy the pearl necklace and bracelet Grayson and I had given Hazel. Morgan's necklace is ready as well. While I'm here, I put together my PANDORA bracelet from Grayson. Checkout is painful. I hand over my black AmEx. I sign my name, laughing to myself about when I was in here with Grayson.

"Thank you, Becca! Have a great day, and give my best to Ray." Eric smiles.

"You too—I will!" I say and head out. I walk past the local gift shop/florist, then stop and turn back. I look in the window and see something special for Ray. Special and funny. I go in and buy it.

Coming out of the gift shop, I realize my feet are killing me, I'm tired, and getting hungry. I look at my watch.

"Geez!" I've been at it for three hours. I pull out my phone to text Ray.

December 30, 2012   11:58 a.m.

Me: Hungry? I'm going to get your Mom's gift then lunch for us. I'll be over by u in 30!

Ray: It's a no go, baby. I'm too busy. I'll see you tonight! :(

Me: What? C'mon, Ray! At least have lunch with me!

Ray: Baby, I love you. I can't.

Me: I'm bringing your lunch.

Ray: No, I'll get something. Don't worry.

Me: C U soon! ;-p

Ray: Becs! I said no, babe! Please, I'm busy!

I ignore his last text and head into the camera store. I get Elise a super-duper lens for her Canon. Next stop, the deli. I order subs for Ray and I as well as grab him some chips and a root beer ... eck! I head back to my truck, happy to unload all of my new treasures. I get in and drive down to Ray's office. I grab our lunch, my purse, and the black Sharpie I found on the floor of the truck. I get off the elevator on the third floor and head through the double glass doors.

"Hi, Becca!" Gwen smiles and hugs me. "Ray's on the phone with a client," she says.

"Oh, well, can you bring this in to him? I need to use the ladies'." I hand her the bag with our lunch.

"Sure." She smiles.

"Thanks!" I head down the hall to the bathroom. As soon as I lock the door behind me, I get to work. I pull my panties off and stick them in my purse. I pull out the Sharpie and close the toilet lid before putting my right foot up. I hike up my dress and begin to write on my inner thigh. I blow on and fan it 'til it's dry. I switch legs and write on the left inner thigh, then follow the same drying regiment. I try to wipe at it. Nothing! I'm good to go. I throw the Sharpie into my purse and head out to Ray's office.

I open the door to find him behind his desk on the other side of the room, his back turned. I quietly close the door behind me and lock it. As if he can sense my presence, he turns around and shakes his head at me. I walk toward him. He sits in his chair, trying to ignore me.

"Rich, we'll do it better than Greerson, and for a quarter-mil less. Yes, one million," he says into the phone. *Go!* he mouths, trying to shoo me away with his hand. I sit atop his desk in front of him instead. "Listen, I'll have the plans drawn up and on your desk by Monday morning. I guarantee you'll like what you see, man." He leans forward and plants a soft kiss on my knee. His free hand travels slowly up my leg, under my dress, and to my hip. His eyes widen and his hand searches around my hip for my panties. He shakes his head in disbelief and smacks his head against my knees gently over and over again. "Yes, Rich. Email me what they want. Nine a.m. Monday morning, not a minute later. Okay, very good. You, too! See you then—bye." He hangs up and presses the button for Gwen.

"Yes, Ray?" she asks.

"Gwen, please hold my calls for a lunch break."

"Will do."

"Thanks." He hits the button again. He slides his hands up my legs, taking my dress with them, then moves back down to hook my knees. He tugs at them, pulling me to the edge of the desk. I feel myself tremble with anticipation. He whips my legs open, then gasps when he reads the message he uncovers. Two simple words seem to ignite him like a volcano. He stands up quickly, pulling at his belt, and I start to unbutton his jeans. He pushes my hands away, taking care of it himself (clearly I'm not moving fast enough). Before I know it, he tilts my hips up and rams inside of me, my "Fuck Me" sign rubbing against his hips as he pounds into me. His hand covers my mouth to stifle my moans. "Shh," he adds. Within minutes, Ray spills himself inside of me. He bites my lip hard as his last quake courses through him. "Jesus Christ, Becca!" He leans his forehead against mine. I trail soft kisses down his cheek to his mouth and cover it purposefully with my own. "Mmm," he groans as he pulls away. "Go clean up in the bathroom and I'll set up our lunch on the couch." He pats my hip.

"Okay, baby." I nudge his lips again with mine. He helps me off his desk and swats my bum as I head off. I swing back around and go to my purse. Diving my hand in, I retrieve my panties and wave them at him, smiling before I head back toward his private bathroom. He bites his smile back and shakes his head at me.

I walk back in to find Ray has already wolfed down half of his sandwich.

"Hungry?" I raise an eyebrow and sit across from him.

"Mmm." He takes another bite. I settle in to my turkey and cheese with extra mayo. Ray thumbs mayo away from the corner of my mouth. I grab his hand and suck the mayo off his thumb, giving him a reminder of the sexual shenanigans that went on in our bed this morning. I watch as he closes his eyes and licks his lips. I kiss his thumb and release his hand.

"So, was that a possible future project you were on the phone about?" I ask before taking another bite of my sub, unaffected by my own teasing.

"Uh, yeah." Ray opens his eyes. "I hope," he adds. "I'm not going to make much of a profit, though."

"Why?" I sip my coffee.

"Because I underbid Greerson, which I never do. Greerson is the one who underbids. He gets a lot of business that way, but the quality sucks. I've been hired often to fix his structural designs. He has a habit of cutting corners that are still within legal limits, but shouldn't be cut." He grabs the other half of my sub and starts eating it like he always does. I don't know where this guy puts it all.

"Well, why did you underbid him?"

"Two reasons," he says with his mouth full like a twelve-year-old boy. He swallows and takes a swig of root beer. "First, I desperately need to line some projects up. I've been a little preoccupied." He ignores the look I give him, because he knows I would've never wanted him to neglect his business. "Second, I've decided to try a different tactic and put my name out there. They'll like my work, and they won't have to pay extra to correct it. That should help get my firm more referrals." He nods like he's agreeing with himself.

"Well, I actually wanted to talk to you about something," I say, a bit unsure as to whether I should bring this up now.

"What's that, baby?" He pops the last bite of my sub into his mouth.

"I'd like to sit down with you and go over what I'd like for the renovations at the inn."

"Becs," he stops me, shaking his head. "We can't do that right now, baby. I'm sorry."

"Why? You said you're trying to line up projects. This would be a huge project for you!" I slap his leg.

"Becca, listen to me, honey. I want to do the renovations for you. I want to give you everything you desire. I just ... I don't have it to give right now. Once I get things rolling again, I'll be able to do it." He rubs my arms up and down.

"Ray, you're not making any sense! You need to get work for your firm, and this is a huge project."

Ray stands up, running his hands through his hair.

"Becca, I don't have the goddamn resources to fucking pay for it!" He can barely restrain his frustration. I stand up and walk over to him.

"Ray. Stop." I grab him. "Grayson is paying for the renovations. He made me promise I would do it. He also told me to tell you to take the money for it, or he will haunt you for the rest of your life." I smile, hoping to provoke one from him. Yeah ... it doesn't work.

"I am not taking your money! I don't care what Grayson made you promise! You are no longer his responsibility—you are mine!" he says through his teeth.

"Well, technically, we're not married, so Morgan and I still fall under the category of being Grayson's responsibility!" *Cautionary*

Sybecca shakes her head and holds up her new ticker board. It reads: "Ohhhhh faaaaaackkk!"

"The answer is *NO!* And I'm going to tell you something else! I am not competing with a dead guy anymore! *YOU HEAR ME? I'M DONE WITH IT!*" he yells. It's so loud, I can sense the people in the office stopping in their tracks.

"A dead guy?" I can hardly believe he referred to Grayson like that.

"*DEAD! D.E.A.D. DEAD!*" he shouts. *I hold Ghetto Sybecca and her brass knuckles back.*

"Well you know what, Ray? You're going to look like a complete idiot when your top competitor, what's his name? Beckett? Yeah, you're going to look like an idiot when Beckett is the one hired to do your fiancée's renovations!" *Ha! Take that, McNeil!*

"Humph ... I don't see a fucking ring on your finger." He grabs my hand to look. "Do you?" he asks, throwing it down. I take in a sharp breath and feel my nose flare to stop my tears—and possibly my heart from shattering into a million pieces.

"Okay," I murmur softly and nod in defeat. I grab my purse and run out of his office. I don't even put the energy into slamming his door. What's the point? Before I reach the double glass doors, I hear Ray yell "Damn it!" and glass breaking in his office. I step into the elevator and press the button for the first floor. As I quietly sob, I decide that today was probably not a good day to bring up the renovations.

I climb into the truck and head back to Ray's house. I know what I have to do. What I need to do.

"Morgan, c'mon, sweetie." I grip her hand.

"What's up, Mom?" she asks as I pull her along.

"You and I are taking a trip. Don't say anything. Just pack what you want from here for now," I say, and leave her at her door. She goes in hesitantly. I head to Ray's room and grab a suitcase to fill with my maternity clothes and toiletries. "Ready?" I ask, and grab her hand.

"Um, yeah." She holds her bag up.

"Where are you two going?" Annie asks as she walks down the hall.

"We have a family emergency, honey. We'll call you later." I hug her and kiss her hair. "I love you."

"I love you too, Mom."

Morgan and I run downstairs and out of the house.

"We have to stop at the inn." I look over at her, ignoring my phone. It's blowing up.

"Mom, Ray's calling you. Aren't you going to answer it?" She holds it up.

"No," I say simply and put the truck in gear.

"Where are we going, Mommy?" She puts the phone down.

"Home," I sigh.

"To the inn?"

"No, baby. To California." I look over at her.

"To our old home with Daddy?!" She smiles excitedly. I nod.

"Claudia." I hug her when I walk in.

"Hey, what are you doing here?" She rubs my back.

"Just grabbing a few things. Morgan and I are heading out to California for a little bit. I need to go get our tickets and set up transportation."

"Um. Okay. Do you need a ride to the airport?" she asks, sounding unsure.

"Yes, please." I sigh and pick up my bags. I almost head to the room Grayson and I were sharing, but am reminded not to do so when a guest walks out of it.

I place the bags on the table in my room.

"Where the hell is my laptop?" I search around, then slap myself on the head. I just wasted several minutes looking for the laptop that Grayson bought me in my subconscious. What the fuck? I grab another bag and put Grayson's Christmas gift to me in it, as well as some other things. My cell pings. I pick it up and take in a deep breath.

December 30, 2012   2:43 p.m.
Ray: Where are you going?
Ray: Please don't leave me, baby. I'm sorry.

I put the phone down. I'll deal with him later. My phone rings, and I look at it.

"Hey, Claudia," I answer.

"Hey, just booked your flights. We have to roll now, though," she says.

"Oh my God, you are awesome!" She totally is! I hang up and grab Morgan's gift from Grayson. *Shit!* I go into my desk drawer and grab the keys to the ranch. I haven't called Susanna or Sam yet. They may be somewhere off with the boys. *Double shit!* If they are, I'm going to have to call Derek to come and get us. His wife may not be too pleased. He only got back two days ago. Oh well, I'll figure it out! I open the next drawer and pull out the checkbook that still has mine and Grayson's name on it. I write Artie a check for fifty grand and a blank check made out to Ray's firm, then quickly pen a letter to Artie and put it in an envelope with both checks for Claudia to give him. Okay, I think that's it. I slam the door and a picture falls out of one of the bill slots. It's a picture of Ray and me, cheek to cheek, smiling. I throw it in my purse. I place Ray's gift on my bed and grab my bag. Locking the door behind me, I answer my phone.

"Derek, hi!" I head down the stairs.

"Becs, what's going on, love? Ray is going out of his bloody mind!"

"Do you know if Susanna and Sam are home, or are they visiting the boys?" I ignore his question.

"With the boys. Why?"

"Okay. I'll need you to pick us up from the airport. I'll call you with the details." I sigh.

"Wait! What?" he yells. Damn it. I had a feeling he was not going to be thrilled.

"I'm leaving now. I'll call you back." I hang up. "C'mon, let's go." I grab Claudia. We run out to the truck and I hand her the keys. Within an hour, she has us at the airport.

"Please give this to Artie without Ray seeing. Tell Ray there's something on my bed for him. Here, Merry Christmas." I hand her the gift certificates I picked up and give her a hug.

"Are you coming back?" she asks, her eyes wide with panic.

"Yes. We won't be gone long. I just need to take care of a few things." I hug her again. "Thank you, Claudia, you're doing a great job!"

"Thanks." She smiles, "Love you!"

"Love you too! C'mon Morgy," I say, and we jump out. I text Derek to be at LAX at five p.m. Morgan and I check in and run to the gate. We're the last to board.

"Mommy, we're in first class?" Morgan asks. Her eyes go wide.

"Yeah, that's all that was left." I half smile.

"Cool." She plops down. "Uh ... Mom." She looks to me, then points to her window. I lean over and see Ray pointing to the door of the gate and begging the clerk at the desk. *Shit!* They close the door to the plane. I watch Ray as the plane backs out. He kneels slowly in front of the window as we taxi away, his hands pulling at his hair. Liz pops into my mind. *Oh, crap! Becca—you asshole!* I take out my cell.

December 30, 2012 4:33 p.m.

Me: I love you! I WILL be back! I need to sort a few things out for me ... for us. I promise. I love you!

I turn my phone off before I get *The Look* from the steward.

Chapter Six

RAY

"Ray ... Ray, baby?" I close my eyes at the sound of my mother's voice.

"Son, where's Becca and Morgan?" Dad asks.

"Gone." I barely recognize my own voice. I stand up and turn around to face my parents and Annie. They're all out of breath from trying to keep up with me.

"What happened, Ray baby?" Mama asks.

"Talk to us, son," my father adds.

"Oh, Dad, I uh ... I really did it now. I screwed up big time today." I sit down and put my head in my hands.

"What happened?" Dad asks again as they all sit across from me.

"Well, I asked Becca not to come today for lunch. I was in the zone with work and trying to line some possibilities up. I didn't want to be distracted by her. She's safe, well, and home. I needed to focus on work. Of course, Becca being Becca, she didn't listen. It was fine though, we were eating lunch and discussing the project I put in a bid for. So she decides to talk about doing renovations at the inn. I told her I'm not in the position to do that right now. 'Bout killed me to tell her that. We went back and forth. She just wasn't getting it!" I sit back, frustrated. "Then she informs me that Grayson is paying for it, that 'technically' she and Morgan are still his responsibility. I told her no, that I'm tired of competing with a dead guy and that I wasn't going to do it anymore."

"Raymond Patrick! Please tell me you did not refer to Grayson as *a dead guy*, literally!" Mama's eyes have daggers aimed at me, waiting to fire.

"Yeah. Not proud of myself, Mama. She repeated me, very hurt, and I actually screamed in her face, *DEAD, D.E.A.D. DEAD*." I shake my head, disgusted with myself.

"Oh, Raymond." Mama's face matches the disgust I feel.

"Wait, it gets better!" I widen my eyes. I tell them about Becca threatening to hire Beckett and how I said in so many words not to call herself my fiancée.

"You fucking *idiot*!" My father, who never says *boo* to anything, looks as if his head just might explode.

"Arthur!" Mama gasps.

"Do you have any idea what you've done? Becca is the best thing that has ever happened to you! You ... ugh ... I could just—" Dad wrings an imaginary neck. I actually feel like I'm ten and am about to get a whoopin'.

"Hey, guys! Phew! I didn't think I'd find you! I saw you pulling in as I was leaving," Claudia says breathlessly.

"Claudia! Claudia!" I jump up. "You dropped them off?" I hold her at arm's length. "What did she say?" I ask, but I'm not sure I can bear to hear the answer.

"She said she needed to take care of a few things, that she needed to sort herself out." I let her sit. "She did say that you two had a terrible fight. That's why she wouldn't answer your calls. That and she didn't want you to try to talk her out of leaving. Ray—" she touches my knee. I look up at her. "She's coming back. She told me so." She offers me a smile.

"She did? She is?" I feel hope bloom inside of me.

"Yes. But she also told me to tell you not to follow her out there. She wants you to concentrate on the plans you need ready for Monday. She left you a gift at the inn on her bed."

"*Idiot!*" Dad interjects again.

"Thanks, Dad, appreciate it!" I smile sarcastically.

"Oh, by the way, Mr. McNeil, can I see you for a second?" She gets up and grabs my father's arm. They walk off and I watch as she passes an envelope to him. My dad opens it, puts something in his pocket, and starts reading a letter. He shakes his head, then gives Claudia a hug and kiss. She waves to us and heads off.

"What's that, Dad?" I ask, feeling a bit calmer now.

"Oh, I'm going to share this with you, and then let me tell you something! When I'm done, you are going to listen to everything I say and do as you are told, or so help me God, Raymond!" I can hear the air release from the can of whoopass my father is itching to bust the seal on. Like a good ten-year-old boy, I nod. He unfolds the letter and clears his throat.

Dear Dad,

Please don't be upset with me. I had to leave abruptly like this, or Ray would've talked me out of it. I realized today that although I'm ready to move on, there is still a lot that I need closure on.

You see, I was married to the most incredible man. He was my whole world. That world came crashing down when I lost him. I know I don't have to explain the severity of my grief to you. You've had front-row seats to it. But a part of me has never let go of the denial phase of grief. There was no proper goodbye to be said. No body to bury. All I had to show for his death were his things as he left them, like he was coming back. So there's a lot I didn't do and/or face because a part of me always felt that if I just left it as it is ... he would come back. I guess a part of me thought, for seven years, that he's been on a deserted island somewhere trying to get back to us. You know, like Tom Hanks in *Castaway*.

Well, I'm ready to accept that this is no longer true. To do this, I must face all of the things I ran from. It's the only way I'm going to be able to give your son everything he needs. He shouldn't have to feel that he's competing with a ghost. I don't want my memories and love for Grayson to overshadow my life with Ray. It has for far too long.

In saying all of this, I must tell you how blessed and thankful I feel every day to have your son's unconditional love. He's the most amazing, talented, thoughtful, funny, intelligent—

Dad puts the letter down, "You're an *asshole*!" he says.
"Oh, did she forget that one, Dad?" I chuckle.
"Humph," he says, and starts reading again.

—handsome, and loving guy I've met since Grayson. I'm so very much in love with him. I promise to always, from this day on, take care of him and his heart. He is my forever.

Okay, done with the mushy stuff! Now on to business! While being mushy, I forgot to mention stubborn and impossible, to put it nicely. This is where you come in! I need your help getting through to your son! As you can see, I've enclosed a blank check to Ray's firm. As you may or may not know, Ray and I had a bit of an argument over the renovations at the inn. His pride got in the way. Surprise, surprise!

Dad shoots me a look. I shrug.

I know where his heart is, and I truly love him for it, but he's being an idiot! I need him to realize that he is taking care of me by accepting the money for the renovations. By pushing his pride aside for a minute, he will help me bring in revenue that will no doubt triple the amount that was put into the renovations in the first place! He will essentially earn my business a lot of money, therefore, he'll be providing for me. Please help him see this! It's a win-win! We're supposed to lean on each other. He won't let me take care of him. We've always been a team when it comes to the girls, and we need to step it up. Our lives are going to be cemented together, our family made bigger. This shouldn't be about what he's bringing to the table, but what we're both bringing and how we can blend it together to help make our life together good, and keep it that way.

I'm rambling. Sorry. I think you know where I'm coming from. Please help Ray see it, too.

Please take care of him and Annie while I'm gone.

Please tell him how much I love him and that I'm doing this for us. Make sure he doesn't follow me out there. I need this time to grieve and let go. Talk soon!

Love Always,

Becca

I take the letter from him. I can vaguely smell the scent of her lotion on it.

"How much am I writing this check for, son?" Dad asks me. I inhale deeply and blow it out through pursed lips, feeling defeated. Christ, that woman could convince a duck it's a lion!

"I don't know what her budget is, Dad. Ask her what it is and write it out." I stand up and grab Annie's hand. "C'mon, let's go home, baby."

"So, you're going to do it then? No more arguments?" he asks.

"Dad, I just got a rude awakening." I point to the window where her plane was. "Sure, it wasn't what I thought it was, but it was still a wake-up call. She's the love of my life. She gets what she wants, whatever she wants. So long as I never again have to feel the way I felt about thirty minutes ago." I sigh, and Dad gives my back a good slap. A dad's code for saying he's proud of you.

"I just don't understand why she wrote you a letter, Artie, instead of me. Becca and I have always been real close." Mama does nothing to hide her disappointment.

"Oh, Mama, Becca needed to get through to me, and she just felt Daddy was right for the job this time. Some things need a man's touch instead of a woman's." I hang my arm around her shoulders and hug her to me as we walk.

"He called you an asshole, Ray!" she states like I'm crazy.

"Yep. Man's touch, Mama." I chuckle. She pushes imaginary nonsense away with her hands.

Once we get into the truck, I grab my phone to text Becca for about the hundredth time. My screen lights up with a message from her. I read it and kiss the screen.

December 30, 2012   5:15 p.m.
Me: Safe flight. Safe journey. Safe home. You are my world. I love you, Becs. Like a love song, baby. And I keep hitting re-peat…peat…peat.peat.peat. peat. ;-p

Pretty sure she'll laugh when she reads that. I put the phone down and start the truck up.

It's five past nine. For the past twenty minutes, I've been pacing and staring at my phone at a rate that even I'm finding annoying. Her plane landed ten minutes ago!

"Ugh!" I sigh and sit back down. A smile comes across my face as I stare at her gift on the coffee table. It's the oddest thing I've ever seen, yet it's so perfect. It's a statue of bare baby feet that go as high as a little bit above the ankles, made out of white porcelain. Becca has always had this amazing talent of finding the most unique and personal gifts. On the other hand, her talent is the reason shopping with her is a fucking nightmare! I jump at the sound of my phone pinging.

December 30, 2012   9:15 p.m.
Becca: Yikes! 38-year-old man reciting Selena Gomez ... little creepy, babe!
Me: Uh ... porcelain baby feet cut off from the rest of the body ... a bit creepier, Becs!
Love the sentiment though, baby! Thank you!
Becca: I knew you were going to make a damn comment about that instead of just seeing

the message! LOL.

Me: Please, I want to hear your voice. Miss you, baby! :(

Becca: I'll call u when I'm in the car. Miss u too! I'm sorry, Ray.

Me: OK.

I throw my phone down and decide to get a beer to take the edge off. Anger is slowly creeping in. Christ, she drives me mad! As I walk back into the family room, my phone plays the intro to "Ice Ice Baby." It always makes me smile. Best first date I've ever had. I pick it up and press the answer key.

"Baby," I sigh.

"Hi." She seems unsure.

"Did you have a good flight?"

"Um. Yes."

"And the weather out there?"

"Little chill in the air, kinda like the one on the phone."

"Derek get there on time?" I continue and take a swig of my beer.

"Yes, Ray!" she snaps.

"Staying with him, or in a hotel?" I keep my voice flat.

"Neither."

"Where are you staying?" I ask before the bottle touches my lips again.

"My house." She's quiet.

"Wow! And the hits just keep coming, huh, babe?" I bait her.

"Ray, what are you playing at?"

"I'm not playing at anything, baby. Just wanted to hear your voice." I sit down and spin the remote around.

"Whatever you are spinning, please stop! Ray, I know the way I left today was terrible. I am sorry. I just knew you would try to stop me." Her voice shakes.

"Becs! It doesn't help me accept the whole barefoot idea when you leave me without a word, and only twenty-four hours into our 'new' life. What do you think that tells me, baby?" I raise my voice.

"Please, baby ... don't yell at me." She speaks in that soft tone that always gets to me. I don't know why, it just stirs something so deep inside.

"I'm sorry, Becs. I'm just upset. I want you here in my arms. I want to smell your hair and kiss your skin. This is all my fault. If I wasn't such an asshole today, you'd be here." I rub my face and sit back with my beer.

"Ray, though your words were awful and harsh, that's not what I took to heart."

I interrupt her. "Baby, I know. Dad read me the letter."

"Oh, he did?" She seems taken aback.

"Yeah. Still, Becs, I shouldn't have. I was letting my pride get in the way. I was such jerk today. Kinda miss Lucy now. At least I'd know I'd get a do over tomorrow." I chuckle a bit.

"Ray, I'm here to make sure 'Lucy' doesn't come back. I need to get full closure. I owe it to both of us."

"I just don't like how this all happened, babe, and I don't like that you are there alone trying to deal with this. Let me fly out," I offer.

"No! I'm sorry, but you are the last person I need here! I have Morgan."

"Morgan's a child, Becca. You need another adult there!" I snap.

"Derek's here."

"Derek's a child, Becca. You need another adult there!" I laugh. She laughs and reports to Derek, who says I definitely shouldn't come if an adult is needed.

"Are we okay, Ray?" She gets serious again.

"Yeah, baby, just come home to me ... soon." I sigh.

"Give me a week, Ray. I love you. You know that, right?" she asks.

"Yes. I love you too." I reply. "Hey?"

"Yeah?"

"You still wearing that dress, baby?" I lick my lips, thinking about this afternoon.

"Uh-huh." I can hear her smile.

"You still have my secret special message in between those lovely legs of yours?"

"Mmm hmm."

"That was fucking hot as hell today, babe! Feel free to stop by for lunch anytime you want, especially if you're gonna pull some hot shit like that. Okay?" I soften my voice.

"Sounds like we've got ourselves a new game to play." She matches my tone.

"Ugh! I love you!"

"Love you, too. We're just getting to Derek's for dinner. Talk to you later, Ray?"

"Yeah, babe. Get settled in and just text me at least, okay?"

"Will do, sweetie. Bye."

"Bye, babe," I hang up. I feel a little better, but I need to set up some support for her. I give Stacey a call and leave her a message, then do the same with Hazel.

BECCA

"I take it Ray's not too happy about this." Derek glances over as he puts his Escalade in park.

"Nope ... not one bit. I just need to do it, though. I can't run from it anymore. If I don't face these things, Ray and I may never make it." I sigh, throwing my phone in the bag.

"It's been a long time coming, Becs." He slaps my leg.

"Becs?" I smile, shaking my head. "C'mon, Morgy. Wake up, baby." I turn and tap her leg. She opens her eyes and grumpily grabs her backpack, but brightens up when she hears Jasper and Diana calling for us excitedly. I open my door.

"Auntie Becca!" They jump up and down. I climb down and pull them both into my arms.

"Would you look at the pair of ya? You've grown so much! Well, except for you, Jasp. It must be tough being the shortest kid in your class!" At almost seven years old, he's already at my shoulders!

"Oh, Auntie Becca! You know I'm the tallest!" He rolls his eyes.

"And Diana, you must be the prettiest girl in your preschool!" I play with her light brown ringlets.

"Becca!" Danielle runs out.

"It's so good to see you, Danni!" I hug her tightly.

℮)❦*

"So, how did you handle waking up from a coma to find ... uh ..." She waves her hand at me.

"Myself four months pregnant?" I ask as I place some roasted potatoes on my plate.

"Uh, yeah. That must've been a shocker." She giggles a bit, more out of discomfort, I think.

"Well, I knew I was pregnant before I woke up," I offer.

"But they didn't discover you were pregnant until almost November. I remember, because Derek was with you, and he wanted to rip Ray's head off," she says quietly. We all look at the kids at the other end of the table. I take in a deep breath, happy that while we're not completely out of earshot, they seem like they couldn't care less about our conversation.

"Did you not tell her?" I glare at Derek.

"No, Becca. You know how Danni rolls!" He widens his eyes at me. Ah, yes! Danni and talk of "the other side" do not mix. It freaks her out. She has phasmophobia—in that she's actually been diagnosed with it. I guess her Great Uncle Herb "visited" her when she was five. It didn't go over too well. She does everything she can to keep her life free of spirits.

"What did he not tell me?" Danni asks quietly, almost as if she's unsure whether she wants to hear it or not. I study her, contemplating. She stares at me, her deep blue eyes wide and innocent. Her long, blonde, curly hair is pulled up in a messy bun. She's about five foot nothing and the size of my pinkie. She's one of those girls that have trouble gaining weight. My heart just breaks for her. *All Sybeccas salute her with their "sight word," except for Cautionary Sybecca. Her ticker board simply says: "Fuck you, skinny bitch!"*

"Danni, I know what I'm about to tell you would be like the equivalent of you throwing me into shark-infested water, so I'll start by saying *sorry.*" I wince. She takes a sip of her wine, looking like she's trying to figure me out. "Um ... I was with Grayson the entire time I was in a coma." I say it quick, like I'm ripping off a Band-Aid. She gulps her wine, grabs the bottle, and refills her glass past even the classless point. *Honestly, at this point, just drink it from the bottle!* She holds her hand up to hold me off as she begins to chug this glass too. I can't help but giggle; it reminds me of myself when Ray would touch me with intent. When I was "Lucy," of course. She closes her eyes—waiting for the intoxication, I'm sure.

"Okay," she says, then exhales through pursed lips. I quietly explain everything, looking every so often at Morgan. I had intended to tell Morgan my first night home, but never did. I thought I would when I had her gift from him. Now that we're back in Cali, I'll talk to her tomorrow.

"Wow. That's amazing, Becca. It's bittersweet, I imagine." She half smiles as I tear up. She asks what provoked our impulsive trip. I take in a very deep breath and tell them.

"He said *what*?!" Derek yells. Yeah, he didn't like the "dead guy" comment either. "Funny, he left that out when he called frantically for help!" He's definitely pissed.

"He didn't tell you, Derek, because he knows what he said was stupid. His pride was getting in the way of his ability to articulate his feelings in a more sensitive, respectful manner. I don't like the way he said it, but I certainly understand where it came from. I've really put him through a lot, and I'm not quite sure how or why he stuck around. I know he loves me, but this has all been a bit much for anybody. Please don't be mad at him." I grab Derek's hand and squeeze for emphasis. He offers me an understanding smile and nods.

"Ready, Becca?" Derek asks. I grab my purse.

"Yes ... no," I sigh. It's been a long time since I've been at the ranch. I know I'm getting ready for a tornado of emotions. A tornado that, up until this moment, I didn't really consider the magnitude of. Fear swells inside of me, so powerful, so raw. "I'm scared." I feel myself become paralyzed.

"Becca, stay here, love. Maybe you shouldn't go tonight. I'll take you tomorrow and stay with you. I don't think you should be there alone." I can sense panic rising in him. Man, I really didn't think this through! What if I catapult myself back into "Lucy"? Oh no ... no, I can't do that. I can't go back! No, that won't happen. Grayson gave us his blessing. The guilt I used to feel is gone. "Sorry, Becca, I have to get this," Derek says, grabbing his phone. I didn't even hear it ring; must've been on vibrate. Derek heads into their study. I stand by the door in the foyer, looking around at their art-work. Contemporary—eh—not my thing. After a few minutes, Derek reappears. "Hear, Becca, for you." He hands me his cell.

"Hello?" I answer.

"Baby, take a deep breath," Ray commands softly. I do as he says, but find myself beginning to cry. I need him. "Baby ... shh, listen to me. Are you listening?" he asks.

"Yes," I murmur.

"There is no one at your house. I would feel much better if you stay with Derek and Danielle tonight, and go to the ranch in the morning." He's speaking very slowly, trying so hard to calm me down. He must be mad as hell at me for doing this.

"But—" I start.

"Becs, I know you, baby. You will get there and be consumed by memories. You won't sleep tonight. Not there. Now, you've had a very long, very emotional day. On top of that, you are pregnant with twins. I need you to think of them, if not yourself or anybody else. You need to keep your stress level down, Becs. Please, baby. Stay with Derek tonight and get rest. I called Stacey. She will be there in the morning. Don't do this without her, please," he begs.

"Ray, I'm sorry. You're the last person I need here, and yet I wish you were by my side." I don't know if it's my hormones or just uncertainty that's got me feeling like an addlepated fool.

"Baby, you say the word and I'm there!" he states with urgency.

"I know that, and I love you so much for it." I smile through my tears.

"Stace will be there in the morning. Will you please stay put? Listen to me, Becca, for once in your life. I'm worried about you and the babies." He sighs with what seems like frustration driven by concern—not irritation.

"Yes, I'll stay put." I wipe my tears. He's right. Besides, I don't think I can do this tonight.

"Oh, Becs ... baby, I'm so very proud of you. This is a huge step for you, and it means so much to me that you would do this for us." I can actually hear the pride in his voice.

"I love you, Ray. I love you so much. Thank you for loving me even though I put you through hell all these years." I wish I could feel his arms around me.

"It was all worth it, baby. I love you. Now get to bed."

"Okay. G'night, sweetie."

"Good night, baby."

I break the news to Morgan, happy with her indifferent attitude about it. We head down the hall to the guest room and get ourselves situated. Ray was right. I'm bone-tired as it is. I would've been an extra mess tonight. I grab my phone to send him one final text before turning in.

December 31, 2012 12:35 a.m.
Me: A theme song to keep your spirits "up." Love Game—Lady Gaga.

I plug my phone in beside me on the nightstand and turn the light off. I lie in the dark, listening to Morgan breathe. She's already fallen asleep. It's been almost six years since I've been back to our house. Well, physically at least. Maybe the fact that I spent over a month there with Grayson will help me with the emotional battle I feel coming. My phone pings and the screen lights up.

December 31, 2012 12:47 a.m.
Ray: Just listened to the theme song and things are definitely looking "up." You're not making it easy to stay away, babe. ;-p G'night.
Me: Thinking about that kink you banged out for me today! :-o
Ray: It's all about the angle and the pressure ...
Me: The size of the tool ...
Ray: The power behind the tool to stretch the area that needs kinks banged out of it.
Me: Sometimes the effects of a large, powerful tool can still be noticed long after the job is done.
Ray: Well the use of a good, large power tool should be very evident afterward, otherwise the client may not want to use it again.
Me: Well, I see this client being a lifetime loyal customer of this said power tool. It knows how to give me a good bang for my buck.

Ray: This power tool loves how you buck to its bang!

Ray: Point goes to Becca James. McNeil throws in the towel, fearing his power tool may get so large, it stretches 3,000 miles to try to bang the buck out of Ms. James!!!

Me: Good thing. Power tool would need a raincoat and galoshes. It's a wet one out here!

Ray: Power tool is waterproof and even comes with a lube dispenser feature to keep areas that should be wet always wet.

Me: Point to McNeil. Becca James cannot continue. She's aching with kinks and has no substitute power tools in her possession. Manual labor is a no go since her daughter is sharing her bed!

Ray: Just got a mental image of you touching yourself. Power tool's lube dispenser just malfunctioned!

Me: Clean up spill in aisle ahem?

Ray: More like oh ... oh ... oh ... shit!

Me: LOL! Seriously just woke Morgan up!

Ray: Becs?

Me: Rays?

He doesn't answer. There are no dots telling me he's texting.

Me: I won't forget that I love you. I promise.

Ray: How can you do that from 3,000 miles away?

Me: I know you. You've been my best friend for over five years and shh ... my secret lova. ;-p

Ray: So secret ... you didn't even know!

Me: Seriously, not to prevent you from fitting your head through a door, but it's been 12 hrs. since we've had sex. HOW COULD I NOT KNOW SOMETHING WAS UP?!

Ray: Literally up! Hee hee! Um, well, you knew something was going on, because you asked Stacey if she ever woke up feeling like she'd had sex.

Me: I did? What did she say?

Ray: She said yes. The morning after having sex.

Me: Well, that was helpful! Did I talk to you about it?

Ray: Uh ... no. Thank God! I don't think I would've kept a straight face! Becs, it's late, baby.

Go to bed.

Me: You wouldn't be saying that if I was there!

Ray: Yeah, well, you're not here, are you?

Me: Ray?

Ray: Sorry. I love you, baby. Go to sleep.

Me: G'night.

Ray: XXXXX

I put my phone back down and close my eyes. It's not a very restful sleep. Every time I drift off, I either dream about Grayson telling me what not to throw out or Ray begging me not to forget him.

"Wakey friggin' wakey, lady!" Stacey walks into the room, shouting. If I were suffering from a hangover, I would be tempted to throw something at her. I look at my phone. Eight a.m. Jesus, I feel like I finally just fell into a good sleep.

"Geez, you're early!" I sigh as I sit up and rub my face, trying to stir some life into my body.

"Yeah, I was on a five a.m. flight this morning, you impulsive, crazy bitch!" She smacks my leg.

"Sorry. Thank you for coming."

"I can't believe you were going to do this by yourself! Ray was a hot mess last night. Becca, honestly, you better stop putting that man on the back burner!" She shakes her head.

"That's why I'm here, Stace!" I bite, feeling tired and grumpy.

"Oh, this is going to be fun. Two cranky pregnant ladies who know how to push each other's buttons!" Sarcasm is her strong suit, as well.

"Well, let's go get some breakfast in us. That might help." I smile as I stand up.

"Becca." Stacey's chin quivers, and I know exactly why. I hug her.

"I'm okay." I rock her back and forth. This is the first time we've seen each other since I came out of the coma.

"I could've killed Ray for not paying attention! Christ, if I lost you, I don't know what I would've done!" she says angrily.

"Well, it wasn't just his fault. C'mon, let me get dressed. I'll be out there in a minute." I pat her arm.

"Yes, please hurry, because if I have to hear that skinny bitch go on about how she can't gain weight any longer, I think I may drop-kick her ass!" she says quietly.

"Stop!" I laugh and head into the bathroom.

Chapter Seven

"Ready?" Stacey looks over at me as we head through the gates to my ranch. *Ranchion*—ranch-mansion—is what she's always called it.

"Yeah." I'm barely audible. I pick up my phone and hit Ray's number. I haven't talked to him yet, and it's already one p.m. on the East Coast.

"Hey, baby." His greeting is soft and calm.

"Hi. I'm sorry I haven't called." Not very considerate, given his insecurities.

"It's okay, babe. Are you at your house now?" I hear him shuffling stuff around.

"Yeah, just got here. Where are you?"

"Work," he sighs.

"Oh, okay. Well, why don't you call me when you're done for the day?" I get out of the car and search my purse for my keys.

"Okay. Good luck today. I'll talk to you later."

I feel like I'm being pushed off the phone. He must really be busy.

"Okay. Love you." I kiss into the receiver.

"Me, too. Bye, babe." He hangs up. *Me, too?* Um. Okay.

"Ready?" Stacey gestures to the door. I put the key in, turn it, and take a deep breath before I open the door.

"C'mon, Mom," Morgan says impatiently, pushing past me. "I want to check out my room," she adds, and runs down the hall. I stand in the foyer, staring down the hall. I'm hit with the calmness of the creamy yellow, faux-textured walls and dark wood. Gosh, my taste hasn't changed much. I've always liked antique, rich-looking things, and colors that complement.

"This still looks relevant, doesn't it?" I ask Stacey as I spin slowly.

"You know, Bec, it totally does. You put a lot of time into this house, and balanced it well enough to keep it in style for a long time." She looks around admiringly.

"Well, I guess I'll bring my stuff to my room." I take in a deep, mindful yoga breath and start to roll my bag down the hall. I open the door to our bedroom and am greeted by the comfort of it. This room is quite different from the rest of the house. Grayson had no problem with allowing me to keep the appearance soft as long as it wasn't frilly. He was very pleased with the cream-colored, coffered ceiling and the sage on the panels between the wood. Another green, just a shade lighter, covers the walls, outlined again by creamy wood. Distressed cream furniture and wrought-iron décor, frames, drapes, and bedding all blended with nature's calming colors keep this room securely on the fine line of masculine and feminine.

Yes, he was very pleased and impressed. It was a little off from our "norm" in the décor department, and yet so very *us*. I still love it seven years later. I feel, though, as if I were *really* here a little over a month ago. I head over to the walk-in closet on my left. Slowly I hit the light switch and open the door.

Once inside, I lose my breath a bit. His clothes all hang the same way, in the same places. I drop my bag's handle and wrap my arms around as many suits as I can, pulling them to me. I just let myself feel what I need to feel. *His blue sweater, the thin one—the one he always looked so delicious in.* I search the drawers and find it. I hug the material to my chest, burying my face in it. I smell it, trying to catch the essence. Gone. Like him. I go into his top drawer, pull out his cologne, and spray it. The chemistry has changed a bit in seven years, but still, I can smell him. I miss his scent. I walk down to my end of the closet. *Well, I won't be fitting my fat ass in those anytime soon!* Where would I wear those gowns anyway ... Ashland's town social? Gosh, my life is so different now—not that Grayson and I were the flashy sort. These gowns were for fundraiser events and weddings. We mostly stayed under the radar.

"Hey, how are you doing in here?" Stacey startles me. She and Morgan are there, staring at me like they expect me to go ballistic. I smile slightly.

"What is that smell?" Morgan asks, walking in further.

"That is Eau de Grayson." Stacey smiles.

"That's Daddy's scent. Well, mostly." I sigh and offer her the bottle. "What did you find in your bedroom?" I put my arm around her shoulders as we head out.

"It's so girly and cute." She smiles.

"Do you want to redecorate it while we're here?" I ask.

"Becca, aren't you selling?" Stacey looks at me quizzically.

"No. Why would I sell this place?" Does she have five heads?

"Bec, that's what Ray told me you were doing. He thinks that's the main reason you are here, to get it market-ready." She picks up a picture of Grayson, Morgan, and me.

"I never told him I was doing that. This is our home. If nothing else, it's Morgan's." I sit on the backless lounge sofa in front of my bed.

"This will be my house, Mommy?" Morgan smiles as she sits next to me.

"Yep!" I slap her leg lightly.

"Bec, does he know about the house in London?" Her eyes go wide. I shake my head. "Oh, Lucy ... you gonna have some es-plainin' to do!" She shakes her head. Great—another notch on my "Lucy" belt!

"Well, I'm gonna have to esplain another time. Who's up for home movies?" I ask, standing up.

"Are you sure, Bec? You haven't watched them since before ..." She trails off.

"Well, then, I guess we better make some popcorn and settle in. I need to do it, Stace. Morgy needs to see her dad and hear his voice. Pictures can only do so much." I hold my hand out to Morgan. She jumps up to take it and the three of us head to the kitchen.

We gather a few drinks and what snacks we can find. I'll need to add grocery shopping to my to-do list! If Susanna had any idea we were coming, this kitchen would've been fully stocked with all of our favorites.

"Go ahead, Morgy. Mommy and I will be right there," Stacey tells Morgan as she pulls me back by my arm. Morgan shrugs and heads off with most of the goods. Stacey takes in a deep breath of apprehension. *Holy shit! Here stands my best friend with a very uncomfortable filter in place.*

"Shit, Stace, how much did that surgery set you back?" I laugh a little, still shocked at the sight.

"What surgery?"

"The one that inserted that filter you suddenly seem to have."

"Oh, shut up!" She smacks my arm and exhales with frustration. "Becca, Ray and I have been talking a lot the past few months," she starts, and I get visions of her behavior in my subconscious. Apparently, this translates across my face, because she smacks me again. "Oh, knock it off! I'm not going all Lavina on your ass! I still can't believe you turned me into her during your coma!"

"Hey, somebody's gotta play the crazy bitch, and let's be honest—you're the craziest bitch I know!" I laugh.

"Yeah, but I'm not crazy like that bitch!" she adds. "Bec, getting back to Ray, please." She puts her drink down on the counter and crosses her arms.

"Yeah, what's up?" I echo her movement and redo my pony-bun.

"He, uh ... well, you know he's a proud man," she starts.

"Ha! Don't I?" I snort.

"Well, he was quite taken aback when he sorted through your finances to keep up with your bills and payroll. He had no idea that Grayson had left you so comfortable. None of us did, really. I always knew you used it to buy the inn and then socked some away for Morgan, but I never knew how much it was. Well, needless to say, Ray was already feeling like he could never give you the things Grayson could—"

"But, Stace," I cut her off. "You know that Grayson and I were not flashy. I never thought about how much money we had!"

"Yes, I know, and I told Ray that, but it didn't help much. Last night it really hit him hard. It started with the talk of renovations, really. Bec, he doesn't want you to know, but his firm is hurting."

"Yes, I know. I overheard him asking to borrow money from Artie. He doesn't know I know." I pull up a chair. Stacey decides to do the same.

"He's been putting money aside the past few years to do the renovations for you. With you in the hospital and not wanting to leave your side, he used the money to keep the firm afloat." She winces. She must know my heart is sinking. I think back to Grayson's "conversation" with Ray, which I didn't realize I was witnessing at the time. *Very bizarre.* Ray talked about putting half a million into the firm to start my renovations.

"Jesus!" I place my head into my hands.

"It about killed him to tell you he couldn't do the renovations right now, and when you told him Grayson was paying for it, it was like a—"

"Slap in the face and a stomp on his pride," I interject.

"Basically. And he noticed you were wearing a bracelet from Grayson. That didn't help." She points to it. I circle it around my wrist. "He had no idea you had this house still. He thinks you're here to flush Grayson out of your system as best as you can. Maybe *flushing* is not a good word."

"I know what you mean."

"You need to tell him that you're not selling, and you need to tell him about London. The longer you wait, the worse it will get."

"I'll talk to him tonight," I say, defeated. "C'mon, Morgy's waiting." I get up. Stacey and I head down to the family room. Morgan's on the couch, looking at the photo albums I left behind.

"Hey, Mama, why did you leave these here?" she asks.

"Well, sweetie, honestly, I didn't think it would take me six years to come back here." I sit and look at them with her. I should've sent for these! Geez—it's like I pretended in some way that I didn't have this whole other life before I moved to New Hampshire. "Ready to watch our videos?" I ask, and head over to the drawers below the built-in bookcases.

"You and Daddy have lots of books, Mom. Did you guys read all of these?" she asks.

"Yes, we did. Well, most of them are Daddy's. He did a lot of reading to grasp new ideas, learn about different cultures, different careers, and so on." I grab the first video.

"Research?"

"Yes. You know, Morgy, there are so many fascinating things in the world. Your education doesn't stop once you get a diploma or a degree. There's always something new to learn. Daddy loved to discover the most unique information and share it with people in his books." An image of Grayson in his Clark Kents with a pencil in his mouth, searching through a book, flashes in my mind. He was always engaging his brain with new wonders. I never knew what he was going to bring home from the bookstore or the library.

"Earth to Becca!" Stacey waves her arms in front of me.

"Sorry, I was remembering Grayson researching." I smile and throw the first DVD in.

"Am I in this one?" Morgan asks.

"No, babe. This is our wedding video."

"Cool! Hey, that's here! You got married here, Mommy?" She

points to the flat-screen.

"Yep, this house holds a lot of my most wonderful memories." I put my arm around her. Grayson's favorite memories were here, too—that's why he brought me back.

"Look how young you were, Mommy! You looked so pretty!" She smiles up at me. It seems like a lifetime ago. "Look how tall Daddy is!"

"And so very handsome." I smile then giggle as Grayson pretends to run for it. Derek pushes him back, shaking a finger at him. God, we were so young! I was barely twenty-three; Grayson only twenty-six. His age always shocked his readers.

"How did you and Daddy meet again?" Morgan grabs a package of pretzels.

"I worked part-time at a Barnes & Noble. He had a signing at my store." I bite my lip and chuckle to myself.

"Was it love at first sight?" She looks at me dreamingly.

"More like irritation at first sight." Stacey says and laughs. We shared an apartment back then. Stacey had to endure countless hours of me ranting on about what a pompous ass he was.

"Your father, being quite the looker and with charm to boot, was pretty used to being able to date whomever he wanted." Stacey tries to explain it the best she can to an almost-eleven-year-old. "Your mother thought he was very full of himself and wasn't shy about telling him so. Your father found this fascinating, and therefore drove your mother crazy!" She grabs some pretzels.

"How did he drive her crazy?" Morgan seems intrigued. I sit back, watching Grayson and I exchange our wedding vows as Stacey continues to talk about Grayson's and my rocky beginnings.

"Well, your father was a very persistent man, if nothing else. He decided that day that he wanted your mom to be his girlfriend. He got Uncle Derek to help him find everything out about her. Your mom worked at a nursing home during the day, and he would magically show up there to 'tour' the facility for his grandmother. He sent her flowers every day."

"Mom's not into flowers," Morgan interjects.

"Well, even if a girl doesn't care for flowers, she still likes to get them at work!" Stacey gives Morgan her best "I know what I'm talking about, kid" face. "I always knew when he'd pay her a visit at either job, because she'd come home irritated and carry on about him and how he purposely baited her."

"What's *baited*?"

"Sorry, *teased* or *riled up*. He would just carry on and, what was it, Bec, a month or so?" She looks over at me.

"Uh, yeah." I nod.

"What?" Morgan crisscrosses her legs.

"Your father declared in so many ways that your mom was his girlfriend."

"How did he do that? What do you mean?"

"Well, I helped him a bit." Stacey and I both laugh. "I was dating Uncle Max, and your mom would go out to dinner with us or to a movie here and there. I knew, as much as she complained about your dad, she liked him a lot, and that's what drove her crazier than any of the shenanigans he pulled. So, when I got her to go out with Uncle Max and me, I would call your Dad a few days ahead of time and tell him where we would be so he could book a flight to Boston immediately. He would then show up and grab her hand when she wasn't looking, acting as if he was supposed to be there the entire time. It would make her furious. But she loved it, too. Just to prove a point to her, I had her go out with us again, but I didn't call your Dad." She points a finger in the air.

"What happened?" Morgan looks at me.

"I spent the whole night looking for him, mad that I was," I say with a smirk. We all get distracted by Stacey toasting us on the TV.

"Look how hot I was! Why did I think I was fat?" She points to the screen.

"Women's curse." I smile.

"So, when did you stop being mad at Daddy for liking you?" Morgan brings her attention back to our conversation.

"I wasn't mad at Daddy, really. I was mad at myself. I didn't want to fall in love with him," I say thoughtfully.

"Why?"

"I was scared. I thought he would break my heart." Petrified, really.

"Is that how you feel about Ray?"

I take in a sharp breath. I wasn't expecting a question like that.

"Um ... no. I've been scared that I would lose Ray like I lost your father," I say truthfully.

"Mommy, Ray really loves you. I like when you let him love you. I like our family then. Everything seems perfect. It's nice having a family with a mom and a dad." She glances down, as if she's feeling a bit ashamed. Stacey and I look at each other. She nods and gets up, turning the TV off. She knows I've been wanting to talk to Morgan about Grayson and Ray. It seems we both agree that now is a good time.

"Morgan, I have a lot to tell you about when I was in the hospital," I start.

"Do you think Daddy would be upset with me for saying Ray is like my dad?" She's still caught up in her previous thought.

"No. That's what I want to talk to you about." I palm her face and thumb away her tears. "Morgan, the three months I was in a coma, I was with Daddy." I smile.

"You were?" Her face lights up. I nod and begin to tell her everything in the most G-rated way I can. I concentrate on how much fun they had together and how much he loves her. Kids are great. She's probably, hands down, the easiest person to tell all of this to. Her eyes widen, fascinated by Grayson's brief description of Heaven.

"Are animals in the same Heaven as people?" she asks.

"I didn't ask him, Morgy, but I think they probably are, or in one adjacent to it. You know, sweetie, Daddy is always watching over us, and we don't have to be sad for him. He'll see me in about a year on Heaven time, and you in two. So he's going to be busy spending time with his dad and everybody else he lost. He'll take a class, maybe teach one, and then, of course, he'll be watching us!" I pat her leg.

"Won't it be hard to see us and not be with us?" She never ceases to amaze me with the depth of her character. Just then, Stacey appears in my peripheral vision. I turn my head more in her direction and take the bag she passes to me.

"Yes. He's very sad about not being here, especially for all of the important things in your life. Morgan, he is so proud of you, and loves you so much. He loves that you still say good night to him out the window. He wanted me to give this to you." I hand her the small gift bag that Stacey just handed me.

"What is it?" She dives in.

"Daddy's special gift to you for Christmas. He asked me to really buy it for you." I feel tears spring to my eyes, my throat tight. She opens it to find the platinum heart necklace that says *Daddy's Little Girl*. Her chin quivers. "Turn it over." I point. She does so, reads the inscription on the back, and starts crying.

"Can you help me?" she asks, holding it open in front of her. I take the necklace from her and latch it at the back of her neck.

"It's perfect." I smile.

"This is the best Christmas gift ever!"

"I agree with you!" I hug her. "I think this calls for a home video with all three of us in it." I pat my knees and get up to find the last video we recorded.

"Mom?"

"Yeah, babe?"

"Are you going to open Daddy's gift?" She seems unsure if she should ask.

"Yes, but later. By myself," I offer.

"Good. I think that's real good, Mom." She smiles as I sit beside her. The video starts with Morgan toddling around the yard. Grayson chases her in slow motion. She thinks this is hysterical and runs away laughing, then runs back, waiting for him to take another giant step. He does, and she dodges out of his path, giggling even louder.

"I'mmmmm goinnnnnnng tooooo getttttt yooooooou, little sweeeeeeethearrrrrrt!" he announces. I chuckle and comment on how silly he looks.

"Grayson!" I yelp as he picks her up and throws her into the air.

"I'm not going to drop her, sweetheart!" he laughs at me.

A huge wave of grief slams into me, and I let myself give in to it.

"Mommy?" Morgan looks at me with concern.

"It's okay for me to cry, Morgy. I need to." I kiss her head.

"Say, 'Hi, Mummy!'" Grayson makes her wave.

"Hi, Mummeee!" She cheeses up her goofy grin.

"Say, 'We love you!'" He makes her blow a kiss.

"Luv ou!" She blows more kisses.

"Ah, Becca, honestly, darling, my heart could stand a few more of her."

"We're trying." I sigh.

"I think we need to try a bit harder!" He waggles his eyebrows and bites his lip. "What do you fancy, Morgan ... a brotha or a sista?" He looks at her.

"Sista!" she yells.

"What? Oh, I see—you want me to be the only man in your life, aye?" he questions her. She nods purposefully. "Well, there we have it! Only girls for us, then—God help me!" Grayson laughs. "C'mere, love."

The picture goes askew as we jumble the camera around, then straightens out. I look through my tears at all three of us on the screen.

"Hello, old Grayson and Becca! Aren't you jealous of us? Look how young and beautiful we are!" he says, a big grin on his face.

"Shut up!" I slap his chest.

"Don't worry, sweetheart, I'll still love that fantastic bum of yours when you're eighty! Of course, I'll probably be half-blind by then, lucky for you!"

I find myself laughing along with my younger self.

"I remember you and Daddy always kissing." Morgan smiles as she watches us lock lips on screen.

"You do?" I look down at her.

"Yes, 'cause I always did that." She points to the screen, where her younger self is trying to get between the two of us. I completely forgot she used to do that. I tell her how Gray and I were laughing about her trying to tickle our eye sockets. "That's so weird!" she laughs.

"It was funny." I can't help laughing, too.

The video fades out. When it comes back, we're in Disneyland. Morgan's on Grayson's shoulders.

"Sweetheart, honestly, you have trouble walking forward, do you think it's really safe for you to be walking backward?" Grayson baits me.

"Shut up, you ass!" I giggle.

"Na nice, Mama!" Morgan points her finger.

"That's okay, Morgy. Mummy will be extra nice to me tonight."
He smirks.

"Gracie!" Hazel smacks him.

"What?!" He acts all innocent. "By the way, darling, that T-shirt you have on has made me acquire a new appreciation for Tinker Bell." He smirks again ... mischievously.

"What does Daddy mean?" Morgan looks up at me.

"I'll explain when you're much older." I sigh and shake my head at the ceiling—well, at Grayson, really. I laugh, knowing he is. This is quite ironic. Morgan doesn't question my laughter, as she is laughing, as well, at Grayson in the video.

We're on the teacups and he's acting very dramatic, as if we're going to spin off. You can clearly see we're not moving that fast. I forgot how much fun we had—how silly we were together. When I think about him, I always think of him as serious, sexy, assertive, and aggressive. I think about him teasing me and us laughing casually. I forgot his goofy side. Maybe because it didn't fully blossom until Morgan was a few months old and would laugh at him. Hazel used to tell me all the time that I was the only one he would act that way around. She also told me that she didn't think Grayson really knew happiness until he met me. I'd tell her it was the same for me.

"Mom, you know what I like most about watching these videos?" Morgan plays with the heart on her necklace, strumming it from side to side on the chain.

"What's that, baby?" I push her hair behind her ear.

"I've always felt very close to Daddy. As I've gotten older, I wondered if it was just because I missed having a dad, and not because we were extra special. Well, these videos prove that we were extra special. Daddy and I were very, very close and it makes me feel happy."

"Oh, Morgy, God put the sun in the sky the day you were born. That's just how he felt. His love for you was—is—amazing. You were his buddy." I hug her to me. We sit back, watching the rest of the video and laughing at different parts. God ... I miss him like crazy. I'm so thankful for the time we had together. Still, the thought of not seeing him for the rest of my life—it breaks my heart all over again. Because I was with him only a week ago, I feel as if he's just on a book tour and he'll be back. I have to keep pushing that feeling out. I know where it leads, and honestly, I don't think Ray could handle me turning back into "Lucy."

"I think this one is over, Mom." She grabs the remote and hits the power button.

"You don't want to watch anymore?" I ask.

"No. I want to save some for later. It's almost lunchtime anyway." She sits back and stares at the ceiling. "Mom?" She glances over.

"Yeah?" I lean my head back and look up as well.

"Can we talk about Ray?" I sense the hesitation in her voice.

"Sure. I'm guessing you have some questions?" I turn more on my side. I pick my head up and glance down the hall, wondering where Stacey went.

"Um, yeah. Is it okay that I ask?"

"Please, Morgan. You can talk to me about anything." I grab her hand.

"Well, I'm confused about why you are the way you are with Ray. Annie and I both are. We know you love him. We just don't understand why you act like you don't sometimes." She looks like she wants to continue, but doesn't.

"Oh. Well, that's a very good question, Morgy. Um. When your dad died so suddenly, it broke my heart. Have you ever heard that saying, that a person died of a broken heart?" I ask.

"Yes, but you didn't die."

"No. But in a sense, I did. A part of my brain that holds my memories—"

"The hippocampus," she interjects quickly, as if she's on a game show.

"Wow, Morgan, that's crazy! You learned that in school already?" I look at her amazed.

"No. *Jeopardy!* with Nana and Pop Pop." She smiles. I can't help but laugh. I have to tell Ray about this later. He'll get a kick out of it, for sure!

"Anywho, my grief over your father was so strong that it made me feel guilty about liking Ray, and I couldn't keep any memories of loving him. So when you saw me holding Ray's hand and kissing him, within a day or two, that memory was gone. I no longer knew I loved him like that." I'm trying my hardest to explain at a level she will understand.

"That's crazy, Mom! So, you didn't remember at all? We thought you just kept breaking up with him. Annie and I got into so many fights about this!" She slaps her head.

"No, I wasn't breaking up with him. I didn't even know we were a couple." I laugh a little. "Why did you guys fight? Oh, you were each defending us, huh?" I half smile.

"Yeah," she sighs.

"Sorry, Morgy."

"So, you remember now?" she asks.

"Yes. That was the main reason your father came to be with me—to help me figure out my feelings for Ray. He concocted this whole storyline to show me the relationship I have with Ray. He gave me a second look at everything."

"Daddy wants you to be with Ray?" she asks, surprise in her voice.

"Yes, honey. Daddy likes Ray a lot. He trusts him with us—to look after us and love us. Daddy wants me to be happy. He doesn't want me to be alone."

"Well, what happens when you go to Heaven and Daddy and Ray are there? Who will be your husband?" *Clearly*, this is panic-worry material for her at the moment.

"They both will be, and I guess we'll just have to figure it out when we're all there together." *Honestly, ten going on eleven, going on thirty!* I take a long sip of my iced tea.

"They'll just have to take turns with you," she says, and my iced tea comes flying out of my mouth and up my nose. I start choking and coughing, my sinuses on fire. Morgan runs to get paper towels.

"I know you're laughing at me, you bastard!" I shout when I'm able to speak, waving my "sight word" around the room to make sure he sees it. Great, I've now gone from "Lucy" to skitzo Becca who talks and yells at her dead husband.

Dead husband? I can't believe I just thought of him like that. Saying it in my head—so weird.

"Here, Mom." Morgan hands me the towels.

"Thanks, babe." I clean up.

"So, are you definitely marrying Ray?" she asks as I blow my nose.

"Well, he hasn't officially asked me yet, but yes. How do you feel about that?" *Nice, Becca. Nice of you to finally ask your daughter how she feels about the new family unit!*

"I'm happy about it, Mom! I love Ray. I wanted to call him 'Dad,' but when I did, it was weird. It didn't feel right. I want to call him something." I see the guilt blanket her face. She's in a very peculiar place. I know why she wants to call him "Dad," and I know why she doesn't. Annie never knew her mom, so it's much easier for her to call me "Mom."

"Why don't you talk to Ray about how you feel, and maybe you two can come up with a different name to call him?" I offer as I wipe myself down. "I need to change." I sigh.

"Go ahead. I'm gonna call Annie." She grabs the phone.

"Hey, wait a second, honey," I say. She turns to me. "Um. I'm sorry, Morgan, everything's been kind of crazy for me since I've been home. I haven't really asked you how you feel about Ray and I having babies." *And the award for Mother of the Year goes to ... yeah ... not me!*

"I'm excited, Mom! I can't wait to see what they look like! Um—just don't forget that you have them!" *Ugh—she is so her father's daughter!*

"Smarty-pants!" I lightly slap her butt, then head off to my room to change. I grab my cell to see if Ray called or texted. Nothing.

December 31, 2012 12:30 p.m.

Me: Can you talk or text?

Ray: Neither. I'm busy.

Me: Okay, sorry. Love you. Can't wait to talk.

Ray: Sound contract so far. Good. Love you.

Me: You got the contract! :)

Ray: Wow, do they bleach your hair once you get to L.A.?

Me: Huh?

Ray: Exactly!

Me: You're impossible!

Ray: Possibly, but you'll manage.

Me: Well, I'll try ...

Ray: You try all the time—my patience, that is.

Me: Back at ya, babe! :| BTW, thought you were busy?

Ray: Thought you were selling?

Me: You ASSumed!

Ray: Sight word, Becca!

Me: Wow ... looks like we really need to have a talk. Call when the stick in your ass has been removed!

He doesn't reply. I throw my phone down and head out into the hall when I hear Stacey.

"You went food shopping?" I grab bags from her.

"Yeah, I wanted to give you and Morgan time to talk." She continues down to the kitchen. I tell her all about my talk with Morgan. "Weren't you wearing something different?" She stares at me blankly.

"Yeah. Morgan came up with a great plan for when I'm in Heaven with Grayson and Ray. They can take turns with me!" I say, widening my eyes for emphasis. "Isn't that a great idea?" Stacey cracks up, the irony not lost on her.

"But what does that have to do—"

"Um, she said that while I was drinking," I say, cutting her off. "Well, I don't know if they'll have to share me. Ray's being an ass-hole again. Did you tell him I'm not selling?" I put the milk and cheese away.

"No. Maybe Derek," she offers.

"Stace, he's been a fucking switch, flipping on and off since I woke up." My nostrils flare.

"Bec, he's just scared. In all honesty, he's out of his element," she adds, throwing pasta in a random cabinet.

"Uh, the pantry is through this door." I take the pasta back out and bring it to the pantry. "What do you mean he's out of his element?" I say, my voice a bit louder.

"Here." She hands me another box and some sauce. "Becca, he's used to dealing with 'Lucy.' He's used to fighting for you. I don't think he knows how to handle you being *on* permanently."

I stare at the shelves, giving her opinion some deep consideration.

"Stace, maybe now that the chase is gone ... maybe his interest is, too, and he's just figuring it out." *My biggest fear.*

"Uh, no—he's very interested! I'm telling ya, he's just insecure. He feels like he's competing with all of this." She waves around as we head back into the kitchen. "And at a time where he's not doing so hot financially."

"Um, because of me!" I mention. She shrugs. "I don't know how to help him with this." I sit, feeling defeated, and spin the nap-kin holder around.

"Just be patient with him. He's given you a lot of himself over the years. Oh, but don't let him treat you like shit, though." She points a spatula at me.

"Grilled cheeses?" I perk up.

"Yep."

"Yay!" I get up to help. I'm starving!

Chapter Eight

"Becca!" Derek calls out.

"In here!" I yell as I wash the dishes from lunch. So much for that nap I was going to take.

"Hey, where's Stacey?" Derek kisses my cheek when he steps into the kitchen.

"Just went for a nap." I turn the faucet off and dry my hands, turning around.

"How are things going?" he asks cautiously.

"Um, okay. It's been a bit emotional, but I think it's a lot better than what it would've been if I didn't just spend three months with him." I cross my arms and lean against the counter. "Derek?" I crook my head sideways.

"Yeah, Bec?" He leans as well.

"Did you tell Ray I'm not selling?"

"Well, yeah. He thought you were, and I corrected him. Was I wrong to do so? Are you selling?" He either knows or can sense we had a bit of an argument.

"No, I'm not. It wasn't even a thought." I shake my head.

"I didn't think so."

"Do me a favor?" I close my eyes for a quick moment. "Unless you already have, please don't tell Ray about our house in London." Derek's face tells me it's too late. "Oh, no! No! No! No!" I practically whine and do actually stomp my foot.

"Sorry, Becs." He shrugs and seems to feel bad about his big mouth.

"When and why did you tell him?" I'm trying not to yell, but I am extremely irritated.

"We were talking this morning, right after you left. He asked me if I was going to help you find a good realtor. That's when I told him you had no plans to sell, at least that I knew of. And I said I didn't think you were selling the London home, either. I didn't realize he didn't know. Why are you trying to keep it a secret from him?" He grabs a beer from the fridge.

"What did he say when you mentioned London?" I ask before I answer him.

"He just said, 'London, huh?'" He pops the cap off and throws it into the sink.

"Dude! What the hell? Now I now you've been hanging out with Ray!" I grab the cap and toss it in the trash. Ray does the same thing. Drives me fucking nuts!

"Yeah ... back atcha, dude," he teases me.

"Did you at least explain that London is Grayson's family home? It has my name on it, but it belongs to Hazel, as well." I'm so frustrated. This wouldn't be such a big deal if Ray wasn't so proud to the ridiculous level of King of the Alpha Males. It's hot and annoying all at once!

"Yeah, I did, actually," Derek says thoughtfully.

"Well, good, that hopefully lessened the blow." I sigh as I sit and hold my head in my hands.

"Becs, what's going on with him? Why do you want to keep this from him?" He sits on the other side of the round table. Suddenly, thoughts of Susanna's Greek omelet come to mind. *When is she coming back?* "Becca?" Derek snaps his fingers in front of my face.

"Sorry, D." I snap out of it. "I think it's safe to say that my ADD has been unaffected by the coma." I laugh a little and shake my head. "Um, to answer your question, Ray never knew about any of this.

He didn't know I still had these homes, and as you know, he wasn't aware that Grayson left me very comfortable."

"Yeah, no one knew, Becs. You never talked about it. I was kinda pissed at Gray when I saw how much you were working to stay—so I thought—afloat." His frustration with me becomes very evident.

"Derek, that was me having denial issues with Gray's passing. I kept thinking he was going to come back. That was ... it's his money. The realistic side of me was keeping it for Morgan," I try to explain.

"Becca, Grayson would have your arse for thinking that way!" Derek raises his voice at me—a first in the thirteen years I've known him.

"Oh, believe me, he did!" I bite back. A slow smirk crosses my lips when my thoughts go from the figurative sense to the literal.

"What?" Derek asks.

"Oh, nothing." I wipe my expression clear. "Grayson screamed his bloody head off at me for it, Derek. I had to promise I would do the renovations and a whole list of things." I rub my face and sit back, crossing my legs.

"So, now, what's going on with Ray?" He grabs the bag of chips we left on the counter and starts eating them.

"Ray is fighting the great internal battle." I roll my eyes.

"Okay, now let's try that in English." Derek pops another chip into his mouth.

"Ray has been taking care of me—as much as I'd let him—for five years. Whenever the inn needed repairs, he took care of them. When we went away to Maine or anywhere else, he paid for it. Ray has always done okay financially, but when I was in the hospital, he dropped everything. He didn't bring in any new projects and ran out of money. So now he's strapped, which is making him insecure. He's always been competing with Grayson for my love, but now you throw in all of this," I wave around, "and now it's like he has to compete with him over who takes care of me, too. He's a very proud man, Derek. He wants to take care of everything. Be the one I depend on. He wanted to do the renovations for me. It was supposed to be a surprise—a gift, if you will—and I come in asking for all these things he now has no money for, and I tell him Grayson said he was paying for it. He's just ... he's having a tough time with it all. So, he's been short with me. That's why I didn't want him to know about the London house. I thought it might send him over the top." I take a deep breath and sigh.

"You know, Becca," he shakes a finger slightly, as if it's pushing his idea along, "let me talk to Ray. I think I may be able to help here." He rolls up the bag of chips and tosses it back onto the counter. "Everything is going to be fine, love." He chucks my chin, then stands and pulls me up with him. "You look tired. Go take a nap."

"You're a great friend, Derek. I love you." I give him a big hug. He clears his throat a bit, like he's uncomfortable.

"I love you, too, Becca." He finally says it.

"Ugh—Grayson!" I gasp.

"Wha ..." Derek lets go of me quickly and turns around, panic in his voice. He turns back to find me in hysterics. "You are an evil woman!" he snaps.

"I'm sorry. It was an opportunity I couldn't pass up!" I laugh. Just then, his phone pings with a text. "I'm sure that's Grayson." I laugh again.

"Ugh—you are so frustrating!" Derek's English accent is extra thick at this accusation. I rub and pat his back. I'm sure Grayson would get a kick out of this. "It's Ray." He looks from his phone to me.

"What did he say?" I look down to his phone.

"He needs to talk. Go for a nap. I'm gonna call him." He gently pushes me along. I fight the urge to eavesdrop and head to my room instead. I see Morgan in her room with Diana, playing with her old toys. Diana is in heaven. Morgan looks up and smiles.

"I'm going to lie down for a bit. Uncle Derek's in the kitchen." I lean against her door frame.

"Okay, Mom. Sleep well." She goes back to whatever scene they are playing out in the dollhouse.

Back in my room, I grab my favorite sweater of Grayson's— which now has a little cologne on it—and climb into our bed. I snuggle with his sweater and quickly drift off.

RAY

"Derek!" I answer on the first ring.

"Hey, Ray." He sounds serious, not like his usual laid-back self.

"Um, how's Becca doing?" I pop the cap off my beer and toss it into the sink.

"Not good, mate!" He clears his throat. "Look, Ray, we need to have a talk."

"What's the matter? Is she okay?" I feel my panic rising.

"She's okay physically, but you're really upsetting her, mate!" He's stern, like a father getting ready to give his son a talking-to.

"I know, D-man." I sigh, angry at myself.

"What is going on with you, man?" he asks with a hint of frustration.

"Christ, I think I'm turning into a hormonal bitch! I feel like I'm walking on eggshells. I want to jump out of my skin!" It amazes me that I'm able to say all of this to Derek without an ounce of discomfort. Carl has been my best friend for years. I even got him to drag his ass down here from Maine. Yet, I wouldn't have this kind of conversation with him if someone paid me. I think it must be because Derek's known Becca for years. He's a link to her past, and from time to time, has the answers I don't always realize I'm searching for.

"Well, Ray," he starts. I hear him popping a cap off a beer as well.

"Cheers, mate!" I tease.

"Cheers!" I hear him take a swig. "Let's talk about the big white elephant in the room," he says to finish his thought.

"What's that?" I sit back at my desk and pull out my credit card.

"The money, the homes, and the private jet," he says slowly.

"A private jet! She has a private jet?" I shoot out of my chair.

"No. Do you feel better now?" Derek chuckles.

"Ugh ... you ass!" I say with relief as I sit back down and bring my computer to life.

"Let me ask you something, mate," he says as I type in my info.

"What's that?" I search for the best offer. *Shit, this is going to hurt!*

"Why are you so bent out of shape over the money?"

I close my eyes, take a deep breath, and sit back.

"I don't know. I guess, well ... it's my job to take care of Becca, and it's a job I like. I want her to depend on me. I know it's very old-fashioned, but that's just how I am. I mean, I certainly don't think she can't have her career and make her own money. I just want to be the one who takes care of our personal stuff, and anything major with her business." I shut up. The more I say, the more I feel like I'm transporting myself back to the 50s.

"Let me ask you this." Another swig. "Who took care of all the repairs and maintenance at the inn since she opened it?"

"Me, but—"

"Who built her store?"

"I charged her for that!" I interject.

"How much of a discount did you give her?"

"Seventy-five percent," I sigh.

"Did she know?"

"No." I choose the best offer and type in my card info.

"Who paid for trips to Maine, amusement parks, zoos, camping, and anything else?"

"Me, Derek! What are you getting at?" I say, my voice flaring

113

with irritation.

"Who's been taking care of her?" His tone matches mine.

"Well, me, but that's before she had all this money!" I argue.

"Dude—she's had the money the entire time! What are you talking about?" He gets louder.

"I don't know! This is what I mean! I'm all over the place, man. I don't understand why she kept so much from me. I feel a bit betrayed—not that I have the right to. If anyone should, it's Becca, after everything I've done to her." I grab the tennis ball on my desk, toss it at the wall, and catch it. I get lost in the rhythm of playing catch, something I do when I'm contemplating ideas for a design. I try not to do it when Becca's around, though—it drives her crazy.

"What the fuck are you doing?" Apparently, Becca's not alone in that.

"Sorry," I offer.

"What have you done to Becca?" he asks me quickly, his voice already accusatory.

"Never mind, she's already forgiven me." *And here I am, acting like Dr. Jekyll and Mr. Hyde!*

"Well, as far as the money, none of us knew. I have been pissed off at Grayson for years, thinking he left Becca to struggle. But that's just Becca. She and Grayson were never flashy people. They have a nice house here, and put a lot of money into it, but other than that, they kept a low profile. Another thing, Ray," he pauses and takes a deep breath. "Did you ever stop to think that Becca let you do those things because she likes having you take care of her? She's very independent, but she's old-fashioned, as well," he states matter-of-factly.

I sit back and think about the different times we went somewhere and Becca would pull out her money. All I would have to do is say, "*Baby ... stop*" in that tone that always affects her. She'd comply and kiss my cheek, thanking me. I'd turn to her and lift her chin with my forefinger. "*You're welcome, baby,*" I'd say softly, letting my lips linger over hers without touching 'til her breath got slightly erratic, then I'd lay one on her. Just a short, sweet kiss that I would reluctantly break.

"McNeil!" Derek snaps me back.

"Ugh, sorry, dude." I hit print and put my card away.

"Well, did you think about what I said?" he presses.

"Yes. You're right. I'm just ... I hate to admit it, man, but I'm feeling a bit insecure right now. I let things go at work, and I can't really do stuff for her. Not that she ever looks for it. It's all me, dude. I know that. I just need to snap out of it. I don't want to push her away. I've been chasing her for five years, and now that she's mine, I can't seem to act normal. I don't know." Derek starts to laugh at me. "What?" I'm on the offense.

"I'm experiencing major déjà vu!" Derek says.

"Huh?"

"Never mind." He laughs.

"Well, speaking of déjà vu, you'll feel that way tomorrow morning at 10:03 a.m.," I inform him.

"Huh, why?"

"Because you'll be at LAX, picking my hormonal ass up. I promise though to try grow my balls back by then." I chuckle.

"No, Ray! She doesn't want you here right now!"

"Dude, ticket is paid for. I'm coming. Becca needs me. She said so herself." I get up and put my designs for Lexter, Inc. into a cylinder container. Rich and I forgot about the New Year's Day observation when we talked, so the plans will now be delivered on Wednesday.

"Yeah, but Ray, you can't behave like a jealous, insecure prick. The moment you do, you are outta here!" He's actually terse with me.

"I promise, dude, as long as you promise to always tell me what you think of me." Slight sarcasm on my part.

"Deal. I'll see you tomorrow. Which airline?" he asks. I give him the details before we hang up. I decide to text Becca. Kiss her butt, really.

December 31, 2012 5:23 p.m.

Me: Babe, happy to report stick has been safely removed. I am now back to being your handsome, charming, loving, and crazy-about-you boyfriend. Call me when you're up from your nap. I love you!!! :)

BECCA

"Sweetheart, I'm so proud of you. You are doing so well." Grayson holds me in his arms.

"This is so hard, Gray," I cry.

"Shh ... there, there, love. You're doing great. I love you, Becca." He kisses me. "Now go and open your present, sweetheart. Please." He smiles down at me. I open my eyes. Grayson's sweater is bunched up by my mouth. I bend my head, plunging my nose into it and inhaling deeply.

"Okay, Gray," I sigh. I get up and head to the dresser where the wrapped gift is. I grab it and sit on the bed, then cross my legs, turn on the bedside lamp, and take in a deep breath. I know it's some sort of book. I think it's a scrapbook. I turn it over and slowly slide my fingers under the taped-down wrapping. It has stuck perfectly for over seven years. My hand slides down the middle to release that tape. This is the first time in my life I have ever unwrapped a gift so slowly. When the paper is off, I see it's a deep purple scrapbook by Creative Memories. Another deep breath and I slowly open to the first page.

It's a picture from our wedding. We're nose to nose. Our eyes are closed. No smiles—just a look of complete contentment. The title says: *OUR LOVE AND LIFE IN PICTURES AND WORDS*. I go on to read his message to me at the bottom of the page.

Sweetheart,

I wanted to do something special for you that I hope you will always cherish. I have to apologise in advance because I came across your old poetry and took liberty in rebutting some of them. I love you, Becca. I love our life. I love our family. You are my "Once Upon a Time" and the happy ending I never thought existed.

I hope I have portrayed my feelings for you, and our life, correctly in this book. You have made me so happy, Becca. My life's mission is to always make sure your happiness outshines mine.

With my heart exploding for you,
Your loving and adoring Husband,
Grayson

I grab some tissues out of the box to wipe away my tears and blow my nose. With a deep breath and shaky hand, I turn the page to find a poem of mine.

I HAVE THIS

I have this pain … It's deep within
I have this pain … It's been my only friend

I have this heartache … It echoes inside
I have this heartache … From it, I cannot hide

I have this memory … Of a smile on my face
I have this memory … Of a smile I cannot trace

I have this voice … It's inside my head
I have this voice … It makes me regret

I have this peace … That wants to get out
I have this peace … So tired, it cannot shout

I have this tear … Who will not shed
I have this tear … Whose secret I've kept

I have this dream … And I will never let go
I have this dream … And it's draining my soul

I have this time … To myself I cry
I have this time … To you, I say goodbye
BKC 1995

The next page is his rebuttal.

I HAVE THIS

I have this love … It's deep within
I have this love …It's a very new friend

I have this butterfly …It flutters inside
I have this butterfly …Your touch, it ignites

I have this memory …Of a smile on your face
I have this memory …Of the warmth in your embrace

I have this voice …It's inside my heart
I have this voice …It's travelled so far

I have this peace …That has gotten out
I have this peace …It's awake and very loud

I have this fear …I want to put to bed
I have this fear …I will not allow to tread

I have this dream …It is my only goal
I have this dream …And I will not hear "No"

I have this time …To show you what's inside
I have this time …Convince you, I will try
Grayson James 2005

I smile, touching his words with my fingertips. I turn the page to find a layout of us in the beginning. The title reads: *TO DATE OR NOT TO DATE?*

Why was that even a question? he wrote underneath, making me giggle and shake my head. On the bottom half of the layout's left side is my poem.

I OFTEN DO

No one will hear me ... No one will listen
I feel so empty ... I'm through with wishin'

I have lost myself ... Don't know what to feel
How can I tell. ... Between fake and real?

So many unanswered questions ... They surround my head
So many decisions ... Their importance, I try to forget

I am numb. ... I am tired
I cannot run. ... My youth has expired

What is love? ... Can it grow?
It is tough ... To really not know

Nothing makes sense ... And neither do I
Even though I've built a fence ... I often do cry
BKC 1996

On the right side are more pictures of us in the beginning. I seem to be warming up to him a little more. On the bottom half of that page is his poem in response to mine.

I OFTEN DO

I'm here to break down your fence
I understand it might take a while
Your sadness has made a lot of sense
But now I think it's time for you to smile

For my feelings are very real
I know that this is love
It's a pretty big deal
The only thing I'm now certain of

GOODBYE UNCERTAINTY

Look at these two kids laughing
Aren't we so young?
Some questions don't need answering
Some reservations can come undone
Grayson James 2005

Before I met Grayson, I was always happy and outgoing, or so it seemed. On the inside, I felt very empty and sad. I always took pen to paper to acknowledge those feelings and have a safe place for them. I was never sure why I felt that way. I think feeling "stuck" as a teenager spilled over into my early twenties. I was always more mature in my thoughts and emotions as a teenager. It's pretty hard to have all of these adult thoughts and not be able to do anything about them, which is why I've always called the teenage years *Purgatory*. Once I was of age, I think I thought life would magically begin! I set out to move to Boston and start my, what was supposed to be, amazing life. It turned out to be an amazing struggle instead. I worked eighty hours a week trying to put myself through college, and waited. Waited for my life to start. Then Grayson happened. My amazing life began, and I fought it tooth and nail until I finally allowed myself to have what I didn't think I deserved.

I turn to the next page. The title says: *COME AWAY WITH ME*. There are pictures of us on different trips we took. A lot of locations were stops on his book tours. It took him two months after we were engaged to get me to quit my jobs and come with him. I find myself laughing at us all decked out in Manchester United garb, cheering. I think that was the first Manchester United game he dragged me to. Derek snapped this shot. God, we all used to have such a good time together. We always considered ourselves lucky when it came to our friends. I became close with Derek, and Grayson with Stacey. We were like one big family.

I turn the page and find a bunch of my shorter poems with his answers beside them. This is really sweet, so thoughtful—and it must've taken him so long. I read my poems, which I haven't looked at in years.

WHISPER

I am a whisper ... That never gets heard
I flow softly through the air ...Seen, but never understood

My fragrance grasps their attention ...But my scent never stays
I wander to find some affection ...Hoping to find it one of these
days

I am a whisper ... That never gets heard
A warm, sweet gesture ... That never seems understood

I fly through the air ...Like a bee on a pollen hunt
Hoping one day they'll care ...Knowing that they won't

I am a whisper ...Will you ever hear me?
Come a little closer ...And maybe we will see
BKC 1996

SOMETIMES I WONDER

Sometimes I wonder why
I hurt so bad
Sometimes I wonder why
I'm always sad

Sometimes I wonder why
I have uncontrollable tears
Sometimes I wonder why
I talk when no one hears

Sometimes I wonder why
My dreams are so real
Sometimes I wonder why

GOODBYE UNCERTAINTY

They always get killed

Sometimes I wonder why
I cry so hard
Sometimes I wonder why
My life is falling apart

Sometimes I wonder why
I wonder so much
Sometimes I wonder why
I seem to lose touch

Sometimes I wonder ... about myself

WHISPER

I've seen you; I've heard you
I've taken you in
I more than understand you
My whispering friend
Grayson James 2005

SOMETIMES I WONDER

Sometimes I wonder why
You don't see what I see
Sometimes I wonder why
You just can't seem to believe

Sometimes I wonder ... about you
Grayson James 2005

The next page is a layout of our engagement photos and our

wedding picture. It's titled: *HAPPIEST DAY OF MY LIFE!*

We look so young, so in love, so full of promise. That was such a beautiful day. I turn the page to find another layout of poetry.

<u>MY CLOUD</u>
There's a cloud that follows me
It throws raindrops at my head
It's gray and awfully mean
I think it wants me dead

It lingers at my house
It hovers over me in the sky
It's there without a doubt
I don't even have to go outside

For my cloud is in my mind
Pouring it's sadness upon me
Draining away all my time
Never letting me be
BKC 1996

He simply drew me an umbrella and wrote, At your service!

WHY, CAN'T I, DO I, WHEN

Why is it all ... I do is cry in my bed?
Why do so many tears fall ... When deep thoughts run through my head?

Why do I write ... Only a sad poem?
Why do I fight ... To know what is unknown?

Can't I ever smile ... And mean the gleam in my eye?
Can't I once in a while ... Have ... a happy cry?

Why am I up so late ... Worrying about the same things?
Why do I always concentrate ... On far-fetched dreams?

Is there some misunderstanding ... To the way that I feel?
Could it be that everything ... Is really not real?

Do my dreams misinterpret ... The way things should be?
Or should I admit to it ... And let the blame fall on me?

Do I have such low self-esteem ... That I'm ready to give up?
Or do I believe in my dreams ... Enough for happiness to develop?

And when does this happen? ... And when do I know why?
See, I was never living ... 'Cause all I did was cry
BKC 1995

WHY, CAN'T I, DO I, WHEN

Why is it all ... I do is imagine you in bed?
Why do I always fall ... When all you see is red?

Why do I write ... This very naughty poem?
It surely wouldn't help in the fight ... To make you see that you are my "home"

Good thing I didn't write it ... Way back when
When you always threw a bloody fit ... And always liked to pretend

Now I can smile ... And mean the gleam in my eye
More than once in a while ... We have an orgasmic cry

You keep me up so late ... You insatiable thing!
Always making me concentrate ... On things that make you scream

Why can't I get enough of you? ... Why can't I keep my thoughts at bay?
I love the way our bodies move ... Christ, Becca, I love to hear you pray!
Grayson James 2005

I giggle and shake my head at his rebuttals. Grayson was always
insatiable!

DREAMS OF MY LOVE

High above in the clouds ... He'll feel the warmth of my love
And all the softness that surrounds ... My heart with so many wonders of

Captured by each other's embrace ... Knowing what we're about to do is
right
I feel my heartbeat race ... While we make love endlessly through the
night

His gentle kisses touch my tickled body ... While he finds his way to my
enthused tongue
Now caressing me passionately ... Again we become one

Feeling a hot sensation ... From his warm juices I'd just received
My happiness has no limitations ... For his child, I've just conceived

And in our dreams it's always like this ... Our love over and over again
becoming new
Living from kiss to kiss ... With each and every ... "I love you"
BKC 1991

Please refer to my version of 'Why, Can't I, Do I, When.' Then please see me to confirm that the date on this poem is indeed a typing error! In the meantime, I'm in panic mode and am now looking for a bubble to place Morgan in!

Being a thirty-five-year-old woman now with an almost-eleven-year-old girl, I'd like very much to say that the date was a typing error. However, I'd be lying. Purgatory, that's all I'll say about that. Well, and that I was a good girl and waited until Grayson. I have nothing to be ashamed of! Humph!

The next layout has our professional pictures of my pregnancy. They are black and white with a black backdrop. I'm wearing a black cardigan and black pants. My cardigan is unbuttoned below my breasts, my belly protruding. One picture is of Grayson behind me. His hands are on my belly, with mine covering them. We're both looking down at it.

The other picture on the page shows Grayson is kneeling in front of me and kissing my belly. I have my right hand in his hair and my left on my belly. I'm smiling down at him. In the third one, my head is back because I'm laughing, and he's smiling up at me. Oh ... that's when Morgan kicked him right in the "kisser." That was funny. The right page of the layout is when Morgan was born. I'm in bed, Grayson's leaning down over near my shoulder, and we're both looking down at her. Next one, we're kissing. The bottom picture is her birth announcement.

THE SECOND HAPPIEST DAY OF MY LIFE! he wrote on the bottom. The next page has all three of us asleep on the couch. Above the picture, I see his words: *HOW CAN IT GET ANY BETTER THAN THIS?* And below, he wrote: *YOU TWO ARE MY SWEET DREAMS.* On the opposite page is more poetry.

GOODBYE UNCERTAINTY

SINGING SOLO

I'm sitting here ... I'm sitting alone
I'm singing solo

Goodbye, my old friend ... I'm saying so long
Never laugh again ... I'm singing solo

I'm trapped in a room ... Faces stare down at me
I'm singing solo ... And only I can hear myself

I look at my dream ... He's so beautiful
I look at me ... And I'm singing solo

I'm sitting here crying ... But no tears will fall
I'm sitting here trying ... But I'm singing solo

My soul floats away ... And my melody picks up
I'm feeling nothing ... I'm singing solo

You were my friend ... And now I'm left
The music never ends ... And I'm singing solo

I'm still sitting here ... I'm still sitting alone
I'm still singing ... solo
BKC 1993

SINGING SOLO

One plus one equals two
No more solos
They're not for you
I need a partner
One who's "English fluent" (Ha ha!)
Hey, you're a good singer
Please be the other half to my duet!

Christ! Sounds more like a cheer than a poem! Oh well! I'm also realizing this would've fit better with our engagement page! What can I say ... I'm an amateur!

Next layouts are of us dressed up for several functions with the title: *THE WAY YOU LOOK TONIGHT*. I turn the page and see us lounging around in pajamas with the title: *GORGEOUS WITHOUT GLAMOUR!* A little note says, You take my breath away no matter what you wear, especially when you have nothing to wear at all! Wink, wink. I can't help but laugh. One-track mind, that guy!

The next few pages are of us with Morgan on various trips, outings, and in the backyard. Then the picture of us with Mickey Mouse and the title: *HAPPIEST FAMILY ON EARTH AT THE HAPPIEST PLACE ON EARTH!* I turn to the last page. It's Grayson's favorite picture of us. We're nose to nose with our lips puckered at each other. Along with it is my "Dear God" poem, then his.

DEAR GOD

I want to write a letter to you
But where do I possibly start?
Do I remind you of my paid dues?
Or show you the broken pieces of my heart?

Sometimes I talk to your angels
Inside my cluttered mind
I ask for a hint that will be helpful
To show me what I wanted to find

I understand that I've been secretly selfish
And don't deserve half of what I ask for
I'm the creator of my own disastrous mess

And unknowingly ask for more
BKC ????

<u>DEAR GOD</u>

I am writing a letter too
And I know just where to start
Please show her that I am the glue
That will mend her broken heart
Grayson James 2005

There's an envelope glued to the back of the book. I lift the flap and pull out a letter. I hold it in my hand for a long time, just staring at it. This is it, I feel—the final step of letting go. I take several deep breaths then slowly open the letter.

My Dear Beautiful Wife,

I am hoping that this book shows you how much I love and adore you. You are the most amazing wife, mother, and friend. I cherish you, sweetheart. You do everything you can to give us all what we need. You are loving, kind, and generous. I honestly don't know a better human being than you.

You are the light bringing me home on my darkest days. You are my voice of reason when I can't see clearly. You are my muse, broadening my imagination to levels I never knew existed.

Sweetheart, please, I'm struggling so hard to be all these things for you. I hurt just like you. I know it's not exactly the same as what you are going through, but I hurt, too.

Becca, you are not at fault, baby. You did everything right! It is so common for this to happen. It's not your fault. I don't blame you. Please stop feeling as if I do. I could never ever find you at fault, love.

When you are ready ... we will try again. We will have the rather large, exhausting family that we have dreamt about. And we will always remember our little angel who's up in Heaven with your parents and my father.

Please, sweetheart, you did everything right with this pregnancy. There was nothing you could have done differently.

I love you and Morgan so much. My heart explodes with it every time I'm with you both. Let us focus on the three of us right now. We'll try again.

I'm so in love with you and I can't wait to hold you in my arms!

> Always,
> Your head-over-heels Husband,
> Grayson

I drop the letter, unable to catch my breath. *Oh my God! Oh my God!* The memory hits me like a harsh smack in the face.

"Grayson." I was barely audible.
"Sweetheart, what's the matter?" His concern was thick, even

over the phone.

"Where are you?" My voice grew louder but shakier.

"Derek's. Becca, what's wrong?" he asked.

"Come home, baby, please. I need you," I cried.

"I'm coming, sweetheart. Can you tell me what's wrong?"

"Just come home." I cried and hung up. I was sitting on the toilet. There was blood everywhere.

Derek lives fifteen minutes away. Grayson was there in ... it had to be seven or eight minutes, tops. I heard him yelling down the hall for me. I couldn't even muster the energy to shout out for him. He crashed through the bathroom door, slamming it into the wall.

"Oh my God, sweetheart! Oh my God!" He pulled out his cell phone and called 911. I just sat there, crying and crying.

At the hospital, we learned the placenta had fully detached from my uterine wall, causing the pregnancy to terminate. I was nine weeks along. No one knew but us. We were going to wait until Christmas to tell everybody. Grayson told everyone that I was sick and in the hospital for dehydration. No one knew I was pregnant, miscarried, and had a DNC. I begged him not to tell anybody. I blamed myself and went into a depression. Grayson tried everything to help me out of it, but I was so distraught. I even accused Grayson of secretly holding me responsible.

Two weeks later, Grayson had to do some book-signing dates. He wanted to cancel, but I wouldn't let him. Then he booked the private jet to get back to us sooner, and he died. If I had let him cancel the trip, he'd be alive. If I didn't lose the baby and go into a depression, he wouldn't have chartered that jet. Grayson was frugal. It was all my fault he died! I thought that then, and on some level, I still do.

This is why my PTSD was so severe that I repressed my memories with Ray. I couldn't bear the thought of any more loss. First my baby, then within a matter of weeks, my husband! Day in and day out, reporters and paparazzi called me and showed up at the house. I wanted to disappear. I wanted to go home. After six months, I sat down and started formulating a plan. Within a year of their deaths, I was in New Hampshire—where no one would bother me.

I pick the letter back up and touch my rounding belly. *How could I forget my baby?* Oh God, the sad look on Grayson's face when we were in the car. I wondered then, if we had a son, would he have looked like Grayson? Now, I'm almost sure it was a boy *because* of his reaction. Is Grayson united with him? Why didn't he tell me when he had the chance?

"Damn it, Gray!" I yell, but he can't yell back. I just sit and cry, cradling the letter in my hands.

"Becca?" Stacey opens the door. "Are you all right?" She walks up to the bed. I fold the letter and put it back into its envelope. She climbs up and sits next to me. I close the book and place it in her lap.

"Another mystery solved," I say, lying back as she opens to the first page. I get up after a minute and go into the bathroom to blow my nose and pee. I get a chill, thinking of what transpired on this very toilet. I finish up and head back into the bedroom.

"Here, your phone keeps lighting up. You have a message." She passes it to me as she continues with the book. I look at my phone.

"It's Ray," I murmur and toss the phone down onto the bed.

"Are you going to answer him?" She glances up.

"No. I'm going to go to the kitchen to make a ridiculously huge bowl of ice cream. Do you want any?" I offer.

"Nope, just had some." She rubs her belly and smiles.

"Okay." I head out and down to the kitchen. *Boyfriend?* I'm trying to sort out how I feel about him saying that instead of *fiancé*. I don't have a ring. He hasn't officially asked. But, since I've been out of the coma, it's been suggested that our intentions are to marry. Maybe he shouldn't marry me. Oh God ... I feel panic rise in me. I grab the edge of the table to brace myself and sit as everything goes white. My heart palpitates wildly. My palms feel clammy and beads of sweat form on my forehead. I think I'm going to vomit. I grab ahold of the silver salt shaker and concentrate on the cold metal. Slowly, I feel myself normalize. Jesus—I haven't had one of those in years!

Chapter Nine

RAY

I jump up and dash to the kitchen when I hear the intro to "Ice Ice Baby" play. I grab my phone and pull the charger from it.

"Hey, baby!" I answer.

"Ray, it's Stacey. Becca and the babies are fine, but you need to get your ass out here now! There is some shit going down, and I'm afraid she's going to fall back into 'Lucy' mode!" Her words are so fast and frantic, I can barely comprehend what she's saying.

"What's going on, Stace?" I try not to panic, given Stacey's long history of exaggeration.

"Becca opened Gray's gift. It's a scrapbook of them through the years, and a bunch of her poems. He wrote replies to them."

"Wait ... Becca writes poetry?" I interrupt her.

"Yes, Ray, that's why I'm calling, because of the fucking poetry! She's walking around now reciting fucking sonnets! Will you stay focused?!" she says flippantly.

"Sorry," I sigh.

"At the end of the book, there's a letter. He's trying to comfort her and encourage her. Ray, she miscarried their second child. I'm guessing a few weeks before Grayson died." She's crying now.

"I didn't know that."

"Ray, nobody did! It seems like they were waiting to tell people, but I think she repressed that, as well." Jesus, she is talking so fast again. "Ray, I'm going to get as much as I can out of her, but you need to get on a plane now!" she demands urgently. I'd say she's at DEFCON 2.

"I've already booked a flight. Derek is picking me up at ten tomorrow morning," I inform her. Looking at the clock, thirteen hours seems too long to wait.

"Can you get here sooner?"

"No. That was the best I could do. Why do you think she's going to go back to 'Lucy'?" I grab the small jewelry box on the counter, flipping it open for the millionth time today.

"She saw your message and tossed her phone down. No emotion. I just, I don't know what to do. I don't want her to pull away from you. This may have sent her right back to how she was feeling when Grayson died. She blamed herself. Ray ... she's drained. She did too much today. She faced too much," she cries. My heart aches. She faced it all for me. I pushed her too much. But this is not what I was pushing for—*damn it!*

"Keep her grounded and focused, Stace. I'll be there in the morning." I close the box.

"Okay, I've got to go," she says. We hang up.

"Shit!" I yell and throw my hands into my hair. I call the airline to see if I can get an earlier flight. It's a no go. Ugh! Why does she have to be so far away?

BECCA

"Mom ... are you okay?" Morgan asks as she walks in.

"Uh, yeah. I'm all right now." I manage a smile. "What do you want for dinner?" I ask and start to get up.

"It's New Year's Eve, Mom. Aren't we having Chinese?" She grabs a water bottle out of the fridge.

"Oh shoot, honey, it's six o'clock. We would've had to order that hours ago. I'm sorry, sweetie. I didn't even realize what day it was." I throw some water on for tea.

"Well, Uncle Derek's picking it up now. He's picking up Aunt Danni and Jasper, too." She leans on the counter near me.

"Oh, good. Glad somebody's on top of things around here." Good ole Derek!

"Mom, you don't look very well. Are you sure you're okay?" She puts the back of her hand against my forehead, and I humor her. God, she's so old for her age—just like I was.

"Morgan, I'm not going to work as much anymore." I grab her hands. Grayson was right to be mad at me for that. Why was I so silly about the money? Even if I didn't want to use his, I have been making more than enough on my own. I shouldn't have been paying extra on the mortgage. I should have had more staff and given them more hours.

"Really?" she asks, her face hopeful.

"Really. I have enough staff now, so I should only have to work a little. My full concentration is going to be on you and Annie, and, of course, the babies when they come." I pat my belly.

"And Ray, Mommy?" It's more of a reminder than a question.

"And Ray, Morgy." I run my hands down her head and kiss her hair. I hug her to me and lay my head on hers. "I love you so much, Morgan. I thank God every day for blessing me with such an amazing daughter. I'm sorry I took so long to snap out of it. It means a lot to me that you are happy with our new family." I bring her face up to look at mine. She has Grayson's chocolate-brown eyes.

"Well, it's not really a new family, Mom. Ray, Annie, Nana, and Pop Pop have been our family for years." She gives me a strange look.

"You're right," I say, tears springing to my eyes. *Oh, my Ray.* I'd give anything to be in his arms right now.

"Lucy! We're home!" I hear Derek call out, the ruckus of his family not far behind him. I laugh at the irony of his word choice.

"Hey there, friend." I smile as he walks into the kitchen. "Where's the army you're feeding with all that food?" I ask as he places four large brown bags on the counter.

"I'm the army, Becs!" he states and starts pulling containers out.

"I brought the fancy china!" Danni says, waving New Year's–themed paper plates. I laugh.

"You guys are awesome!" I give them each a kiss and a hug. "Hey, I'll let Stacey know it's time to eat. I have to call Ray. I'll be out in a bit."

Derek nods, and I leave the kitchen.

"Bec?" Stacey's already halfway down the hall.

"Following your nose?" I tease.

"Bec ... why didn't you tell anyone?" Her face is red, and I can see she's trying hard to hold back her tears.

"I was only nine weeks. We were waiting for Christmas to announce it." I pull her aside. "I was devastated, Stace. I was miserable to be around. I pushed Grayson away, positive he thought I was somehow to blame. Then he ..." I trail off, choking on my tears. "I blamed myself again. Stace ... how could I forget about my baby?" I shake my head in disbelief.

"Bec, you know firsthand the tricks grief can play on your mind." She rubs my arms, trying to console me.

"Well, Ray will be happy to know he's not the only one I forgot about."

"Wow, Bec. I'm pretty sure that this is not something Ray would be happy about!" she snaps.

I wince. "Christ ... I don't even know why I just said that, Stace."

"Well, make sure you don't say it to him!" She crosses her arms.

"I won't. I'm actually going to call him now." I take in a deep, shaky breath.

"You do remember that he's your boyfriend, right?" she asks, seemingly unsure.

"Who's my boyfriend?" I shoot her a strange look.

"Becca?" A look of panic comes across her face.

"Just kidding." I bite my lip to stifle my giggle.

"You asshole!" She slaps my arm.

"Sorry, I couldn't pass it up! Yes, Mr. McNeil has made it abundantly clear several times that he's just my boyfriend." I sigh, thinking about his text and the comment he made before I stormed out of his office.

"What do you mean?"

"Never mind. Look, go ahead to the kitchen before Derek eats everything. I'll be down in a minute." I pat her arm and head to my room.

"Bec?" She calls after me. I look over my shoulder at her.

"Go ... I'm all right," I say. "Hey, Stace ... thanks for being here with me. It's New Year's Eve; you should be home with Max. It means a lot to me." I smile.

"Max is fine. Somebody's got to be the 'Ethel' to your 'Lucy'!" she says. I hear the appreciation in her voice.

"Just glad you're not Lavina ... that bitch be crazy, yo!" I laugh. She shakes her head at me.

"Go call him!" She waves and heads down to the kitchen.

It's almost ten on the East Coast. Ray's definitely up. I grab my phone and dial his number.

"Stace?" he answers, panic in his voice.

"If your phone is ringing 'Ice Ice Baby' for Stacey ... we have a problem, McNeil!" A spark of jealousy hits me. *Damn! Where did that come from?*

"Wow, that's fucking hot, babe! I should make you jealous more often," he adds.

"Ray, why would you expect Stacey? Did she call you from my phone?" I sit on my bed.

"Yeah, baby, she did." His voice is soft and patient.

"She told you, didn't she?" I ask, knowing the answer already.

"Becs, I'm so sorry that happened to you guys," he says. I take in a sharp breath at his condolence. He referred to Grayson and me both. I'm in awe at this—at him. "Hold on, I'm getting a text." I sit in silence. "Oh, Becca—c'mon, baby." He sighs with what sounds like frustration.

"What?" I sit up straight.

"Would you rather I continue to refer to myself as your *best friend*, like you have been doing for five years?" he asks.

"Fucking Stacey," I sigh.

"Well?"

"No." I have no argument. "I'll just call you *my baby daddy*," I laugh.

"Yeah, there we go." He laughs. "I'm going to marry you, baby. Let me be your boyfriend for a little bit first," he says.

"Rings or no rings, you'll always be my boyfriend."

"Hey, baby, that's ... I think that's one of the sweetest things you've ever said to me." His voice is soft.

"Oh, come on, Ray! That can't be!" I defend myself.

"Well, no, I just mean the sentiment of me always being your boyfriend even when I'm your husband. That's really ... I like that." I can hear the thought he's putting into it.

"Did you eat dinner yet?"

"And here we have Becca James coming in from left field. McNeil must have overwhelmed her, folks." He laughs when he hears me giggle.

"I love you, Ray."

"I love you, Becca, and I miss you. Yes, I ate ... four hours ago," he says.

"I wish you were here, but I'm glad your surgery went well and you're back to being my loving, patient boyfriend," I tease as I fight off becoming *verklempt*.

"Um, handsome and sexy as hell, don't forget those."

"Mmm ... you *are* sexy as hell, baby," I agree.

"Ugh! I can't wait until you're back in my arms ... in my bed." He makes no attempt at hiding the desire in his voice.

"I'll be home soon," I say with promise. "Ray, I need to go eat dinner. Will you call me for the ball drop?" I ask.

"Yeah, babe," he finally manages to say after laughing a moment. He's such a guy!

"Ugh, you're ridiculous!" I grumble.

"Go eat, baby. I love you. Give Morgan and our babies a kiss for me."

"Love you, too." I kiss into the phone and hang up.

I take in a deep, cleansing breath. I've been through a lot today—a lot more than I was prepared for, really. I text Ray.

December 31, 2012   7:04 p.m.

Me: "Love" by John Lennon and the Plastic Ono Band. Just heard this today and thought of

you. So good hearing your voice. You always know what to say ... most of the time.

Love you!

Ray: Research! Research! Where do you find these songs? Thank you for loving me again

today! :)

Ray: Love your Boyfriend, Best Friend, Secret Lova :-o

Me: Not much of a secret anymore (pats rounded belly) ;-p

Ray: Hmm ... quite the scandal!

Me: Yes ... Nanarazzi has been off the hook since I've been home.

Ray: Nanarazzi knows no boundaries!

Me: Clearly!

Ray: Go eat, baby! I'll call you soon!

Me: McNeil benches his best player ...

Ray: That's a good one, baby! Now go feed my children! :|

Me: Yes, Coach! :)

"Did you guys leave me anything?" I ask as I walk in.

"Nope!" Derek teases. I smack his shoulder and grab a white Styrofoam container with God knows what in it.

"How's Ray?" Danni asks.

"He's good. Back to his old charming self!" I sit and open up my mystery dinner. Not quite sure what it is, but there's no fish and there is pork-fried rice, so ... it's a go!

"No arguments?" Stacey asks nervously.

"No, your text did not cause an argument." I give her my best "thanks for meddling, bitch!" smirk. She mouths, *Sorry*. I shrug it off. I'm not mad, really.

"So, what do you wild preggos have planned for tonight's festivities?" Derek asks, wiping his mouth.

"Sleep!" we say in unison.

"Wild enough for you?" Stacey adds.

"You and Grayson threw the best New Year's Eve parties! People still talk about them!" Danni pipes up. The three of us look at her. I don't know if we're all thinking the same thing, but our collective stares clearly make her feel uncomfortable. Danni only went to one of our parties—the last one, and she was so shitfaced, she threw herself at Grayson. She and Derek were broken up for a few months after that.

"Well, Mom throws a great party! That's why people love when she does their weddings," Morgan says proudly, melting my glacial stare.

"Thanks, sweetie!" I smile her way.

Danni excuses herself from the table and heads to the bathroom. Derek lets out a huge, frustrated sigh.

"D ... why would she mention that? Is she Daffy Duck, or what?" Stacey asks, making Derek and I erupt into a fit of giggles.

"Shit, Stace! I haven't heard that in years!" Derek says through his laughter and grasps his stomach. He takes a deep breath like he's trying to control himself. Nothing like watching a six foot something, three-hundred-pound black man giggling himself silly.

"Christ, Derek, you sound like a little girl!" Stacey teases him. *Daffy Duck* has been a long-standing joke in our circle that Stacey started many moons ago. Stacey thought she had been around Grayson and Derek long enough master to their British lingo. One night we were out for drinks, and some chick was flirting—or at least trying to flirt—with Grayson, Derek, and Max. Stacey, having enough, grabbed her arm and yelled, "Get out of here you, daffy cow!" This put the rest of us in stitches. I don't know if she'd already had too much to drink, or she really thought it was *daffy* and not *daft*.

The girl asked, "What the hell is a daffy cow?" All snarky.

"One level worse than the duck," Grayson stated seriously, causing another ripple of laughter from us. The girl walked away, confused—or pretty sure we were all nuts. From that day forward, *daft cow* became *Daffy Duck* amongst us. It's funny how the stupidest things can stick for years.

"Shit ... I miss the old days!" Derek's been saying that a lot. I know he misses Grayson as much as I do. We don't see each other as much as we used to. It's a painful reminder.

"Well, Stacey and Max are moving back to New England! That makes it a lot easier for all of us to get together more. I know it's not the same without Grayson, Derek, but ... I miss you. I miss all of us together." My nostrils flare.

"Hey, hey, Becs." He rubs my back.

"Sorry," I offer, and blow my nose.

"No ... it's okay. I feel the same way you do. Before you leave, we'll sit down and try to set up some plans to get together every few months, at least. But you need to bring Ray out here, Bec. If you're going to keep this house, you're going to have to learn how to share it with him." *Oh, Christ ... Father Derek is slowly stepping into sermon mode.*

"Yes, Father D," I tease him.

"Oh, Bec!" He shakes his head slowly, then starts chuckling.

"What?" I smile, knowing it's obviously over a memory.

"Grayson ... he used to say, 'I don't know why she calls you *Father D*. I'm the one who makes her say her prayers!'" His shoulders shake. I'd try to be offended, but it was true, and poor Derek unintentionally caught us in the middle of my prayers several times.

"Yes ... he made me talk to the Lord a lot." I put a forkful in my mouth.

"Uh, let's put another quarter in the jukebox, people!" Stacey says, nodding toward Morgan, Diana, and Jasper. Morgan looks around the room as if she's searching for something. I realize ... she's looking for the "jukebox."

"Oh, Morgy, Aunt Stacey just means we should change the subject."

"Another inside joke?" she asks.

"Yeah, sorta." I smile.

I actually started that one when Grayson and I were officially dating. We fought a lot in the beginning. He lived in L.A., I in Boston. It was difficult. He always expected me to drop everything when he came to town. It was one thing when it was planned; I always cleared my schedule. Quite often, though, he would fly in randomly and expect me to drop everything. Not just plans with friends, but work as well. I was struggling to get by as it was, and I couldn't afford to lose either of my jobs. Oh man, did we used to get into it over this! One day, I just yelled at him to put another quarter in the jukebox, I was tired of hearing the same song. Stacey walked in on me saying it and interrupted us long enough to inform me that she was stealing that line. True to her word, she's been using it ever since!

"Hey, Danni." I give her a sympathetic smile when she walks back in.

"Hey." Her voice is quiet. I feel bad now. She was just trying to compliment me. Do her part in cheering me up. When she sits, I reach across the table for her hand and squeeze it. *Sorry*, without words. She manages a half smile.

"I have a question," Stacey announces, looking around the table for the duck sauce. "Why the hell are we all squeezing around this small-ass table in here when you have a huge dining-room table that can accommodate all seven of us?" She dips her egg roll.

"Um, I'd say a bunch of lazy asses didn't want to bother carrying it out there," I suggest, taking my very last bite. And I mean *very* last, or I'm going to burst.

"Sounds about right," Derek agrees and attacks another wing.

"Seriously, how are you all still eating?" I feel sick watching them. Nope ... ugh, I just feel plain sick! I jump up and run to the bathroom, barely making it. Stacey knocks on the door as I give my last heave.

"You okay, Becs?" she asks.

"I think I may need an exorcism," I groan. Ugh ... yuck. I flush, wash my face in the sink, and rinse my mouth out.

"Mommy, it's Ray." Morgan passes me my cell when I come back out.

"I'm not going back in there," I tell Stacey and nod toward the kitchen before bringing the phone up to my ear. "So, the babies are not a fan of Chinese food," is how I greet him.

"Eck, sorry, babe. Maybe you should have some soup."

"Well, right now, I need to stay out of the kitchen. Sorry ... hi," I sigh.

"Hi. I hate this," he states.

"I know." I head into the study and turn on the lamp. I plop into the corner of the plush sofa and throw my feet up. "Hey, sometimes you like my impulsive behavior," I add, thinking again about yesterday's shenanigans on his office desk.

"I do, but Christ, Becca, I feel like you've been gone for a week, and it's only been a day. Your timing is really off, baby. I mean, I'm happy you're doing what you need to do and that you are handling it so well, but ..." he trails off. "We've missed all the holidays together now," he adds. I feel like his switch is pushing hard to flip. This really wasn't fair to him, especially time-wise.

"You're right to be upset with me about today, but I had no control over the others," I say defensively.

"I know that, babe," he says, his frustration showing no signs of dissipating. "I didn't call you to fight, Becs." He keeps his voice soft and steady.

"I don't want to fight, either. How's the design for that company coming along?" I inquire, looking for anything to talk about besides how my trip has disappointed him.

"I finished it today. It's amazing how much a man can get done when he's not distracted by his girl flashing signs in his face. Demanding signs." I can sense his slow, sexy smirk. The one he usually makes before blowing a kiss and winking at me.

"See ... silver lining," I say.

"I'd rather the distraction," he murmurs.

"Hmm, hey, you know what I was thinking?" I ask, and wonder why we all ask that instead of just saying what we're thinking.

"What?" I hear a cap pop off. Into the sink it goes!

"McNeil! I better not come home to a sink full of beer-bottle caps!" I snap. I hate when he does that!

"There's no way I could fill it in a week." I hear him take a swig.

"You've got Derek doing it now! Why is it so hard to throw it in the garbage?" *Wow ... hormonal much?*

"It makes the beer taste better when you toss the cap into the sink," he answers.

"That doesn't make any damn sense!" I say, even though I know he's baiting me!

"Sure it does!" he starts. "See, you open your beer and toss the cap into the sink. This aggravates the piss out of your girlfriend, causing her to nag you. Makes that first sip that much more enjoyable as you tune her out."

"You're an ass!" I giggle. Can't help it!

"I've been called worse, and without the effectiveness of a giggle," he says. "It's good to hear you giggle, baby."

"So, back to what I was saying." I push myself up straighter on the couch so my back gets more support from the armrest.

"What's that?"

"What would've been your fair bid on this project if your firm's situation were different?"

"Uh, probably one-point-five mil. Why?"

"Hear me out, Ray, all right?"

"Go ahead," he says, humoring me.

"I think you should try a different approach. Tell them that, while you'd love to do the design and build for them, you can't possibly give them the type of quality you stand by. Tell them you have to renege on your original bid and raise it by five hundred thousand. Tell them you understand if they want to go with Greerson, but that they should talk with these companies first. Then, give them the list of companies that came to you to correct his work. Then tell them to get back to you ASAP, because you are getting ready to hire people to handle another project you have lined up. You want to make sure you have enough guys to accommodate their needs, as well."

Did he fall asleep? "Ray?" I ask.

"Uh ... yeah, babe, I'm listening."

"Well?" I wave my hand for emphasis.

"Well, what if they go to Greerson? I don't know if I can do that, babe ..." he sounds defeated.

"Wow ... do you have any idea where they might have gone?" I ask in disbelief.

"Where what might have gone?" he asks, sounding confused.

"Your balls, Ray. Where did they go? I mean, Jesus! Next thing, you'll be asking me if your butt looks big in your jeans." I sigh. I'm saying this in jest, but honestly, this is not my Ray.

"I guess I left my balls at Mass General when I made you my number-one priority for three months!" he yells.

"Hey! Don't put this on me! I didn't ask you to stay by my side and ignore your business! It was your choice to flush it down the tubes!" I yell back.

"I stayed by your side because I love you! Nothing else takes priority over you!" He's even louder now. "Then you say some shit like that, and I wonder why the hell I bother to stick around at all!" He starts to lower his voice. "I know you're not a heartless bitch, baby, but sometimes you come off that way. The ball just dropped ... Happy New Year." His tone has changed to flat ... lifeless ... done.

"Ray ... I'm—" I start.

"G'night, Becs." He cuts me off.

"Wait!" I say, but he hangs up. I text him.

December 31, 2012   9:01 p.m.
Me: Ray, I'm sorry. Please love me tomorrow. :(
Ray: Always. G'night.
Me: G'night.

Chapter Ten

I open my eyes and look at the clock. It's 10:30 a.m. Wow. I could lay here for another hour. I was up late last night laughing with Derek, Danni, and Stacey. We were reminiscing some more. Because of my long nap yesterday, I wasn't tired when everyone went to bed. I stayed up reading the rest of an old novel by Judith McNaught. I snuggle deeper into Grayson's sweater and inhale deeply. I'm disappointed that he didn't visit me in my dreams last night.

My eyes shoot open quickly when I feel fingers caressing my face. Ray sits on the side of the bed.

"Hi," he says, his voice soft. His hand palms my cheek.

"Ray?" I sit up. I've already begun to cry. "Are you really here?" I ask, leaning forward and grasping his face in my hands.

"Yeah, baby, I'm here." He pulls me to him and captures my lips. My mouth opens at his tongue's beckoning. My tongue meets his and softly they caress each other. Ray begins to climb on top of me.

"No, Ray, don't," I gasp, pulling away.

"What?" he whispers in disbelief.

"No, no. I want to." I kiss him. "Just not in here. This is ... it's Grayson's and my bed. This is where I made love to him. I can't, it just wouldn't be right." I search his stormy eyes for understanding.

"Okay. Where can we go?" He stands and pulls me up. I swing my legs around. "Do you need this?" He grabs Grayson's sweater.

He gives me a strange look and raises it to his nose.

"Here, I'll take it," I say quickly, trying to reach for it. He pulls away and shakes it open.

"What's this, Becca?" His nostrils are flaring.

"My favorite sweater of Grayson's," I say quietly.

"You put his cologne on it and slept with it?" His jaw twitches now to complement that nose flaring.

"Ray, please." It's all I can say because I'm too busy crying. He closes his eyes. I think he's trying to control his anger. He opens them and tosses the sweater back onto the bed. He grabs my hands.

"Come on. Show me where I can have you." His voice is low ... sexy. He pecks my lips. "Now, baby." He squeezes my hand. I grab the clothes on my chaise lounge before I lead him out of the room and head to the guest room that Gray and I never christened.

It seems to take forever to get there. I watch as Ray takes in the architectural design of the house. Habit. He's finding what he's impressed by and what he can improve on. As I lead him down a long hall, a memory hits me. A T-shirt of Ray's is hidden in the back of the third middle drawer of my dresser at the inn. A slow smile comes across my lips. I speed up to walk backward in front of him. I grab his other hand and lead him in. He studies my sudden change of mood, like he's trying to figure me out.

"I just had a memory of something that has nothing to do with my alter 'Lucy' personality." My smile becomes huge. It ignites a hint of one at the corner of his mouth.

"What is the memory?" He pulls me to him.

"Whenever you sleep over, I swap out your T-shirts." I bite back my smile. "It all started when you forgot one. I kept it and slept in it so I could smell you. Then, the next time you came over, I swapped them because the first one lost your scent. I keep it in a ziplock bag in my third drawer to hold the scent." I look up at him as I slowly unbutton his shirt.

"You wore it even when you weren't 'on'?" He makes air

quotation marks and continues to study me.

"Yes. All the time. It makes me feel safe and loved." My hands run up his chest to his shoulders and slowly I guide his shirt off. Amusement flickers in his eyes. "What?" I lean up and kiss his lips, thankful his mood seems to be changing.

"I caught you once." He nudges my lips with his. "I came over early one morning to have breakfast with you. Remember? The girls were with my parents for their yearly Cape Cod trip." He shakes my hips a bit. I shift my eyes as I try to remember. "I went upstairs to wake you. I was surprised you weren't helping Hazel with break-fast—thought maybe you weren't feeling well." He closes his eyes. "I unlocked your door and walked in."

"How did you get a key to my room?" I interject.

"I made a copy of it, baby." His smile is mischievous. I just shake my head at him.

"So I walk in and goddamn it, Becca, there you were. Fast asleep on your belly, facing away from the door. You were wearing my shirt, hugging your pillow, with your right leg bent straddling the blanket on the outside. My shirt had risen above your ass, and your panties hugged your cheek in just the right place. I knew right there, this was either going to be a very good day or one of our worst, because there was no way I could find you like that and not touch you." He thumbs my lip and collects it. A low groan escapes my throat as he sucks purposefully on it.

"Ray, please tell me more." I pull away. "I want my memories back." I turn my face away.

"Just this one, baby, then I want to make love." He leans his forehead against my temple.

"Okay." I'm breathless. His fingertips softly strum over my nip-ples through the fabric of my pajamas. "Ray, please." I place my hands on his forearms and stare into his eyes. I watch as they dart left to right, taking me in, his fingers still working. My breathing becomes more erratic by the minute—second, really. "Ray." I close my eyes, getting lost in the erotic feeling of his fingers, the fabric, his blue-gray eyes. "Ah ... Ray, please!" I gasp as he tweaks my nipples harshly, tightly kneading them between his fingertips. My panties are like the Hoover Dam. I squeeze his arms for support as my knees get weak.

"Open your eyes, baby." His voice is sexy and low. I open my eyes as he continues his torturous play at my nipples. He gives them one last long tug, pulling them toward him and rubbing the tips. I gasp and try to steady my breath. Abruptly, he releases them. My hands lose hold as he drops his arms. He practically jumps on top of the bed.

"So, I took my coat off and tossed it onto your chair," he continues, unaffected while I stand there dizzy with desire. "C'mere." He holds his hand out to me as I turn toward the bed. I take it, climb up, and lie on my left side to face him. His hand rests on my right hip. "You okay, baby?" he asks, as if I stubbed my toe or something. I nod and rest my head on my left arm. "So, I climbed in next to you and very slowly traced the edge of your panties, then caressed your cheek. You woke and looked over your shoulder. You put your head back down and didn't say anything. 'Becs, baby, you have the most fantastic ass,' I said near your ear. Then I said, 'Is this my shirt?' and tugged on it a bit. You looked back at me and said, 'No. It's my boyfriend's shirt.' You said it so nonchalantly, I took you seriously and a flicker of anger came over me. I swatted your ass. The sound of my hand hitting your skin, the sound that came from you ... Jesus! Something ignited in me that I couldn't cage. I got off of the bed and ripped my shirt off. You turned, watching me strip down. I could see you becoming more and more nervous. Your eyes widened when I went Full Monty. It was hard to keep the predator look going."

"Is that what that is?" I touch his face. He smiles.

"I climbed onto the bed and told you I was going to take your panties off. You didn't utter a word. You lifted your hips when I reached to pull them down. I climbed between your legs and rubbed my dick up and down. Christ, you were so wet, Becca." He closes his eyes. "I said, 'Who's your boyfriend, Becca?' I waited for your answer. You said, 'You are, Ray.' I asked you again. You repeated yourself and pushed toward me, begging. 'Who?' I asked again. You said, 'You, baby.' And I slammed inside of you. God, baby ... I fucked you so hard—so deep. All the while I kept asking and you kept answering. It was so hot ..." He trails off, lost in the memory. "We stayed in bed that whole day. Oh man, you were so fucking *on* that day, baby!" He opens his eyes to look at me.

"Like Donkey Kong?" I smile.

"Yeah." He leans over and grasps my lips with his.

"That's because you're sexy as hell, McNeil," I say before I fully give in to his lips and his needs.

My right arm rests leisurely over my closed eyes as we bask in our post-coital glow. I feel hypnotized by Ray's fingers trailing up and down my belly, his lips planting kisses.

"I still can't believe we're finally having a baby. Well two," he adds.

"Hmm ... I know." I open my eyes and let my left hand play with his hair. He sits up and takes in the guest bedroom. It's large, but pretty plain. I never did get to this room. The walls are white and textured. Linens are a light cocoa cream and grayish blue. Nothing but a mirror on the wall.

"Bec, this room doesn't say *you* at all." He looks back to me.

"No, I never got to it."

"Well, I'm guessing this will be our room from now on so you should probably get to it." He pats my knee.

"Well, for now, not forever." I sit up with him and kiss his shoulder.

"Baby, I can't give you anything like this. Not yet, at least." He looks straight ahead.

"Ray, I love the house you bought for us. It's special to me. We picked it out together." Another kiss on the shoulder.

"I bought that house for Annie and me," he says, trying to hide his playful smile.

"Uh-uh, you bought that house for *me*." I turn his face toward me. "That's why you had me decorate everything the way I wanted to."

"No. I just like your taste," he states flatly.

"I love your taste, McNeil," I whisper in his ear before I bite at it.

"Stop." He shrugs away. He gets off the bed and starts to dress himself. I stand and throw my clothes on.

"You know what? I'm dealing with enough shit here!" I say. Ray rushes toward me and grabs my arm when I start to push him away.

"Baby ... baby, stop." He stills me. "Stop," he says again in *that* tone. I lean my head on his chest and let myself have a good cry. "Shh ... shh, baby ... okay, it's okay." He rubs my back and kisses my head.

"Please, Ray. Please stop. I need you. Please stop flipping your switch." I look up at him. He nods.

"Sorry," he whispers. "C'mon, finish getting dressed. I want a tour." He palms my face and kisses me. I throw my top on and head into the bathroom to blow my nose and do the usual business. I walk back out.

"I have one question, baby," he says, his back turned to me.

"What?" I ask.

"Does my butt look big in these?" He looks over his shoulder. I can't help but laugh.

"No. It looks fucking hot!" I smack it hard.

"Mmm," he moans and grabs my hand. We head out and I give him the tour of my six-bedroom Mediterranean ranch, or *Ranchion*, as Stacey calls it.

"What's up these stairs?" he asks.

"Grayson's office." I glance up. I haven't gone in there yet.

"Can I use it to work on the designs for your renovations?" Ray seems unsure about asking me.

"You're going to do the renovations?" I ask in disbelief and excitement.

"Of course, baby." He pulls me to him by my hips. "My job is to give you everything you want. Even if it's not how I planned." His index finger hooks under my chin to lift my face for a kiss. *Humph ... I wanted him again, but he wouldn't give me that.* He pulls back and tries to figure me out.

"I'm not ready to go up there." I sigh and turn away.

"Okay. Well, you don't have to." He grabs my hand as I bring him into the kitchen.

"Ray!" Morgan jumps up and runs to him.

"Hey, Morgy!" He hugs her and kisses her head.

"I didn't know you were coming!" She smiles up at him. It's so weird to see this. I'm used to her being indifferent to him. I'm glad she loves him.

"It was a surprise, sweetie! Have you been taking good care of Mommy?" He pushes her hair behind her ears.

"Yes. I'm trying." She looks over to me.

"You've been doing a great job," I say as I pull eggs out of the fridge. "You guys hungry?" I look over my shoulder as I pull out ham, sausage, bacon ... oh, and cheese!

"Starved." Ray pats his belly.

"I'm good, Mom. Can I watch some more home videos?"

"Sure. Babe, do you want breakfast or lunch?" I cut open the package of Jimmy Dean sausage and toss some into the pan to fry. I gasp when Ray's arms come around my waist from behind.

"Whatever you're making, I'll eat. You. Know. That. Baby," he says between the kisses he plants on my neck. "Becs, call me old-fashioned, but I love watching you in the kitchen, especially when I know you are cooking for me. I love when you wash my clothes. I love when you iron them and put them away." He rests his chin on my shoulder as he reveals things to me I was already very aware of.

"Very brave of you to say that to a woman in the year 2013," I tease.

"I know, but I needed to tell you. Oh, and I especially love that you will come over before the guys show up to watch a game and make a platter of sandwiches and all kinds of dips. They're all jealous," he laughs.

"Is that why you end up hosting more than anybody else?" I turn my head and kiss his cheek.

"Yep!" He squeezes me.

"Well, since we're being honest," I start as I throw the bacon in another pan. "I love that you handle all of the cosmetic and mechanical issues at the inn. I love that you keep up with the maintenance on my truck, and my Honda Pilot before that. I love that you come over when I'm expecting a delivery so I'm not lifting anything too heavy. Should I go on?" I nudge his head with my shoulder.

"No. It's clear we were both born in the wrong generation. I'm just glad we're stuck here together, Mrs. Cleaver." He kisses my neck again. "Call me when it's ready." He pats my bottom and heads out of the kitchen.

RAY

I decide to head down and watch these home videos with Morgan. With the exception of him visiting me in my dreams last night, I've never seen how Grayson was. What his personality was like. I've heard from others that I'm like the American version of him in a lot of ways. I'm not quite sure how to take that. I certainly don't want to just be his "replacement," especially for Becca.

"What's this one?" I sit beside her.

"Um ... " She looks down at the cover. "It says *Becca pregnant*." The first scene shows Becca sleeping on a hammock.

"There she is," Grayson whispers as he tapes her. "The most beautiful woman on the planet."

Jesus ... she's so young. She hasn't changed much, though. She's still the most beautiful woman on the planet.

"Honestly, have you ever seen anything so lovely in your life?" he asks.

No.

"And there ... in there grows the most beautiful, intelligent baby." He zooms in on Becca's slightly rounded belly.
"What are you doing?" Becca smiles and holds her hand over her eyes to look up at him.

The video gets jumbled around. Then you see both of them on the hammock.

"I'm recording you so I have proof that I've married the most hideous woman on the planet," he says, straight-faced. Becca smiles warmly at him. "Honestly, it's awful ... the torture I go through hav-ing to look at you. I mean, really, did you hit every branch coming down?" he asks her. "Jesus H. Christ! I really took one for the team, fellas!" He looks into the camera.
"Grayson!" She bites her smile back and puts his hand on her belly. Her smile takes over her eyes.
"That's amazing, sweetheart!" He looks at her, awe on his face. "See," he brings his attention back to the camera, "she's so ugly, the baby is trying to kick its way out!"

"Oh, would you shut it?!" She smacks him and lets out a delayed giggle.

"Ah, Becca ... I'm the luckiest bloke in the world, sweetheart." He pecks at her lips.

"And you'll do well to remember that, Mr. James." She taps his nose.

"I remember every day, Mrs. James." He leans down.

I watch them kiss. It's very difficult and weird to watch Becca respond to another man the way she responds to me.

"Mrs. James! Honestly!" He pulls away, sounding appalled. "This is a G-rated family production! Please stop making these sorts of advances toward me." Becca shakes her head like she's trying to keep from laughing. "Stop it! Stop it right now! Seriously —knock it off!" He taps her hand lightly.

"I will as soon as you tell me what I'm doing," she says.

God, she's so cute!

"Look at you, acting all doe-eyed and innocent while undressing me with your eyes! Ugh—there goes my belt! Honestly! You're insatiable!"

She giggles and reaches for his belt.

"Mr. James ... what shall we do about that?" Giggling gone.

Oh, damn ... seductive Becca.

"Sorry, mates, I've got to take another one for the team!" he says as Becca trails kisses down his neck. She's pulling his shirt free from his pants as he turns the camera off.

"Awkward!" Morgan announces.

"Yeah ... just a bit." I agree. The video comes back on, and

Grayson appears.

"I've been awoken by the sound of an awful beast. I thought I should video for solid proof, given the history of Bigfoot and the Loch Ness Monster. Let's see if we can locate the beast this hideous noise is coming from." He walks further into their bedroom. *"There's Becca, sleeping soundly. Apparently, the beast hasn't woken her or our unborn child."* He zooms in on Becca's face. *"Wait for it ... wait for it,"* he coaches the viewers. *Within seconds, Becca makes the most ungodly snoring sound. Grayson starts giggling.*

I hate to admit it, but I'm joining him.

"Beauty by day ... beast by night," he states.

His British accent somehow makes the comment funnier.

She starts to do it again, and Grayson reaches toward her nose and pinches it. An even more hideous noise comes out of her mouth.

"My God! It cannot be stopped!" he says with exaggerated panic in his voice.

I'm rolling! I throw my mental white flag up. He and I would've definitely been great friends! I have a newfound respect for him. The video fades and comes back to a calm Becca in a hospital bed.

"Today is the day, sweetheart!" Grayson announces. *Becca flashes him an excited smile. A nurse comes in and starts up her IVs.* *"A little induction for the introduction of one sure-to-be very beautiful Morgan Alexa James. You are awfully quiet, Mum."* Grayson swats Becca's arm from behind the camera.

"It's six in the morning, baby." She yawns, then makes an "ow" face as the nurse twists the tubes and tapes them down.

The video fades and comes back. Becca's on a birthing ball, breathing through a contraction.

"How are things coming along, sweetheart?" Grayson asks. Becca lifts her head off of the bed and looks over at him. "Ready for drugs yet?"
"No, but maybe they could supply you with a tranquilizer." She shoots him a look.
"You think you could hurry this along, darling? I'm getting a bit bored watching you huff and puff."

I can't believe he just said that to her! It makes Becca giggle, though.

"Would you like me to juggle while I do this?" she asks.
"I'd say you're already doing that, sweetheart! You're juggling labor and putting up with the likes of me. You're amazing, Becca. I love you." You can hear it in his voice.
"I love putting up with the likes of you. I love you ... too," she says, and begins breathing through another contraction.

The video fades again, and when it comes back, Becca is pushing.

"You're doing an amazing job, sweetheart!" Grayson cheers her on. She looks up at him mid-push.
"Grayson James, if you put that camera in my crotch, I will rip your balls off and eat them for lunch!" she screams at him. Grayson turns the camera on himself and makes an exaggerated look of panic. "Turn it off!" Becca screams as she begins to push again.

I look over at Morgan. Her eyes are wide, her face a little pale. "Are you okay?" I ask.

"I think I hurt Mommy," she says, tearing her eyes away from the screen.

"It's painful to give birth, but it's worth it. You were worth it, Morgan. You'll see Mommy happy in a moment." I put my arm around her. "Your dad was a pretty funny guy." I smile down at her. She nods and snuggles into me. My heart leaps. I haven't been a good enough dad to her. From now on, I'm gonna give a hundred and fifty percent. I kiss her hair.

"Look at her, sweetheart!" Grayson says softly, his finger touching Morgan's little cheek. "She's perfect ... absolutely beautiful. Just like her Mum. Aw, Becca, sweetheart ... you make my heart explode," he says with a sigh.

Know the feeling, dude! I agree in my head.

"Does my mom do that to your heart?" Morgan asks.

"Absolutely, every time I look at her," I admit. "See how happy she is now?" I point.

"Yeah. You wouldn't know I caused her any pain," she says.

"You were a beautiful baby, Morgs. And your mom ... wow. Look at her. Never a moment she's not beautiful." I sigh in awe at the fresh-faced beauty on the TV.

I turn my head, sensing her presence. She's leaning on the door-frame. Her face is red and wet with tears.

"Morgy, let's turn this off for right now." I lift my arm from her shoulders to reach the remote. The TV goes black. I get up quickly to join Becca. "Baby?" I palm her face. Her green eyes stare up at me. I don't like to see her cry, but I'm always in awe of the color of her eyes when she does. Normally emerald, they are an amazing blue-green now. I want to kiss her, but hesitate. This is all very strange. Here we are, standing in the house she shared with her husband—a man she loved very much. Seeing them together in videos must make her miss him even more. I don't think she'll really want me to kiss her.

"I'm sorry, Becs." I lay my forehead against hers. "I'm sorry for all of the pain you have gone through, losing Grayson the way you did," I say softly. "The baby," I whisper. "I can see from the video how much you two really loved each other. I just hope that one day I can make you as happy as he made you." This provokes a strange look from her.

"Ray ... you do make me happy." Her face softens.

"No, baby. Ever since you've come out of the coma, I've been all over the place emotionally. Christ, I think you're right. I may need a tampon," I say. Becca starts laughing. Her hands cup my face and she leans up for a kiss.

"C'mon, Rachel, your breakfast is ready." She taps the side of my face.

"No, you didn't just call me Rachel!" I act hurt. "Here I am, pouring my heart out to you and all you do is—" I stop to wave at my eyes, "—poke fun at me."

"Knock it off!" She smacks my shoulder and starts down the hall, but I grab her hand and pull her back to me. I study her face. She looks at me thoughtfully, waiting patiently to see what I'm playing at. I wipe the last bit of tears away from the corners of her eyes.

"Ray?" She places her hands on top of mine.

"What, baby?" I lean forward and kiss her again.

"I did get emotional over the video, but what really got to me was watching you and Morgan. Um, that was the first time I've ever see you have a father-daughter moment with her ... alone. It was ..." She trails off.

"Shh." I place my finger over her lips. "I promise more of that from now on." I collect her lips again.

"C'mon, your food is getting cold." She gives me another quick peck.

I slowly climb the stairs to Grayson's office, wondering what I'll find up there. Becca hasn't stepped foot in it since he died. His words in my dream echo in my mind.

"Ray ... use my office, mate! Don't be such a stubborn arse! The money's there, man. Turn this renovation into your baby! If you just get over the bullshit you're hung up on, the inspiration will hit you. I'm telling you, man! This is the project that will "make you"! It's going to make the Digest, *and you will become one of the top names in architectural design! Get your head out of your arse, man! You want to take care of our girl? This is how you are going to do it!"*

Persistent pain in the ass wouldn't leave me alone all night!

I open the door.

Ah, yes! A sophisticated man cave ... love it! Built-in book-shelves in dark Peruvian walnut take up the entire right wall from floor to ceiling, and the beams across the ceiling and window frames match the wood's color. The walls are a calming grayish-blue. I look at the books—the many, many books. Almost every room in this house has built-ins filled to the brim. There are even stacks on the floor. Derek said Grayson's thirst for knowledge was insatiable.

There are several framed pictures on various shelves showing Becca and Grayson, just Becca, all three of them, Gray with Hazel, and one with him and both of his parents, I'm assuming. There is a framed Manchester United poster with a signature on it. The room gets great light from the huge picture windows on the walls across from the entrance and to the left. I head over to his large desk and place my bag on it. His chair is plush leather.

"Oh ... sweet!" I sit. I rev up his computer and drum my fingers on his desk. *To look or not to look?* I wonder as I stare at the drawers. Oh, what the heck? I open the bottom-right drawer and find a box, sort of like a shoebox. I pull it out and open it. Notes. Notes from Becca. I pick up the first one and read it.

Baby,   06/08/01

Church was exceptionally moving last night. As Nine Inch Nails would say ... you keep me closer to God!

XXXXX

Becca

I grab another.

Becca Sweetheart,   06-10-01

Please read over these chapters while I'm away. I'm sure you will not be shy with your thoughts!

Love your prayers,

Gracie

Gracie,   06/12/01

Sure you're checking in on my opinion 1st to determine which way service will go tonight! The chapters were spot-on, but I still don't like your heroine's name! Please change it!

Now come to bed, I miss you and I need help saying my prayers!

Love you x 5,

Becca

Dearest Husband,   11/14/03

If my smile was any bigger, it would swallow my face! XXXXX Becca

Becca Sweetheart,

Please, darling, I don't know what came over me. I'm so sorry. I promise. I will never do that again. Please forgive me ... please. I'm so in love with you. Please tell me I haven't lost you. I will do anything. Tell me what I must do for your forgiveness.

With a heavy heart,

Grayson

Just time ... please. Becca   05/20/02

What the hell did he do to her?! I search through the pile of notes to see if any of them indicate what happened. Nothing. Just all cutesy notes or inquiries about opinions on things. I put the lid on. My blood is boiling. Did he hurt her physically? Did he cheat on her? I shake my head. No way this dude cheated on her. Ugh ... Ray, just let it go! It was over ten years ago. Clearly she forgave him!

It's been three hours since I stepped into Grayson's office. All I've managed to do is stare at the list of essentials for the design and build. How many rooms, which have king-sized beds, which have doubles. Office. Store. Kitchen. Three hours, a list, and a note I wish I never saw! Now I understand the phrase "curiosity killed the cat"! I get up and head over to the bookshelves. I take my time glancing over the inventory, waiting for something to scream, *Pick me! Pick me!* Nothing. *Damn it!* "Ugh ... forget it. I'm thinking too hard!" I say aloud and finally decide to leave the room.

"Hey I was just coming up to get you." Becca smiles at me from halfway up the stairs.

"Ugh, baby, I've been staring at the goddamn walls for three hours!" I complain and throw my arm around her shoulders when I reach her. I kiss her hair and head down with her.

"Can I help you, Ray?" She looks up and over to me.

"No, you already told me what you'd like. I just need to catch the essence of something. If I'm gonna do this, I want to make it my baby." I pull her to face me. "My services will be very expensive, Ms. James ... I hope they will exceed your expectations."

"I have no doubt they will. I don't want you to hold back on anything, sweetie," she says, then her eyes widen. She grabs my hand. "I don't know if you'll be able to feel this." She places my palm against the side of her belly. We stand there and wait. The anticipation actually makes me feel a little *verklempt*. Liz never did this. I had to ask her. She was never thrilled about any of it. "Did you feel that?" she asks excitedly. I shake my head and feel disappointed. "Well, you'll feel it soon. It's just because they're so little. Strong, though," she adds, looking up. "I should only feel butterflies still, but that was definitely a field goal." She's glowing.

A son? I wonder if there's a boy in there. I haven't really thought about it. I mean, the family has taken bets, but this is the first time I've really thought about it.

"What?" Becca tilts her head sideways like she's trying to figure me out.

"Do you think we're having a boy?" I plant both hands on her stomach.

"Could be. Maybe it's two boys," she offers.

"Two boys?" I repeat, lost in the wonder and awe.

"McNeil, I see future sporting events flashing in your eyes." Becca laughs and taps my face with her hand.

"Sorry. I just ... I really want a boy." I wince.

"Me, too." She leans up to kiss me. "Come, let's take a walk outside. I want to show you the guesthouse and yard." She pulls me along.

"Do you want your coat, baby?" I offer before we head out the double glass doors.

"No, it's sixty degrees out, I'm good." She slips on flip-flops.

"So, Grayson, he, uh ... bounced a lot of ideas off of you?" I ask once we step out onto the outdoor patio. Jesus, this is sweet! It's a large rectangular area with a high beamed ceiling, amber-colored textured wall, and fireplace. The dark cherrywood from the ceiling comes down in large posts. The outdoor seating has plush amber and rust-orange cushions. "Can we sit?" I ask and point to the sofa.

"Yeah, sure," she replies. We do so, and I wrap her in my arms. "So, to answer your question," she says as she leans her head against my shoulder. "Yes. Grayson came to me about everything in his novels."

"Why? He did fine before he met you."

"Because I was blatantly honest with my opinions. He valued that. A lot of times, when you reach a certain level of success, you find that either people placate you or they don't know enough about what you are doing to give you a proper opinion. That's one of the things that drew Grayson to me in the first place." She closes her eyes and a soft, amused smile crosses her face.

"Care to share, babe?" I nip at her ear.

"Hmm." She snuggles in more. "I was working part-time at Barnes & Noble when I first met Grayson. He was there for a book signing. I had read his latest novel two days before, like I always did when an author was coming in. Well, the dust jacket didn't have his picture, and I wasn't impressed enough with the book to bother looking him up. So, when he approached me in the store, I was clueless as to who he was. Besides, he was like an hour early. As you can see from our house, Grayson either had his nose in a book or was in a bookstore buying another book. Hence the early arrival." She shifts a bit, crossing her legs away from me.

"Well, I was putting some new gardening books out, not even realizing he was kneeling down on the floor looking at several different gardening books. 'Excuse me, can you help me?' he called out. I said, 'Sure!' and walked over to where he was."

"I bet he took a double take when he glanced up at you." I squeeze her.

"Uh, I don't know, why?" She shoots me a strange look.

"Because, that's exactly what I did when I walked into the girls' classroom and saw you for the first time," I say, and think back to that night. Christ, the moment I looked at her, my mouth went dry and my palms got sweaty. Sometimes she still affects me that way.

"Oh." She shrugs, oblivious to the compliment I just gave her. "Well, he asked me if I liked gardens. I said they were okay, then he asked if I would be interested in gardens and flowers. I said, 'Not particularly.' He said, 'Fantastic! As a woman with no interest in gardening or gardens, which one of these do you find most appealing?' I knelt down next to him to look at the books he had open. 'This one,' I said pointing to the French Country garden. 'Why that one?' he asked. 'I don't know ... it's appealing.' I shrugged and stood, but he pulled me back down. 'No! Come here, please! What makes this appealing over all the rest?' I looked again. 'The design and the color scheme.' 'And do you have a flower that you find appealing, even though you're not into them?' He began writing in a notebook. 'Um, hydrangeas.' 'Why?' 'I don't know. I guess because they are full.' 'What color?' he asked. 'All of them, especially the ones with green.' 'Really ... that's very interesting.' I started to laugh. I thought he was very odd. 'Aren't they scentless?' he continued to ask. 'Yes.' 'Well, why is that appealing?' He looked at me strangely. 'The look is appealing.' I shrugged again. 'I like peonies, too ... they smell nice,' I offered. 'But you don't buy the flowers or get excited about them?' 'No.' 'What do you do if someone sends them to you? Do you get excited then?' 'No. I appreciate them, but that's about it.' I didn't move because he was furrowing his brow. 'Well now, let me ask you this. Would a woman who is not particularly fond of flowers, such as yourself, be against or for receiving flowers at work?' 'Oh, that's different. Always send them to work. Even if she hates them. It's not about the flowers.' I reached out and touched his arm for emphasis.

"My manager came over and mentioned to me that they really needed help with the set-up for Grayson James. I said okay, then as he walked away, I mumbled, 'Ho hum ... snore.' Grayson jerked his head up from his notes. 'Did you say *ho hum snore* in reference to Grayson James?'"

I cut her off. "*Ho hum snore* is right! Jesus, I can't believe he talked to you that long about fucking flowers knowing you had no interest in the topic!"

"Yeah, you and me both!" she laughs. "So, anyway, I said yes. He asked me if I've even read any of his novels. I said, 'I just read the new one two days ago.' 'You didn't like it?' He seemed shocked. 'Well, it was written well enough. I just wasn't fond of the heroine ... if you could even call her that.' I rolled my eyes and got up. He shuffled all of his books together and stood as well. Or, towered, I should say—he was six-four."

"I'm not short!" I interject.

"Didn't say you were." She smiles at me. "But he did have six inches on you."

"Not where it counts, baby." I nip her ear again. She rolls her eyes at me and continues.

"'Well, why do you say that?' he asked, following me. 'I often wondered if Jessica knew how to even tie her shoes! And Garrett kept telling her how "strong" she was. Give me a break! Strong for what ... breathing?' 'Well, she was a bit of a damsel in distress,' he offered. 'Yeah, on crack! Even if a woman feels weak, she doesn't broadcast it all the time! It's pathetic! This guy wouldn't know a strong woman if she smacked him in the face.' I started putting the rest of the books away. 'Well, what did you think of Garrett?' he asked, handing me a book to shelve. 'He was well-written and appealing, except that he fell for that brainless idiot. Kind of makes you wonder if he's as brilliant as he's written.' I turned to him when he spoke again. 'Well, I have a different view on the matter. I think most women want to be a damsel in distress and have a strong-minded guy come along!' He seemed a bit on the offense. 'Look, even if a woman wanted that, she wouldn't broadcast it. Not a strong woman. It's just my opinion as a woman. Sorry if you're a big fan of his. What's with all the questions about flowers? Research, or a girl?' I changed the subject. I could tell I was infuriating him. The feeling was mutual. He opened his mouth to say something, then closed it like he was thinking about it. He looked at me again and said, 'Well, it was for research purposes, but now you've got me thinking of a girl I'd like to date. Do you suppose I should send her favorite flowers to her work?' He picked up one of the books I dropped. 'Oh yes, definitely. Good luck with her.' I smiled and thought, *And good luck to her!* 'Yes, I think I'll need it.' He turned away, then back to me. 'By the way, I find you most helpful and infuriating all at once.' 'Well, I'm no Jessica, that's for sure,' was all I could say, otherwise I would've been fired. 'No ... you most certainly are not, sweetheart.'"

"Can you speed this up, baby?" I tap her leg impatiently.

"Oh. Sorry." She looks at me hesitantly. I nod.

"So, needless to say, I sort of flipped out on him because he touched my face when he called me *sweetheart*. We baited each other back and forth 'til my manager came over to see what the problem was. Grayson assured him that everything was fine. My manager sent me to lunch. I said to Grayson before I left, 'You should have Mr. James sign your book, *From one pompous ass to another*!' And I walked away. When I came back from lunch, there was a hydrangea arrangement on the counter behind the register. I was told it was for me. I looked at the card and it said, Because it's not about the flowers! Under your spell — The Pompous Ass. I glanced around the store and finally locked eyes with him. He was at the table signing books. He picked up one of his books and mouthed *Want one?* then imitated signing it. I picked up a trash can, pointed to it, and mouthed *Full* as I shrugged."

"That must've pissed him off!" I would've been pissed.

"No ... he actually laughed." She smiles at the memory.

"And so began his stalking?" I ask.

"Yep ... Derek tell you?"

"Yeah. Well, now that I know you won't placate me, maybe I can pick your brain about the renovations," I say with a sigh.

"Sure. What's going on?" She snuggles in to me, crossing her legs toward mine.

"I know I was only at it for three hours, but I can't seem to get an idea about anything. I want this to represent both of us, but I can't come up with a way to incorporate us." I blather on like an idiot.

"Well, first things first, don't rush the thought. It will come to you. I told your dad to put the check in so you won't have to worry about that. Take your time." She yawns as the end of her statement.

"How much did you tell him?" A budget in mind will definitely help me.

"Um ... I wasn't sure, so I told him three million. Is that a good amount to start out with?" *Wow! She just said 'three million' like it was nothing.*

"Do you have a cap?" I ask, feeling a bit uncomfortable.

"Well, try not to go past ten."

I feel sweat form at my brow.

"Becs, when's the last time you met with your finance guy?" I rub my palm back and forth on my knee to dry off the sweat.

"Um, last month," she says after much thought.

"Last month ... while you were in a coma?" I'm snarky. I can't help it.

She laughs and shakes her head. "No, I meant August."

"And you can comfortably put ten million into this project?" I unwrap her from my arm.

"Well, it's never comfortable putting ten million into anything," she states, looking at me wearily, "but I can do it if need be." I'm pretty sure she can sense me wanting to flip my switch.

"I need to go for a walk." I jump up.

"Shall I wait here?" She uncrosses her legs and shifts forward, looking up at me.

"Um, yeah ... I'll be back in a few," I say.

"I love you, Ray."

"I know." Half smile.

"You take good care of me," she says, as I hold up my hand for her to stop.

"Baby, please ... ten minutes." I run my hand through my hair and head off.

I resist the urge to fight an invisible opponent as I walk away. I pass the pool and guesthouse, ending up in the garden. It's extensive and obviously professionally maintained. I'd bet my eyes it's a fucking French Country garden! "All right, focus, McNeil!" I snap at myself. I hate that she has all this money. More than that, I hate that I knew nothing about it. I'm used to the girl who clips coupons and cuts corners to save a buck. The first night I met her, she was worried about going over her budget! Now she cuts me a check for three million like it's fucking pocket change?!

"Ray," she sighs, walking up behind me.

"Becs, I told you I need a few minutes." She never friggin' listens!

"I know you did, but I think this is something we need to sort out together. Come sit on the bench with me, baby." She grabs my hand and we sit on the white wrought iron bench. "Ray, none of this changes me. Who I am, who you fell in love with. All of this," she waves around, "this is not me."

"Becs, it is you. Everything says *you*. I walked into this house this morning and got hit in the face with your essence." I stand up and pace.

"Ray. Yes, I decorated the house." She inhales deeply to either gather the right words or gain some patience for me. "But this," she says, waving around again, "this is Grayson. The money is Grayson's."

"The money is yours, whether or not Grayson's the one who brought it. It's yours now, and you kept it from me! And everybody else, for that matter. You kept us in the dark about it!" I seethe. I'm trying so hard to "get over" her hiding all of this, but it's a battle I fear I'm losing.

"Why does it matter?" She stands and raises her voice as well. "The money is not who I am!"

"I can't compete with all of this, Becca! I don't know if I'll ever be able to!" And there it is: my insecurity, once again smacking us both in the face. Becca stands there, staring at me. Her nostrils flare to hold back her tears—unsuccessfully, I might add. She shakes her head and turns to walk away.

"No! No, I won't let you do this to us!" She turns back and walks toward me. "Listen to me, you stubborn, thick-headed son of a bitch!" She's all teeth and tears. I feel I should prepare to duck at any moment. "First of all, what you said is insulting to me! Grayson didn't win me with his money, and it's certainly not the reason he managed to keep me! To say that suggests you don't really know me at all!"

"Becs ... baby, I know you." I reach for her. She pulls away from me.

"Then you would know what it means to me." She takes a deep, shaky breath. "What it would mean to me to see you put your heart and soul into these renovations. It sounds silly." She puts her hand up to keep me quiet. "Ray, if someone else did it, it would be a big square with rooms. It may look nice, but I won't feel anything from it. I know when you design it, the talent will be wrapped with love. I know I will feel the essence of us. Yes, technically Grayson is supplying the money, but he couldn't do what you do. Something like this, he could only pay someone to try to capture 'us.' But you, you are molding it all from scratch ... it's all you, coming from your heart. The sky's the limit, baby. I want you to put everything you've got into this. It's yours, too. I am not your employer, I'm your partner. The money is only a tool, it can't compare to or compete with you! Please stop letting it affect you like this.

"Ray," she says, holding me at arm's length, "do the renovations. When it's done, I'll put the rest of the money in a trust for Morgan to have when she reaches a certain age, as well as this home. I don't want this money coming between us. I don't need the money. I need you."

Her chin quivers, and her eyes are that gorgeous blue-green they turn when she cries. She licks her lips before she bites the bottom one. I pull it away from her teeth and hook my index finger under her chin to raise her mouth up to mine. I nudge her lips with mine reluctantly, overwhelmed by her words. I've waited five years for such affirmation of her love. *Bare feet ... bare feet,* I chant to myself, slowly deepening the kiss with a slip of my tongue.

"*Vous avez mon Cœur. S'il vous plait me faire confiance avec les vôtres. Avoir foi en mon amour.*" Her voice is just above a whisper.

"You haven't spoken French to me in a long time, baby. What did you say?" I touch her face and rest my forehead against hers.

"You have my heart. Please trust me with yours. Have faith in my love." I attack her mouth with my own once more.

"Baby?" I pull away, panting.

"Let's go." She grabs my hand and we head back to the house, on a mission.

Chapter Eleven

Becca sharply turns to me, reaching to unbutton my shirt once we're in the room. I push her hair behind her ears and occupy her lips with mine. My hands move quickly for the hem of her shirt.

"Arms up."

I pull away and lift her shirt up and off as she complies. I smile, still trying to get used to her wearing pants with stretch panels.

"Don't say a fucking word, McNeil," she warns me as she helps me out of my shirt.

"You look cute, baby." I can't help grinning. Getting down on my knees, I hook my fingers under the elastic to pull her jeans off, chuckling as I do.

"Stop, you're making me feel self-conscious," she complains.

"Baby, stop, you're beautiful. Hello in there. Daddy loves you!" I talk into her belly button. There's a shift in Becca's mood. I glance up at her. *Oh shit!* She has that look. "Becs!" I jump up. "Baby ... please," I beg.

"Sorry." She snaps out of it and looks down.

"What is it?" I ask. She shakes her head. "Are you thinking about him?" I'm a little aggravated by the possible cock block happening here.

"I'm sorry," she says again.

"Uggghh!" I groan loudly, pulling at my hair as I walk away. "Damn it, Becca! I'm not going to compete for the rest of my life with a goddamn ghost!" I turn back to her. "I know you'll always love him. Damn it, when you're with me, stay focused on *me*!"

"It wasn't anything sexual," she interjects.

"I don't care!" I yell. "When we're having an intimate moment, there should be no thought of him whatsoever!" I close my eyes and try to calm down. "Becs ... baby, you don't understand. You say 'bare feet,' but it's hard for me to accept that. I'm trying very hard. When you still like that, and get that look on your face ..." I run my hand through my hair again. "That's what you do right before you pull away from me." I push her hands off my chest.

"Okay," she breathes and touches my face. "I'll try harder. Ray, things are going to be rocky for us for a little while. We're both adjusting to our new relationship."

"It's not new! We've been together for five years." I try to control my temper.

"Are you chasing me?" she asks.

"No."

"Am I running?"

"No."

"It's new then, isn't it? When's the last time I was 'on' a whole week with you?" she asks, brushing my lips with hers. I stare off into the distance, thinking about her question.

"Mmm ... Montreal," I say, licking my lips. My purpose renewed, I back Becca up to the bed. She sits and goes to work at my jeans. "Baby ... you were so hot in Montreal." I caress her cheek.

"Seems to me, McNeil," she says, whipping my belt off, "any situation that finds me naked and underneath you, you consider 'hot.'" She laughs, biting playfully at my stomach as she pulls my jeans down.

"Uh, yeah, pretty much."

I can't disagree. It's all hot in my mind.

"Well, you'll have to fill me in on Montreal after you, uh ..." She trails off, smiling as we climb back on the bed together.

"Fill you in," I say, chuckling as I finish her sentence.

"Exactly. Cliff notes, please." She nudges my hip with her knee.

"Really? Again? You're becoming very impatient, baby." I smirk.

"Well, this pregnancy has me horny as hell. It's giving me an itch that needs immediate scratching, if you will."

She plays with the hair at the base of my neck, waiting for me to approve her request.

"No," I whisper. Her eyes look up to mine.

"No?" she asks quietly, lifting her head up for me as I pull her hair tie out. I grab a handful of her hair, bringing it to my face. I inhale deeply.

"Mmm ..." I exhale and look back into her beautiful green eyes. "I love you. I'm so in love with you, Becca. You're right, baby; none of this matters. Just you, me, and our family. I love how you believe in me. How you now believe in us. I'm going to work my hardest. I won't disappoint you." I grab her hand from my face and plant a kiss in her palm. Slowly, I work my way up her arm.

"You never disappoint me, sweetie." she speaks softly in my ear. She knows how that tone affects me. Her open mouth welcomes mine. I pin her arms down on either side of her head. Her knee nudges my hip again.

"No," I say sternly.

"Please, baby," she begs. I ignore her and enjoy the taste of her skin instead.

"Feel good, baby?"

I catch her nipple in my mouth again. My right hand teases her, softly caressing the inside of her thighs with a light tickle. Up and down the apex of her groin, I trace along her plumping lips. My fingers go everywhere but where she encourages with her hips. Her lips become slick.

"Go ahead ... see what you do to me."

She moves her hips over so that my fingers slide against her.

"Jesus, baby!" I gasp. I may need the galoshes and raincoat she talked about a few nights ago! I bring my face back to hers as I plunge my fingers inside. I enjoy the sounds that escape her throat.

"Oh, baby," she moans against my lips. "Don't you want to take what's yours?"

The use of my own words against me dizzies me with the need to explode. I sit up and pull her with me.

"Straddle me with your back to my chest," I say. She turns and climbs back, then rises up on her knees. "Come down, baby," I instruct, holding myself at her entrance. My paradise. My home. Slowly, she slides down on me, releasing a whimper as I stretch her. Christ, she's still so tight. I gasp. "Gotta love Kegels," I mumble as I guide her hips down fully. I grab her arms and pull them back to me, forcing her to arch her body. She cries from the fullness. "Come on, baby." I nip at her ear. My left hand wraps around both of her wrists, and my right hand travels up her thigh and into the source of both of our pleasure.

"Ugh ... oh," she cries as I pull back on her wall to help her take more of me in.

"That's it, baby, c'mon now." My fingers glide up to her clit. The teasing sends her hips into action and she begins to ride me at a slow pace, making sure to get her "fill" of me every time she lowers herself. "Faster, baby," I command after a few minutes of her agonizing pace. Dutifully, she responds to my request. "Faster!" I say, releasing her arms. Supporting myself on my left arm, I grasp her right hip and guide her at the pace I'm looking for.

"Oh, Ray ... baby ... ugh."

I wrap my right arm around her, pulling her close to me. I bite along her shoulder and neck as she rides the waves of her orgasm.

"Ah!" I groan as I feel the buildup coming on and the surge climbing up and into my dick. "Becs, baby ... yes!" I gasp as she tightens around me, helping me explode like a volcano. It's so intense I almost forget to exhale. I gasp for air against her back. My hands rest on her belly, which tightens every few minutes. "Is that normal? Your belly tensing up like this?" I raise my head and lay my chin on her shoulder.

"Hmm-mmm, from the orgasm. It's okay, sweetie." She turns her head and gives me a warm, content smile. She rises one last time to pull me out of her, taking in a sharp breath. We lie on our sides, facing each other. Like a magnet, my hand automatically reaches to caress her stomach. "We're amazing together, Ray," she says, leaning in for a kiss.

"Yeah ... been trying to tell you that for five years now," I tease.

"It's just too mind-blowing, that's why I forgot." She giggles lightly.

"Oh, Becs. God, I love you, baby. You are everything I never knew existed. You're like a dream, a fairytale." I trace her jawline, then her lips, with my index finger. She takes in a shaky breath and her eyes fill up. "Oh, baby, don't. Why are you crying?" I kiss her eyelids.

"You just say the most wonderful things to me."

She licks her lips and kisses me.

"Not always. I've said my share of pretty terrible things to you over the years."

I close my eyes as regret consumes me.

"Stop. It doesn't matter anymore. I know where it came from." Her finger taps my lips. I kiss it, and her eyes light up. "So, do you want to tell me about Montreal?"

"You don't remember anything?" I ask.

"I remember going with you. You were taking a course in French architecture. You asked me to go because you didn't want to be there all by yourself. We had a great time."

"Shit, baby," I say, "this is so frustrating."

"Well, tell me and maybe it will trigger my memory." She scrunches her pillow under her head, anticipating the revelation of a forgotten memory.

"Well, we drove up on a Saturday," I start.

"You made me go dancing when we got there." She rolls her eyes.

"Yes, I wanted to take you out dancing. It wasn't so bad, I recall you having a good time." I poke her shoulder.

"I did. You're right."

She grabs my hand.

"When we got back, you took a shower while I went to meet a colleague for a quick drink downstairs. I actually went to give you time. I knew you were going to flip out when you went to get dressed for bed."

"Why?"

"Um ... because, I bought you several different nighties, from a few silk gowns to some more risqué, see-through sorts of things. I had Stacey replace your SRPs with them before you left." I grin at my cleverness.

"Hey! I packed nice pajamas! They weren't sex-repellant pajamas!" she defends herself. I raise my eyebrows at her. She gives in, letting her smile hit her eyes.

"So, when I came back, you were wrapped in a towel in the bedroom, looking through your suitcase, pissed as hell. I decided to jump in the other bathroom for a quick shower. When I was done, I walked over to the bedroom. Your back was to me. You were wearing the long, red silk gown, just like I knew you would."

"How did you know I would wear that one?"

She reaches for the covers.

"Because, while it was very sexy—especially on you, baby—it was elegant, simple, and could pass as something you might normally wear to bed. Anyway, I was leaning against the doorframe, watching you iron my shirt for the next day."

"Oh, Mr. Cleaver ... me in a gown like that, ironing your shirt ... you must've been fighting off a case of possible premature ejaculation," she says, giggling.

"Oh, Mrs. Cleaver ... you have no idea," I agree.

"Did I have your pipe and slippers waiting for you?" she teases. I love that she understands me and doesn't get offended by it like most women would. I love that she's kind of old-fashioned with certain things, like I am. "C'mon, McNeil." She nudges me. "Carry on, please!"

"Well, you were on the phone with Stacey, asking her why she switched out your PJs. Then you said, 'Ray did not buy these for me!' I came up from behind you. 'Yes I did,' I said, placing my hands on your hips. You turned around quickly, your mouth open in shock. You scanned me with your eyes. 'Say good night to Stacey, babe.' You just stared at me doe-eyed. I grabbed the phone from you, 'Night, Stace,' I said, sighing into the phone. Stacey almost had me in a fit of laughter."

"Why?"

"She said to me, 'Now be gentle ... remember, this is her first time with you.' I just said 'Yep' and tried not to laugh. I hung up on her and tossed your phone onto the chair. 'Jesus, baby, you're so beautiful.' I held your face with my left hand and let my fingers on my free hand travel down like this."

I run my fingers down her neck and across her shoulder.

"Mmm ... I remember. It's a bit fuzzy, but I remember feeling nervous and unsure. Most of all, I felt desire. I wanted you to touch me. I've always wanted you to touch me. There was always something there for you, Ray. My feelings gnawed at me constantly," she confesses. "Please go on. My memory is hazy."

"Well, you did what you normally do when you're nervous."

"Left field?"

"Yep! You said, 'Um, I ironed some of your shirts.' I glanced over at the shirts and back at you. 'Thanks, baby.' I leaned in closer. 'You always take good care of me.' My lips were barely touching yours. Your breathing was so erratic. I swept your lips gently, over and over again, with mine. I pulled your hair out of your hair tie and dove my hand into it. I rubbed my nose against yours as my fingers

183

migrated to your nipple. I slowly traced around it, affecting you like I am right now." I watch as she takes in a sharp breath and closes her eyes. "I kissed you like this." I lean in and grasp her lips gently, taking my time to deepen the kiss. "'Ray, wait,' you said, pulling away."

"Don't wait, Ray." Becca smiles and pulls me back to her.

"No, no. I'm in the middle of a story here ... frustrating, though, isn't it?" I smirk. She nods. I can see she feels bad again. "So you said, 'I don't want to lose our friendship. What if things go bad between us? I know we're both not seeing anyone, and we have needs, but I don't think we should chance our friendship just to have sex.'"

Becca winces. "Oh, yikes."

"Yeah. I was prepared for you to say something like that." I tap her nose with my index finger. "I said, 'Becs, you are indeed my very best friend. That aside, you are also the only woman I've been seeing for a few years. You are the only woman I want to see for the rest of my life. I'm in love with you, baby, and I know that you love me. So let's stop worrying about our friendship, because we have a whole lot more going on here than just friendship. We should nurture all of it. Now, I'm going to kiss you again, baby. Don't pull away, just let it happen.'

You said, 'Ray, I'm scared,' and looked away. I pulled your face back to mine and said, 'Becca, I'm scared too. For my own reasons.' Your eyes darted up to mine as you realized I was referring to my past with Liz. I think, at that moment, you truly realized that I was left alone too, to figure everything out on my own. It wasn't for the same reasons, but it had a lot of the same outcomes. I said, 'Becs, you're the only one I trust to mend my broken heart. Will you please trust me with yours?' You said, 'I do. I'm just afraid I'm going to lose you.'

'Baby, we're both afraid of that. But it could still happen, even if we push the idea of us aside. Then we'd be left with the regret over wasted time when we could've been making each other happy.

We've wasted three years already! Baby, I don't want to do this anymore. I want us. I want our family. Please, don't push me away.' I rested my forehead against yours. In true Becca James style, you planted your hands on my shoulders and said, 'Wow, McNeil ... you are working very, very hard at getting laid tonight!'

I shook my head and said, 'Overwhelmed, huh? Well, let me tell you something: In a minute, I'm going to have you up against that wall with your legs wrapped around my waist as I overwhelm the shit out of you, and the only goddamn thing that will be coming out of that smart mouth of yours is my fucking name!' I was ready for you to go ballistic, but instead you said, 'McNeil, Jesus ... that was fucking hot! Let's do that our second time though, not our first.' I must've had a shocked look on my face. You just laughed and started kissing me. Totally brought me from boiling over to a nice simmer."

"Mmm ... we were so good together that night." She grabs my hand and kisses my palm before she snuggles it to her chest.

"Baby, we're always good together!" I jerk my head, looking at her oddly.

"Yes, but there was something about that night. It may have been a combination of your words, your touch, the French music you played, the French wine I drank, and Old Montreal. I felt as if I was under a completely wonderful spell."

"You remembering better now?" I lay my head back down in front of hers. "Do you remember the next day?"

"Yes. We spent it walking the cobblestone streets, taking in the architecture and whatever sites we happened across."

"Our favorite coffee shop," I add.

"Our favorite little bistro." She beams. "It was so beautiful and romantic. I loved being there with you." Her eyes fill up.

"What, baby?" I thumb the tears away.

"I just hate that I blocked all of these memories out. You trusted me to mend your heart, but I just kept breaking it. How could you continue to love me and wait for me? I didn't deserve you," she cries.

"So, on Monday I had to leave you to your own devices while I went to class."

"Ray!" Becca cuts in.

"Becca, please. Bare feet, right? I just want you to get these memories back so they become 'ours' again. Promise me one thing, though." I palm her left cheek.

"What, sweetie?" She takes in a deep, shaky breath.

"When and if you get a memory back that shines a bad light on me, will you please try to look past it? This relationship has been stressful, emotionally draining, and painful for me at times. I didn't always handle it well."

"So, you went off to class and I spent the morning at a spa getting my lady parts waxed and my hair done." She goes back to the memory. I thank her with a kiss.

"Why did you get waxed?" I say, cringing.

"I didn't want to worry about missed patches of hair. It had been a while since I'd done all that waxing—had me singing like a virgin!" She crosses her eyes and makes a goofy face. I laugh a little. "So, I was twenty minutes late to meet you since I went to get lunch for us. You were sitting on that little cement wall by the stairs looking like your dog died."

"Uh, yeah, thought 'Lucy' was back with a vengeance! Then I looked up and you were running toward me saying 'Sorry.' You plopped on my lap and kissed me. 'Hungry?' you asked, and I finally felt myself calm down. You pulled out our lunch just as Kyle came up and said, 'Hey, Ray, that was a great pointer you gave the class this morning! Is this the Mrs.?' But I didn't get a chance to answer because Vivian then appeared and complimented me. I was talking for a few minutes and realized I hadn't introduced you yet when Vivian introduced herself. I said, 'Sorry, guys, this is my—' and you cut me off and said, '—wife, Becca.' It took me a moment to register what you said."

Becca smirks, "I had to, fucking Vivian was batting her damn eyes at you and hanging on to your every word. It was nauseating."

"Wow, still jealous, huh? It's very rare that you get jealous. I find it extremely hot, baby." I play with her bottom lip before I kiss her. "So you became Mrs. McNeil. I loved calling you that all week. I even picked up a diamond band for you to wear."

"Uh, yeah, because Vivian was all 'Where are your rings? If Ray were my husband, I'd make sure everyone knew I was his and he was mine.'" She imitates her with some exaggeration.

"Yes, I recall you staring daggers at her. Before you got up to strangle her, I told her we must've forgotten to put them back on that morning. That it's usually not a question we're a couple. Just for you ... but I didn't say that." I chuckle and receive a smack to my chest.

"I loved the night we took a bath together and we were holding our hands out, looking at the new additions to our ring fingers. We were so relaxed and content. Mmm ..."

I'm waiting for her to say more because something very significant happened at that moment. She doesn't, though. She still doesn't remember. I feel that same terrible pang in my heart.

"What is it?" she asks, touching my face.

"Do you remember anything else?" I already know the answer, but I have to probe anyway.

"No." She leans up on her elbow. "What happened?"

"I, um ..." I exhale harshly through pursed lips. "I asked you to marry me. I said, 'You play the role of Mrs. McNeil very well. I'd love for you to permanently play her for the rest of your life. Will you marry me, Becca?' You turned to me and without the slightest hesitation, said yes, and threw your arms around me. I was so happy, I forgot that it ... the moment ... wouldn't exist anymore once we got back. I was stupidly, stupidly happy! Becca, I don't want to go over this memory anymore. It is one of my favorite times with you because it was just us. Alone, together, without other distractions. It was amazing to fall in love with you all over again. I wish we could've stayed there forever." I get off the bed and get dressed. "I need to go for a walk. I'm sorry."

I look over at her and see the remorse swallow her whole, even though I know she couldn't help what happened. I can't even bring myself to comfort her. It took a lot for me to come back from the pain she caused me. I'm not about to wrap my arms around her and tell her it's all right because it wasn't. It was—is—my pain, and I have the right to it. I won't allow myself to feel selfish for thinking this way. I walk out of the bedroom, closing the door behind me.

BECCA

I've been lying on this bed crying for at least ten minutes now. One of the babies gives me a good wallop. Clearly they want me to cut it out. I sit up and get dressed. The bathroom light hums when I flick on the switch. I look a mess, tired and pale. My hair is wild and my eyes are puffy. I tie my hair back and rinse my face. I'm not going to discuss memories with Ray anymore. I can't help my previous behavior. I know I've hurt him, but the only thing I can do is give him my all now.

Stacey told me to be patient with him. I'm going to, but I'm not going to allow our relationship to be built on a foundation of guilt and remorse. He's going to have to work through his reservations on his own. I have my own, and right now, I also have dinner to work through.

"Hey, Stace, I haven't seen you all day." I smile, walking into the kitchen.

"Whoa, what's wrong with you?" she asks, looking up from her sudoku.

"Oh, same ole same ole." I wave my hand to dismiss it. "Chicken and pasta okay?" I ask, pulling it out of the fridge.

"Yeah. Hey, what's going on with you and Ray?"

"It's been a roller-coaster day." I grab some zucchini and summer squash and rinse them off. Stacey pulls out a chopping board for me. I cut them into thin to medium slivers, then throw them in a pan.

"Do you wish he didn't come out here?"

"Part of me feels that way. Most of me is glad he's here. I just ... I know what I've put him through is awful, but I didn't know I was doing it. I'm beginning to feel very overwhelmed. I'm trying to work through my grief over Grayson and let go of some things, but now my focus has shifted to Ray and his insecurities. I'm not used to him acting like this. He's always so strong and confident. That's the Ray I need right now. If he stays here this week and continues to behave this way, I'm not going to get anything accomplished." I smack the bottle of Greek dressing to get the last bit onto the vegetables. I throw the lid on the pan and place it on the simmer burner.

"Here, I'll fill it." She grabs the big pot from me and heads to the sink. "Bec, maybe you should just ask him to go home, then. You definitely don't need the added stress! Your body has been through a lot these past few months. You need to worry about those babies first, not about licking Ray's goddamn wounds." She brings the pot over to the other burner.

"Can you get me the multicolored bow-tie pasta from the pantry?" I ask as I cut up the chicken. "Stace," I add, "I can't ask him to leave. If I did that, I may not have a Ray to go home to. I don't want to lose him."

"He is not going to leave you if you ask him to go home!" she states flippantly.

"I think you're wrong. I think he's had enough. The rehashing of memories is stirring up a lot of pain for him. Then there's the money. He's a proud man. It's all too hard for him to swallow." I throw the chicken in another pan and season it. "Did you know he asked me to marry him in Montreal?" I look over my shoulder at her.

"Yes," she says simply as she places things in the sink. "I spent hours on the phone with him after his bubble burst when you two got home. He was really crushed."

"I know. That's probably why he's not rushing to put a ring on my finger now." I throw the pasta into the boiling water and give the veggies a quick stir.

"Becca, he wants to marry you." She tries to reassure me.

"I don't think he really wants to anymore. We'll probably be rolling like Goldie Hawn and Kurt Russell. I think I'm okay with that. Besides, I'm not really ready to give up Grayson's name yet." I look over to find Stacey, her eyes wide and panicked as she looks to the entrance of the kitchen. I take in a deep "oh God" breath and wait for the shitstorm that is about to take over.

My heart races as Ray slides his hands onto my hips.

"What are you making?" He kisses down my neck. *Cue erratic breathing.*

"Um, my chicken and pasta dish," I say, carefully walking on mental eggshells.

"Mmm ... the one with the dressing and the cheeses?" His voice is low and soft. Honestly, I find its effect on me rather irritating. How is it that he can seduce me with a normal conversation over what's for dinner?

"Yes." I close my eyes and try to pull myself together.

"You haven't made that in a long time. I'm gonna go upstairs and work. Call me when it's ready." He pats my left hip and kisses my neck again. He walks away. "By the way, baby," he says and comes back over to me, his mouth to my ear. "You better get yourself ready to give up Grayson's name, because it's going to happen real soon." His fingers gently grasp my chin, making me turn my face to his. I gasp as his mouth hits mine hard. He pulls away abruptly and swats my ass before he walks away.

The chicken makes a popping sound in the pan, which brings my focus back to the task at hand. I stir it and look over at Stacey.

"Who are you calling?" I ask.

"Max! I'm going to tell him to get his ass out here now!" she says adamantly.

"Why?"

"So he can get a goddamn refresher course on how to be hot as hell!"

I chuckle to myself as she walks out of the room with her phone. *McNeil is pretty fucking hot!*

I combine the pasta, chicken, and zucchini in one pan, folding it over as I add grated Parmesan and a blend of four shredded Italian cheeses. I keep mixing until the cheese is melted. A forkful tells me it needs some more dressing. I add. I taste. I add more Parmesan. I taste. Mmm ... perfect! I head over to the cabinet with my serving dishes. Great. The pasta bowl I can usually snatch from my tippy toes is no longer in reach, thanks to my swelling belly. I look around, then grab a chair from the table and slide it over. I take a deep breath and climb up.

"What the *hell* are you doing?" Ray yells and grabs ahold of me.

"Getting the pasta bowl—why?" I shoot him a strange look and pass the bowl down to him. He puts it on the counter and hooks his right arm around the small of my back, his left under my knees, and swoops me off the chair before I can yell, "Hey!"

"Don't do that again! Ask for help, please. You're almost five months pregnant. Use your fucking head, babe!" He sweeps my lips with his.

"McNeil, it's a chair, not a damn tightrope." I roll my eyes.

"And you tend to be clumsy." He lets my feet hit the ground.

"Hmm," is all I can offer as I pull away from him and pour the food into the bowl.

"I'm going to take mine upstairs, if you don't mind. I may have an idea, and I want to jump on it."

"Do you want bread?" I glance over as I grab a dish for him.

"No." He studies me. "Becs?"

"Beer?"

"No, I need to think clearly. Baby?"

"What do you want to drink?" I go to the fridge.

"This is fine." He reaches around me and grabs a flavored water. "Becs." He turns me to him.

"Ray, I don't want to discuss what happened earlier. Please." I gaze up into the storm of Ray McNeil's eyes.

"Okay," he sighs after a few moments. He pushes back off the fridge and lets me go back to the food.

"Here." I hand him his dish. "I'll have Morgan bring your dessert up."

"Do you want me to leave?" He crooks his head sideways to gain my attention back.

"No. I don't." I look over at him. "It's pretty rude, McNeil, to listen to other people's conversations," I add as I pull three more dishes down.

"It's pretty rude to talk behind someone's back, babe."

"I didn't say anything I haven't said to your face," I snap.

"Really?" His eyes go wide. "Sure about that, baby? Oh, I'm sorry, I mean *Mrs. James.*"

"Don't start." I close my eyes and take in a deep breath.

"I'm not. I'm going to head upstairs now, Mrs. James." He heads to the door. "Don't wait up for me, Mrs. James."

"Oh, I won't!" I snap. *Country Sybecca holds onto her lap bar and screams as the coaster goes downhill again.*

Stacey and Morgan walk into the kitchen as I set dinner on the table.

"I wish Ray brought Annie," Morgan complains.

"Do you want me to see if Grammy will fly out here with her?" Speaking of Hazel, she hasn't returned any of my phone calls the past few days!

"No, she won't, Mommy. She went with Charlie to meet his

family," Morgan says.

"You've talked to her?" I ask, feeling hurt and shocked.

"Yeah, every day. Why?"

I shrug and shoot Stacey a "what the hell?" look. She knows I've been trying to reach Hazel. Neither one of us have the slightest idea why she may be avoiding me.

It's eleven o'clock in the evening. I stand at the bottom of the staircase, looking up. The light is still on. Morgan told me Ray was in a drawing frenzy, that he barely noticed her when she said good night. When he finally paid her any attention, he made sure he told her to say, "Sleep well, Mrs. James" for him. *Asshole!* I walk away and go to my room, locking the door behind me. Before I head to bed, I step into my glorious shower. Oh, how I've missed this shower! The water pelts my worries away.

I apply my lotion before putting on one of the nightgowns that Grayson loved best. I'm surprised the fabric is forgiving of my belly. I pull back the duvet and jump when I hear a knock at the door. I open it.

"You're sleeping in here?" Ray asks, his jawline twitching.

"Well ... this is where Mrs. James sleeps," I say, as condescendingly as possible.

"All right, then. Good night, Mrs. James!" His smile is not friendly. It's more like his "sit and spin" smile. He turns and walks away.

I climb into bed and snuggle up to Grayson's sweater. It's been a long, stressful, crazy day. Tomorrow will be better. We both just need some sleep.

Nine a.m. feels like six a.m. I inhale deeply the smell of Grayson James and feel a terrible pang of guilt. I shouldn't be doing this. I should be breathing Ray's smell. Luckily, my bladder overrules the guilt. The usual morning ritual ensues in the bathroom. Pee, brush teeth, wash face and tie hair. I get dressed and head out to greet the world. Hopefully, no tomatoes will be thrown at my head for the decrease in my maturity level last night.

Humph ... I seem to be the only one up. I check Morgan's room. Not there. I check Stacey's room. Not there. I take a grand tour around the house. Unable to locate anyone, I give in to technology and call Stacey to see where she is in the house.

"Hey," she answers.

"Where are you?"

"Out to breakfast with Ray and Morgan—why?" she asks, as if I should already know this.

"When did you guys leave?"

"Half an hour ago."

"Well, why didn't anyone ask me if I wanted to go?" I ask, somewhat hurt.

"Ray said you weren't coming. I thought he asked you." She lowers her voice.

"No, It's okay. I'm not feeling well anyway. I'll see you when you guys get back. Please don't say anything to him. I've had about enough of our behavior." I listen for her "okay" and hang up with her.

I don't remember Ray and I ever arguing this much. Then again, I was "Lucy." But no, this was much simpler when we were just "friends," at least for me. I head into the room we're supposed to share. I take in a deep breath, observe the mess, and head back to the closet with all the cleaning supplies to grab the broom and dust-pan. Apparently, the wall decided not to move out of the way of the vase Ray threw at it. I clean up the mess, including the clothes he dumped all over the place. I put everything away and take his shirts down to the laundry room to iron them.

I used to hate to iron, but now I find it relaxing. I get a lot of thinking done while I'm ironing. I hang up his last shirt, grab them all off the rack, and head to the room to hang them up. I notice Ray out of the corner of my eye, stopping dead in his tracks. I ignore him and hang the shirts in the closet. As I walk out, Ray blocks my path. I stand there, avoiding his eyes. I fear the silence is killing me, so I finally look up.

"I don't remember arguing with you this much," I say.

"That actually makes sense, because we didn't."

"I don't want to argue with you anymore, Ray."

"At some point we're going to argue, Becca."

"I know. I just ... I don't want to argue this much."

"You know what I don't want, Becca?" He's terse.

"What?"

"I don't want to *ever* ... *ever*," he yells in my face, "find you snuggling up to and sleeping with Grayson's sweater while purpose-fully *avoiding* me!"

"I locked the door."

Obviously, I manage to always say the right thing.

"Wow, Becs! Really? First of all, I design and build shit! You don't think I'd know how to unlock a goddamn door? Like an idiot, I came in to apologize and bring you back to bed, and there you were! You might as well have been in another man's arms," he says, sighing and walking away.

I can't help but giggle.

"A man, I think, would have quite a different effect than a sweater."

"Really? So then it's okay if I snuggle with one of Liz's old shirts?"

"No. No, it's not. You're right, Ray. I realized what I did was wrong when I woke up this morning. It won't happen again." I reach for his hand.

"I felt like you wished he were here and not me. You told me you chose him over me in your subconscious. Lying in bed—with his sweater—was better than being with me?"

"Ray, I told you what happened during my coma. As soon as I started remembering us, you were the only one I could think about. Last night was just me being a smartass." I grab his other hand.

"You kept calling out for him before you woke up. You were saying, 'I love you, Grayson.' Over and over."

"I was saying goodbye. I never got to do that. You remember me saying that." I take in a shaky breath. "Do you remember how happy and relieved I was to see you?"

"Yeah. I do." He nods. "Becca, we're both just getting hit with so many things at once. Most families that join together have a hard time situating the kids and housing. That's the easy part for us. Why do we have to have all of this other crazy shit?" He pulls me to him. "We need to both slow down and figure all of this out. One step at a time. I think we're both jumping feet first into everything, and I don't want to lose us."

He pecks at my lips and pulls away.

I wince. "Wow ... really? You can't do better than that, McNeil?"

"Ugh—c'mere!" He attacks my lips. After a few minutes, he pulls away. "Did you eat anything?"

"No."

"I didn't think so. I brought you home an omelet. C'mon."

He pats my bottom and we head out.

Chapter Twelve

It's been four days since Ray and I had our last talk. We've been doing great since. Back to our old selves; joking and laughing. He's been working hard up in the office. I'm getting a little impatient with him because he won't show me until it's done.

With the help of Stacey, Derek, and Danni, I've gotten a lot done as well. Most of Grayson's clothes and shoes have been donated, with the exception of the infamous sweater and some T-shirts Morgan wanted. We've done a re-shifting of most framed pictures, giving them central location in the study.

I've had several breakdowns during the purge. Ray's jumped by my side each time, holding me and letting me cry. Sometimes he cries with me. At night we take turns reading chapters aloud from Grayson's last book, the one I coauthored. Every night he says the same thing: "Becs, please publish this."

"I will," I reply. "Soon."

"Becs? You all right?" Ray's voice pulls me back from my thoughts.

"Yeah," I say, smiling. "Just thinking about how well we've been doing the past few days."

I stand up, away from the books I'm packing, and give him a quick kiss.

"It's been a record-breaking four days!" He smirks playfully, then gets serious. "I wanted to ask you something. I'm not sure it's my place, and I probably shouldn't bring it up, but it's been gnawing at me all week." He sits on the sofa. I sit beside him, eyeing the box in his hands.

"What is it?"

"I ... came across this the first day I was here. I opened it and found all these little notes you and Grayson wrote back and forth to each other."

My eyes light up as he opens it.

"I can't believe he kept these!"

I grab a few and start reading, then I laugh. Grayson was always a romantic. Even the first day we met.

"Well, I came across this one and it's bothered me." He hands it to me cautiously. I open and read it. My heart sinks; I haven't thought about this in years.

"I'm sorry, Ray. This is between Grayson and me. All you need to know is that he made a very big mistake that we both worked hard to get through. I'm pretty sure he kept this specific note as a re-minder to himself. I forgave him, and that's all you need to know." I remain as calm as I can.

"Did he cheat on you?"

"No. Grayson never so much as looked at another woman. It wasn't anything like that. Well, not entirely. Please, can we drop it?" I beg.

"Okay, baby. I'm sorry." I can see he truly feels bad about bringing it up. "Hey, before I let you get back to work here, I wanted to tell you something!" He pats my knee.

"What?" I try to perk up again and erase the images in my head.

"I did what you told me to do, like a good boy." His boyish grin makes me laugh. "Lexter agreed and gave me the bid at one and a half mil!"

"Ray!" I scream and hug him. "That's terrific, baby!" I kiss him all over his face. "I'm so proud of you!"

"Yeah, well, I took a page out of Grayson's book and listened to your advice. Don't go getting a big head now!" He smirks. "It's a small project, but that's actually good, considering the renovations are going to be such a big undertaking."

"Well, every job that puts your name in a good light is important, so don't downplay it. Especially in this economy!" I sigh. He nods in agreement. "Thank you for listening." I kiss his lips again. "Shall we go out to celebrate?" I ask.

"Arrangements have already been made, baby!" He kisses my forehead. "We'll have an early dinner here. You need to pack for the weekend. We're going on a little road trip."

"Where to?"

"Northern California, for the weekend."

"You're taking your girlfriend, who loves wine, to wine country?" I ask him, wide-eyed.

"Yes."

"Oh," I say as I wince. "Did you not get the memo?" I ask. "I'm a little pregnant."

"You are? I thought you were just getting comfortable with me." He laughs. "There are other things to do, you lush! Come on, get packed." He pats my knee.

"Ray, we're supposed to go home in two days." I sit back.

"Plans have changed. Stacey will be flying back with Morgan so she doesn't miss any more school. Everything is all set." He leans in.

"Who's going to take care of Morgan?" I ask. "Hazel's away."

"The same two people who've been taking care of Annie," he states, sounding frustrated.

"Right." I grab his hand and give myself a mental head-slap. "Sorry. How far away is it?"

"GPS says almost seven hours, so probably six."

"Why don't we just fly?" I ask.

Ray stares at me.

"Make something easy for dinner tonight," he says flatly as he gets up to leave.

"Ray?" I call after him.

"I'll be upstairs," he calls back. All righty then. Ugh! *What the hell did I say?*

෨෬ඏ෫ඏ෪ඏ

"Holy shit, Becs!" Derek gasps, looking over to the right side of the foyer lined with boxes of books for donation.

"Yeah, I know. And yet, it looks as if I haven't gotten rid of any."

"Grayson would roll over in his grave if he saw this!"

"Well, good thing he doesn't have a grave," I snap.

"Shit, Becca, I'm sorry. Just a figure of speech."

"Oh, Derek. I'm sorry too. I've been jumpy all day." I pat his shoulder, and he hugs me to him.

"What's going on?" he lowers his voice. I look around.

"Ray. He told me he's taking me up north for the weekend. I suggested we fly, and it turned his mood sour."

"Becca, would you have suggested that to him six months ago?" Derek raises an eyebrow, encouraging me to think about it. I open my mouth to say *yes*, but stop myself. No, no. I wouldn't have. Ray and I love to take drives. It's our thing. Grayson would've wanted us to fly. He didn't know that, though. It's the money. Six months ago, I was still acting like I didn't have all of this money. "Why don't we fly?" wouldn't have even been a thought.

"No," I finally say. "Give me a minute." I head down the hall to the stairs leading to the office.

Slowly I walk up. I've still managed not to set foot in there. Too many memories in such a confined space. Grayson and I could easily spend an entire day in there. Working ... and, ahem, other stuff. I take in a deep breath and knock.

"Yeah, Morgy?" Ray calls.

"It's me, Ray. Can I come in?"

"Uh, hold on."

After a few minutes, he opens the door and the smell of books, wood, and leather smacks me in the face.

"Are you burning incense?" I almost want to cry.

"Yeah. I thought it smelled nice."

"It does. We used to burn that all the time." It's woodsy vanilla.

"Sorry," he says lightly.

"No, baby, it's okay. I'm sorry I mentioned flying. It's not really *us*. I wasn't thinking. I'm looking forward to road-trippin' it with you, McNeil." I wrap my arms around his neck and kiss his smile.

"And you came to that conclusion all by your lonesome?" He arches a brow at me.

"Yes, I did!"

I try not to smile.

"Still a terrible liar, babe." He nudges my nose.

"Derek only shifted my thoughts in the right direction."

"Yeah, that's what I thought." He sways side to side with me.

"So, what's going on in here?" I peek over his shoulder.

"I'll show you this weekend. Stop it, Becca." He forces me to walk backward, away from the door.

"I'm very excited to see your vision, Mr. Cleaver." I play with the button at the top of his shirt.

"You'll see it soon, Mrs. Cleaver. I just hope you like it," he says, sounding hesitant.

"I won't! I'll love it, I just know!" I give him my sternest look.

"Ah, I don't know. It might be too much. I can fix whatever you don't want."

"Stop it!" I smack his chest.

"Hmm ... promises, promises." A mischievous grin forms at his lips.

"Ugh, get away!" I laugh and pull away from him.

"C'mon, I'll walk you back down the stairs." He grabs my hand.

"Seriously? I'm not that clumsy, McNeil!"

"Uh-huh." He continues down the stairs with me.

"That everything?" Ray looks over to me before closing the trunk door.

"That was nice of Danni to lend us her MDX." I sigh with some guilt at blowing her off so much this week.

"Yes, it was. I don't think there's even a thousand miles on it yet. Probably why Derek had to pry the keys out of her hands."

He smiles. Guilt lifted, thanks to one Ray McNeil.

I give Morgan and Stacey each one more kiss and hug. "Now, Susanna and Sam will be here in the morning. Be good for them, both of you!"

"We'll try." Stacey makes a face at me.

"I'll see you when we get home." I kiss Morgan again.

"Okay, Mom, have a great time!" She hugs me once more to humor me, then heads in.

"Have a nice, *stress-free* weekend," Stacey emphasizes toward Ray. I turn toward him in time to catch him flipping her off. I know he's just playing with her.

"We taking I-5?" I ask as he drives around the fountain in the middle of the circular driveway.

"Yep. You have the iPod, babe?" He glances over before hitting the button for the gate.

"Yes, I do. I made you a futuristic mixtape." I smile.

"Mixtape? Perpetually stuck in the nineties, babe." He slaps my knee, teasing me as he takes a left out of the driveway.

"It's not on a cassette!" I defend myself.

"Baby, it's called a playlist now." He grins wide at me, looking at me through his aviators.

"Well, when you're making it for someone else, it should honor the original name somehow, like ... DMT!" I say excitedly.

"DMT ..." He trails off, trying to figure it out.

"Digital mixtape," I say.

"You know what? I like that, Becs. DMTs," he says after a brief pause.

I plug in the iPod after I rename Ray's songs to "Ray's DMT."

"Do you want it in order or shuffled?"

"Shuffle it. Is there a lot on there?"

He turns right.

"Yeah. I started it the first day I got home from the hospital. I wanted to remember all of our songs—the ones we mentioned in my subconscious. Then I put a lot on here that I remember from the video you will make me. Lastly, I added songs that just make me think of you." I hit shuffle. The first song that comes on is Biz Markie's "Just a Friend." I laugh at Ray's expression.

"Wow ... this is romantic, babe!"

I hit pause to tell him all about the day downtown when I texted him about this being my theme song. Ray catches on quickly to the irony and legitimate reason behind the song. I skip it and "Warning Sign" by Coldplay comes on. Ray looks over, grabbing my hand. His thumb caresses the top of it slowly as we listen to the words.

"From the video?" he asks.

"Yes," I say. He nods as he heads onto I-5N. Next song is "The Show" by Lenka. A cute song I just heard that reminded me of us. Ray's left thumb drums on the wheel to the beat.

"What do you think of this car, babe?" he asks as he switches lanes.

"It's nice."

I look around.

"I figured we'd go car shopping for you when we get home. We're going to need a family car now. I'll take your truck. What do you think?"

"I think you've already taken over my truck." I shoot him a

look.

"Well, you weren't using it, and mine got totaled."

"I see all of your CDs survived, along with your tools, your boots, et cetera, et cetera," I tease. My truck no longer looked like my truck when I got into it. There was a nice surprise, though, when I lowered my visor. He has a picture of us plastered to it, looking happy and in love. I lift his hand to kiss it. "*Mi trucka es su trucka.*"

"Fluent in Spanglish, too!" he chuckles.

"Yes. Okay. We'll buy me a new car." I sigh.

Ray's smile gets huge. He's like a kid in a toy store whenever we're car shopping or at Home Depot. We make a good team, though. He makes sure it's loaded with everything he thinks I'll need—or he'll need, because really, who are we kidding here?—and I manage to get a few thousand knocked off the price. The nagging, "we don't need another toy" wife always plays the salesman to our advantage.

"So, are you done with the renovation plans?" I lower the music more.

"Yes, they're all done. I'll show you tomorrow morning."

"Ugh! I can't wait!" I say as I yawn.

"That excited, huh?" He smirks.

"Sorry. I just get hit with a wave of exhaustion at this time of day."

"Well, lie back and take a nap, baby. I'll listen to my DMT."

He turns the volume up.

"Sure?"

"Yeah, go ahead. Grab your pillow back there." I lean over and kiss his cheek.

"Mmm ... you smell good, McNeil," I whisper against his ear before I nip it.

"Better stop it," he warns.

"Yes, dear," I say, reaching for my pillow. Lying back, my eye-lids get heavy as I listen to "Near to You" by A Fine Frenzy. This song is probably the most meaningful, being the closest to our situation. I notice Ray glance over at me several times as he listens to the lyrics.

I stir when I hear Ray yell at some asshole who cuts us off. "Sorry, Becs." He looks over as I sit up. It's dark now, with snow whispering through the air.

"It's okay, I'm good. Did you listen to every song?" I notice the Sirius radio is on.

"No, babe. You had some French music on there, which was nice, but it was making me drowsy."

"Sorry. Explains why I was dreaming in French, though." I laugh through a yawn. "When do you start the build for Lexter?"

"We break ground in two months. I've got a lot of hiring to do. I just hope the weather cooperates. It's not easy starting a build in the winter. We may have to push it back if March gives us a bitch of a time. Your renovations will have to wait until April. I've already told Claudia not to book any more events for the barn."

"I can still board horses though, right?" I ask before taking a sip of water.

"Oh yeah. I still need to talk to Charlie and do some more research to renovate the stables. My plans may involve moving the stables' location. Don't worry, baby. I'll have everything figured out!" He grabs my hand.

For the next four hours, we talk about our other plans. Things we want to do with our house. With the ranch. Our businesses. Our kids. Our conversation hits a level it's never really been able to because of my PTSD.

"I know it's only been like two weeks, but do you miss 'Lucy'? I mean, the whole 'first time' part?" I'm nervous because a part of me still fears that, deep down inside, he does.

"No, not really. I think if you reacted to me differently, I might. But you don't, so I don't."

"What do you mean?" I ask.

He pulls my hand up to his mouth and nips lightly at my wrist, then down my arm. I find it difficult to steady my breath.

"I mean *that*," he says softly, bringing my hand back down to rest with his.

"Oh," is all I can manage as he takes the Yountville exit and turns right. He turns left onto Washington Street and keeps right at the fork in the road. Taking a left, we arrive at *Maison Fleurie*. I read it aloud. "Ray, it's so pretty. Did you let them know we'd be checking in late?" I ask as he turns the car off.

"Of course I did." He hits me with the "give me some credit" look.

"Okay! Okay." I hold up my hands. Ray gets out and comes around to open my door. Always the gentleman! *"Merci!"* I smile up at him as he helps me down, a much shorter trip than the truck. Ray holds my hips while studying my face. "What?" I ask, feeling self-conscious.

"I just love you. I want to make this weekend special for you."

"I'm with you. I'd say it's special already." I lean up and press my lips to his over and over 'til we deepen the kiss.

"Oh, Mrs. Cleaver, we'd better get you inside."

"Need something ironed out?" I ask softly near his ear.

"Jesus Christ, baby ... that was so fucking hot!"

He closes his eyes. I'm sure he's doing a mental replay of me wearing only my shirt and panties in the laundry room yesterday. I was ironing my pants. Before I knew it, my panties were flying off and I was grasping the sides of the sit tub as one Mr. Ray McNeil had his way with me.

"I think we redefined the meaning of 'dirty laundry.'" I giggle.

"C'mon, before we end up airing our 'dirty laundry' out here." He smirks, pulling me away from the car to shut the door.

Inside, we're greeted by Rose and handed a key to our room in the bakery building, adjacent to the main house. Ray gives me the key so I can head over while he parks the car and grabs our stuff.

I open the door and feel welcomed by the buttercup-yellow walls. I head directly to the gas fireplace and turn it on to take the chill out of the air. I remove my coat and place it on one of the flowery, plush chairs sitting in front of the window.

Ray walks in and closes the door behind him. "This is nice, isn't it?"

"Yes. It's very charming." I smile at him.

He reads from the pamphlet. "Go look in the bathroom, there should be a jetted spa tub."

"Jetted spa tub? Not a Jacuzzi?" I laugh.

"Ugh ... that's so nineties." He rolls his eyes. I open the bathroom door and suddenly wish I could have wine with bath time. "Do you want to take one now?" He rubs my back.

"No. I may just shower quickly." I turn to him. "Want to join me?"

He nods and slowly undresses me.

"McNeil, can you grab my bag for me?" I ask as he steps out of the shower.

"Sure, babe."

Within a few minutes, he brings it in. I can hardly contain the giggle that's bubbling up over the little joke I'm about to play on him. After drying off, I open my bag and get out my medium-length pink and black silk nightie. Given my rounded belly, I forego panties. The rising giggle finally bursts and I have to cover my mouth to stifle it as I pull out the most God-awful flannel nightgown I could find. It's blue and covered in moose with ornaments hanging from their antlers. The sleeves ruffle at my wrists, and the bottom near my ankles. There is a strip of white, lacy fabric across the front top part of the chest. Three faux buttons go from the neckline to the lace in the center.

I turn to the mirror and put on my high-top slippers. I can barely contain myself as I pull my hair tie out and brush my hair. Finally, I pull it together. Opening the door, I head to our room, which is only lit by the fireplace and some candles. Ray turns around and blows a match out.

"Cold tonight, isn't it?" I ask as I place my bag down and rub my arms. "This is nice, sweetie." I look up at him. He stands there speechless, staring at me.

"Babe," he sighs, sounding confused. "I don't know whether to laugh or cry. Did the SRP store have a massive sale? You've got to be fucking kidding me." He walks over. "What the hell is this? What are these?" He pulls at the material.

"Moose," I say, as though my feelings are hurt. "With ornaments on their antlers. I thought they were cute," I add.

"Moose? With ornaments?" he asks. I nod. "Wow, babe." He stares at me in disbelief. I bite my lip to stifle a laugh and finally give in when he starts to look pissed. I roll my eyes and start to pull the nightgown off, but Ray gets to it first. He rips it aggressively down the center, and I step out of it. "Slippers too, please," he says. I comply.

"Is that better?" I try to steady my breath as I slide my hands up his bare chest.

"That was really mean!" He tries to pout. "Some poor grandmother in her eighties is sleeping without a warm moose nightgown out there!" He chuckles.

"Oh, there were plenty on the rack," I say.

"I can't imagine why." He acts stupefied. "I have to say," he starts, sliding his knuckles down the silk nightie's strap and onto my left breast. "This looks wonderful on your rack." I close my eyes and relish in his touch as he circles my nipple.

"Oh, McNeil ... Shakespeare has nothing on you," I say, as if it could even be questioned.

"Thanks, baby!" He grins widely for a moment, then stops.

Yeah, dude ... wasn't a compliment! "Come here, Becs. I have a little picnic for us." He brings me over to the middle of the floor, between all the furniture. There are strawberries, grapes, and cheese on a red and white checked blanket. Flavored sparkling water peeks out from the ice bucket. Two champagne glasses wait to be filled.

"Wow." I sit down on my left side, letting my legs rest to the right.

"We won't stay down here long, but I know how you hate food in bed."

He's right. It grosses me out for some reason. I watch as he opens the sparkling water and pours some for both of us.

"Mmm ... I'm hungry. This looks good." I put strawberries on his plate.

"Stop, don't touch!" He taps my hand, then hands me my glass. "To the magic of a redo." He clinks my glass and takes a sip. I look at him quizzically before I bring my glass up to my lips. "Now, what would you like?" he asks as he takes my glass and places it aside. "This?" He raises an eyebrow as he holds up a large, ripe strawberry. I nod, biting my lip as he leans closer to me. He takes the first bite of it. "Mmm ... so good," he says softly as he chews. He lifts the strawberry to my mouth. I move to take a bite. "Uh-uh." He pulls it away, then brings it back and rubs my lips with it. Pulling it away again, he slowly kisses me, sucking on my lower lip with purpose before breaking away. "Mmm ... that's even better." He licks his lips before he feeds me the strawberry. "Becs." His voice is just above a whisper.

"Yes?" I say, then swallow.

"No cliff notes tonight, baby." He pushes a few strands of my hair behind my ear before leaning in. "I want to taste every inch of you," he murmurs against it.

Country Sybecca showers her naked body with a bottle of honey. Horny, Ghetto, Porn, and Submissive follow her lead—there may even be some chocolate syrup involved. Cautionary Sybecca holds her ticker board up. In bright red letters, it reads: BITCHES BE CRAZY!

A little laugh escapes my throat. Ray jerks his head back.

"Tickled my ear." I smile as his face softens. *Ha! I'm not a terrible liar!* Wait, should I really be proud of that? Ah, harmless ones are okay!

"Eat up, babe. As soon as you've had enough, I want to get my fill." His eyes scan me, letting me know he's ready to pounce at any time. *Operatic Sybecca starts stuffing her face ... that fat lady really wants to sing!* I pop a piece of cheese in my mouth and chase it with a bite of strawberry. I close my eyes, chewing slowly and savoring the taste. Oh ... so good. I open my eyes to reach for my glass, only to find Ray holding it up to me. I watch him watching me. As with Grayson, I think I may be Ray's favorite subject to study. I eat faster. "Take your time, baby, we've got all night." He smiles before taking another sip.

"Don't you want any more?" I ask before having another bite.

"No. I'm hungry for something else." He licks his lips and finishes his glass.

"I'm all set," I say, wiping my mouth.

"You sure?" He grabs my plate.

"Yes. I'm sticky though, I need to wash my hands." I go to get up. Ray helps me and leads me to the bed. "Ray. Still need to wash my hands," I say again.

"I'll take care of that." He kisses my nose and pulls the bedcovers back. His hands slide up the side of my thighs, bringing my gown up with them. He jerks his head back when he realizes I have no panties on. "Jesus! You don't have a 'Fuck Me' sign in there again, do you?"

"No. Hard to find sexy preggo panties." I laugh.

"Arms up," he instructs. "You look sexy in just about anything, except for that moose nightmare over there." He smirks, shaking his head. "You look especially sexy with my babies in here." He palms my belly. I lean up and taste his lips. His right hand comes up to hold the back of my neck, steadying me as he deepens the kiss. My fingers reach the top of his PJ bottoms. I trace the skin above the waistband. "No." He pulls away quickly and grabs my hand. "Lie down." He stares into my eyes. "Now, baby." My heart is racing. I sit and scoot back, swinging my legs in. He climbs in next to me. "Close your eyes." His right thumb and forefinger slide down my eyelids softly. "Don't open them." He pecks at my lips. "Hands first, due to stickiness," he teases.

He takes my right hand first and gently licks the palm, then slides my pinky into his mouth and sucks purposefully. He follows suit with my other fingers. I feel him lift my left hand as he lays the first one down. He begins the same process, but this time starts with my thumb. After my pinky, he brings my ring finger into his mouth, then out. He brings it in again, but I feel it slipping through the center of a ring. I inhale a deep, shaky breath. Ray releases my finger from his mouth, then attacks my lips. My hands thrust into his thick hair. His question ... my answer ... apparent in our passion.

Ray pulls his mouth away and starts its expedition across my body. As much as I want to goggle at my ring, I show self-control and concentrate my efforts on encouraging Ray's motions. As his mouth departs my breast and travels down my torso, I begin to pon-der.

How odd is it that it doesn't bother me not to hear the words "Will you marry me?" Is that weird? Most girls dream about their proposals—what he'll say, how she'll react (usually in an annoy-ingly weepy *yes*). Are they weeping because they're really emo-tional, or because it's what's expected? I suspect the latter. What's more annoying than watching a future bride pretend to weep with joy is the groom-to-be proposing in a public place, like a restaurant, or in front of family. Awkward! I mean, I'm a sensitive, sentimental girl, but please, put your fucking neon sign that says *Looks at us! Looks at us!* away and have your special moment in private!　211

Nope! I've decided—I'm not weird! Well, when it comes to this. I've possibly become a little cynical in this area ... just a little. A smidge, if you will.

Suddenly, I feel impressed with Ray. He knew exactly what to do, and how to do it! Wow—he rocks! Of course, Grayson doing a trial run for him some months back may have helped.

"Uh ... babe? Please tell me you're at least devising a plan for world peace in that head of yours." He's trying not to sound frustrated, but I see right through it.

"Sorry. I was deciding that I'm not weird. I'm all done now. Head's back in the game. Sorry," I say again.

"I may have to debate you on that later," he says, climbing back up.

"You want cliff notes now?" I ask before he kisses me.

"No. I'm starting over. Try to stay focused, or I will—start—all—over—again," he says between kisses. And so his journey begins anew. This time, his tongue travels at a quicker pace until he gets to the place he finds most delicious. *Country Sybecca curls her toes in approval at the solid tongue-lashing we're receiving.*

"Jesus!" I gasp as I feel myself start climbing. My hands clutch the sheets. My breathing becomes more rapid, my hips fight the intensity. *Rising. Rising.* My head is spinning. *Rising. Rising. Huh?* I lift my head and watch Ray slip down the inside of my right thigh. "Um ... Ray," I say, my voice a gasping whisper.

"Shh ... head back, baby." He continues down my thigh.

"But—"

"Shh."

"Not nice," I say under my breath as I lay my head back. He bites and licks behind my knee, sending me into a fit of giggles. He does it again. "Stop!" I beg, laughing.

"Wow ... that's awesome." He grins. "I found your Kryptonite." He kneels on the bed and hooks his hands under my knees.

"Ray ... don't."

"Sorry ... what did you say?" Thus begins the torture. "I can't hear you over the loud, girlish giggles in this room."

"Ray!" I scream and try to sit so I can stop him. He lifts my knees up, forcing me to flop down onto my back.

"Now, now, Mrs. Cleaver, do keep it down, or there may be some complaints about us."

He hovers over me.

"Well, Mr. Cleaver, you should stop instigating things and remember to be more careful with the pregnant Mrs. Cleaver." I tap his nose and bring my knees up to his sides.

"I like instigating you. I like the things it leads to." He rubs his nose against mine.

"What sorts of things?"

"Things like you laughing." He tickles my side, prompting a giggle. "You gasping." His tone is softer, more serious.

"Gasping?" I ask. Ray enters me quickly. "Ah!" I gasp. "Oh ... gasping," I say, understanding now.

"Mmm ... gasping," he repeats before his mouth devours mine. His hips pull back and slowly dive in deeper. He clasps my hands, lacing our fingers together, and holds them down on either side of my head. We lose ourselves in each other, in our taste, our touch, our lovemaking.

∼◦◦◦∼

"Missionary is starting to prove difficult, babe," he says, rubbing my belly as I try to collect myself.

"I concur." I smile at him. "We're not strangers to creativity, so I don't see that posing a problem for us." I turn onto my side and glide my hands over the hair on his chest. Just the right amount.

"No, we should be fine. Do you want to look at your ring?" He sits up and grabs the pillar candle from the bedside table. I push myself up and lean into his chest. He grabs my hand and holds it under the light. It takes my breath away. It's round and halo-styled. Seventeen small diamonds glisten at the edges of the frame. I giggle a little bit.

"What?" He gives me a strange look.

"It almost resembles a flower."

"Hmm ... well, this one doesn't wilt. It lasts forever." He holds my finger to examine it. "Just don't expect me to send one of these to you at work every day."

"Well, you know, it wouldn't be about the diamonds." I play off his comment.

"Yeah, but it will turn out to be about bankruptcy."

"Okay, no daily diamonds." I kiss him. "I love it, Ray. It's beautiful. I love the Victorian setting. Thank you." I look at it again, then at him for another kiss, then back to the ring. Ray chuckles, so I give him a strange look.

"Our love has finally," he starts, looks up to the ceiling like he's thanking God, then says, "gone platinum, baby." He shakes my finger.

"You should put that in your vows, McNeil."

"I just may! Now go on into the bathroom. I'm sure you have to pee, preggo," he teases. "We need to get some sleep. We have a busy day tomorrow." He kisses my temple.

"Okay," I sigh, then get up and grab my nightgown.

In the bathroom light, I check out my ring in all its glory. Stunning and so ... me. Amazing. It's a decent size. I'd say the center diamond has to be at least a whole carat, but then again, I'm not one of those girls who knows her diamonds. Whenever somebody talks to me about what letter diamond they have in which color, I go completely into Charlie Brown mode. I think this happens for two reasons. One, I have no idea what any of it means. Two, quite frankly, I don't give a shit. I know what kind of setting I have only because Stacey told me. A ring like this caught my eye several months ago when we were out shopping for a gift for her mother-in-law. Fucking

Stacey! She's always been Ray's secret sidekick! *Thankfully.*

How did he pay for this, though? I'm pretty sure he had it before he came out here, before the money was deposited in his firm's account. Well, as Ray would recommend, I'm going to "use my fucking head" and not even question him about it!

Bathroom ritual complete, I head out and climb back into bed with Ray. He snuggles up to me on our side and wraps his arms around me.

"I love you, Mrs. Cleaver ... soon-to-be Mrs. McNeil. Good night," he whispers in my ear and kisses my hair.

"Love you too. Good night, baby."

Chapter Thirteen

My eyes shoot open as Ray's cell phone alarm springs into action.

"Very rude gadget ... must be thrown at a wall and broken into a gazillion pieces," I grumble. Ray reaches over across my head to grab it off the bedside table and turn it off.

"I have another gadget here you may find a little ruder first thing in the morning." He nibbles at my ear. I feel my pink nightie slowly creep up my leg.

"There's a difference between that rude gadget and this rude gadget." I reach my left hand back and gently caress him.

"Mmm ... what's that?" he murmurs against my ear.

"That little rude gadget makes me get out of bed, which is not very pleasurable. This rude gadget here," another stroke, "makes me stay in bed longer, which *is* very pleasurable."

"I could put this one on vibrate," he offers.

"Not the same." I smile and turn my head to kiss his lips. He lifts my left leg and slowly enters me. We get lost in each other. No thoughts of time, place, or past arguments. Just Ray and me, and our love. I reach back and hook my arm around his neck, grabbing a fistful of hair. I moan against his lips, grasping at them urgently to relieve my orgasm's intensity. As I come down from my peak, Ray begins the final climb to his. He takes in a sharp breath through his teeth. Just as he finds his release, there is a knock on the door.

"Jesus ... what the?" he gasps. He finishes and collapses behind me.

Another knock.

"Room service!"

"Hold on a second, please!" he yells and leans over me to grab his cell. "Christ, they're fucking ten minutes early." He grabs one of the plush Maison Fleurie robes as he climbs out of bed and takes some money from his wallet on the way to the door.

"Sorry we're a bit early, Mr. McNeil."

Ray has the door open so it blocks me from view.

"That's okay," Ray says.

"Would you like me to bring this in for you?"

"No, man, that's all right. My wife is not up and about yet, so I'll just take it from you. Here you go. Thanks, dude." Ray turns with a huge tray and closes the door with his foot.

"Jesus, McNeil! Did you order everything they offered?" I move my feet so he can place it on the bed.

"Well, everything I knew we'd like, baby. C'mon, get up." He pats my leg.

"Yes, husband, dear," I tease. This warrants a very unusual shy smile from Ray. He's not one to ever be shy about anything. I stay in bed another minute and study him as he uncovers dishes and puts them on the little table.

"What?" he asks in a very un-Ray-like, self-conscious way.

"McNeil, what is going on with you, baby?" I ask, my tone half playful, half serious as I climb out of bed and go to him. I stand behind him and slide my arms around his waist, hugging him to me. "You okay?" I crook my head sideways and wait for him to look back at me. He doesn't. He takes in a deep breath and covers my hands with his.

"I've called you my wife several times over the years, as you know." Another breath. "But that was the first time you've ever called me *husband*. I know you were teasing me, but it was nice to hear. I've waited a long time for you to refer to me that way." He turns to me and stares into my eyes.

"Last week at the butcher shop, I referred to you as my husband to Will." I smile.

"You did? Wait! *What?*" His mood switches when he realizes whose name I said. "Why the hell were you talking to him?" *Oh crap!*

"Ray, please calm down." I palm his face.

"Why were you talking to him, Becca?" He's all teeth and anger.

"I was in the butcher shop buying filets. Al asked how 'my husband' was doing," I start. "I didn't know Will had walked in. He overheard Al and questioned whether you were my husband. I said you were. Then he saw I'm pregnant and made a stupid comment about how you must've knocked me up to get me to commit to you. Some stupid shit like that."

"What did you say?" He now seems less angry with me, but still angry. Probably at Will.

"I told him he better shut his mouth about us, or you'll finish what you started," I say. Ray's eyes widen. "And I told him that you are a very well-liked and respected member of the community. Everybody's pal. Whereas no one can stand him, so the chance of cheeks turning the other way while you kick the crap out of him is high. Then Al shooed him out of the shop." I laugh. Ray just stares at me—in disbelief, I think.

"I'm sorry, Becs," he finally says, looking disappointed.

"For what, sweetie?" I furrow my brow. *Cautionary Sybecca holds up her ticker board, which reads: You're furrowing straight to a bottle of Botox! Stop it!* I immediately relax my face and rub out the crease that may have formed ... casually, of course.

"Hi ... welcome back," Ray teases me. Ugh! He can always tell when I follow a thought somewhere else!

"Good to be back," I say to humor him.

"I'm sorry I ever doubted you. I'm sorry I believed it was a possibility."

"Huh?" Now I'm confused.

"Sleeping with Will. I know you better than that."

"Oh."

"It's just ... well, if you didn't remember having sex with me, why would you remember it with him? I thought he could've possibly been telling the truth." He looks down.

"Yeah, I get that, Ray. But, even though I repressed those memories of us, I've always been completely comfortable with you. You could say anything off-color or over the line, and it never bothered me. If Will did, or got too touchy-feely, it totally freaked me out. I was never comfortable with him." I pour cement on Will's lie to make sure it stays buried and never resurfaces again.

"Baby, you don't have to explain yourself. I shouldn't have let that asshole get to me. Fucking prick! I hate that guy!"

"Well then, let's not waste any more time on him. C'mon, let's eat." I pull him toward the table.

"Is it okay that I had them bring it up? I didn't feel like socializing. I just wanted this time to be ours." He sits across from me. I nod in agreement as I chew on a strip of bacon.

And thus begins our breakfast ritual. Ray puts sugar and cream in both of our coffees while I give him half of my omelet and take a piece of French toast from his plate. He scoops out my yogurt into a smaller bowl and sprinkles granola on top. I spread strawberry jam on his English muffin. We pass plates back and forth to each other. One sausage link for me, two for him. Three pieces of bacon for me, two for him. He takes the pancakes and places the pumpkin muffin on my plate. Anyone watching us would think we'd been married for fifty years. We're a well-oiled breakfast machine. We know what the other will eat, and how much, without saying a word. He makes my coffee perfect every time ... *every time*.

"Baby, there is no way we are going to eat all of this!" Mr. "You gonna finish that?" looks overwhelmed.

"Well, we can only do what we can do!" I sigh and dig in. "Ray?"

"Yeah, babe?" He sips his coffee.

"Have you talked to Hazel recently?" I ask as I pick apart my bacon. I wish it were a tad bit crispier.

"I talked to her last week, but that's about it. Why?" He shovels the last bite—which could easily pass as three bites—of omelet into his mouth.

"Smaller bites, Ray, you're going to choke!" I sigh lightly. "Well, I haven't talked to her since I got out of the hospital. I feel like she's avoiding me. Actually, I know she's avoiding me. I've left her several messages, and she hasn't returned a single call. Yet she talks to Morgan every day!" If there's anything that moves me from *upset* to *pissed* quickly, it's stuff like this!

"Becs, I think she's just giving us some space to get on the right track here," he says.

"But, Ray, she's my family. She will always be family. I hope she's not feeling like I'll push her aside. I would never."

"Why don't I give her a call for you today?"

"Can't hurt. I just want to know what's going on with her."

"Baby, don't cry. Everything will be fine." He reaches to caress my cheek.

"It's just so upsetting." I try to shake it off.

"Well I'll talk to her," he reiterates. "Now, finish up so I can show you what you've been impatiently waiting for all week." He thumbs a free-running tear away from my face.

"Ooh!" I get excited and refocus my efforts on breakfast.

"All done?" he asks as he grabs my plate.

"Mmm-hmm." I nod as I chew the last bit of food. I get up and pile the remaining dishes on the tray. "Okay, c'mon!" I clap my hands and bounce with excitement.

"Wait. Do that again." He smirks, his eyes making a beeline for my breasts.

"Shut up, McNeil!" I smack his arm and head over to get the long cylindrical tube.

"Hey, hey—give me that, lady!" He grabs it from me and swats my ass. He tosses the tube on the bed and moves the breakfast tray to the table.

"C'mon! C'mon!" I'm like a kid on Christmas morning. He hops onto the left side of the bed and I grip his arm as he starts to open it.

"Now, before I show these to you, I want to explain my thought process," he says.

"Why don't you show me and see if I can figure it out?" I smile over at him.

"Um ..." he thinks. "Okay. I hope you like it." He exhales through pursed lips.

"I'm sure I will love it! Now let me see it, *damn it*!" I bounce and tap his hand.

"Kiss?" he asks, leaning in. I lay a big one on him.

"C'mon, now!" I say. He chuckles at me and pulls out several rolled-up sheets of paper.

"Close your eyes." He holds them away and tosses the tube onto the floor.

"Christ, McNeil, you're torturing me now!" I complain, but close my eyes just the same. I hear him unroll the papers. "Can I look?" I ask.

"Not yet," he sighs. I don't hear him doing anything or feel him moving around.

"Ray!" I snap impatiently.

"Okay," he says quietly. "Open your eyes, baby."

I open them and gasp. "Ray!" I cover my mouth. "It's ... it's gorgeous—amazing!" I stare down at it. It's going to take me hours to catch all the details. "Montreal," I say.

"Yes ... Montreal." He pushes my hair behind my ear before tracing my cheek with his finger. "The idea came to me after we talked about our trip. That was—is—my favorite time with you. It was just us, and we were so in love."

"Is that what this weekend is about?" I turn to him.

"A redo? Yes. I love you, Becca." He leans in and kisses me again.

"I love you so very, very much." I collect his face in my palms and sweep his lips again. "Really, Ray, this is amazing." I look back to the sketches.

It looks like an oversized French Canadian country home with tray ceilings and European ambiance. The area out front is cobble-stoned like Old Montreal.

"Now, let's look inside." He reveals the next sheet. "Let me just explain my thoughts here. I did change some of your original ideas. Just wait for me to finish if you have any issues." He glances over at me, waiting for my okay. I smile and nod. "Okay, so, the cobble-stones continue inside, because I wanted it to be like walking down a street in Old Montreal. These storefronts in here will be real. A coffee shop. A bakery. A gift shop, et cetera, et cetera. There's room for five small shops that you can rent out. This here," he points to the back of the building behind the fountain, "is where the restaurant will be. You'll be able to open to the public, not just guests. The elevators are here, and the rooms wrap around the whole place. There are spiral staircases at the building's side corners, as well. The tray ceilings have huge beams going across to give them that Old World feel. A large wrought iron chandelier will hang down from the center beam, adding stronger lighting than the sconces and street lamps. There will be skylights for daytime light. What do you think so far?"

"It's gorgeous. I love the curved wrought iron railing that goes around the second floor. I love that you can look down from upstairs to faux Old Montreal. I love the idea of little shops. That's awesome! I love the cobblestone and the street lamps, the fountain ... wow. I don't think there is one thing I don't like." I'm in awe.

"Really?" he asks, sounding unsure.
"Really, babe."

"Okay, well, let me show you the rooms." He picks up the next paper. There are eight doubles, four kings, and four king deluxe suites. "A lot of the detail will be in the tile and fixtures that we'll select."

"So now, how big is the place?"

"Oh, ten thousand square feet." He shows me the page with the main interior design. "Your office is right here." He points.

"The infamous office." I laugh, showing my teeth. "But now, where will my scrappers scrap?"

"Oh. Well, that's one of the things I've changed. I thought you could keep the scrappers in the original inn and convert the dining room permanently into the crop room. That way, you can leave the lounge alone. All of your guests will come over here for their meals. You can use one of these little stores, too, as an additional scrap-booking store for the regular guests. I thought maybe Talia would want to rent space from you and have a second coffee shop."

I just sit and listen to him. He's so passionate, so completely in his element.

"I'm so proud of you." I run my hand through the hair above his left ear, then tug playfully on his ear and lean in to kiss his cheek.

"Thanks, baby." He turns for a proper kiss. "Is there anything you want to change? Do you have any questions?"

"No. Well, the only thing I can think of right now is the infor-mation desk. I'm guessing people will check in at the original inn. Once they are over here, though, they should be able to talk to a staff person about their needs, and ask questions about local stuff. I don't think they should have to go to the main inn or up to their room to call. What do you think?" I look at the sketch to see where that could possibly go.

"We could use this spot over here and create a reception desk. Anything else, Becs?"

"Laundry and cleaning supplies?"

"Basement. Anything else in the main area? Did I forget

anything?"

"No, Ray. Honestly, it's amazing. So, what are we looking at price-wise?"

"Good news or bad news?" He winces.

"Ugh ... just tell me."

"Well, we're looking at five to six million, seven at the max. Good news is it's three million under your cap. The other good news is you'll be pulling about two million in a year after renovations." I act as if I'm going to pass out. "Well, you could go with Greerson," he teases.

"Oh, sure!" I laugh.

"I still have to talk to Charlie about the stables, like I said, but I projected an approximate cost and added that in."

"Oh, okay. That's good." I pretend to wipe the sweat from my brow. "Really, Ray ... this is great. Montreal was a very special time for us, and this is such a beautiful reminder. Thank you, baby." I lean in for another kiss. "I don't know why you were so worried. You know me, sweetie. You had to know I would fall in love with this." I rub my nose against his.

"I did, but I didn't want to get cocky either, just in case." He pulls all the sketches together and rerolls them. After placing them back in the tube, he tosses it on the floor and scoots into bed, resting his head on the pillow. I lean my head on his chest and let our synchronized breathing hypnotize me.

"What are the plans for today?" I finally ask.

"Well, I didn't think it would be fair to take you to the wineries, so that's off the list. I thought we could just relax today, maybe do a little shopping before we go out to dinner. We have early reservations, so we can't be out too long." His fingers trail up and down my arm.

"Where are we going for dinner?"

"Oh, a little place called The French Laundry."

"Ray!" My head shoots back up. "How did you get us in there

on short notice? They book up months in advance!"

"Hey, what can I tell you?" He shrugs. "I know people who know people who know people, babe." He smirks playfully.

"You dropped Grayson's name!" I gasp in shock.

"Nooo. Derek knows the owner and *he* dropped Grayson's name. See. People who know people who know people." He smiles and sweeps my lips with his. I roll my eyes and giggle a bit before I rest my head back down. I inhale deeply the scent of one very fine Ray McNeil.

"Becs ... baby, I need to tell you something. Please try not to get mad at me."

"What is it?" I lift my head again.

"Um, I asked Hazel to give us some space."

"Why would you do that, Ray?" I sit up.

"Because."

"Because why?" *Because? What the hell kind of answer is "because"?*

"I just ... sometimes I feel that a lot of your guilt stems from Hazel being around. She reminds you of Grayson, and it doesn't help anyone. Then I think you're worried she'll feel like you forgot her, which you just confirmed over breakfast. This helps you push me away." He sits up too. I stare at my hands, playing with my ring as I contemplate his concerns.

"Ray." I look up. "I understand. I have to tell you, though, that this does upset me. Hazel has been my mom and my best friend since Grayson introduced us. She's a blessing in my life. She dropped everything to be with Morgan and me after Grayson died. With the exception of her sister, we're her only family. What you did is hurtful, Ray. Not just to me, but to her. We're a package deal, babe." I'm amazed, actually, at how calm I am. I think he is, too.

"I didn't intend to hurt either of you. I just wanted to do everything I could to make this stick. I'm done chasing you." He runs his hand through his hair.

"I know you'll have your guard up for a while." I get off the bed and head to my bag.

"What are you doing?"

"I started this when I woke up. I recorded everything that happened while I was the coma, and every day since. I am determined to never forget again. Here." I hand him my journal. He takes it hesitantly and begins to flip through it.

"You've written a lot." He glances up.

"Every page will be filled with our story. If there is ever, *ever* a time I forget, hand this to me. Make me read it." I sit next to him and watch as he scans the pages.

"Jesus, that was fucking hot," he says under his breath, reading a section I'm sure contains sex. I can't help my laughter. "You could get pissed off at me and rip my pages out, or toss the book entirely." He flips to another page.

"I type it up every night and save it on a flash drive." I kiss his shoulder. He looks at the beginning.

"I thought you said you wrote about the whole coma." He points to the date.

I show him the inside cover of the book. "This is book six. The others are back at home."

"Can I read them?"

"Well ... it has a lot about Grayson and me."

"I know. I want to read it."

"Um, okay." I feel a bit unsure. "Hey." I turn his chin, trying to pry his eyes away from the book. "Thanks for being honest with me about Hazel. Will you call her today?"

"Yeah, baby. I'm sorry." He pecks my lips.

"Just try to think of her as my mother, not Grayson's. I'd love for you to consider her your mother-in-law."

Ray looks at me thoughtfully. "I think I will. That is a nice way to look at it. You know I love Hazel. It's nothing against her. I'll call her today and apologize."

"Thank you." I hug him.

"Okay, can I get back to my soft porn over here?" He shakes the book.

"Yes. I'm going to take a shower." I kiss his cheek and head off.

Chapter Fourteen

"Mmm ... you smell good, baby," Ray breathes against my left ear as he buckles me into my seat. The weight of his lips presses on mine before I feel a slight breeze and hear him close the door. I part my lips and take in a slow, steady breath. My heart is still racing, my face flushed from the acrobatics we performed over the past hour. Apparently, my journal ignites a fire in him that takes some effort to extinguish. "Becs." His hand covers my left knee and slides up my thigh. "You okay?" I open my eyes to look over at him. I didn't even realize he got into the car.

"Yeah." I smile softly and nod for emphasis. A slow, sexy smirk crosses his lips, accompanied by his signature air kiss and wink. He throws on his aviators, starts up the car, shifts into drive, and coasts us slowly out of the parking lot.

"When do you want to go back East?" he asks as he hits play on the iPod. "Blue Jeans" by Lana Del Rey comes on. Christ, this song makes me hot for him. *Country Sybecca is walking funny. She holds her crotch and shakes her head. One of her pigtails has come undone. Porn Sybecca hands her an ice pack to soothe her lady parts.* Lucky bitch! I wish I had an ice pack to soothe *my* lady parts! "Baby?" Ray grabs my hand and shakes it.

"Sorry, sweetie." I lace my fingers with his. "Maybe Wednesday or so. I really want you to meet Susanna and Sam. I'd like to spend some time with them." I sigh and feel guilt blanket me. I haven't been very fair to them, staying away this long. They've been like family to us, and I haven't done my part in making them feel that way lately. "I have to reschedule my ultrasound to the following week," I add.

"Well, I'm in no rush to get back to our life at home."

"Bubble's not going to burst, baby." I squeeze his hand. "I'm yours." He glances over at me, but those damn sunglasses are blocking his eyes. I can't see what he's thinking.

"I just like having this time to ourselves. I love our girls, baby, but we needed Ray and Becca time." His lips paint kisses on the back of my hand.

"Well, it's going to get harder once the twins are here. I'm not going to feel comfortable leaving them for a while."

"Becca, you are not going to work like you did before. Part-time only. I mean it, baby. Twenty hours max. I don't even want you to do that much!" he says. I bite back my smile and decide to watch him go on with his rant instead of interjecting. "I have certain expectations, Becs," he continues, his voice softer. I raise my eyebrow. "I want to come home from work every night to kids finishing up homework or setting the table. My wife in the kitchen, doing last-minute preparations for dinner and smacking my hand away when I start picking at things."

"Should I wear a frilly apron for you?" I tease him.

"Only with nothing else on, when the kids aren't home." He smiles.

"Shall I ask you how you day was, dear?" My smile is full of mirth. He says nothing. I study him some more. His fantasy is so simple, so sweet and innocent. Most women might be appalled, and if I didn't know Ray like I do, I would probably roll my eyes at him and flash my "sight word." But I do know him. These ideas do not stem from being a chauvinistic pig, but from a deep appreciation of being taken care of. He's never made me feel like my place was only in the home. Granted, we haven't really had your typical conventional relationship, but the foundation has always been there. I love when Ray came to the inn for dinner on Wednesdays after work, when he wrapped his arms around my waist and kissed me hello. Even when I wasn't "on," I loved it. Maybe a part of me was always "on," at least a little.

"I know it can't be helped when people call in. But I don't want to hear, 'Mom said to order a pizza, she had to work' a lot." He pulls into a space at the outlets and turns the car off. "Weekends off. That's our time," he states, staring ahead. I think he's waiting for me to go apeshit on him. It's taking a lot for me not to laugh.

"Except for crop weekends." I remain calm.

"Okay. I can live with that," he says thoughtfully.

I lean over to him and run my index finger down his jawline. "I won't work the Friday before or the Monday after the crop weekends. Okay, baby?" I speak softly in his ear, and his breathing becomes erratic. "Okay, baby?" I ask again.

"Um ... yes."

I smile against his skin, my lips following the trail of my finger.

"Jesus, Becca, you've gotta stop, baby." He's barely audible. I pull away. He takes in a deep breath and shivers.

"C'mon, let's get you a jacket for tonight." I unbuckle myself, satisfied by the way I affect him. Ray climbs out and comes around to open my door. I slide out.

"One to two hours a day—that's it." He stares down at me, my reflection glaring back at me from the lenses of his aviators. I can't help my laughter. "Don't laugh," he says with a sigh.

"Ray." I wrap my arms around his neck. "I'm not going to argue with you, sweetie. Two hours a day unless someone calls out. Every other weekend off, every other Monday and Friday off. Home-cooked meals most nights. Weekends away together when I'm comfortable leaving the babies. Besides all that, I promise that you will always be the sun—at—the—center—of—my—universe." I peck at his lips between the last few words.

"Sorry," he sighs. "I don't know why I'm acting like this. I'm not trying to argue, I just ... " He trails off as he closes the car door.

"You just don't want me to get swallowed up by work and forget about our family or push you guys off. I know where it's coming from. I understand. That's kind of been my history." I grab his hand and we head off to the first store. "Things will be different. I promise. Bare feet, baby," I reiterate.

"I believe you, Becca. I'm feeling selfish. I can't help it. I finally have all of you. I don't want to share you with anything or anyone right now." He pulls my hand around to the small of his back. His arm drapes over my shoulder, pulling me close as we walk. I slip my hand into his back pocket and rest my head below his shoulder.

"Four kids, McNeil ... you'll have to be a big boy and share me." I glance up at him.

"Damn kids," he teases.

We walk into Barneys New York. Alexander approaches us at approximately our fifteenth step into the store.

"Yes, Alexander, please measure my husband for a sport coat," I say, before he can even welcome us—and before Ray can look at a single price tag.

"Right this way, sir." He turns on his heels immediately.

I cringe at Alexander's shiny, swamp-green suit as I watch him walk ahead. The color isn't the problem for me, though. If there's one thing I consider more of an eyesore than skinny jeans on men, it's skinny suit pants on men. They hug his bony legs proudly, and I want to scream *Stop the insanity!* like that crazy chick ... what's her name? Ugh!

"Susan Powter!" I do a mental head slap.

"Huh?" Ray shoots me a look.

"Oh, never mind." I shake my head.

Alexander approaches Ray with measuring tape and stands him in front of a mirror. While he measures, I start fishing around.

"I'd go with a 40 regular," Alexander states. I grab the tan, velvet Dolce & Gabbana sport coat. It has a single button, front-flap pockets, and peaked lapels. I hide the $1,825.00 price tag and help Ray into it. "This coat goes fabulously with jeans and a plain tee," Alexander says.

"Hmm ... I agree, although I think you should wear a dress shirt with it tonight," I say, circling Ray. "What do you think, McNeil?" I ask.

"It's comfortable, and different from what I already have. What do you think, baby?"

He studies my face in the mirror.

"This makes me want to write in my journal." I smile mischievously.

"We'll take it!" Ray says quickly. He takes it off and hands it to me to put back on the hanger.

"Ray, let me get this for you as part of your Christmas present," I say. He shrugs. "Can you get me a decaf coffee from that shop over there while Alex here rings me up? I'll meet you outside." I kiss his cheek.

"Okay, babe. Do you want anything to eat?" I shake my head. Ray heads off.

When it comes to clothes, there are several types of men on this planet. Ray, thankfully, is the kind that dresses affordably well. As far as labels and the price that comes with them, well, that's completely off his radar. Now, if this jacket were a power saw of some sort, he would know the brand and the price without looking at the tag. If this jacket were a power saw, he wouldn't flip out at the total like he would for one tan sport coat—hence my sudden need for a cup of coffee. I hand Alexander my AmEx Black Card and ask him to pull the tag off. He smiles. I suspect he's fielded similar requests.

"Thank you, Mrs. James. Please come again." He smiles.

"Sure. Thanks for your help," I say. What I want to say is, *Dude, burn the suit and eat a sub!* But, alas, I smile and turn on my heel.

I walk up to the glass doors of Barneys and spot Ray outside with my coffee, lid off, blowing on it to cool it down. *Shit.* I think I just fell more in love with him at this very moment. It's the little things that keep everything glued together. So few people realize it, or remember how *big* little things are. Ray glances up quickly and his eyes lock with mine. His beautiful, stormy eyes. His smile hits them and he jerks his head slightly, beckoning for me to come join him.

"They had pumpkin for you, baby." He puts the lid back on and exchanges it for the bag from Barneys.

"Just for me?" I tease before taking a sip. *Perfect.* "Mmm ... thank you." I lean up to kiss him.

"Where next?" He grabs my hand. I shrug.

We stroll around for the next two hours, wandering in and out of different stores. Ray gets a new pair of jeans and a shirt for dinner tonight, plus new boots at Kenneth Cole. I splurged on a Coach purse and matching wallet. Well, Ray splurged. Had I known he was going to offer, then proceed to give me *The Look* when I tried to argue, I never would've walked into the store. I didn't know whether to laugh or cry when the clerk told him the total was six hundred. Ray's eyes grew wider than I had ever seen them before. He swallowed hard and handed over his Visa.

"Ray," I say when we get outside, "I don't usually spend that kind of money on a purse and wallet."

"Becs, stop. It's okay," he interjects. "I'm getting off easy here! You'll use the same purse for two years or so. Other women change them out constantly. Even if you bought twelve reasonably priced purses, they would end up costing more than what I just spent."

I'm speechless.

"Uh ... that's a good way of looking at it," I finally say.

"It's the only way I can look at it. Otherwise, I wouldn't be able to stomach dropping six bills like that." His statement makes me wince. "Besides, it's okay. I have this wicked-rich client now. I can afford it," he teases, nudging my arm.

"I'm not wicked rich, I'm uncomfortably comfortable," I say.

"Well, a lot of families in our area will enjoy sharing in your comfort when I do all of that hiring." He throws our bags into the back of the MDX.

"Oh! Tanya Smith! She was Morgan and Annie's favorite teacher. Her husband has been out of work for a while. They're really struggling. I think he's in computers. I want to give him a job. Grayson said he'd be very valuable to our company."

"Reggie, babe?" He closes the trunk.

"Oh, I don't remember his first name."

"They have three children, right?"

"Yeah, that's them!" I tap his arm.

"His resume is impressive. He came to me right before our accident, but I didn't have anything to fit his qualifications. I'll give him a call this week. If he's still looking, we could definitely use him."

"I'm glad. So many people are struggling."

"I know, babe, it's awful. Puts some things into perspective, especially for me. Here I was, being a proud prick, instead of thinking about how much you and I alone will be helping our local economy with this build." He sighs, shaking his head.

"You know what part of the problem is, sweetie?" I cross my arms.

"What?" A slow smile forms at his lips. He's getting ready for one of my rants.

"We've gotten so detached from our neighbors, we can't seem to truly grasp that sense of community I know most people really want."

"What do you mean, Becs?" He leans against the SUV.

"Well, you know, we tease each other calling ourselves Mr. and Mrs. Cleaver." I mirror his action. "But that generation is known and respectfully referred to as *the Greatest Generation*. When I think of our grandparents, I think of their sense of community. When times got hard, they rolled up their sleeves and did whatever they could to help each other and the country out. Three generations later, we can all still feel the essence of their pride. A lot of things were organized on the town, state, or federal level. The point is, just about everyone who could do his or her part went ahead and did so. They were all basically in the same boat, working together to get to dry land. They leaned on each other and learned how to 'scratch one another's backs,' if you will. Did you know that by the end of World War II, unemployment was virtually nonexistent?" I finally take a breath. "Yes, there are groups who try different things to help, but we need something bigger. I think our generation has been so spoiled—we're too busy trying to look like we're still 'keeping with the Joneses' to admit we're struggling and ask for help. Then there's the other side of that: chronically complaining about our situation and expecting things to be handed to us. Of course, there are the people in the middle, hanging in limbo or just retracting completely. Maybe we can get something started in our town. A back-to-basics plan. Get the people talking and plan as a community. Find out people's needs versus what they can do to help others. Start rowing the boat together in our community." I pause for a sip of my coffee.

"You know, baby, I think you're on to something. Most of the people in our town want to feel that sense of community. We all get involved in local events, but we haven't fully grasped that old sentiment. A lot of it has to do with people's attitudes and trust issues. Technology is a beautiful thing, but on the other hand, it's doing a number on people socially. You know, I'm going to get us in with Mayor Brewster. You and I are pretty well known in town. We may just be the two to get the ball rolling." He pulls my hips, bringing me to him. "And then we will solve world peace." He smiles.

"One small New England town at a time," I laugh.

"This is good for our girls, too. You're an amazing woman, Becca. You make me so proud in so many ways." He seals his compliment with a kiss.

I'll feel prouder of myself when I talk to Rev. Johnson about anonymously making someone's mortgage payment this month. Christ, I just spent that much on a sport coat! That's where the *uncomfortable* part of my comfortable life comes in. Grayson and I used to get into it a lot over my discomfort with our situation. He hated that I couldn't get over the guilt of being successful and just enjoy it a little. I don't know, I guess I was always worried about forgetting what it felt like to struggle. Now that I'm older, I don't think I ever will. It's too much a part of me and who I've become as a person. Ray's right; this build will help many people enjoy in my comforts. Never mind Ray's company—I'm going to need a lot more staff. The shops in the new building will be hiring. We'll create a ton of local jobs between us. Suddenly, I don't feel so uncomfortable anymore!

"Now, we have a half an hour. We can either head back," his eyebrows rise, hinting at an idea or two he may have, "or we can spend that time in the Gymboree store you've been eyeing for the past ten minutes."

I bite my lip. I really want to go look at the baby clothes. I don't want to disappoint him, either, though I haven't fully recovered from our earlier shenanigans.

"The Gymboree it is." He smirks, pulling my lip away from my teeth before he collects it for himself. My heart races as he sucks on my lip before he deepens the kiss.

"C'mon, we need to hurry now!" Ray rushes us into our room.

"Sorry!" I say for the millionth time.

"I told you half an hour, babe!" he says again, tossing bags onto the bed and kicking his shoes off. I close the door. "Forget it. We're here, just get dressed. Our reservation is in fifteen minutes." He undresses while pulling his clothes out of the bags. I go to my suitcase for my new favorite sweaterdress. Quickly, I change outfits and throw on my knee-high black boots. I stand up and let my hair down on the way to the mirror, and it falls down past my shoulders. *Ah ... thank you for cooperating.* I grab my makeup bag and apply with haste. A glance in the mirror shows Ray turning around behind me as he slides his arms into his new jacket. He stills, taking in my outfit. I can see something igniting in his eyes from way over here. He looks at his watch, then to me, then back to the watch.

"McNeil, we only have ten minutes! Knock it off!" I apply my lipstick.

"You must know how fond of that dress I am, Becs." His voice is soft and seductive, matching his facial expression as he prowls closer to me. He reaches up and moves my hair over my shoulder. I close my eyes and focus on controlling my breathing as his lips take advantage of having full access to my neck. I breathe sharply as his hands slide up the outside of my thighs, dragging the hem of the dress with them. "I have a theme song, baby," he murmurs into my ear before he nips at the skin below my earlobe. My heart leaps from the electric current.

"What is it?" My voice shakes as I try to fight off the desire building in me.

"'The Sign' by Ace of Base." His voice is full of mirth as he grasps my inner thighs. I turn my head and let my smile hit my eyes.

"Ray." I gasp as he pushes my panties to the side. A single finger circles around my opening before plunging deep. I rest my forehead against his temple, feeling hypnotized by the rhythm of his one rather intrusive finger.

"Oh, baby, you're so ready for me," he says in almost a whisper. Slowly, he pulls out entirely and adjusts my panties. He stares at me in the mirror. No need for blush now! "You look beautiful," he says before he sucks my taste off his finger. "Mmm ... so good. C'mon, baby." He grabs my coat and helps me into it. I watch him in the mirror. His brown hair is choppy—at the length I love. His blue-gray eyes are rich. Christ, he is so handsome. There's strength in his jawline and chin, without it being overpowering. Strong cheekbones. Honestly, he could've been a model. He flashes me his big, boyish grin, and I can picture him in a high school letter jacket.

"Were you captain of your high school baseball team?" I ask, matching his smile.

"Yeah, why?" He seems caught off guard by my out-of-the-blue question.

"No reason," I say. "Random inquiry." I lace my fingers with his to walk with him out the door.

"Shit, we're going to be late now," Ray says as I plug the address into the GPS.

"Only a couple of minutes. It's fine." I tap his arm. "We wouldn't be late at all if you had just stayed focused on the task at hand," I add.

"I believe we're late because I was focusing on a beautiful, seductive task that required my hands." He pulls my hand to his lips as he turns onto Yount Street.

"I wasn't doing anything seductive." I give him a strange look.

"Baby," he says, glancing over, "the moment you're in my view, I'm seduced." He plants a kiss on every one of my knuckles. Butterflies burst out of their cocoons in my belly. I sit, speechlessly bathing in his words. Ray takes a left on Humbold Street, then a right onto Washington, and within seconds, we're parking. "Ready?" His forefinger caresses beneath my chin. My eyes find his and I'm overcome with the intensity of my love for him. I never thought I would ever feel this way about another man. "Baby?" Ray touches my face. "What's the matter?" He wipes the tears that escape the corners of my eyes.

"Happy tears."

I rest my hands on top of his.

"Good," he says softly.

"Do you mind being one more minute late? I just ... I want to kiss you." I lean forward.

"Becca James, you mean to tell me you want to air our dirty laundry in front of The French Laundry? Oh, the irony." He smiles.

"Shut up and kiss me, McNeil." My hand slides into his hair. I grasp it, pulling his mouth to mine. Ray deepens the kiss with the slip of his tongue. I get lost in it, his smell, his touch, and ... the sounds that escape his throat.

"Baby, we have to stop." Ray says, sounding somewhat on the edge as he pulls away.

"Okay, okay." I try to catch my breath. "Let's go." I turn to open my door.

"Becs, wait," he says, and climbs out. Coming around, he opens my door.

"Mr. Cleaver." I nod and smile.

"Mrs. Cleaver." He grabs my hand and helps me out. "Christ, what you do to me, baby." He rests his forehead against mine.

"Back atcha, McNeil." I nudge his nose with mine before sweeping his lips quickly.

"Come on." He grabs my hand and pulls me away from the car. He shuts the door and locks it as we head into The French Laundry.

"Hi. Reservation for James," Ray tells the maître d'. I give him an odd look.

"Mrs. Becca James?" Christophe asks.

"Yes." I smile.

"We have a lovely table waiting for you. Please, let me take your coat." He walks over to help me.

"Thank you." I smile, but it fades when I catch Ray studying him intently. We follow Christophe's lead. "Knock it off, he's gay," I whisper in his ear.

"He doesn't seem like he is." His jawline twitches.

"And you would know this, how?" I ask with concern before I laugh. Yeah ... I just visualized him as the construction guy in the Village People. "Is it fun to stay at the YMCA, Ray?"

"Shut up." He chuckles. "Smartass."

"Claudette will be with you in a moment. I will let Thomas know you are here." He places a menu card in front of us.

"Thank you, Christophe."

"Who's Thomas?" Ray asks, looking over the menu.

"Thomas Keller ... the owner."

"You know him?"

"Well, we've met a few times. Grayson was the one who really knew him. He frequented his restaurants and worked with him for research on his character Clive in *Winter's Baby*. The character was a world-renowned French chef."

I smile as Thomas approaches our table.

"Thomas!" I stand up with my arms outstretched.

"Becca, so good to see you!" He matches my excitement as he hugs me. "Finally. After all these years, you finally made it in here!" He holds me at arm's length.

"I know. I'm sorry, Thomas." I sigh. "But, alas, I'm here and ready to eat for three." I rub my belly.

"Twins?" he asks, his eyes wide.

"Yes," I answer. "Thomas, I'd like to introduce you to my fiancé, Ray McNeil." I hold my hand out to Ray, who stands and shakes Thomas's hand. They exchange pleasantries, talking about the sites we'd like to visit and whatnot.

He turns back to me, then lowers his voice. "I'm so sorry about Grayson, Becca. He was a good man ... a great man!"

"Yes, he was," I agree. "Thank you."

We talk for a few more minutes before he heads back to the kitchen.

"Recommend anything, Becs?" Ray resumes looking over the menu.

"Whatever catches your eye, babe. Thomas is a culinary genius; anything you order is going to be one hundred percent better than your expectations." Myself, I want to eat everything on the menu!

Claudette arrives, giving us a well-rehearsed, detailed description of tonight's specials. The words parade from her mouth so romantically, you can envision the love affair between the entrées and sauces that complement them.

"Baby?" Ray is gentlemanly, allowing me to order first. No one but me would know there's another part to his gesture—the part that says, *I have no idea what she just said or what I would like on this menu*. His wide eyes confirm my thoughts.

"Thank you, Claudette. It all sounds lovely. I will have the pan-roasted breast of squab with Swiss chard."

"Very good," she says, then looks to Ray. "And you, sir?"

He looks down at his menu.

"Why don't you go with your first choice, sweetie? I bet you'll love the *pot-au-feu*."

Ray looks up. "She's right. *Pot-au-feu* it is. I'll have a Coke and she'll have ginger ale." He hands her the menu. She nods and walks away. "Christ, I feel like I'm five."

"It's the sauces throwing you off."

I smile as I grab my phone and open Google.

"What are you doing?" He scoots his chair closer to me.

"Looking up 'squab,'" I whisper, trying not to laugh.

"You don't know what you ordered?" Relief underscores his smile.

I playfully wince and shake my head, then look at the screen. My heart sinks. Four-week-old pigeon. I instinctively rub my belly. Ray looks over my shoulder.

"Silver lining, babe ... it's not fish." He hits the circle on my phone to close the app. "So," he says, his mouth close to my ear. The back of his hand caresses my cheek gently, hypnotically. "When will you write about this weekend?"

"This weekend is still happening." I kiss his finger as it traces my lips.

"Becs, when you describe what my touch does to you ... what

241

your body experiences ... Jesus, baby." He shakes his head, like he's trying to push the thought away. "Well, I think you know firsthand how that affects me."

Yep, completely recall him trying to bang me into next week when I returned from my shower! I gasp and turn my face to his as his hand slides up the inside of my thigh. Our backs face any eyes that may scan over us, and the length of the tablecloth conceals his naughty behavior. Finding relief in this, I gradually part my legs for him and look up to meet his stare.

"Was it hot for you?" I barely whisper, using his description of choice.

He exhales through pursed lips. "It always is, baby." Our breath becomes unsteady as the memory of this morning comes back to both of us.

One minute, I was walking out of the bathroom at a carefree pace, wrapped in my towel. The next, Ray forced me onto my back and stripped me naked. The mattress dipped as he knelt in front of me, aggressively pulling my legs apart. My initial panicked reaction dissipated when I saw his expression was full of desire. His member saluted me in a rock-hard stance. Before I could take another breath, Ray lifted my hips in the air and rammed into me deep and hard. My neck arched back so violently, I swear it could've snapped in two.

His pounding was relentless, unforgiving. My hips remained in the air, keeping me at an angle that allowed him to engage me at the deepest and fullest capacity. I had nothing to use for leverage. Because of my protruding abdomen, I couldn't reach him. I had no way to help him reach the place he wanted. Then again, he seemed to be doing fine on his own. I could barely handle the task of remembering to breathe. Instead, I encouraged him with my whimpering moans, then my pleas as I felt myself begin to climb. Ray's teeth clenched together hard and his nose scrunched up. His next thrust was the magical one—the one that released me. I tightened around him greedily to savor it.

"Becca!" His voice was an aching roar as he came undone. I'm pretty sure everyone at the inn is very aware of my first name now.

A burst of laughter from the table behind us brings my focus back. Ray rubs my belly, a pertinent expression on his face. I crook my head and furrow my brow as I try to figure him out. His eyes come back up to catch mine. "I'll be gentler tonight." His voice is soft and low, so only I can hear him.

"Yes, that was a bit rude, McNeil," I tease.

The corners of his mouth curve up and his eyes take on a playful look. "You have no idea how rude I wanted to be."

He palms my cheek as he leans in for a kiss. Claudette comes and places our salads before us.

"Thank you." I smile, immediately giving her my attention.

"So, Grayson never brought you here?" he asks before taking a forkful of salad.

"Um, no. We wanted to, but plans for a long weekend here always fell through."

"Well, next time we come, we'll make sure you're in a condition to enjoy the wineries."

"That may lead me back to this condition," I say, nudging him.

"Probably," he says with a wink. "I'm glad he didn't bring you here," he adds. "It can be ours."

"We have a lot of things that are 'ours,' babe." I rest my head on his shoulder and hug his arm.

"Yeah, we do. It's just being here in California. It's silly, but I feel like the whole state is Grayson territory." He looks over at my plate and nudges me. "C'mon, eat, baby."

I sit back up, reclaiming my fork. "I think Grayson felt the same way in New Hampshire. He was very aware of your presence there. That's why he shuffled us off to California."

"But Becca, that wasn't real," he says.

"It was real!" I snap at him.

"I know. I mean, I wasn't really there in the flesh." McNeil backpedals carefully.

"Well, he's not really here in the flesh, so it's the same thing."
One point: Becca James.

"Okay, baby."

Ray sighs and looks away. I know he's rolling his eyes. Luckily
for him, Claudette brings us our sorbet. He plays with it a little after
his first bite.

"So," he says, looking back to me, "I was thinking we could go
do something that's 'ours' after this."

"What's that?" I take my last bite.

"It's a surprise, as long as you're up for it."

I shrug, pushing my sorbet dish away.

"Don't be mad at me, Becs." He tucks my hair behind my ear
and slides his hand down to rub my back.

"I'm not."

"Hmm ... well then, what caused your drastic change in mood?"

"I don't know. Hormones," I point out.

"Yeah, I'm not buying it. But at least dinner's coming."

He nods as Claudette and a runner come our way. They clear
our dishes and replace them with masterpieces that look and smell
divine.

"Do you want me to share in your guilt and take the first bite of
yours?" He leans over. I cut into it and feed him. "Wow," he says,
his mouth still full.

"Yeah?"

"Oh yeah." He shakes his head. I take a bite and it melts in my
mouth. We sit in silence, enjoying our meals. The mood lightens—
well, mine does—as we chow down.

Ray eats off my plate when he finishes his. Honestly, I don't
know where he puts it all! I place my fork on the table and let him
have the last bite.

"Making sure I have room for dessert?" I tease.

"Of course! Always looking out for you, babe!" He kisses me.

"So, back to the inn after here?"

"No. We'll go out." I smile, grabbing his hand. Claudette comes back to take our order.

"We'll have the chocolate cake with red-beet ice cream and toasted walnut sauce, and the vanilla-bean roasted figs with wild-flower-honey vanilla ice cream."

My mouth waters as Ray speaks.

I turn to Ray. "I don't even like beets, but I've heard it's delicious."

"Sounds interesting. You're being very brave with your choices tonight," he says.

"Ray?"

"Hmm?" He swirls the spoon in my coffee around.

"Thank you for this weekend. This has been a wonderful day; this getaway is just what we needed." I take my cup from him.

"It's nice just focusing on us, isn't it?" He rests his head on his propped-up fist. He studies me as I drink my coffee.

"Mmm-hmm," I agree. "What?" I ask after a few minutes of him staring at me.

"I'm going to be fighting for your attention again in a few months, once these guys are born." His fingers graze my belly.

"Oh, stop it! You'll still have plenty of attention."

He shakes his head as I try to convince him.

"McNeil, you've never had difficulty getting my attention. If anything, my senses go through the roof when you're around. It's pretty hard to ignore." I lean in to rub his nose with mine before kissing him.

"I think I read something about that somewhere." He looks up at the ceiling quizzically, acting as if he's trying to retrieve exactly where he read it. I smack his chest playfully. We break at the sound of Claudette placing dishes on the table.

"Sorry. Thanks," I say once again.

Half an hour later, we head back out to the car. Snow blusters around, all bark but no bite.

"You sure you're still up for going out, Becs?" he asks as he climbs into the driver's seat.

"Yes, it's only eight o'clock." I turn up the heat.

"Okay. Well, we won't stay long." He starts up the car and plugs the address into the GPS. "I have a song for you that I keep forgetting to play." He grabs the iPod and searches.

"What is it?"

"'Who'd Have Known' by Lily Allen. I think you'll find it very fitting for us. Actually, I think it may have been written for us." He smirks and hits play. We head back to Washington Street. Within a minute, the chorus hits and I can't help but giggle. Ray laughs with me. He's right—this song was written for us. Within ten minutes, we pull up to a pub.

"You're taking your pregnant fiancée to a pub?" I look at him like he has five heads.

"Yep," he states before getting out of the car. He comes around to let me out. As we walk toward the pub, I see the sign for karaoke.

"We haven't done this in a while." I look up at him.

"No, we haven't." He squeezes me to him as we walk in and find a table near the stage area.

"I'll get us some drinks," Ray says as I take a seat. A woman is singing "Respect" by Aretha Franklin—and not doing a very good job of it, either. Several minutes later, Ray makes his way back to our table. "Sorry, it took forever to get the bartender's attention." He hands me my drink. "Ginger ale and cranberry," he says. I take a swig as he sits. For the next twenty minutes, we watch people sing, then comment on their performances.

"Next up, we have Ray!" The DJ announces. I look over at Ray. I didn't realize he'd even put in for a song. He smiles and runs up.

"I'd like to dedicate this to my beautiful fiancée, Becca," he announces into the microphone before "Hey, Soul Sister" by Train comes on. As he starts singing, my smile grows so big, it could swallow my face.

As usual, Ray gets the room going with him. He's got a great voice and not a shy bone in his body. I almost go into hysterics when he sings about us having a game-show love connection. The faces he's making are classic Ray. I laugh again when he sings about us being gangsta and thumbs his nose at me. This song is so *us*. Christ, I love the hell out of him!

When he stops, stares directly at me, and sings, "I want the world to see you be ... with me," my eyes well up.

He continues parading around the stage and this overwhelming feeling of completeness comes over me. At this moment, I know for sure we're going to have a good life together. We have endured so much and still have so many obstacles to overcome. And we will overcome them all. Together.

As long as he's by my side, I can overcome anything.

Epilogue

January 16, 2015

"Is it on?" I ask, walking into the family room.

"Yeah, c'mon, baby." Ray places his left foot on the floor and pats between his legs on the sofa. I hand him his beer and my wine, then pull the coffee table close so we can set them down on it.

"Sorry. If I didn't fold those clothes, I would've been buried tomorrow." I sigh and sit where Ray indicated. He wraps his arms around me. I turn my head up to him for a kiss. I refocus onto the TV and Ray hits play. Barbara Walters appears on the screen for a special segment of *20/20*.

"It's been nine years since the tragic death of the young and talented international best-selling author, Grayson James," Barbara starts. "Tonight, we will talk with his widow, Becca, about her life since that devastating day in December 2005. This is Becca's first interview about her husband, his life, his death, and the novel they wrote together ten years ago, which she's finally brought herself to publish. Take a look as we travel to Becca's home in New Hampshire."

The picture goes dark, then comes back to Barbara and me sitting in the office of the newly renovated part of the inn.

"Becca, how old were you when you met Grayson James?" Barbara asks.

"I was just barely twenty-two."

"So young. How did you meet?"

"Well, I was working part-time at a Barnes & Noble when he came in for a signing."

"Was it love at first sight?"

"Not exactly. I mean, I found him to be extremely handsome, but quite irritating." I giggle.

"A lethal combination?"

"Apparently it was for me." I shake my laughter away.

She inquires more about our meeting. Our courting.

"So persistence definitely paid off here." She laughs lightly.

"Oh yes, Grayson was a very persistent man."

"Within a year, they were engaged and married."

They show pictures of our wedding, then some of us at different functions and traveling to promote his books.

When I interviewed Grayson in 2001, this is what he had to say about his relationship with Becca."

It switches to their old interview.

"Why so many number-one best sellers? Where do these ideas come from? What's your inspiration?" She fires off a round of questions as if she knew they all had the same answer.

"That's easy, Barbara. My wife, Becca, is my muse. She's brought my imagination to a level I never realized existed. She's there with me through the whole process."

There's such passion in his conviction—it takes my breath away. I had no idea they were going to show this interview. Silly on my part, really. Ray squeezes me as I take in a very deep breath. My tears fall freely.

It took a lot of work over the past two years for Ray to accept my everlasting love for Grayson and be okay with it. He no longer feels threatened by my memory of Grayson or our life together. He asked me, hypothetically, "If Grayson actually survived the plane crash and walked through the door, who would you choose?" My answer was always the same: I would walk away from both of them, because I could no sooner choose which of my limbs to cut off. He didn't believe me, and my journals certainly didn't help. It wasn't until I made love to Ray in Grayson's and my room that he finally dropped it. I sobbed terribly afterward, feeling like I betrayed Grayson. It was silly to feel that way, but I couldn't help it. Ray was so good about it. He just held me and let me cry. I think, to him, it was the final step to me being completely his.

"So," Barbara starts. "Any thoughts of children?"

"Most definitely! Becca and I would love an absurd amount of kids." Grayson laughs.

"Grayson and Becca started their family the very next year with the birth of their daughter, Morgan. Unfortunately, she would be the only child that would come of their union. When we come back ... family life with Grayson James, his untimely death, and Becca's long and painful journey back to happiness," Barbara says.

The TV fades to a commercial, and Ray hits pause.

"You okay, baby?" He rubs my arms up and down.

"Yes, I just ... I wasn't prepared for that interview. I forgot he even did it."

"Well, there's no doubt that you were his world."

"He was mine, too." I sigh as I grab a few tissues. "Oh, Ray," I gasp, realizing how my words might affect him.

"Becs, it's okay. I know you feel the same way about me." He pulls me closer.

"I do." I snuggle into his arms.

"Ready?" he asks. I nod and he fast-forwards through the commercials. The show fades back in with home videos of Grayson, Morgan, and me—various ones from when she was born up until before his death.

"Not really a side of Grayson James that many people saw," Barbara states.

"No. We teased each other a lot, but our daughter really brought his goofy side out," I say, tears in my eyes as I watch the video on-screen.

"What happened? Walk us through those last few days." Barbara leans in.

"Um ... well, Barbara, what most people don't know is that two weeks before his plane exploded, I miscarried our second child." I'm quiet, looking down at my hands.

"No one knew? Did Grayson?" she asks.

"Oh yes, of course Grayson knew," I say quickly. "We were waiting until Christmas to tell everyone we were expecting. I was nine weeks along, and it was devastating for me. For both of us. I blamed myself, though, and it sent me into a depression. Grayson wanted to reschedule his book tour around Texas, but I wouldn't let him. He was able to cancel the last event due to a flooding situation at the store."

"So, instead of waiting, he booked the private jet to race back home to you." She finishes for me.

"Yes." I'm barely audible, my eyes glistening. Barbara gives me a moment to collect myself.

"Was hiring a private jet a common practice of Grayson's?"

"Never, Barbara. That was the first time he used one in the almost seven years I was with him. Grayson was more of the parsimonious type. We weren't flashy people, and we didn't take on

unnecessary expenses without serious justification."

"You were his justification." Barbara gives me her famous poker-faced stare as she states the question that's meant to be asked.

"Persistent as always," I say.

"Very persistent," she agrees. "When we return, life after Grayson James and what Becca is doing now," she narrates before the picture fades.

Ray fast-forwards again until it's back on.

"Tonight we are sitting with Becca James, widow of international best-selling author Grayson James in her first interview. So young and so very much in love. Their love was one worthy of fairy-tale status. But their happily ever after came to a close far sooner than any fairy-tale ending would suggest. On December 23, 2005, the private jet Grayson James chartered exploded an hour after takeoff," Barbara narrates as they show pictures of Grayson, Grayson and me, and then all three of us.

"You lost your baby, then two weeks later, your husband," Barbara starts. "What got you through?"

"One can only imagine how I blamed myself, Barbara. I was the reason he went. I was the reason he came back early. The guilt was ... unbearable." I start crying again.

"How old were you, Becca?" she asks.

"Twenty-eight," I say, pulling myself together. "To answer your question, my daughter got me through. I put all my focus into her. Grayson's mom, my best friend Stacey, and Grayson's best friend Derek were all there for me. I had a wonderful support system. But the trauma was so severe." I shake my head to push the tears away.

"You were diagnosed with PTSD."

"Yes, I was."

"When?"

"Two years after—maybe a little more."

"People hear of PTSD and they think mainly of military men and women who were in combat," she says.

"Yes, it's most often associated with people who have been in battle. But Barbara, some of the greatest battles people fight are the ones without guns in their hands."

"For those who don't know, what is PTSD, and how did it affect you?"

"Post-traumatic stress disorder. For me, it suppressed my ability to form certain short-term memories."

"Well, let's come back to that in a moment. In the meantime, what did you do after Grayson's death?" She leans forward again.

"I dodged the media for six months, then moved back to the East Coast. Being in our house was just too painful. I needed to get away." I take in a deep breath.

"So you opened a bed-and-breakfast in New Hampshire." She smiles.

"I did—one that caters to scrapbookers on crop weekends." I smile.

"Something else happened after you moved back." Barbara verbally nudges me.

"Yes. I met Ray McNeil."

"Your husband?"

"Yes." My face lights up.

Ray tightens his arms around me again.

"When we come back, we'll meet Becca's husband, Ray McNeil, and hear about how they met and fell in love. We'll also discuss her PTSD and how it affected their relationship, and the fateful accident that changed their lives. Stay with us."

"You okay, baby? Do you need a break?"

"I'm going to get more wine," is my answer. He grabs my empty wineglass.

"I'll get it, Becs." He kisses my cheek and climbs out from behind me.

The house phone rings and I grab it quickly to avoid waking the twins.

"Hey, Stace!" I answer, glad I checked the caller ID.

"Oh, Becca, you did so well! I cried so much." Her voice is so sincere; I can practically feel her hug through the phone.

"Thanks. Yeah, we haven't finished it yet. Started late and had to take two breaks," I say, looking over at the paused TV. I hear Cole fussing in the background. "What's wrong with my godson?" I ask, suddenly concerned. He's not usually up this late.

"Oh, he's coming down with something," she says. "Has a ... Cole Edward Bergman! *Damn it!*" she snaps, and he cries more.

"What happened?"

"He hit the medicine out of my hand," she says, sighing with frustration. "Would I be a rotten mother if I say I feel sorrier for myself?" she asks. I hear her shush him.

"No, not at all. It's draining when they're sick or teething. I'd offer to give you a break, but I don't need my two getting sick, especially with Ray traveling so much." I stand and stretch.

"Well, I hate to tell you this, but now that his work got national recognition from this broadcast, his firm will be booked solid for the next ten years!"

"I don't know how much more they can handle. Ever since the *Digest* named him one of the top ten architects on the East Coast, we've both been crazy busy! I don't have to tell you that," I say with a laugh. Ray and I hired Stacey a year ago as our companies' public-relations manager.

"No, you don't," she agrees. I feel Ray's hands on my hips.

"Stace, can I call you tomorrow? Ray and I want to finish watching this."

"Yeah, I gotta go to bed anyhow. Cole better sleep through the night, or I'm checking in at the inn!"

I can hear her exhaustion, and it makes me feel terrible. We say our good nights and hang up.

"Was that Stace?"

"Yeah, Cole's sick and she's at her wit's end," I say.

"Why isn't Max helping her? She's pregnant," Ray snaps.

Ray and Max get along all right, but never really "clicked." Max was very fond of Grayson, and he has a difficult time with change. I can understand that, but Ray's been in my life for over seven years now. The warranty on Max's difficulty with the situation ran out ... like five years ago. Seriously, dude, get over it!

"In his defense, he's in Florida visiting his sick father."

"Becs, he might as well be in Florida when he's here!" Ray rolls his eyes.

"Stop it. Come on, let's finish watching." I pull his arm and lead him over to the couch.

"You know, I'm not really mad at Max. I'm mad at myself." He sits and props his elbows on his knees, then places his head in his hands. I rub his back. "I hate being away from you guys so much, babe. It sucks!" He sighs and looks forward. "I mean, the money is rolling in like crazy, but it doesn't make it any easier. I've got to figure out a better way to do this. If I'm not flying to be with clients, I'm spending my time designing for them."

I can't disagree with him. This is the first time I've seen him in five days.

"Maybe you need to do more video conferencing," I suggest.

"I do—when clients are set up for it. Besides, I have to bring them their plans."

"Hire a courier and go over it via conference call," I tell him for the millionth time.

"Everyone wants me in the flesh now that I'm sought after. I just have to cut back on projects." He leans back. *Yeah right, he won't do that!* "Why are you making that face?" He smirks because he *knows* why. "I promise, Becs, I'm going to add to my team. I can't do it all myself anymore." He pulls me back down between his legs. "No more talking," he says softly in my ear as he presses play. I take a long sip of my wine. "That's it, baby ... drink up."

"You're insatiable, McNeil!" I slap his roaming hand.

"Shh. Pay attention."

I look up and see Barbara, Ray, and me.

"So, tell me. How did you two meet?" Barbara asks.

I look over at Ray and nod. He explains that we met at parent-teacher night. We clicked right away—so much so that we went on our first date that very night.

Did you have any idea you would end up together?" She looks to both of us, but focuses mostly on Ray.

"Oh, I knew that night!" he says quickly. "I woke my poor mother out of a sound sleep at two in the morning."

"And what did you say to her?"

"I said, 'Mama, I've just met the woman I'm going to marry! You're going to love her!'"

"Becca, you're looking at Ray strangely. Why?"

"He never told me that."

Ray winks and smiles shyly at me.

"So, you had your first date."

"Best first date ever," Ray says. I nod, smiling.

"Completely smitten?" Barbara asks. She's smiling, too.

"Completely," Ray agrees. "Couldn't wait to see her again."

"When did you see her again?"

"Next day. Our girls had a playdate."

"And?" Barbara encourages.

"And ... nothing. Lights out," Ray says. His eyes go wide.

"What do you mean?"

"I went to kiss her and she flipped out. I mentioned our kiss the

night before, and she looked at me like I had five heads. Told me I must've had too much to drink, because we certainly didn't kiss. Oh, but she was glad I got home from the pub safely." Ray looks over at me as I chuckle.

"What did you do?" Barbara asks.

"Her best friend, Stacey, was visiting her," Ray continues. She pulled me aside to talk." He takes a sip of water and explains the conversation he had with her, our five-year relationship, and what he had to put up with.

"Five years," Barbara says in disbelief. "How did you manage?"

"I fell deeply in love with her. It wasn't easy. I tried to walk away, but I missed her every time. She's the air that I breathe. It was more painful to be without her." Ray lifts my hand and kisses it. "I always felt hopeful that one day it wouldn't be like that anymore," he adds.

"What happened September 22, 2012?" Barbara asks, keeping a steady gaze on both of us. Ray nods at me.

"Um, I woke up in Ray's bed, completely naked. Completely freaked out."

"What did you do, Ray?"

"Tried to comfort her, to get her to accept that it was okay."

"Didn't work." She offers a slight smile.

"Nope. We argued all the way downstairs and outside. Becca tried to leave, but her truck's battery was completely dead. I had to drive her home."

"You never made it, though."

"No. We were so busy arguing, I didn't see the dump truck coming." Ray shakes his head at the memory.

"You were almost pronounced dead at the scene," Barbara says to me.

"Yes." I nod.

"I begged them to try one more time," Ray interjects.

"You saved her life." Barbara smiles warmly, and Ray takes in a sharp breath.

"In more ways than one, Barbara," I say. I smile at Ray; his eyes are filling up, just like mine.

"The EMTs saved her," he says, shaking away his emotion.

"Yes, but only because," she pauses, *"they followed your lead."*

I look toward Ray. His eyes are wet with unshed tears. I kiss his cheek and squeeze his arms to me.

"You survived, but you were in a coma."

"Yes."

"How long?"

"Three months."

"When we come back, we'll hear about Becca's and Ray's separate journeys during Becca's coma, and how and why their life changed when she woke up."

"You okay?" I turn to him again when he pauses the TV.

"Christ! She really does make everyone cry," Ray says, looking angry with himself.

"Ray, that was a very scary memory to relive. It was traumatic."

"I still think about that day all of the time. Jesus, baby, if they didn't take pity on me and shock you one last time ... you ... our boys ... " He exhales through pursed lips.

"They did. We're here. We're safe, and it's all because of you." I turn completely around to kneel between his legs and palm his face. "Damn, you're handsome." I bite my bottom lip as I take the sight of him in. I lean in and brush my lips against his.

"Are you trying for an intermission here, baby?" he asks before he attacks my lips, rendering me breathless. I find it so difficult to pull away from him. Death grip followed by wandering hands, then erratic breathing. *Damn*. Even after seven years, we're still completely hot for each other.

"C'mon, Ray." I turn my head. "Let's finish watching. Then you, sir, may have my full and complete attention." I look back and tap his lips with my right index finger. He bites at it playfully as he gives my bum a good squeeze.

"Ugh! Becs, can't we finish it tomorrow? I haven't seen you, touched you, for five whole days." He gives me his best pouty face.

"And you survived. Imagine that." I look at him in disbelief. "Twenty more minutes, sweetie, and I promise, you'll have one—hot—very—hot—evening with your wife," I say between kisses.

"It's always hot with you, baby." He smiles against my lips.

"Well, then, you know you won't be disappointed with your reward for waiting a whole 'nother twenty minutes." I nudge his nose with mine.

"All right, turn around," he says. I raise a playful brow. "To watch the rest of the show," he clarifies, patting my bum. "You've got a dirty mind there, Mrs. McNeil." He smirks.

"Well, a dirty mind is a terrible thing to wash," I say thoughtfully.

"I agree. I love that dirty mind of yours." He hugs me tightly to him as I reseat myself, then grabs the remote and fast-forwards.

"After the almost-fatal car crash, Becca James spent three months in a coma at Massachusetts General Hospital," Barbara narrates, showing a picture of me in the hospital bed right after the accident.

I cringe at how bad I looked.

"Ray." She focuses on him. *"What was life like for you?"*

"Hell," he says quietly and runs a hand through his hair. *"The love of my life was lying defenseless in a hospital bed. I sat next to*

her, waiting and praying. The longer she was in the coma, the worse the prognosis looked."

"Her prognosis did take a surprising change in November." Barbara looks like she wants to smile as she eggs him on. Ray gives a shy smile and a nod. "What did the doctors tell you about Becca's condition? What changed?"

"They told me she was pregnant with twins."

"Now you had three to worry about." Barbara's eyes widen to match Ray's. He nods. She then talks to Ray about how he kept vigilance at my side the entire three months, allowing his business to suffer. "Becca," she turns her attention to me once again, "physically, you were lying in your hospital bed, but that's not where you were ... should we say spiritually, emotionally ... what?" she asks, seemingly unsure of how to describe my state.

"Well, let's just say I was busy taking a trip down memory lane."

Before the interview, Ray and I discussed what I would say. We decided it would be best to tell a different—possibly more believable—version of what happened in my subconscious. We didn't need the world thinking I was off my rocker. Besides, if I ever decide to pursue writing, what an awesome "fictional" story would that make?!

"How so?" Barbara shifts in her seat.

"Basically, it was like a movie. All of my memories with Ray came back. Everything I had forgotten or repressed resurfaced. I remembered." I smile sheepishly at Ray.

"What happened at the end, right before you woke up?" She squints a little, encouraging me.

"Grayson came up from behind me and grabbed my hand. He told me how proud he was, and how much he loved Morgan and me." My chin quivers.

"What else did he say?"

"That he will always love me and that he wants me to be happy. That I should enjoy the rest of my life with Ray."

"Do you find a lot of people rolling their eyes at your story?"

"No, but then again, I've only told a handful of people." Now I shift in my seat. *"I'm sure there will be people who don't believe me, but I don't care. I got to say goodbye to my husband, the man I loved so very deeply. I never got to do that in real life, and I needed the closure. He gave me his blessing, and that's all I care about. That's what matters to me."*

"Becca got something else, too," Barbara narrates. *"She came out of the coma remembering her relationship with Ray, and was even aware of her pregnancy. When we come back, we'll find out how Ray and Becca put all of the pieces of their five-year history together and where they are now."*

Ray wastes no time fast-forwarding once the show fades to a commercial. When it comes back, we're walking with Barbara along the pathway to the new portion of the inn and talking about all of the issues we faced when I woke up.

"Le Maison de Montreal," Barbara reads aloud as we approach Ray's beautiful creation. *"Amazing. So warm and inviting ... enchanting, really. Such detail."* She looks around inside. *"This must've been quite the undertaking,"* she says to Ray.

"On more levels than one can imagine," he replies. *"This was the most important project of my life. Becca gave me full carte blanche. I wanted to design something that spoke to us and captured our essence."* We continue to give her the tour, making sure to stop at *"Boulangerie de Grand-Mère"* for some delectable treats.

"Grandma's Bakery?" Barbara asks before Hazel and Elise, the proud owners, come out to greet her.

Hazel and Elise approached Ray and I when we were preparing to advertise the space in the building for small, tourist-friendly businesses. It was actually more of a presentation—an over-the-top presentation. They had the girls help create a plethora of charts and pictures to showcase why their business plan would succeed. Ray gave me a quick wink and we sat back to listen. Miraculously, our stolid expressions remained intact as they nattered on about the French bakery they wanted to open.

I came across some of the "charts" a few weeks earlier in the girls' room. I put everything back the way it was and immediately called Ray.

"Hey, baby, everything all right?" His usual greeting for whenever I call him shortly after he's left for work.

"Uh, yeah. You got a minute, sweetie?" I spoke softly before peeking into the twins' room to make sure they were still napping.

"Yeah, I just pulled up to the inn. What's going on, Becs?" I could hear him shuffling papers around, meaning he didn't put the manila folder right into his briefcase when he got into the truck, like I told him to. I rolled my eyes instead of mentioning it. I knew he had a lot going on that day, what with all of the inspections scheduled. He didn't need my nagging on top of it.

"I stumbled upon some information that tells me we already have some interest in one of the shops that'll be available." What fun would it be, stating what I know from the start? None, I tell you!

"Really? That's great! What is it, and who's interested? Shit!" He added the last word under his breath.

"Drop something?" I asked. I was sure something had fallen to the truck floor again.

"Yeah," he said. "I got it. Go ahead." I could hear the clasp lock on his briefcase.

"Good thing you put that folder right in your briefcase like I suggested. I'd hate to think what kind of mess would've ensued if all of those papers flew out everywhere," I said nonchalantly. I tried to hold back, but I just couldn't help myself.

Ray laughed. "I'm pretty sure it would've been cringe-worthy, with an elongated *Faaaccckkk* added for emphasis."

"Good thing you always listen to me, McNeil." I smiled and shook my head as I walked down the stairs.

"Yup, always." I could sense his smile. "So, tell me what you know, baby. I've got to head in."

"Sorry," I said quickly as I sat on the couch, curling my legs beneath me. "It's a French bakery, or so I presume. It's called *Boulangerie de Grand-Mère*. Simply: Grandma's Bakery."

"Well, that's cool! It sticks with the whole Montreal motif," he said.

"Yep," I said. "Any idea who the *Grand-Mères* may be?"

"No," he stated. I could hear him open the truck door. He didn't even think about it!

"Really?"

"No, babe—who?" he asked impatiently as he slammed the door.

"Why, none other than *Grand-Mère* Elise and *Grand-Mère* Hazel." I sighed, ignoring his impatience.

"You're kidding?" He almost laughed. I continued on to tell him what I found in the girls' room. "You know, now that I think about it, the four of them have been having lots of hushed conversations lately. I thought they were just planning a surprise for us."

"Hmm. Well, what do you think about it?"

"Actually, I think it's good. We'll talk about it tonight. I'm sure there will be more pros than cons. Baby, I'm sorry, I've got to go," he said quickly. I could hear some of the guys nearby asking him questions.

"Go ahead. I love you. See you tonight." I heard one of the boys over the monitor, which hastened my need to get off the phone as well.

"Love you, too! Bye, babe," he said before hanging up.

That night, we did discuss it, and compiled a pros and cons list. Ray was right—there were more pros. First, Hazel and Elise both cook and bake like nobody's business. There would be no problem gaining interest in their product, we were sure of that. Second, they would be responsible for their upkeep and rental payments which, of course, we wouldn't want to charge them. However, we knew they wouldn't hear of us giving them space rent-free. Thirdly, it would mean Elise and Artie possibly giving in to the idea of living with us on a more permanent basis and treating their house in Maine more like a vacation home.

Ray's men had just put the finishing touches on the in-law suite he built off of our house for them. They would have their own entrance and privacy, leaving us with ours. He offered to build one for Hazel on the other side of the house, but she declined.

Charlie proposed to her in the spring and she said yes. In response to this wonderful news, I clasped my hands together, looked up, and said, "*Finally!*" I was, and still am, certain that a divine intervention took place. Put that in your hat, Hazel!

Charlie owns a small, cottage-style house not ten minutes away from us. We helped Hazel move there before the babies were born. Of course, Ray being Ray, he went through the house with his guys, making a list of all the maintenance and repairs that he needed to make. Free of charge—against Charlie's wishes. It was Ray's way of apologizing again to Hazel. He vowed that he'd always take care of her in honor of Grayson—and my love for her, of course. They've become quite close again, and she adores the fact that he calls her 'Mum.'

Yes, Hazel and Elise are now quite the dynamic duo! They became friendly over the years, but my being in a coma solidified their friendship on a level it may never have reached had that not happened. Now they're inseparable. They remind me of older versions of Stacey and me.

"Eh." Ray cringed when they finally finished. "Don't take this the wrong way, MaMums." MaMums is what Ray started calling them when he had to address them simultaneously. He felt 'Mama and Mum' was too long-winded, so he smashed the two together. It's caught on, really; we all call them that when we're talking to them both. "Your business plan sounds wonderful, and Lord knows you two know your way around a kitchen, but ..." He trailed off.

"But what, son?" Elise asked, not hiding her disappointment.

"Becca and I have enough on our plate without worrying about complaints of nepotism! Besides, you girls are getting up there in years. Not really a good idea for you to start a new business."

Elise and Hazel both gasped. I decided to join Ray in his raillery efforts.

"If we're going to be honest here," I began, "yes, you two know your way around a kitchen. Ray knows his way around a kitchen too, but it doesn't mean he should cook. Now, what you two make for the family is fine. We love you, so we eat what you put in front of us and smile to protect your feelings. This is a business though, ladies, and while what we're saying may seem harsh, it's meant to protect you from embarrassment. I don't think anyone will buy your baked goods." I looked down at my hands.

"Baby, they'll buy them ... they just won't come back for more," Ray added. He and I looked up at them again, and I felt the urge to run and get my camera. To make one of these ladies speechless was quite the feat, but to get the pair of 'em in that state at the same time was nothing short of a phenomenon! I was sure it would never happen again, like witnessing a total solar eclipse in your lifetime.

For several minutes—which actually felt like hours—the deafening silence became a test of wills between the four of us.

Artie and Charlie entered the room. "How are things going in here?"

"You were right, Artie." Elise slowly turned her head to him. I could've sworn I saw steam escaping her ears. "Our son is an asshole!" she stated in a matter-of-fact tone.

Ray pretended to be hurt. "Mama, that's not a very nice thing to say about your son. Or your landlord, for that matter."

"What?" Hazel finally spoke up. I gave in to my girlish need to giggle. "Why are you laughing?" She looked to me with noticeable irritation.

"Maybe you ladies should change the name of the bakery from *Boulangerie de Grand-Mère* to *Boulangerie de Credules*." I laughed. "You are both so gullible!"

"Is that what that means, baby?" Ray smiled my way. I nodded, having another laugh.

"You two are awful!" Elise yelled, but smiled in spite of herself. They both started flinging markers at our heads when we gave into the fit of laughter we tried to bury.

"Mmm ... delicious." Barbara groans with delight. We bid Hazel and Elise adieu and continue our tour of the shops. We get coffee from the Java Café, sister to the town's Java Joint. The Mini Mad Scrapper is next, where Morgan and Annie present Barbara with a bag full of scrapbooking supplies for her to start an album. Next, we come up to The Book Nook, which, of course, carries all of Grayson's books, as well as those by many other wonderful authors. Barbara picks up her book, Audition. *"I heard this is a wonderful read." She smiles.*

"Only the best in this shop," I say with a wink. Finally, we arrive at the shop Ray and I are most proud of and excited to talk about.

"Back to Basics." Barbara reads the sign aloud before we walk in. The works and talents of some local and not-so-local hands greet us. There are quilts, knitted and crotched blankets, sweaters, and hats ... you name it. There are hand-carved cabinets, shelves, and even toys by Eddie Lewis, who does woodworking as his pastime. We have jams and preserves from Elsie Cartwright. We even have pure maple syrup from a local farm. "A quaint little craft store,"

Barbara notes as she admires a baby sweater that my own Aunt Tess made.

"It's so much more than that, Barbara." I smile.

"Oh?" She focuses her gaze on me.

"Well, when Ray and I decided to renovate the inn, we got to talking about how many jobs would come of it." I glance over to him and he nods for me to continue. "That conversation led to one about getting the community involved in helping each other out during these difficult economic times. So we met with the Mayor and had a town meeting. Ray and I, along with many others, started the Back to Basics Foundation locally. Basically, we involved everyone we could in creating a plan of action to get people back on their feet, or at least lighten their burden. A town local and friend of ours, Reggie Smith, created a program to help us."

I stop, noting Barbara's need to interject.

"What does this program do?" She smiles—I think she's thanking me for providing her the window to ask. I can be quite the chatterbox when discussing something I'm passionate about.

"It's a wonderful program. The best way to explain it is to give you an example," I start. She nods. "Okay. So say, Barbara, you are an avid gardener and have a wonderful garden filled with vegetables or herbs, maybe both. But, hypothetically of course, you don't have the money to make repairs on your home or car. Now, you come to me. I'm a single mother who barely makes ends meet. There's only so much my coupon clipping will do, and coupons for vegetables and fresh herbs are a rarity. Thankfully, you've given me enough vegetables and herbs over the summer for me to freeze a portion of them for winter. You've helped me out quite a bit. I'd help you, but I can't do any of the things you need done. Sorry, Barbara." I pat her hand gently. "What I can do is help Ray. He's a bachelor, and with that title usually comes the need for a home-cooked meal here and there, a dusting of his house, possibly his clothes leaving the washer machine the same color they went in. I can do that! I

don't even have to worry about my kids, because I've received free babysitting services from someone else while I help Ray out. By the way, Barbara, you're in luck!" I throw my hands up with enthusiasm. "Ray is quite the handyman, and he's been popping in on the weekends, crossing off one or two items off your to-do list while I'm working at his house. I may even be leaving him a casserole or quiche with your wonderful vegetables in it! That's the Foundation's plan. We're all learning how to scratch each other's backs." You can see the pride beaming from my face.

"What a wonderful idea! So ... this store?" she asks.

"Everything you see in here was handmade or donated by locals. Some are even from other states! People involved in the program run the store, and all proceeds go to help families with their everyday bills, mortgages—whatever they need. We don't charge rent and everyone who works volunteers their time," Ray explains.

"You've gotten a lot of recognition for your efforts. Other communities have been asking you about the program."

"Yes! That makes it even more rewarding. To see people in other areas taking a page from our book. Well, really ... it's quite the accomplishment to all of us involved." My eyes fill with tears.

"It's also a well-deserved compliment. In talking to many locals, we've heard quite the buzz around town about you two. Talk of you running for mayor, Ray, when Mayor Brewster's term is up." She smiles, as if she knows she'll catch Ray off guard.

"Uh ... yes. I have been approached about it." His smile implies he's both shy and embarrassed. "While I'm flattered, I know that right now would not be a good time for me, personally, to take on such an endeavor."

She brings her attention to me. "You're frowning, Becca."

"Yes."

"Why?"

"Well, Ray's right. It's not a good time. That's what I find so disappointing, because he'd make a hell of a mayor. Who knows,

though? Maybe in the future?"

I smile at him, my pride again beaming off my face.

"Well, being recognized as one of Architectural Digest*'s top ten architects on the East Coast is nothing to scoff at, and has probably demanded your attention as much, if not more, than any political office." She plugs Ray's accomplishment as we leave the shop—not that he needed it.*

"Yes, it's a wonderful burden," he says.

"I'm sure many people tonight will find your story encouraging in so many ways. You went through so much, and yet you're able to leave an amazing legacy for your children." She smiles as Morgan and Annie approach us with the boys. "Speaking of children, we've met your darling daughters already, but your sons have yet to be introduced."

"Barbara," Ray starts. "I'd like for you to meet Grayson Arthur McNeil." He puts Gracie's hand out to wave at Barbara. Her eyes widen.

"This is Troy Everett McNeil," I say, making Troy wave as well. He immediately goes for her necklace. Gracie follows suit, but finds her earring more interesting.

"They're beautiful. Look at their curly brown hair. Hi. Yes, hi!" She gives them her attention. "You know I'm going to ask, because many people besides me would want to know. Grayson? How did that come about, and how does that make you feel, Ray?"

"I named him," Ray states. "It was ... is ... an honor to name our son after him. He was a great man." Ray kisses Gracie's cheek. Barbara turns to me.

"Becca, what, if any, reservations did you have?"

"None. I didn't have a chance." I laugh. "He named him in the delivery room. He asked me if he could name our firstborn. I knew the middle name would be after his father, but I didn't know the first name until delivery. Of course, I reminded him of my power of veto if I didn't like it."

"No need for a veto?" She plays with Troy's hand.

"No. It was the most powerful, overwhelming moment for me. I am married to an amazingly wonderful man." I look to Ray again, my eyes glistening.

On the couch, Ray hugs me tightly.

"I think he may feel the same way about you, dear. Call it a hunch." She winks at me.

"You think?" I laugh.

Barbara is back in the studio. "Yes I do, Becca," she answers, then looks away from me and begins to narrate. "I can't begin to tell you what a pleasure it was to interview Becca James McNeil and her lovely family. They are truly an inspiration to us all. We wish them the best and only the happiest of times ahead. If you would like more information about the Back to Basics Foundation, please con-tact them at the number or email address below. Good night, and thank you for watching. I'm Barbara Walters, and this is 20/20."

Ray hits the power button and the screen goes black.

"I'm proud of the message we sent." I turn my face to his.

"I was just thinking the same thing, baby. I'm sure the phones at Back to Basics will be inundated with calls tomorrow." He kisses my temple.

"How awesome would that be?" I ask, in awe at the possibility. We sit back, marinating in the idea for two whole minutes before the green dots on the baby monitor all light up frantically, complementing the effects of the sudden screaming wail blaring from it.

Ray jumps. "What the ...?"

"Shit, guess that answers my earlier suspicion." I exhale forcefully and shake my head as I get up.

"What? Are they getting sick?" Ray stands up with me and turns off the lamp.

"No. Troy must be getting his two-year molars." I sigh and head straight out of the family room and up the stairs. Ray follows me as I open the door to the boys' room. Troy is standing in his crib, a pacifier dangling from his mouth even through his painful cries.

"Mama!" he sobs, lifting his arms for me with a binky tightly fisted in each hand.

"Aw, poor baby." I pout and pick him up to bring him to the changing table.

"Here, baby," Ray says softly behind me, placing the infant Motrin on the flat, raised surface to my right.

"Thanks," I say as I start working on getting a dose ready.

"Hey, buddy," Ray says, caressing Troy's cheek softly. Troy responds with a whimper. "Shh, shh ... Mama will make it all better, she always does," he tells him, and then kisses at my neck. *Country Sybecca whips her shirt off, deciding spit-up stains and "God knows what else" stains are, in fact, not sexy!* Ray nuzzles into my neck, releasing an appreciative sigh. *Country Sybecca pulls several Cheerios (now of various flavors) out of her hair. Cautionary Sybecca whips a medicine bottle at Country Sybecca's head. Her ticker board reads: FOCUS BEFORE YOU OVERDOSE YOUR CHILD!!!*

Shit! I shake my head to refocus and double-check the dosage before I give it to him. He sucks on the syringe and immediately calms down. My son is a genius; he knows yummy, sugary grape-flavored stuff equals pain relief! I wipe his face and change him while Ray checks in on Gracie.

"This kid can sleep through anything," Ray says, shaking his head. "Just like his mother," he adds. I can tell he's smirking.

"Well, that's not entirely true, now is it?" I turn with Troy in my arms and an eyebrow arched. Ray's boyish grin proudly stakes its claim on his face.

"No, it isn't. There are definitely some things you and your salacious appetite wake eagerly for." Signature wink and air kiss ensue.

"Pot-kettle, sweetie." I smile while laying Troy back down and kissing his head. He flips onto his belly and tucks his knees beneath him. His cute little butt sticks up into the air.

"Comfy, Troy?" Ray asks softly, sweeping the baby's loose curls away from his eyes. "Yes ... Mommy likes that position, too," he adds.

"You are just beyond ridiculous, McNeil!" I gasp, appalled. I slap his chest for good measure.

"You got some bite to back up that bark, baby?" he asks in that tone that always gets me. His mouth against my ear, he nips playfully at my earlobe for emphasis. My breath hitches before shifting to a more erratic tempo. I gave up the search for willpower a long time ago!

Ray hooks a couple of fingers in my back pocket as he begins walking backward and tugging me along with him. "Come," he commands in that tone that makes me need a panty change.

"Oh, I fully intend to, McNeil." I hold my smile back and grab his hand, following his lead out of the room.

"Do you, now?" He smirks and pulls me to him.

"Mmm-hmm." I let out a small, nervous giggle. I can't believe he still affects me like this.

"Shh." He places his thumb on my lips as he reaches his other hand past my hip to grab the knob, closing the door to their room. My back is against the door. Ray stares at me intently, stormy ocean to emerald sea. After a beat, his face takes on a more somber look.

"Ray ... what is it?" I ask as his thumb softly caresses my cheek.

He places a prolonged kiss on my forehead. "C'mon, baby," he says, grabbing my hand and leading me once more to our room.

"What, sweetie? What are you thinking?" I press further as we enter our room.

"Do you have a crop planned for this weekend?" He tugs at the hem of my shirt.

"No. Why?" I tilt my head sideways, trying to figure him out.

"I'm clearing my schedule. We're going away for the week-end—don't argue!" he states vehemently, pulling my shirt off.

"Uh ... well," I start, my finger fidgeting with the buttons on his shirt.

"Becs, no!" he snaps. "The boys are twenty months old—enough is enough! I need time with my wife!" His hands squeeze my hips emphatically.

I guess I have been somewhat ridiculous in this department, but it's not entirely my fault. We've been too busy. The *both* of us!

"You're right. This weekend it is." I nod with a half smile and finally manage to get some buttons undone.

"No canceling at the last minute, either." He chucks my chin. Eh, I *have* done that the last three times he's tried to take me away.

"I won't. I promise."

I wrap my arms around his neck.

"Damn straight! I won't cave in—so don't even think about it! No tears. No *But, Ray*s," he says between kisses.

"I said I promise." I give him a playful pout, then widen my eyes. "I know just the place for us to go!" I enthusiastically tap his shoulder.

"Where?" He humors me, but I see caution in his eyes.

"It's a nice bed-and-breakfast not too far from here. Everyone I know raves about it."

"Really?" He plays along.

I smile. "Yes. They've recently added on a whole other building that is positively gorgeous! I think it was recently showcased on a 20/20 special."

"You don't say?" He smirks while running his index finger across my skin, just above the waist of my pants. My heart triples its beat, causing quite the ruckus in my eardrums.

"Yeah ... apparently the owner is quite the woman."

"Quite," he says.

"Her husband is a very attractive, capable man, whose many talents extend generously to the bedroom." My eyes scan his face. I run my tongue along my upper lip before biting down on my lower one. He pops the button of my jeans open.

"I'm sure his generosity is due to the fact that his wife comes so sweetly for him." My breath hitches at his words. *Christ, he is so hot! Country Sybecca is on her back, dry-humping the air and pulling her pigtails whilst coming undone.* "Gasping already, babe? I've barely touched you." He touches my face and teases my lips with his, taking forever to let their full weight press down onto mine. As if someone walked into the room and flipped a switch, the small fire we were slowly building becomes an inferno. An involuntary five-day separation is proving to be quite the explosive fuel. Our clothes fly off, hastily landing in random places as my backside greets various places in the room—the dresser, the side of his armoire, and a final thrust into the wall. I rip my mouth away from his in a panic when his arm hits a framed picture on the wall—we both catch it in time. Ray grabs it and tosses it onto the cream plush chair.

"Baby, enough with the choreography. Put me on the bed," I manage to say as he bites down my neck.

"Yes, ma'am!"

He smiles against my neck and turns with me wrapped around him, bringing us to the bed. We collapse onto it (without an ounce of grace, may I add).

"Shh, shh ..." Ray's thumb finds my lips again to stifle my laughter. I stare into his playful, amused eyes and I feel myself fall for him all over again. I may not be "Lucy" anymore, but the essence of her is still very present in my feelings for him. Everything still seems new to me, at least sometimes. Ray softly nudges my nose before his lips fall to mine, collecting them again. "Christ—I've missed the hell out of you, baby," he says, breathing against my lips.

His mouth travels down my jawline and onto my neck. Our

hands meet and our fingers lace. Ray guides our clasped hands up to either side of my head. He puts his full weight on them, forcing them to sink into the mattress as he shifts himself to carefully enter me. My head arches from the fullness. "Oh, Becs ... you feel so good, baby." He nips at the skin right behind my earlobe. "Breathe, baby," he whispers. Like magic, I finally exhale. Ray pulls his hips back ever so slowly. I squeeze his hands hard, bracing myself. Before my lungs expand to full capacity, Ray slams into me harshly, knocking the attempt to inhale out of me. My head pops back quickly, giving him access to my neck again. He pulls back only once he's certain he's filled me to the max.

Ray and I have many different ways we make love, depending on our mood. We've even dubbed some of them with specific names. This right here is the "Rolling Thunder." I'm the one who named it that, because it reminds me of my favorite wooden roller coaster at Great Adventure (Six Flags Great Adventure, to anyone born after Generation X). The slow climb, the hitch and bucking of the break, the lingering at the top, the thrilling anticipation through-out. It's intense and harsh, rattling every bone in your body with a delicious delight that makes you want to stay on forever.

"Please, baby, please." I finally beg him. The lingering-at-the-top part is driving me mad.

"Ready? You want it?" He bites at my earlobe.

"Mmm-hmm." I turn my head and attack his lips. His hips roll skillfully into me at a aggressive, relentless pace. "Yes, Ray, yes!" I cry as I quickly rise. The tingling deep inside gets stronger, almost too intense for me to bear.

"No, baby ... you're not going anywhere." Ray pushes down harder on my hands as he slows his pace. Apparently, I was trying to escape the intensity, as usual. He rolls his hips again, and the spark from the friction sets my body ablaze—I'm wild beneath him. Ray's mouth crashes into mine to quiet my sounds. His hand re-leases mine to touch my face. I grasp his hair to steady him, my tongue meticulously caressing his. I tighten around him fiercely, causing an increase in my own pleasure as I bring him past the point of no return. Ray pulls his face back, scrunching his nose at the intensity of his orgasm.

"God, Becs," he groans.

The tip of his tongue curls and holds its position over his top teeth.

"Mmm ... Ray," I moan lightly as he spills inside me. It always feels so good.

One last pump and Ray collapses on top of me. Gradually, his breath returns to a normal rate. When he raises his head to look into my eyes, I push his damp hair off his forehead before leaning up for a kiss. He leisurely pulls out, watching me wince—and his usual satisfied smirk graces his face.

"We're not staying at the inn," he says, finally speaking up.

"Where are we going?" I ask, strumming my index finger up and down over his bottom lip.

"It's a surprise."

He kisses my finger and rests his head against my chest.

"Can't wait." I try to hide my reservations in leaving the twins for a whole weekend.

"Ugh ... terrible liar." He rolls onto his back, pulling me toward him. "But I do appreciate you trying to sound sure about leaving the boys." He squeezes me.

I look at him. "How far away will we be?"

"Nope, not telling you. Now get some sleep, baby. We've got a busy day tomorrow."

He leans in for a kiss. I lay my head back down, trying to think about where he'll take me. Probably Maine. Satisfied with my conclusion, I give in to a much-needed deep sleep.

RAY

One week later ...

"Becca ... stop it, baby. They'll be fine." I try again. She continues staring out the window, tears streaming down her face. Christ! I wish they would get this plane down the runway already! "Baby, c'mon." I caress her cheek with the back of my index finger.

"Ray, please—I'm so mad," she says, closing her eyes.

"It's two nights, Becca! Jesus!" I can't help but snap at her. She's completely overreacting!

"Yes, Ray, two nights, but Tennessee?!" She holds her hands out in disbelief.

I rest my head back and exhale deeply as our plane finally heads down the runway. I'm just gonna keep my mouth shut and let Tropical Storm Becca blow over. Hopefully her disposition will be better once she sees we're spending the weekend in Gatlinburg. She's men-tioned her interest in going there several times over the years. God, I hope she's not like this the entire weekend ...

"Ray ... baby, wake up." I open my eyes to find hers gazing at me. "We're about to land." She leans in and brushes my lips with hers. "I'm sorry," she adds in a whisper.

Christ, she's beautiful. She's as beautiful as the day I met her, if not more. I caress her cheek with my thumb and she leans into my touch. The way she is looking at me, I can't help but think of her on our wedding day.

I remember how my breath hitched at the sight of her when I lifted my eyes as the "Wedding March" began. Her gown was simple, yet so elegant. It was an ivory-colored vintage number, which went perfectly with the theme of our wedding.

Becca is truly amazing at planning weddings. It was her idea to do a vintage-style wedding, replicating the era of time we know our souls are from. It was so us—Mr. and Mrs. Cleaver. Even if most didn't know the meaning behind the theme, we did, and it made our wedding that much more special to us. Of course, no one but the people closest to us understood the *shoes are optional* part. Anyone who caught us at the alter, greeting each other's bare feet with our own, may have thought we both had foot fetishes. Alas, no one asked. But we felt some things were better left unexplained. It was our secret, private moment, and with almost two hundred people in attendance, we were glad to have it.

"Ray," she said, beginning her vows. "You are the beacon of light shining brightly, always guiding me home no matter how lost I am. You're the warmth that blankets my heart, keeping it on beat, safe, full of life. You're the guardian of my happiness, encouraging my laughter, making my eyes smile, the reason behind the goofy grin on my face—even when you're not in front of me. I cherish you. On so many different levels—it's hard to describe in words." Her voice trembled, but she pushed through. "I promise to love and cherish you today and for all our tomorrows. I promise to never forget to remember and remember to never forget how we got here and how deeply in love with you I am." Her tears finally released from the pools in her eyes and slipped slowly down her cheeks. I couldn't help but release her hands to thumb them away. She closed her eyes, relishing in my touch.

Reverend Johnson moved her through the regular vows. Then it was my turn, only I was still trying to pull myself together mentally. Her words squeezed around my heart, sending it up to my throat. I don't know what I was prepared to hear from that lovely mouth of hers, but it certainly wasn't what she said. Not that Becca ever falls short on saying the sweetest things to me, but to say all of that ... in front of all those people ... with barely a joke in sight to mask her discomfort—that's what floored me the most!

I was speechless. Not a good thing when I didn't bother to write my vows down. I'm never without words and I've certainly never had a problem articulating my feelings for Becca, no matter who was around. But there I stood before her, our guests silent as they anticipated my declaration of love, and I felt as if I couldn't even mutter my name. I looked at Becca with a sense of panic—stage fright, really. Becca hid her smile, shaking her head. Her eyes filled with warmth and humor at my situation. I could practically hear her thoughts, as if she were announcing them through a megaphone: "I told you not to wing it!" I suddenly felt myself relax and a chuckle escaped my mouth. Everyone chuckled with me. I'm not sure whom they were trying to make feel better in light of my awkwardness, themselves or me.

"Sorry." I looked out at the crowd. "It's hard to talk when the love of your life takes your breath away."

Becca gasped at my words, and I turned my focus back to her. Her nostrils were flaring to hold back her tears, just like they always do. I gave her my "sit and spin" look in the most loving fashion I could muster. Becca giggled and pushed at my hands as she squeezed them. Suddenly, my words—my feelings—came out of me like a freight train.

"It's always amazed me, your ability to do that. To take my breath away at the drop of a dime. I realized a long time ago—it's because you are the air that I breathe. Of course you have the ability—the power—to take it away. Since the first day I met you, you've filled me to capacity—my heart, my mind, my soul. You are my calm waters in the storm of life. You are my right when all things are going wrong. You are the reason behind the man I am today, and the man I will be tomorrow. Last but not least, you are the 'Lucy' to my Charlie Brown, the 'Lucy' to my Henry Roth, and the 'Lucy' to my Ricky Ricardo. In saying that, I promise to always come to you for advice, knowing it's worth more than the nickel you charge. I promise to always trust you blindly and try not to imagine you ever pulling the football away." I paused to let our guests finish their

slight laughter. "I promise to remind you every day that you love me by doing something to make you fall for me even more. Lastly, I promise to accept, if not encourage, your impulsive behavior, which sometimes gets you into precarious situations you weren't planning on. I promise to try to keep my irascibility at bay—knowing it'll all end up being some sort of silly misunderstanding in the end."

Becca's tears flowed again, this time from laughter.

"That's one of my favorite sounds in the world, baby—your laughter. I promise to work my hardest to make sure your laughter never fades, but only grows stronger and more frequent over the years. I love you, baby. I cherish you and I'm going to zip my lip now so I can get that ring on your finger. I can't wait another minute to call you my wife." I pressed my lips together and my heart practically exploded from a full-wattage Becca James (almost McNeil) smile.

Within the next few minutes, it was official. She was finally mine, after almost six years of waiting. I would've held her tighter during our kiss if it weren't for her protruding belly. Poor thing, she was seven months pregnant. I was so worried the day would exhaust her beyond what would be deemed acceptable. She was a trooper, though. I like to think it was her happiness that supplied her with all that energy.

A month later, our sons were born via C-section at thirty-six weeks. She was mad that she and the doctors couldn't keep her blood pressure under control. Thankfully, everything went all right—the boys healthy, mama healthy ... all was right with the world.

Since then, life has been chaotic, to say the least. I haven't had Becca all to myself since our honeymoon—almost two years ago, damn it! She doesn't know it, but this is basically a dry run. I'm getting her ready for what I have planned for our two-year anniversary—Paris!

Ah, nothing like springtime in Paris with your girl in your arms.

GOODBYE UNCERTAINTY

A man can dream ... but how many men really have their dreams come true? I'm one lucky bastard! I lean in toward Becca and seal that affirmation with a kiss.

And they lived ... well ... you know!

Acknowledgements

I'd like to thank my family and friends who've supported and encouraged me since I wrote the first sentence of this series. Obviously, my biggest thanks are to my three children for cheering me on and trying to understand this work from home thing. :)

I started a street team a few months back. If you are not aware of what that is, it's like an online fan club. Only, I talk to most of these women every day. They support me, encourage me, and pimp the hell out of me! They've become dear friends, and honestly, I don't know if I would've followed through, publishing the series as quickly as I have without them. So a very special thanks to (in no particular order) Debbie Baardsen, Wendy Colby, Jennifer Ingle-hart, Tammy Becraft, Heather Routh, Nicola Spears and the rest of the beautiful ladies on The G-Team. I love you all so much. Your support has meant the world to me!

There are certain people that I would just really be lost without. Wendy Shatwell and Claire Allmendinger are two of them. They keep me in line, they keep me laughing, and they encourage my dreams. I couldn't have asked for better friends. Thank you both so very much. I love you, ladies!

Jess Huckins has been with me on every project as my editor. I swear we could publish a book filled with our back and forth comments during the editing process and it would be a hit! I can't sing your praises enough! Thank you a million times over for taking me on and coming back for more! Love you, lady!

Stacey Blake makes my books look so pretty. She also laughs

at me when I'm stuck in three feet of snow while she prances around in flip flops! *blows raspberries* Thank you for all of the gorgeous work you do!

A big thank you to Robin Harper for making another gorgeous cover for me! You rock, chicky!

Thank you to Becky Carnahan, my friend and one of the first readers of this series. Your shared excitement over my books and love of my characters really helped fuel the fire to get this thing going. I am so grateful to you. Love you!

Jennifer Bedet, the final count is in! I'd like to thank you fifteen times! You have always been the Stacey to my Becca, the Ethel to my Lucy and Shirley to my LaVerne. I love you more than there are words capable of expressing. My life wouldn't be the same without you.

Last, but not least! I would like to thank all of the readers who have followed Becca on her journey! I wasn't sure what to expect. I can tell you right now, I did not expect so many of you to have such a strong love for Grayson after book one! I am still floored by this. I can't tell you what it means to me to read a review, stating how my books have affected you in a positive way. It inspires me to keep going. Thank you all so much!

Want to see what I'm up to? You can stalk me here at these spots!

Twitter: @JacquelynAyres
Facebook: https://www.facebook.com/JacquelynAyresAuthor
Pinterest: http://www.pinterest.com/jacquelynayres/
Spotify: Goodbye Uncertainty

Coming Summer 2014!
UNDER CONTRACT
The GEG Series #1
~ Unedited ~

Chapter One

Retrieving a compact out of my small clutch purse, I finally bring my eyes up for one last good look in the mirror. I told myself—convinced myself, really—that I was just popping into the bathroom to give one last final check on my appearance. As I stare into my green eyes (my first qualification for this job), I now realize I'm in here to have a conference call with my sanity. Clearly it went bankrupt and closed up shop like most of the country because there's no answer. My sanity is gone ... replaced by desperation and a mother's instinctive need to provide for her children.

I lay my palms on the cool marble counter top and take in a few cleansing Yoga breaths like my friend Ava always recommends. Apparently—I freak out too much—so she says.

"Ok, Charley ... put your big girl pants on. You can do this." Sometimes you need to just act brave so well, you convince yourself that you are. Of course, I have to push off the thought of my big girl pants being pulled off later. I sweep a few whispers of hair off my temple. Thank God Ava was able to do my hair. *Must be sophisticated looking, yet, approachable.* One of many qualifications needed for this job. Ava had parted my long brown hair on the left side. She then crowned the sides with tight French braids till all of my hair was pulled to the back. There, it is involved in a mass production of neat pin curls at the top of my neck. It looks great for the office or a night out on the town. "Sophisticated, yet approachable." *Good job, Ava!*

I step back for one final look to make sure everything is in place. I'm wearing a black silk draped dress by Alice + Olivia. I would've never randomly spent this much on a designer dress, but luckily my Aunt Clara has more money than sense. She loves her some Saks Fifth Avenue! However, Aunt Clara shops for people blindly. I don't know about my cousins, but my sisters and I always end up with a store credit of anywhere from three hundred to fifteen hundred dollars, depending on the occasion for the gift we received.

The last big "occasion" was my husband leaving me six months ago with three kids and no pot to piss in. Said he was tired of society and government. He didn't want this—any of this. He was going to live off the land. I've since learned that in Europe, they call this going for "A Walk About". To this day, I have no idea about where he's been walking. *Asshole!*

Aunt Clara, out of the goodness of her heart, sent me an Armani silk jumpsuit for my hardship; only cost her $1700.00. Problem solved! I now had something special to wear to all my "special" appointments, you know, W.I.C., fuel assistance, food stamps, and TANF. What would I possibly do with $1700.00 in my pocket—pay the mortgage? More money than sense, that one!

Punctuality is a must! Shit! I look at my phone—phew! Two minutes to spare. One more deep breath before I walk out of the bathroom and head to the bar in the Ames Hotel. Funny, until a few days ago, I never even knew this hotel existed. Then again, I don't usually have a reason to stay overnight in Boston's financial district. "Please don't be old and bald ... or creepy ... or ... eck ..." I try to chant to myself. "Please have kind eyes and a kind heart." I lower the bar—small steps.

I head over to the table in the far left corner as instructed and take a seat. So much for "punctuality"—where the hell is he?

MITCH

"Scotch on the rocks and a glass of your best Merlot," I sigh, looking up from my phone. The bartender nods and goes about my order. I throw my phone into the inside pocket of my jacket and glance at my watch, impatiently. She better be punctual! Biggest pet peeve— one minute late and I'm out of here! I grab my scotch from the guy before he can place it down, swirl it around, and take a good swig.

"Waiting on a girl?" he asks.

"Aren't we all?" I smirk.

"Pretty much," he laughs. "Well this one must be special ... you seem nervous."

"It's complicated." I offer.

"When isn't it, dude?" He shakes his head wiping the bar down.

"True." I smile partly because he has no idea about my type of complicated.

"Damn," he sighs. I look up at him. His mouth is open in disbelief and his eyes are wild with desire. I follow his eyes and my breath hitches. *Holy shit ... please be Charlotte.* I think to myself as I watch her make her way through the lounge. I feel my lips curve up at the corners with satisfaction before the information really hits my brain.

"That, my friend, would be my complication." I turn back to him.

"I will gladly release you, sir, from such a burden. It's all part of the great customer service I like to give around here." He tries to remain serious.

"Thank you ... eh, Jim ... I appreciate your thoughtfulness. But, alas, this is a burden I must carry alone. Try not to feel sorry for me." I lift my glass to him and nod before I head over to her.

"I can't—I'm too busy feeling sorry for myself," he mutters.

"Charlotte?" I ask softly. She turns her neck and looks up at me.

"Mitch?" She smiles.

"Mitchell." I correct her.

"Mitchell. Hi." She nods.

"Merlot?" I place her wine in front of her before taking my seat.

"Oh ... thank you." She picks it up to take a sip.

"Very punctual—that's good," I say as I take in the sight of her. I was very specific in my ad about the type of woman I wanted to "employ". So far, she's a vision more perfect than what my own imagination could conjure up.

"I try to be. I'm not always successful, I must admit." I watch as her smile hits her eyes with ease after she speaks. "Mitch? Everything alright?" She leans her head to the side.

"Yes. Why?" I sit up a little straighter and take another sip of my scotch.

"You were just staring at me ... for a while." She breaks eye contact and plays with the charm on the stem of her glass.

"Sorry. You're just ... you're a very beautiful woman." I swirl the cubes around and take my last swig.

"Um—thank you," she says hesitantly while now fidgeting with a napkin. I place my hand on top of hers to stop said fidgeting. Her eyes fly up quickly to meet mine. Shit—did she just feel that, too? No. What am I thinking? She's a professional. Then again, I'm not quite sure why I felt a flutter of electricity—this isn't my first time around, either.

"Please call me Mitchell, Charlotte." I pull my hand away.

"Isn't that what I called you?"

"You called me Mitch a moment ago; only close friends and family call me that." I sigh half expecting her to roll her eyes at me.

"Well, I'm a little less formal; you can call me Charley." She smiles. There's something playful about her smile; as if she's teasing me.

"Charlotte is such a beautiful name, why do you go by Charley?" I sit back, studying her again.

"Oh, that's my dad's doing." She takes another sip of her wine and leans back in her chair, as well. "I'm the youngest of five girls. My dad, like most men, really wanted a son. My mom told him she was done. No more after me. So he asked if he could name me Charlotte. Of course, she didn't know it was so he could call me Charley. But it stuck. Everyone calls me Charley." She takes another sip.

"Did he ever get over not having a son?"

"Oh yeah. Turns out, he named me perfectly. I was quite the tomboy and his constant sidekick." She shakes her head, seemingly laughing at herself.

"Is he still alive?" I set my empty glass down.

"Oh yeah; healthy as a horse, that guy! I think he'll out live me!" I watch how her face lights up, thinking about him. I wonder if "Dear old Dad's" health would be so good if he knew what his precious sidekick did for a living.

"The waitress is right over there. Do you want me to wave her down for another drink?" she asks just before she opens her purse. "Excuse me," she says and quickly texts. "Sorry." She puts the phone back.

"Turn it off."

"Sorry?" She looks up.

"No phone when you're with me," I say calmly.

"Ok, well, I uh ... put it on vibrate. I will not turn it off, but I can assure you that we won't be interrupted again unless there is an emergency. I only answered to let my friend know that I arrived safely." She seems a bit perturbed. "Why are you smiling like that?" Now she's just plain irritated and I think my smug smile just got a little bigger.

"Finish your wine, Charlotte. I want to go upstairs and go over my contract with you." I push her glass forward.

"Contract? What sort of contract?" Her eyes go ridiculously wide. I can't help but laugh.

"Don't worry; it's not that sort of contract." I open my eyes wide to match hers and she laughs again.

"I don't have to call you sir?" she asks playfully.

"Hmm ... nope. No." I shake my head.

"Do I need a safeword?"

"Nope." Jesus, she's cute. She's perfect. Just what I wanted. I hope she'll agree to my terms.

"Any chains, whips, floggers, canes or paddles involved?" She rattles off as she pushes back on a finger for each thing she thinks of.

"Jesus—I may need a safeword!" I give her a playful, horrified look. She laughs again and I think it's the loveliest sound I've heard in a long time. Charlotte takes the last sip of her wine. I stand up and hold my hand out to her. She smiles up at me and takes my offer. I pull her up to me. I'm caught a little off guard by her nervousness. Is she always like this with clients or is it me? I tilt my head slightly as I lean in and sweep her lips with a kiss. *Mm ... soft.* "Let's go." I nudge her nose with mine.

CHARLOTTE

Mitch hits the button for the ninth floor as I try to collect my wits about me. *Mitchell ...* that's going to be hard for me. He looks like a Mitch, but not a Mitchell, if that makes any sense.

He's a handsome man. Not drop dead gorgeous, but definitely handsome. I'd peg him to be in his early forties and just under six feet tall. He has dark dirty blond hair. His eyes are hazel, and they are kind eyes. His smile hits them and like magic, I can see him as a little boy. I have to keep reminding myself that this isn't a regular first date. Although, if I was my friend Julie, the end result would be a regular first date. AND ... he's taking me upstairs to sign a contract amongst other things. What did his ad say? *If upon initial interview I feel that you are right for the position, you will fill out all necessary paperwork and begin immediately. Length of employment, as well as salary, will be discussed at that time.* So, I'm guaranteed a phone call after our first "date". Definitely a step up from Julie's regular first dates. That, coupled with the fact that I instinctively like him, makes me feel a smidge better.

"What's going on in there?" he asks, pulling me out of my thoughts as his left index finger softly taps at my right temple.

"Well, I was trying to find that out myself but ..." I trail off.

"But what?" Smiling eyes. *Not a regular date, Charley—stop it!*

"I was rudely interrupted by someone knocking and asking me 'what was going on in there?' before I could even find out." I state in a matter of fact tone.

"Rudely, huh?" He bites back his smile.

"Hmm ... yes. Probably not the last rude thing you will do to me tonight." I sigh playfully and watch as the numbers light up in the elevator. It stops but it's only the seventh floor.

"You think I'm going to do rude things to you tonight?" His voice full of mirth. I open my mouth to say something but am distracted by the door opening. Mitch yanks my hand, pulling me to the back of the elevator as two older couples get on. The door closes.

"Frank! This is going up!" The one lady hits her husband's arm as her utter irritation pierces his ear drums, I'm sure.

"So what?" He shrugs.

"Charlotte," Mitch nips at my right ear. "You didn't answer my question."

"That's because Frank got on the wrong elevator." I whisper and hold an accusatory hand out in the direction of poor Frank.

"Charlotte." He raises an eyebrow.

"Charley." I correct him. He places his hands on my hips.

"Charlotte." He says insistently as he squeezes my hips and pulls me back against him aggressively. I gasp—*Christ, I'm such a girl!* Frank's wife shoots me a look—*Christ, she's such a bitch!*

"Do you think I'm going to do rude things to you?" he asks again in a whisper.

"Well, I guess it depends," I say.

"Depends on what?" He crooks his neck to look at me. I turn

my neck and look up at him.

"If our definition of what is rude is the same." I smirk.

"Christ ... I think I'm going to enjoy the hell out of finding out!" he says in his regular volume. "Excuse us, please," he says just as everybody turns to look at us. Luckily, we don't have to endure their stares; Mitch leads the way through the older couples, holding my hand. "Good luck, Frank!" Mitch says loudly as we head down the hall. We hear Frank's friend laughing.

"Mitch!" I smack his arm. "He's going to get holy hell for that!" I say with a bit of exacerbation. Mitch ignores me as he opens the door to the room. I no sooner step in and he's slamming the door shut and pushing me up against it.

"This is the last time I'm telling you—Mitchell!" he says through his teeth with a subtle mixture of anger and irritation.

"Oh, honey, you must've had a little too much to drink. I'm Charlotte." I place my hand on my chest. "You're Mitchell." I place my hand on his chest. Mitch looks down and shakes his head. He backs away from me a little.

"Forget it. This isn't going to work. I'll pay you for tonight, but you can leave." He pulls out his wallet. I'm trying to decide which action is offending me more—his dismissal or the wallet reaching? Of course, getting pissed about either and walking (storming really) out of here is not going to put food in front of my kids and a roof over their heads. AND ... I like him. Yeah, he seems to have some quirks—we all do. But I like him. I feel ok with him. Ok with what I'm going to do with him. Well—was going to do unless I rectify this situation.

"Whoa ... wait." I reach out and touch his arm. "I'm sorry." I take a step or two closer to him. He stares down at me intently. "You made me nervous. I joke when I get nervous. I can't help it." He tosses his wallet on the table and places his hands on my hips pulling me closer to him.

"I made you nervous?" he asks before he plants a light kiss on my nose.

"Well, yeah. You slammed me up against the door and yelled in my face." I pull my head back from his advances. "Third rude thing you've done to me in the hour that I've known you, by the way."

"Third?" he questions with a smile.

"Yes."

"When was the second time?" He leans in to kiss me.

"You made me gasp in the elevator ... in front of other people." I pull my head back again.

"The horror!" He widens his eyes. "Well," he starts before he palms my face, "I can do better than that." He leans down and captures my lips. My knees weaken as I part my lips allowing him to deepen the kiss. *Holy shit—this guy can kiss!* I hear a slow waltz playing in my head. Our mouths keep in perfect hold while our tongues dance skillfully together as if this was their millionth waltz and not their first.

Mitch pulls away—abruptly. He stares down into my eyes again; his left thumb strumming across my bottom lip.

"What?" I ask, feeling a bit self-conscious.

"You're different," he finally says after a few more moments of awkward silence.

"What do you mean?"

"Nothing." He shakes his head. "Come. Let's look at the contract." He leads me over to the sofa. The sofa has a bajillion pillows on it. It looks nice but you have to pull off half of them just to sit. I scan over the room while Mitch gets the contract out of his briefcase. *Must remember to call him Mitchell!* God forbid! What's up with that anyway?

The Ames (A Morgan Original) is quite the contemporary hotel. Not too overbearing though; there is more of a softness to it than a sterile feel. The walls are gray. There's a beautiful white decorative engraved fireplace. I'm not sure if it's real, though. The room is very calming with its gray, white and deep purplish tones. I'd love to curl up on that chaise lounge over there, in the corner, and read a good book.

"Charlotte ... here." He hands me a manila envelope. I turn it over and open it up. The first paper I see in a Non-Disclosure. I look up at him. "This is to protect both of us, really." He leans in so that we're almost cheek to cheek as he looks on with me. "Basically, this states that you can tell people about us. However, you cannot tell anyone about our business arrangement or our real one." I can't help my confusion or the fact that it's blanketing my face. "You'll under-stand in a minute. Do you have any questions about what you can say or can't?" he asks getting ready to hand me the pen. I read it over. "C'mon, Charlotte," Mitch breathes a bit of impatience. "I just explained it to you. Sign so we can move on."

"Excuse me." I look over at him. 'Do you have a lot of contracts handed to you at work that you have to make decisions on?"

"Sometimes several a day. Why?"

"Do you read them over or do you just go by whatever they tell you?" I look back down at the paper.

"I read them over. That's different. It's business." I jerk my head back up at him and give him "The Look". "Yeah ok, but you haven't even gotten to the contract, yet." He points for emphasis.

"Pen." I hold out my hand. He gives me the pen and I quickly sign. I hand the Non-Disclosure to him and move onto the contract.

It's only a page long. I don't know what I was expecting, but I find this odd. Instead of questioning it, I decide to read.

Holy shit! I jump up out of my seat and walk over to the fire-place to continue to read. Most people need to sit when they are re-ceiving information that is life altering—not me! I need to feel the ground under my feet.

"Charlotte?" Mitch walks up behind me.

"Shh." I wave my hand and continue to read. I feel his arms slip around my waist. His lips fall to the back of my neck gradually working their way to the right side of it.

"Baby, it'll be so good, I promise." He murmurs between kisses. Wait! Did Mr. Formal just call me baby?"

"So I can't have any other clients?" I ask.

"No. I'm your only client and as you can see." He points to the retainer fee of $25,000. "I compensate you well for it."

"And this is a monthly fee?" I turn to him.

"Yes. Did you read it all?" He flicks the paper.

"Yes ... but ... I'm not quite sure what to make of it. Am I right to believe that you are contracting me to be your girlfriend?" I wince unsure.

"You are very right. Come. Let's sit down and I'll explain this in my words—not my lawyer's." He grabs my hand and leads me back to the couch. I sit down crossing my right leg over my left. Leaning my left elbow on the back of the sofa, I rest my head against my hand.

"Ok?" he asks. I nod. "The reason why I'm doing this is because I'm the owner and CEO of Colton Technologies. Unless you're big into cars and technology for their parts, you probably haven't heard of us," he starts.

"Actually, I have," I say thoughtfully.

"You have?" He's seems taken aback. "Did you Google or Wiki me?"

"Not you, your company. I had no idea you were the owner. I was helping my dad research companies for his stock portfolio. You have a very impressive company, Mr. Colton." I smile.

"Yes, I think so." You can see his sense of pride in his accomplishments. "Well, then you know that we serve more than a hundred countries. I'm always traveling. I don't have time for the whole courting process. I take a girl out on a date then I don't see her for two months. It doesn't go over too well. If they do stick it out—it's usually for my money. If it's not entirely for my money and they do actually like me, I get the nagging about never being there. So ..."

He takes a deep breath. "I've decided enough is enough. I know what I want and if I have to pay for it to get it ... so be it." He slaps his knee.

"But, Mitchell, you're a good looking guy and you seem nice to be around," I start but he cuts me off.

"Charlotte, I want to know every inch of your body. I will tonight. There's no waiting, there's no wondering, and there's no bullshit. I don't have time for that stuff. I let you know when I'm in town and I expect all of your focus to be on me. It's simple, Charlotte. You've got it made. Even if I was a complete asshole—you still have it made." His argument is compelling.

"This says something about a house." I glance back down to the paper.

"I have a house in Andover. You will live there as long as we are under agreement." His left hand rests on my outer right thigh and he squeezes. "You get a house, twenty-five thousand a month plus double the going rate for each night we spend together and health insurance."

"Uh ... health insurance?" I ask.

"Yes." He laughs a little. "I can't just give you a personal check each month for you to deposit in your bank. It'll raise red flags with IRS. You'll be on my company's payroll ... hence the medical benefits."

"Do you offer a 401k plan and how much do you match?" I ask in the most serious way as one would during contract negotiations.

"You're quite the smartass, aren't you?" He grins and squeezes my thigh again.

"Well, your ad did say you wanted an educated woman." I shrug. He laughs lightly and rolls his eyes at me.

"Do you have any other questions?" he asks as his right hand starts playing with the back of my hair. I feel him slowly pulling a pin out.

"What are you doing?" I instinctively reach back.

"Is your hair long?" He pulls another pin out.

"Yes ... stop." I lean forward.

"Please try to leave your hair down for me and never cut it shorter than just below your shoulders." He pulls out another pin.

"Mitchell! It took Ava almost two hours to do this with my hair." I try to push his hand away.

"I want it down." He states calmly. "Who's Ava?" he asks as he continues on with the destruction of her masterpiece.

"One of my best friends," I offer in defeat.

"The one who texted you earlier?" he asks. I nod slightly.

"Does she know what you are doing here ... the nature of your business?" he asks. "Turn." He commands and taps my leg.

"No. Yes, she knows I'm here for a date, but she doesn't know what kind of date." I uncross my legs and turn away giving him full access to my hair. I can't help but smile at how careful he's being not to pull my hair. It's kind of sweet.

"Charlotte."

"Yes?"

"As soon as I'm done here, I'm going to bring you into the bedroom whether you sign the contract or not. If you have any questions—now's the time to ask." his voice is soft yet assertive. I feel as if there are little gymnasts in my stomach, flying around a bar, getting ready to do a triple mound or whatever the hell it is gymnasts do!

"Right!" I finally find my voice. "I have my own home. I won't need to live in yours."

"I want you to live there. It's part of the condition." He stops pulling pins out.

"I can't. I won't. I am willing to compromise." I add quickly.

"Compromise how?" I can tell he's working hard at not becoming irritated.

"When you call me to say you will be here, I will make sure I am at your house for when you arrive and stay with you the entire time." I wait for him to shoot my offer down. Slowly he works at pulling pins out again.

"I'll deal with that for now, but it's not off the table. We will revisit this subject later." He pulls on the hair that's loose for emphasis. I decide it's best to carry on with my other questions.

"You mentioned you will be paying me double the going rate each day that we spend together."

"Yes."

"Why?" That seems excessive. I mean, I'm sure I can make it on twenty-five thousand a month. Christ ... is he related to my Aunt Clara?

"I've learned that loyalty comes with a big price tag. You sign that contract, Charlotte, and you become mine. I don't want another man's hands on you whether a client or not. I'm willing to pay you a lot of money to guarantee that you comply." He runs his fingers through my hair combing out the curls he's released.

"Have you done this before? If so, how long do you usually stay with the same woman?" I try to hide the sadness I'm feeling for him.

"Just once; it didn't work out well. Apparently, I didn't pay her enough to stay loyal. To be quite honest, I realized she wasn't really for me." He sighs then continues on with my hair.

"How so?" I turn my head to look at him.

"I wasn't picky enough; wasn't clear enough about my expectations. But, I chock it up as a learning experience. By the way, I will be having my people randomly checking in on you to make sure you are complying." He stops again, I think, waiting for my reaction to this information.

"From what I've read, your expectations are just for me to be your girlfriend in every way—not just sex." I move along in my questioning, noting that he almost has all of the pins out.

"Yes. I want a companion too. It's not just about sex. Although, I should warn you, I have quite the salacious appetite. I'm sure, given your line of work, that won't be a problem for you." *Huh?* Oh right ... yes, I almost forgot, I'm supposed to be a high priced whore—only I'm not and now thanks to Mitch—I won't be. Well, I'll be high priced but not a whore. I can't very well be a whore if I'm sleeping with only one man. Right? Eh, these moral conflicts, I fear, will be the death of me.

"I'm sure I'll be able to keep up with you." I smile.

"Does that mean you will sign?" He asks as he lightly grabs my chin and turns my head to face him again.

"How long is the contract for and will there be others around the world?" The last of my questions—for now.

"Indefinitely—as long as we are both happy and content with it. And no; you will be the only one. It's only fair of me to bestow the same courtesy I expect from you. Besides, like I said, my free time is limited." He pulls the last pin out. "Beautiful," he whispers before undoing the braids at the top.

"Can I have the pen?" I hold my hand out again.

"I need to see your physical and blood results first." He hands me my purse. "You did bring them, right?"

"Yes, yes of course." I sit straight up. I didn't even realize I was leaning up against him. I open my purse and hand him the papers.

I remember Dr. Timmins' look of confusion when I asked to be tested for every STD known to man. I was prepared for that, considering the man has known me most of my life. I told him I just wanted peace of mind with Josh's odd behavior the last year of our marriage. Like a light bulb quickly flashing on; he got it.

"Here is mine." He hands me the paper. "Are you on birth control?"

"Yes." I nod and scan the paper.

"And you're good about taking it properly?"

"Yes." Geez ... this is now finally starting to sound like a business deal. I feel my stomach turning a bit. "I get the shot."

"Oh ok. Good." He nods. "Before you sign I feel the need to remind you again that you will be at my beck and call. I also want to make it clear that it will never be more than this. I will never want more. I will never give more. I'm not trying to sound like a cocky or arrogant bastard but if you find you feel more for me and want more from me—our contract will be through. I don't do the marriage thing, I don't do the kid thing and I certainly won't do the falling in love thing. Sorry, I just want to make myself clear." He holds the pen back from me.

I smirk playfully and grab the pen from him, "Cocky Bastard." I murmur loud enough for him to hear me.

"Smartass!" he murmurs back, grabbing the pen and paper from me so he can sign as well.

"Now what?" I widen my eyes and bite back my smile.

"Now," he stands up and grabs my hand to pull me up as well, "I finally get to peel you out of this dress." He grasps my lips with his and unzips my dress at the same time.

"Don't you want to know my favorite color?" I pull away and tease.

"No." He pulls me back.

"Flower? School I went to? Names of my sisters? My philosophy on life?" I keep my hands on his shoulders, holding him at arm's length to continue my teasing.

He takes in a deep breath. "There's only one thing I want to know right now." He pulls my hands away and holds them behind my back.

"What's that?"

"What you sound like when you come." He pulls me to him aggressively not allowing an inch between us. His mouth lingers over mine. His eyes telling me to knock it the fuck off. My only response to his behavior seems to be erratic breathing.

"Well," I kiss him, "good luck with that." Good luck indeed! I can't remember the last time I "came" naturally.

"Good luck? You don't think I'll be able to make you come?" His brows arch up.

"Probably not but, since you're paying me so well, I'll make sure to fake in a believable manner." I say thoughtfully.

"I don't want you to fake anything!" He snaps lightly. *Except our relationship.* A slow smile embraces his lips abating his temper. "So ... a challenge?"

"Quite." I sigh with a mixture of sentience and disappointment.

"Hmm ..." A flicker of amusement hits his eyes. "Have a little faith, baby." He nudges my nose with his before planting a quick sweet kiss on my lips. Bringing my hands back around to the front of me, he continues the lead to the bedroom.

"What happened to the formality you insisted on, Mr. Colton? That's twice you've called me baby." I tug on his hand.

"You've signed the contract ... you're officially my baby." He tugs back forcing me onward at a quicker pace.

"You called me baby before I signed." I remind him.

"Yes, but I knew you would capitulate to the terms quickly given the position you are in." He says upon entrance to the bedroom.

"And what kind of position do you think I'm in?" I pull my hands away swiftly. Honestly, what an offensive thing to say!

"Charlotte," he pulls me to him, "I don't know exactly what position you are in outside of this room." His fingers push my hair behind my ears. "But ... in this room ... I can think of several positions you will find yourself in tonight, baby." He licks his lips before claiming mine again. *Holy Shit!* He certainly doesn't fall short on saying the hottest things ... effortlessly, if I may add.

Slowly, my lips part enough to allow his tongue entrance. A small moan escapes my throat as his tongue explores my mouth skillfully. I feel him slip my dress off of my shoulders.

Crap—this is it—the moment Charlotte McKendrick, A.K.A. "Pollyanna" turns into a dirty whore! *No, no! You are not dirty! Stop it, Charley! And one John certainly doesn't make you a whore.* Christ—did I just call him "a John"? I've been watching way too much *Law & Order: SVU*!

"Very rude, Charlotte," Mitch sighs as he kisses down my neck.

"What?" I refocus.

"Exactly. This is your one and only warning. I'm paying you way too much for you to get lost in your thoughts." His eyes find mine and wait for my nod of understanding.

"Sorry." I frown slightly as I reach up to the top button of his dress shirt. I start to unbutton it and continue down to the next. Mitch watches my every move like unbuttoning his shirt is the most fascinating thing he's ever seen.

"Stop." I finally say.

"Stop?" He chucks my chin so I'm looking back up at him. "Charlotte ... is this part of your "act"—the innocence ... the reluctance?" He almost seems unsure. I'm almost certain I already suck at my new "job" and not the kind of sucking that involved in my "job".

"Do you want me to stop?" I play into his idea.

"No ... actually, I'm finding it to be quite the turn on." His grin is laced with a bit of surprise. Aha! I don't suck at my job! Well, metaphorically speaking. "I almost feel as if I'm about to take away your virginity." He chuckles a little.

"Oh ..." I laugh. "Well, I can assure you that you won't be doing that." I don't know why but I feel even calmer with him than before. There's just something about him. Maybe it's the whole "knight in shining armor" thing. I'm relieved and beyond grateful. He and his little contract will be saving me from God knows what kind of trauma I may have ensued. I slip my hands inside of his unbuttoned shirt and slide them up to his shoulders slowly pushing it off of them. I step out of my dress and toe it to the side. Mitch reaches his left hand around the back of my neck bringing my hair to sit on my right shoulder. He leans down. His lips trail kisses down and into the curve of my neck.

"Set the scene for me, baby; I want to play along," his voice is soft and sexy. It sends my little gymnasts back into action.

"It's a simple scene really." I pull at the hem of his undershirt. He takes a step back letting me pull it up and over his head. I toss it on top of my dress. He's fit. I can tell he works out—when he can. There are no ridiculous muscles to outline with my tongue like I've read in so many of my favorite romance novels. Nope ... he's just a regular guy. I like that—makes him even more appealing to me for some reason. I place my hands on his strong shoulders. "I'm your girlfriend and this is the first time I'm letting you have all of me." I continue. "I'm nervous. While this is not my first time; it's my first time with you. I want to be perfect for you. I want to do everything right. I want to be more than you imagined." I bring my eyes up to find his.

His kind eyes. I begged for kind eyes before I met him but I'm not so sure I knew exactly what I was asking for or if it really existed. Now I know and it does exist. They are laced with warmth, generosity and concern, held in place by small lines in the corners showing off many years of laughter and playfulness. At the moment, I am most certain, that I can trust this man. The irony, of course, is not lost on me—I'm trusting in a man who pays for sex—not the usual sort I put my trust into.

"Jesus, Charlotte," his hand palms my left cheek. "I feel like you're staring into my soul."

"I am." I almost whisper. Leaning up a bit on my toes, I brush my lips against his and note the slight change in the tempo of his breathing. His left hand wraps around the small of my back pulling me close to him as he properly attacks my lips. I play at the belt of suit pants and whip it off of him. Mitch unhooks my bra. Cool air hits my lips. I open my eyes; watching him watching me. I quickly glance to my right shoulder. Mitch guides the straps of my bra off my shoulders and down my arms; his eyes focused on mine. Sad to say, but—I think this is the most erotic moment of my life. My bra falls to the floor.

"You ok, baby?" His left index finger traces the slight prominence of my right clavicle bone. I almost think he's asking for real but then I remember ... he's "playing along".

"Hmm mm ... yes."

"I'll stop if you need me to," he offers before leaning down near my ear, "not really," he whispers and I can't help but laugh a little. He straightens up with smiling eyes. I reach up with my right hand and lightly touch the laugh lines at the corner of his eye with my fingertips.

"What are you doing?"

"Admiring the evidence of joy in your life; no matter how great or small—it's all right here." I strum my fingers over the tiny lines. "I find that very attractive." I smile shyly.

"I find your thoughts overwhelming," he says grabbing my hand. He kisses the tip of each finger. I give him a quizzical look. He shakes his head dismissively. "Enough stalling, baby," he begins to back me up towards the bed.

"You started it." I arch a brow and pop the button on his pants.

"Yeah, well—I'm gonna finish it, too." And with that he turns me around swiftly so that I'm facing the bed. *Holy hell!* His breath hits my neck hot and full of promise. His hands fall onto my sides. Slowly they push forward to my stomach and travel up.

"Ah!" I gasp from the bolt of electricity surging to my groin. Mitch rolls and tugs my nipples with skill and precision. I lean my head back against his chest. Hooking my arm around his neck, I bring his mouth down to mine. After a beat, his hands quickly slide down to my panties. His fingers hook under the elastic. He pulls away from mouth and whips my panties down to the floor. *Good God!* He nips affectionately at my bum. He holds my hips and slowly turns me back around as he comes back up to a standing position. He pulls the duvet back.

"Lie down." He nods towards the bed. I hear the unzipping of his pants while I sit and gracefully (I hope!) crawl back onto the bed.

Laying my head back, I take to Yoga breathing once again only I don't exhale with lion's breath. *Shit ... I'm not exhaling at all! Breathe, Charley. Breathe.* My lungs finally give into the pressure and the feeling of Mitch's teeth lightly biting at the inside of my leg during the travels of his mouth. He pulls my legs apart—wide. I feel so overwhelmed—the exposure—the vulnerability. I gasp again as he tenderly bites and licks at the apex of my groin. My hips rise encouraging him. Mitch's finger traces ever so slowly over my cleft. I think I hear him whispering something but I'm not certain; the pounding of my heart is deafening. Just when I think I can't handle any more of the tantalizing torture of his hesitation, his tongue glides over—tasting me. A slight moan escapes from my throat.

"Damn it, Charlotte!" he snaps just above a whisper—over the pounding in my ears. *Damn it, Charlotte? What's that about?* Did I do something oh ... Oh. My. God.

"Ugh ... Mitch ... please," I beg. The fingers of his left hand hold me open; his mouth violently attacking my vulnerability. The swirling, the biting, the plunging—it's more than I can bear. I'm in sensory overload and his right hand holds my pelvis down, forcing me to endure it all with no relief in sight. "Please ... oh please, Mitch." I practically cry. I feel—I know—I'm on the verge of some sort of break through here. Mitch brings his hunger to a savoring pace. I feel a finger circling my entrance; plotting its plan of attack. He slips two fingers in at the pace of a Sunday drive. Meticulously, they massage the upper front wall of my vagina. My body goes on a leisurely hike to Heaven—I think. A delicious tightening occurs deep inside, traveling up to the pit of my stomach. I close my eyes tightly as my body celebrates the joyous occasion of my first orgasm not supplied by a battery operated object. A rocket shoots off a burst of purple. Another burst of white ... blue ... green ...

"Ugh ... oh ... Mitch ... Mitch ..." I don't even recognize my voice; the rockets are coming so quick—one explosion after another.

"That's it, baby ... let me hear you," he encourages and works me through the last of my quakes. My body stills—having just given him the last of my whimpering cries. I stare at the ceiling, trying to steady my breathing. I feel tears rolling out of the corners of my eyes. I quickly wipe them away while Mitch begins his climb up my body. My breast rise up to greet his mouth. My hands dive into his hair for encouragement. I grasp his chin with my right hand. Lifting my neck, I pull his mouth away from my nipple and attack his lips. He finishes his climb allowing me to rest my head back down; his tongue exploring my mouth. He rips his lips from mine and gazes into my eyes; his thumb strumming my bottom lip purposefully. Mitch shifts ever so slightly never losing eye contact. I raise my hips for him and I realize at this moment—I have never wanted someone this bad in my life. My neck involuntarily bends back as I feel myself stretching around him.

"Charlotte," he gasps. A small sob flies out of my mouth and hangs over us like a secret that never meant to be discovered. "Charlotte ... baby, look at me," he whispers. My neck relaxes and my eyes find his confused ones. "Charlotte?"

"Shh." I lean up and kiss him. Our kiss turns from soft and reluctant to urgent ... desperate even. Mitch rolls his hips again, skillfully, if I may add. Within moments, we are in perfect rhythm. I relish in the feeling of my body finally accommodating his with ease. I turn my head swiftly away from him. My eyes go wide in disbelief as the newly familiar feeling creeps up on me once again.

"Look at me," he commands. It's meant to be assertive sounding but it translates almost like a plea. I comply—eyes still wide, ready to be transported someplace incredible. "You're mine," his right hand palms my face and I feel as if I'm hanging by a thread. "Say it!" he demands.

"I'm yours ... I'm ... oh ..." I'm gone—wild underneath him.

"That's it, baby ... tell me ... show me you're mine," he eggs me on. I comply in every way. Sound. Touch. I'm his ... contract or no contract. I tighten myself around him; my final proclamation. The sound that escapes his throat brings me to my knees (metaphorically). "Char—goddamn." His nose scrunches up and his lips form an "O" shape. The tip of his tongue slides over the top of his teeth and pushes against them as if it's life depended on it. "Ugh!" He grunts one last time and falls to my chest, panting. Mitch lifts his head.

"I'm sorry." I say quickly.

"About?"

"I called you Mitch." I wince.

"Christ, Charlotte, that's the furthest from my mind right now," he says with a hint of irritation. I don't know what to say so ... I say nothing. He shakes his head slightly and takes in a deep breath. "Right now I just want to bask in our post-coital glow."

"But?" I ask shakily, showcasing my nervousness.

"*But* ... we are going to have a *very* in depth conversation tomorrow morning." He grabs my chin and rocks my head side to side gently for emphasis. I reply by swallowing hard—it's all I've got. He dips down and sweeps my lips lightly before pulling out. I wince from the sudden emptiness I feel. Mitch rolls onto his back and pulls me with him. His fingers glide up and down my back, into my hair and back down again. The strumming of his fingers, the effects of two amazing orgasms, the stress and worry about what was to come of tonight and the fact that I was up at four in the morning with a feverish Brooklynn—I find myself in a soporific state that I can't fight anymore.

BARELY SURVIVING
By: Courtney Cross

PROLOGUE
CHICAGO, ILLINOIS - USA

I longed for death with every painful thud of my uncontrollably raging heart. Death would bring solace to a body and soul that knew only pain, violence and cruelty. Death would be relief to an existence that no longer wanted any part of this fucking hell on earth. Right there, right then, if death decided to descend upon me I knew without a shadow of a doubt that I would embrace it.

Summoning all the remaining inner strength I could muster, I dragged my beaten body from the pool of blood I'd been laid in, which stained and covered my bed linen, across the room to my dressing table chair. Sitting down tentatively, I winced at the stab of pain that came from my behind, pain that reminded me of the unwarranted violation that had taken place inside there. Slowly placing my bruised elbows on the table, my hands cradled my throbbing head.

I had no comprehension of what just happened. One minute I was enjoying the only birthday party I'd ever had thrown, the next minute Alexander Matthews was viciously dragging me into the privacy and confines of my bedroom. Lifting my head from out of my hands, my gaze fell upon the antique white mirror that adorned my equally antique and expensive dressing table. I gasped loudly with horror at the battered and bruised face staring back at me. Hot tears welled profusely in my eyes whilst surveying the damage. Removed was the sparkle from my usually vivid emerald green eyes. Swollen slits remained that stung as the tears fell. My naturally high cheek bones wore dark bruising and brutal scratches, visual remnants of Alex's fierce onslaught. Usually full, pink lips were swollen, bleeding and painful as I skimmed two fingertips across them. The feel of his mouth on mine, biting and nipping brutally at my lips and tongue made me gag. The vile stench of strong whiskey and tobacco enveloped my senses making my stomach roll. A shaking hand ran over my long, straight auburn hair that was now wild and clumped and hurt like hell at the scalp. He had pulled and tore at my hair as he pinned me down, holding me in place. I struggled for survival, desperate to stop him from taking me. God, I had fought like a caged animal fighting for its freedom but all to no avail. Alex was larger and stronger and had felt unbearably heavy when laid over my small, slender frame. Moving or stopping him had been in vain but I'd tried my damn hardest anyway.

Alexander Matthews was my adoptive step father, a heartless bastard and the sole reason my spineless, weak mother had taken her pathetic waste of a life and ended it. For ten solitary years I'd survived the humiliation, loneliness and the brunt of his unwavering and volatile temper. Her act of selfishness and maternal negligence left me at his mercy, tonight's attack proved that.

For years I'd handled everything he threw at me by remaining detached and unemotional to life. A tireless string of young nannies and hired staff raised me. Void of attachments to any one of them made it all the easier to deal with when Alex screwed them then moved them on. I lived alone in the world, always had been and functioned happiest that way.......until now. Tonight, a lonely vulnerability set in. There was no-one to take me away from the bastard who had just taken the last shred of life and dignity I possessed. There was no-one. Nobody would come to help me. Nobody out there gave a shit about me or my life and that was a hard, bitter truth to swallow.

Alex was a seriously successful, self-made exec with international connections. If confided in, none would ever believe what he had subjected me to tonight. All they saw was the tortured man who bravely grieved the loss of his beloved young, beautiful wife to suicide and then selflessly continued to raise her emotionally detached daughter. That lie of a notion made Alexander Matthews seem a man to be admired and revered by anyone acquainted with him. He was a man that men aspired to replicate and emulate. Women sought to snare the wealth and lifestyle by fucking the man whatever the cost. Not a single soul would choose to believe that Alexander Steven Matthews was a brutal wife beater who drove his glamorous wife to her grave and had mercilessly terrorised his eight year old stepdaughter in her absence ever since. I would never be believed. Nobody would give a shit. And that thought alone ripped my damaged soul and beaten spirit to shreds, finally finishing me off.

Yelping in pain, I pushed up off the dressing table into a standing position. Gritting my teeth I inhaled and exhaled deeply, my chest expanding and deflating in agony around possible cracked ribs as I headed for my en-suite. Sudden clarity and the way to exit off the never ending carousel of barely surviving hit me full on. This had to stop. It just wasn't within me to carry on. Reaching up to my mirrored wall cabinet I caught one last glimpse of myself before opening the cabinet door. My looks had always haunted me and Alex. I was without question the image of my dead mother. There was no mistaking I was Gina Dawson-Matthews daughter. My auburn waves and memorable green eyes were exactly like Gina's, eyes which now adopted that same haunted glaze my mother's had always worn. Eyes made to bare that look by the man who had systematically destroyed both of our lives.

My vision slid over the various items and cosmetics adorning the four shelves of the cabinet and settled upon the answer I was looking for, a bottle of pain killers. They were exactly what I needed. Grasping the bottle of pills that sat on the bottom shelf of the cabinet I was surprised by the overwhelming feeling of calmness that washed over me in waves for the first time in my life. As I stood there, bottle in hand I wondered if Gina had experienced the same inviting sense of peace when she decided to end things by killing herself, leaving me behind. For the first time since she committed suicide, I felt a faint tinge of empathy with Gina. It was fleeting and for no more than a second but I most definitely felt it all the same. I hated myself for feeling any kind of sympathetic feelings or maternal connection to the woman who bore and then abandoned me. A connection that now seemed to share a pre-determined destiny.

Gripping the bottle tightly I became aware that my hands were rock steady as I removed the lid. Not a single shake to be seen. Maybe fate was informing me it was my time to leave, convincing me to end the suffering just as my mother had. Nobody would care if I did it. I had no-one to mourn for my eighteen years of wasted life so I decided; it would be better this way.

The first few pills were really hard to swallow down. My throat was sore and dry from the constant screaming and pleading with Alex to stop. But my piercing screams remained unheard and nobody had come rushing to my aid. That thought made the rest of the pills in the bottle slide through the dryness to my stomach so much easier. The cool refreshing water that washed them down was soothing to my throat. I drank it thirstily; savoring the quenching sensation in my mouth until reaching the very final drop I knew would be my last. After consuming all the tablets in the bottle, the now empty container fell into the sink. Inhaling a deep breath, I closed my eyes and turned towards my bed. Taking the somber last steps towards the bed seemed to take me an age; there was no turning back now. Sinking slowly onto the bed, my limbs heavy and weary, I found myself making peace with the big guy in the sky. Why I began silently praying to him for forgiveness I had no explanation for. I'd never had religious inclinations or a belief in any kind of God, but saying the words, begging for his redemption and urging him take me to a better place filled my mind, body and soul with calmness. So this is what death felt like? I warmed to the feelings death was offering me, welcoming it with two very open arms.

I lay on the bed still and silent with no idea of how long for. Short-lived panic eased as the pills took a hold. The intense throbbing in my head subsided, replaced by an increasing need to sleep. As the burn from my lungs becoming deprived of air calmed, the racing thud of my pulse slowed down. Paralysis took over my body as my mind slipped in and out of its conscious state. The end was near, my life ebbing, my spirit diminishing. I felt no fear; no regret only floods of exhausted relief.

The silence was deafening, the gradual slowing of my pulse the only sound to be heard in my ears. This was it. I was really going to die here, right now, tonight. Unwanted thoughts of what I could have had and now never would swamped my mind as my focus and attention began to waiver. Clear, unwanted images of innocent hopes, aspirations and dreams that would never materialise rushed through me. As the feeling spread, I was unable to tell if I was feeling regrets for rushing into taking the tablets or just self-pity for the easy discarding of such an unlived life. Was this really the answer? I'd always firmly believed without a hint of doubt that suicide had to be the coward's way out. My hasty actions now making me a coward just like my fuck up of a mother had been. Oh god, I didn't really want to die did I? Just as the panic started to spread further through my weakening body like poisonous venom, I heard HIS unmistakable booming voice shouting my name. He'd come back to finish what he'd started no doubt. Not intent with the abuse he had already inflicted on me, he was coming back for more. "Screw you Alex," I screamed silently in my scrambled and distorted head, "Damn you to fucking hell." The sound of his authoritative tone chased away any brief feeling of doubt. Satisfied with my decision and content with what I had done, reclaiming control of my life was liberating. Impending darkness began to take me, spreading through my veins and stemming the blood flow. I barely felt the repulsion of rough hands skimming my arms and skin, barely heard his yells of panic commanding me to open my eyes. Taking back my soul with thoughts of dazzling white clouds and the clearest of blue skies beckoning me to join them, the darkness finally claimed me. As my breathing ceased, blood stopped pumping the shriveled organ called my heart. Death was imminent and the pain over. And for the first time in a very, very long time, I was internally smiling my peachy ass off.

CHAPTER ONE
FOUR YEARS LATER – LONDON, UK

Breathing in the fresh, crisp spring air made me feel truly alive. I loved London. It had become my home over the last four years and I loved it with the affection and loyalty you would have for someone you cherished. London was my family, my saviour and my place of sanctuary. I embraced the vibrancy and pulsating energy it emanated as it invigorated my soul. London was a metropolis of wealth and power. Its tall skyscraper buildings, theatres, and wealth of untold possibilities were simply inspiring. Moving here had been the best decision of my life. It was a decision that undoubtedly saved me.

I never tired of taking a moment just to stand and survey my surroundings. Awe filled my spirit with the visions of bustling life from the rise of the sun to the falling of it. London lived and breathed as if it was alive and I thanked god for being here to witness and embrace that life every single day.

From the opulence of Kings Road and Knightsbridge and its vast array of designer stores, to the simple yet enticing second hand markets of Portobello Road and Noting Hill, everything about the city screamed of diversity and culture and I was proud to call it home. I could never imagine being as happy anywhere else on the face of the earth as I was here and felt nothing but privileged to be a part of it.

I'd lived in seclusion and loneliness until I moved here. Many people despised the overcrowding and loud bustle but I thrived on it. It filled me with a sense of belonging and rightfulness and I needed that. I'd felt a connection to this cosmopolitan oasis the moment I stepped off the flight from Chicago and the connection had continued to grow ever since.

Standing on the small pathway to my modest but perfect Kensington apartment, I watched as everyday life unfolded before me.

Impeccably dressed executives rushed out from their up market apartments to their awaiting taxis or expensive sports cars in a bid to survive the early morning traffic while making their way to work. The odd well known celebrity, hiding behind oversized sunglasses and swamped by security as they tried in vain to be invisible took their morning run. My road was warm and inviting with its picturesque apartments and homes but was also full of the daily bustle of life and I stood there silently drinking it all in. London was the comfort blanket that covered me in protection and warmth and I had no intention of ever walking away from that or giving it up.

Making my way down the path towards the little wrought iron gate at the bottom, I grimaced to myself as the reason for my unreasonably early start today hit me like a sledgehammer. Fuck, I hated lawyers or 'solicitors' as I'd learned they were referred to in the UK. As passionate as I was about my adopted home city, I was as equally passionate in my hatred for solicitors. Men and women dressed in bespoke suits with the power to change lives at their will filled me with complete loathing. Solicitors were false, indifferent creatures and I'd no intention of spending a second more in the company of such people than I had to.

I exited through the gate onto the pavement, just as the taxi pulled up. Confirming with the driver that I was his pick up and reminding him that I was heading to Canary Wharf, I slipped into the large rear leather seat. As the taxi pulled out into the road, I settled back into the seat and sighed heavily. Just the mere fact that I was going through with this spoke volumes of my recovery and just how far I had come emotionally and mentally over the last four years. Cold memories hit me, detailing the last time I'd sat in a Solicitors office and the treatment I had then suffered at their hands. The sickly sweet stench of the females perfume and the cold, accusing eyes of the male that had sat across from me that day flittered through my mind. They were precise, calculating and unrepentant in covering up Alex's mess landing the blame and shame of his actions at my feet. They were clear; the fault was mine, my lies despicable. Thick, burning bile crept into my throat remembering the uncontrollable shake in my hand as I signed their damn piece of paper. I'd sobbed violently, damaged and fragile, while listening to their imperious demands receiving only mock smiles, barely audible expressions of false sympathy and sly eye rolls in return for my meltdown. Any thought of reliving that experience would have made me violently sick before relocating here. Mentally stronger, physically healed and emotionally stable now, I readied myself for battle if the situation presented itself and the need was warranted.

My spirit plummeted with wishing that Charlotte was here right now. The vivacious Charlotte Collins was my housemate, my fierce best friend and my beacon of hope when black moments of despair crashed down on me. She was my rock and my reserves of strength at times when the darkness seemed to fall over me again. Those types of moments were much fewer and further between these days, but all the same, she was always on hand to bring me out of my funk when they hit. She was currently vacating with family, had been for two weeks and we had barely spoken twice since the day she left. She was unaware I'd received the letter requiring my attendance at the meeting today, yet her support was needed more than ever. Charlotte would know how to best handle today and would have stood beside me without question and without a single ounce of reserve. The sordid details regarding every aspect of my life had been spilled to her during a rare moment of weakness, which admittedly, had been entirely vodka fuelled. Charlotte had listened to the outpour of my heart in silence, without judgment and held me tightly for numerous hours afterwards until my tears and sobs subsided. That night had sealed our friendship and Charlotte had been firmly by my side ever since. I never begrudged or resented the frequent trips she took with her family, but on this occasion I couldn't help but wish she was here with me and not having the time of her life in Barbados with them.

After first receiving mail from Jacobson and Fitzgerald, the huge firm of solicitors based in Canary Wharf I was heading to, my life had been placed on hold. I'd lived a little over four, blissfully naive years since that night and until now, Alex had maintained his end of our bargain and kept well away from me and without any contact of any kind. Apart from the substantial monthly allowance he deposited into my bank account that remained untouched to this day, all reminders of him had been wiped from my life. But the moment I'd picked up the luxury envelope with my name and address typed neat and precise on the front and the solicitor's details on the rear, I knew this was down to him. Determined to just throw the letter out with the day's rubbish, I was infuriated at the thought of Alex rescinding on the agreement he himself had demanded me to agree to. He could gladly have every penny of money he deposited into that account back with my blessing. I'd never wanted his god damn conscience money which is why it was unspent and sat collecting huge amounts of interest on a monthly basis. Fear of the unknown, of having to deal with anything vaguely related with my previous tormenter whipped up storms of anxiety that I was struggling to control. Whatever awaited me would be unpleasant, unnecessary and difficult to deal with. Shifting with nerves, my mind became crazed with the unknown as disjointed images of life under Alex's rule hit me thick, fast and threatened to pull me back under.....again.

The taxi pulling over to the side of the road wrenched me from my memory fog. After informing me I was at my destination, the driver took his fare and generous tip with a smile and a bow of his flat cap and wished me a good day. Mustering a faint smile, I jumped out of the taxi and onto the pavement. I was in an area of the city that exuded wealth and power more than others. Industry and commerce were rife here, millionaires were ten a penny. Streets lined with the power houses of marketing and commercial enterprises alongside Michelin star restaurants, world famous art galleries and museums were an overload to the system. This area was a young entrepreneur's Mecca, the backyard of the filthy rich and astronomically successful. Multi storey buildings sprawled upwards as far as the eye could see. The choking whirl of fog and fumes from the exhausts of the never ending line of traffic rose into the air. As much as I adored this city, in all its rawness and glory, these parts were intimidating. A shudder of respect and foreboding crept ominously down my spine. Standing in front of an imposing twenty storey building that seemed to stretch upwards into the breaking blue of the morning sky, my heart thumped wildly behind my breast bone. Built from grey, harsh looking stone, with large windows scattered across it on every floor, the structure was powerful and imposing. The only decoration the dark framed windows wore was a single venetian blind or the name of the company emblazed on the glass. The building smacked of efficiency and productivity and as expected Jacobson and Fitzgerald inhabited the top two floors of the colossal feat of engineering. Straightening my spine, lifting my chin and inhaling a few sharp breaths of refreshing spring air, I placed one foot in front of the other and strode confidently into the building to face my awaiting audience while also confronting my gruesome past.

About The Author

I am a domestic engineer (born and raised in New Jersey) whose sole responsibility is guiding three young, impressionable kids into becoming phenomenal adults. This challenging yet rewarding work requires a lot of love (coffee), patience (wine), and determination (periodic exorcisms). I work all of this magic from the beautiful state of New Hampshire.

Before becoming a domestic goddess (not really), I spent over a decade working in the medical field, where I wore more hats than the queen.

I have loved the written word and the great escape it provides since I was a little girl. When I wasn't reading about people and the places they lived, I created my own characters and adventures. Finally, I started putting a pen to paper and allowing my characters to come to life. When I don't have a pen in hand, you can often find me laughing at the conversations my characters are having in my head.

www.ingramcontent.com/pod-product-compliance
Lightning Source LLC
Chambersburg PA
CBHW021309250626
47155CB00002B/452